PRAISE
THE SHORTEST DISTANCE BETWEEN TWO WOMEN

"Radish displays an intimate understanding of boisterous families."
—*Publishers Weekly*

"Popular and prolific Radish offers a touching story about strong women and family bonds."
—*Booklist*

"Through the women in her popular novels, author Kris Radish reveals what has value and meaning in life for her—friendships and a passion for living."
—*Albuquerque Journal*

SEARCHING FOR PARADISE IN PARKER, PA

"Girl-power readers will get a kick. . . . Women will surely connect with Radish's empowered femmes."
—*Publishers Weekly*

"Slyly comic . . . Radish is a good writer to get to know, creator of terrific characters and warm and tangled relationships and a world that's a pleasure to visit."
—*Sullivan County Democrat*

"Radish unrolls a rollicking yet reflective read that adds to her robust repertoire of beloved fiction. . . . When an author reaches out to draw you into her pages and the intimate lives of her characters, like Addy Lipton and her hapless husband Lucky, then what's a reader to do but relish the ride?"
—*BookPage*

"Funny, insightful . . . Radish's writing is deft, humorous, and right on target. This book would be an excellent choice for a book group, bound to spark discussion and laughter."
—Greensboro *News & Record*

THE SUNDAY LIST OF DREAMS
CHOSEN AS A BOOK SENSE PICK FOR THE MONTH OF
FEBRUARY 2007!

"An inspirational story about making amends and the power of mother-daughter love . . . Every page contains a warm fuzzy."
—*Publishers Weekly*

ALSO BY KRIS RADISH

The Elegant Gathering of White Snows
Dancing Naked at the Edge of Dawn
Annie Freeman's Fabulous Traveling Funeral
The Sunday List of Dreams
Searching for Paradise in Parker, PA
The Shortest Distance Between Two Women

Hearts
on a String

Hearts
on a String

a novel

KRIS RADISH

❦ BANTAM BOOKS TRADE PAPERBACKS | NEW YORK

A Bantam Books Trade Paperback Original

11/3/10   15 00

Published in the United States by Bantam Books, an imprint of The Random House Publishing Group, a division of Random House, Inc., New York.

BANTAM BOOKS and the rooster colophon are registered trademarks of Random House, Inc.

Library of Congress Cataloging-in-Publication Data
Radish, Kris.
Hearts on a string : a novel / Kris Radish.
p.   cm.
ISBN 978-0-553-38475-8 (trade pbk.)
eBook ISBN 978-0-553-90778-0
1. Women travelers—Fiction.   2. Strangers—Fiction.   3. Women—Fiction.
4. Female friendship—Fiction.   5. Chick lit.   I. Title.
PS3618.A35H43 2010′
813′.6—dc22   2010001834

Printed in the United States of America

www.bantamdell.com

2 4 6 8 9 7 5 3 1

Book design by Steve Kennedy

Title page art by Penny Jackson

This novel is for my beloved editor, Kate Miciak.
She has always had her hand on my writer's heart.
Thank you, Kate, for never letting go of the string.

Hearts on a String

prologue

The story her great-grandmother told was simple, lovely, and unforgettable.

It is spring when the story is shared and the sights and smells of the sweet earth coming back to life are intoxicating.

Her great-grandma comes often, but this day she wants to see only her, the youngest daughter. She takes the small child by the hand and they walk right down the middle of the freshly seeded field until they hit a meandering stream that the girl will forever love.

This great-grandma looks at the sweet child who has wild eyes and a heart that beats with the rhythms of her own. She smiles so openly that her ill-fitting false teeth drop a tiny bit and the girl laughs. The child is afraid of nothing. And then the girl, tired of waiting, implores, "Tell me, Nana."

And Nana begins.

Nana takes the girl's warm hand and places it above her own heart. She asks the precocious eight-year-old to stand still for just a moment, because a moment is all it will take.

"Someday," Nana tells her, "you will know this is an important passage. You will know that it is your turn, you will know that you can see what so many others cannot see until they are older."

And then Nana holds the adorable girl's hand there, over a heart that will very soon slow until it completes its wonderful circle of life. The woman tells the attentive girl about the precious, beautiful, sweet string that connects all women. She tells her great-granddaughter that the string is so pure and light that many women cannot see it. If those women get lost, or walk too fast, or think before dancing, the string that connects them all will still be there, but they won't be able to see it.

"The string is a powerful force, my sweet girl. It allows women to lean into one another and find a sister when they need one. The string can never be broken. You can use it to pull yourself up, to pull yourself forward, or to steady the place where you must remain."

The little girl instantly understands everything that her great-grandmother is saying. Sometimes, at night, when she is frightened by a bad dream, she raises her hand, and feels something soft move through her fingers that makes her feel safe and loved.

The girl has only one question, and she asks it while they are walking back through the field.

"Are you sure all women see this string, Nana?" she asks.

"Oh yes!" her great-grandmother exclaims. "If they dare to see and feel, if they build a world for their hearts and lives that comes from the designs of their own souls. They can see it. But sometimes, my little dove, these women need help. And sometimes you may need a little help too."

"Nana," the great-granddaughter exclaims proudly, "I can see the string already."

"I know, my darling, I know," Nana says softly, moving her free hand through the air as if she were catching the nearly invisible string and holding it tight.

one

THE AIRPORT

EARLY SUNDAY AFTERNOON

The soft rumble of the toilet sucks away the people, places, events, and details of her life as Nan's iPhone slips from her pocket. It splashes into the white porcelain toilet in Airside A at Tampa International Airport and turns Nan Telvid into a woman possessed.

"Son-of-a-bitch!" Nan screams as she bends at the waist, drives her hand into the toilet bowl, and tries to rescue her lifeline. Then, "Shit!" she yells as she begins kicking the pedestal of the toilet.

The four other women in the restroom freeze as if someone has just slapped them. Then they turn to face Nan's stall. Two are at the sinks, hands dripping. One has just walked out of the stall next to Nan's. The fourth woman clutches her lipstick as if it is a weapon. She takes a timid step forward.

Whatever is going on in stall number three sounds serious.

It's early afternoon on the first Sunday in April and every single one of these five women would rather be anywhere but in the bathroom across from the Jose Cuervo Tequileria in yet another airport. The busy terminal is a madhouse of men, women, and children coming to the beach, leaving the beach, heading back to reality after another interminable business trip, or just leaving for one. And all the women in this bathroom at this particular moment could suddenly turn vicious from the stress of simply standing still amidst the swirling masses. The now ancient joys of airplane travel, minus airport bars, have all but vanished for them.

The profane woman in the center stall obviously needs help and the brassy blonde with the lipstick in her hand makes the first move.

"Nan, what in the world is going on in there?"

The blonde clicks her lipstick shut, throws it into a purse large enough to hold a small child, and pushes her bony hip into the side of the metal door. "Nan?"

"I dropped my damn phone into the toilet and it's wedged down there," comes the snarl on the other side of the door. "I bet Steve Jobs never bothered to measure the width of a public toilet drain when he designed this wonderful phone," Nan seethes.

"Open the door," the blonde commands.

The women can hear Nan step backward, unclick the door, and then, before the blonde can move, one of the women at the sink shouts, "Nobody *flush*!"

The other two women move without thinking to block the other stalls in case someone new comes into the bathroom.

"I dated a commercial plumber once," the woman at the sink shares. "He told me the suction from these public toilets could rip off my underwear if more than a few of them were flushed at the same time. My name's Patti, by the way."

Patti has a voice that demands attention. It's a throaty, sexy rumble that would make even a dying man want to take off his clothes. Nan decides right away that Patti's either a singer or has been working as a test smoker for a tobacco company most of her life. She looks like she's pushed past sixty but she's one of those older women who clearly gets more attractive daily. Patti the plumbing expert has on a two-piece blue suit that looks hand-stitched; whoever dyes her hair is a goddess because the specks of gray blend perfectly with her light brunette tones; her bracelets, necklace, and rings are lovely strands of gold; and there's a funky bold scarf around her neck that says, "I'm hip but don't push your luck, honey."

"I'm Cathy," the blonde says. "Do you by chance have any plumbing tools in your purse?"

"No, sweetie," Patti answers, without blinking an eyelash. "The plumber took his tools with him when he left. And let me tell you, he didn't need a very big bag when he packed."

One of the women guarding two other stalls starts to laugh, just as a newcomer pushes into the restroom, sees Nan, Cathy, and Patti standing in one stall and two other women with their backs pressed flat against two of the other five stall doors, as if they are about to be frisked. The newcomer freezes.

"Is this a kind of restroom theatrical play or something?" the woman at the door asks. "Can I pee in here?"

"We're having a bit of a crisis," the woman who'd laughed tells her. "It's probably best if you go down the hall. There's a bathroom right across from Sam Snead's Grill & Tavern. They're having a pre-boarding happy hour that I highly recommend."

"Well, aren't you a fun group," the woman at the door snips as she turns away. "You five look like a bunch of fruitcakes."

Everyone laughs but Nan. Patti peels off her jacket, hands it to Cathy, and orders someone to figure out how to block the door before another cranky woman with a full bladder tries to pop in.

"I'll do it," the laughing woman tells Patti. "I'm Margo."

"That leaves me." The fifth woman speaks so softly it's almost impossible to hear her. "I'm Holly."

"Nice hair," Margo says, looking at Holly's wispy spikes and lovely frosted tips. The curves of Holly's hair seem to dance perfectly whenever she moves her head.

"I did it myself. I'm a hairstylist."

"Okay, girls," Patti announces. "Enough about the hair already. Let's think about this. I'm a bit older than most of you but even *I'm* addicted to my damn cell phone, especially when I travel. Not so much when I'm not on the road, but unfortunately I travel a lot. I do have to tell you that for three cents I'd throw my phone in there. Phones are nothing but a waste of time, unless, of course, you *really* need one."

Margo asks if anyone has gum or anything sticky in their purse. She yanks a piece of paper out of a notebook, scrawls *Closed for Repairs* on it. When Holly hands her a stick of gum, she chews it for a second, sticks it on the back of the note, and thumps it on the outside door. Margo is about as big as a large toothpick but somehow she pushes a big garbage can against the door so no one else can open it.

Holly with the perfect hair looks as if she's spotted a dead relative. She's trying very hard to decide what to do. She turns nervously to look at herself in the mirror and wonders how these women, all obviously older and more capable, see her. What she sees is a sort of slightly overweight woman under the age of thirty with really great hair who wouldn't know how to fix a toilet, keep intruders out of a bathroom, or organize a bunch of unknown frequent flyers to do any or all of the above if someone held a gun to her head.

"Geez," she mutters under her breath, not loud enough for any of the others to hear her. She's thinking that from the looks of things each of these women has more of a life than she does. Styling hair in Aberdeen, Ohio, is probably not on any Top Ten List of career experiences. Holly darts her eyes from one woman to the next and assumes she is not just outclassed but already in over her head and she's not even near the toilet bowl.

"Hey," Patti says, turning to look at Holly. "Can you hold the stall door open while Margo there guards the garbage can?"

Holly obediently pushes her weight against the door. Patti is now standing in front of the toilet, hands on hips, looking exactly as if she'd pee like a man if she had the proper equipment. Nan is to her right, hands dripping toilet water and red in the face from panic and anger. Cathy straddles the bowl. Holly can now see why the poor woman who'd simply wanted to go to the bathroom looked so terrified.

"You two know each other?" Patti asks, looking from Cathy to Nan.

"Kind of," Cathy answers. "I've actually met Nan's husband through work. I was just throwing down some wine at the bar across the hall and there was Nan, sitting right next to me."

"We just started talking—you know, about what a small world it is and stuff like that," Nan adds impatiently. "What about my phone?"

"So you don't know if Nan here regularly drops her phones into the toilet?" Patti cannot help herself. She breaks out into a huge smile.

"That's a stupid question." Nan is now clearly even more ir- ritated.

Margo momentarily moves away from her trash can–guarding duties. She tells Nan it's not really a stupid question because she herself happens to have three teenagers and she washes their iPods and phones and other electronic devices all the time.

Patti looks at her and ignores the part about her washing her electronics.

"Three teenagers? Are you serious? I hope you were at the bar too."

Margo informs Patti she was down the hall at Snead's, throwing back gin and tonics. It wasn't so much because of the teenagers, she shares, as it is the six days she just spent visiting her parents in their trailer park community, her father's inability not to fall down every two hours, and the fact that even though Margo's pushing forty her mother showed her how to vacuum and put dishes properly into the dishwasher *every damn day* she was visiting. Not to mention the number of times she was almost killed by bald men driving golf carts.

"Am I the only one who wasn't at a bar?" Holly asks bravely in her whisper-thin voice.

"I was on my way there when I made this unfortunate pit stop," Patti confesses. "Let's get back to the phone here, sugar. If we do get it out of the toilet, it probably won't work, unless you have a freezer or an oven handy. One of those is supposed to fix a wet phone, but I can never remember which. I just throw my cell away when this happens to me."

Margo then announces that she has figured out you can wash a variety of cell phones and iPods four times before they quit working, because she's done that with numerous devices. She says she's afraid to tell Apple, for fear they'll make the iPod less waterproof.

"Grab us some paper towels," Patti orders Margo, ignoring the phone-washing update. "Girls, I think we should try and get that damn thing out of there for Nan. I've read where some phones survive even in the ocean. Is there good stuff on that phone, Nan?"

Nan opens her eyes as wide as saucers. She raises up her hands, spreads her fingers. She looks half-crazy.

"I'm in banking," she tells the other women. "Investments. I have clients all over the country. Do not ask me if I backed everything up yesterday or the day before, when I was in so many meetings I wanted to puke. It's not life-or-death down there," she says, moving her head in the direction of the submerged phone, "but if there's a chance we can save it, I'm going back in. And besides, I hate to give up, you know?"

Holly wonders if she should say something. After Nan the banker's words, the other women have all grown quiet—probably thinking about their lost investments during the past few years, through the fall and rise and fall and finally the rise yet again of the economy. Leaning against the stall door, Holly feels like a money virgin. The economic mess didn't affect her too much because she's never had anything to affect. When the economy hit bottom, her clients would have sold their husband's last pair of shoes so they could still come in for their cuts and colors. And Holly's one-bedroom condo could probably fit inside of Nan's car. Leftover money in the bank or for buying stocks and bonds? Aberdeen is not exactly the high-tipping capital of the world.

What she really wants to say is, "It's a *phone,* for pity's sake! Yank it out, flush it down, let me have a go at it with one of my hairbrushes, or call a plumber—but it's *just* a phone."

But she's silent. Patti appears to be the one who's in charge of phone wrangling and Holly's a little afraid of this stranger with her gravelly voice and bossy manner. Holly would never have the courage, she knew, to drink alone at an airport bar. Tomorrow she'd be right back in flipping Ohio chopping hair and begging a client to try a new hairstyle after having the same bangs for twenty-five years. Why in the hell couldn't she break out of her own airport routine and go to a bar alone?

Patti finally breaks the spell by saying, "Girls, should we flush Banker Nan?"

"Let's take a vote," Margo pipes up, clearly feeling the effects of her trip to the happy hour bar.

Cathy, still straddling the toilet, doesn't move.

Nan sucks in her breath. She is about to let all four of them have it when Patti leans toward her, jabs her shoulder, and tells her she's just kidding. Investment jokes are already passé, she assures Nan, what with those Obama kids now loping toward adolescence, the rebirth of the stock market, and people realizing it's just as much fun to read or go to a state park as it is to buy one more damn telephone or fly to Paris.

Despite Patti's pseudo apology, Nan snaps. She suddenly pushes Patti aside and plunges her hands into the toilet again, trying not to think about who may have been in this particular stall just before her. Water splashes onto her arms, drips down the side of the toilet, and creeps toward her expensive leather high heels. She gags and backs up.

Patti starts laughing.

"It's clean water, really," Patti snorts. "The inside of your mouth is probably dirtier, honey."

Margo starts to laugh too and so, to her own surprise, does Holly. Cathy decides to side with Nan and says she gives her barmate credit for at least trying. "Give her a break, people," Cathy barks. "I think the shoes cost more than the phone."

Patti has on lovely well-built but trendy open-toe shoes, Margo is wearing dark green cork-soled sandals even though she knows her feet will freeze when she gets off the plane in frozen Wisconsin. Holly has on her traveling Nikes.

Patti has an idea, but now she wants to see what the big shot with the fancy shoes and the skinny-ass and very fit blonde who looks like a hip version of a woman she once met in Hollywood (who turned out to be a classy hooker) can contribute to this phone retrieval ceremony.

"What did you say you did again?" Patti asks Cathy.

"I didn't say. But I work for Wendy's."

"Wendy's? The fast-food Wendy's?" Holly asks, thinking Cathy absolutely does not look like a Wendy's kind of gal.

"I'm upper-level management. Development and special events."

"I'll bet you are," Patti mutters as she puts her hands on her hips.

"What the hell does that mean?" Cathy is clearly offended.

Margo's thinking. She still has more than an hour before her flight boards. That could mean at least two more gin and tonics, and instead here she is, in a women's restroom with a bunch of strangers, arguing about how to help some brassy chick get her phone out of a toilet.

"This looks like a scene from a sitcom, for heaven's sake," Margo says, loud enough to get their attention. "Everyone but Holly seems to be just the other side of tense. Looks to me like we are all just trying to help. Does anyone have an idea about getting the phone out of that toilet so we can get back to our lives and I can go back to the bar before I have to get on the damn airplane?"

Nan suggests they take a few minutes, just for the hell of it, to see if there's anything, like maybe a hanger, in one of their carry-on bags that she can use to leverage the phone out of its watery nesting spot.

"I think if I can get something under it I can wedge it out," Nan suggests, shaking her hands as if she's a surgeon about to snap on latex gloves. "It's a mean little bastard."

"It's because you flushed," Patti tells Nan with a hint of delight. "I heard you. But a hanger is a brilliant idea. I was actually thinking the same thing. If we find one and can get it under there, you may be on to something, Ms. Nan. At ease, everyone. Hangers have been saving women for so long it isn't even funny. We should have thought of this sooner."

This sobering fact changes the entire direction of the phone-salvaging operation. Outside the restroom the five women can hear people parading as if there is a live circus under way in the airport corridors. Babies who should never be forced to fly in an airplane are screaming. Carts with elderly people, who should also never be forced to fly, are zipping by and beeping in twenty-second intervals. Every other man and woman walking past the restroom seems to be arguing. Although the noisy unemotional ambivalence of the airport is just inches away, there's at least a door, a garbage can, and five women between all that chaos and the temporary sanctuary of the women's restroom.

The five look at one another. Holly looks at Cathy. Cathy looks at Patti. Patti looks at Nan. Nan looks at Margo. Margo looks at Holly. It is a simple, mute circle of amazement that jerks them back to the daunting task at hand. But not before each one of them silently wonders what could possibly be keeping them all insanely connected like this in a public restroom in an unknown city on an April afternoon.

The hanger.

Triumphantly Patti plunges a hand into the suitcase that holds clothes that startle even the high heel–wearing Cathy and Nan. Patti paws through two sequin gowns, seamed nylons, a crimson cocktail dress, a handful of scarves, and what they can only imagine must be a bag of uncut diamonds.

"What the hell," Cathy says as Patti rises with the hanger as if she's just won a gold medal. "What's with the Las Vegas clothes?"

"I'm a singer," Patti answers without hesitation. "Just finished a gig. But enough about me. This is all about Nan and her phone. If this doesn't work, I'm determined to smash the toilet to hell and run for my plane."

Patti uncoils the throat of the hanger, pulls it into one long piece, and then hands one end to Nan. And without saying a word Patty and Nan back away from each other so they can stretch it open before they try to curve it into the toilet and under the drowning phone.

They take the hanger into the toilet stall as if they are in a sacred procession. Patti goes in first, closely followed by Nan. Holly pushes open the door as wide as it can go, Cathy hugs the left side, Margo reclaims her position against the trash can.

Patti peers inside the toilet, then at the hanger, back in the toilet, and then starts bending the hanger wire into a small curve that she thinks will fit into the bottom of the bowl, around the phone, and up the other side.

"This is suspenseful," Cathy remarks, breaking the longest spell of silence the women have had since they'd slammed the bathroom entrance shut. "What's the plan if it doesn't work?"

"I already told you," Patti replies in total seriousness.

"Smash the toilet," Holly repeats.

"Come on," Cathy says with a whine.

"It's going to work," Nan breathes as Patti angles the hanger into place. Holly edges closer and then is nudged by Margo, who has abandoned her post.

Nan grabs one end of the hanger and Patti grabs the other.

Patti explains that she is going to force it under the phone and then she will count to three and they must both pull like hell.

"Sweet Jesus. I feel as if we should pray or chant," Margo says. "I mean, we've been in here, like, twenty minutes or so and we are about to do something almost miraculous."

Holly turns to look at Margo because she's trying to see if the other woman is serious or not. Holly's kind of miracles, especially the one she has been praying for during the past three years, would not include the resurrection of a cell phone. But then Margo smiles, and Holly assumes she's kidding about the praying.

Well, *maybe* she's kidding.

So far, all anyone knows for sure is that there's a singer, an investment banker, a hamburger developer, a hairdresser, and a mom trying to get a phone out of a toilet in the Tampa airport women's restroom.

They might also know that a couple of these women have control issues, one looks a little skankie with her tight-fitting clothing, they all like to drink at airports—except Holly—and they all took a seemingly ridiculous chance to help a stranger by willingly participating in this Airside A restroom event.

And at this point nothing really matters but getting the phone out of there and catching a plane.

"Ready?" Nan asks, bracing herself.

"Yep. I'll count to three and then you pull like you're as angry as you have ever been in your entire life," Patti says, squaring her feet and rolling back her shoulders as she desperately tries not to imagine how Nan would react to a really serious disaster.

"Here we go. One. Two. *Three!*"

The phone pops straight up just as Patti falls back and Holly catches her. Nan and Cathy yelp and reach for the phone at the same time; they miss, and it drops right back into the toilet. But this time it falls sideways and Nan dives in, scoops it up, and there is a loud round of cheering and high-fives. And then, before they can finish celebrating, the airport loudspeaker goes off as if the announcer is standing on the bathroom sink.

"*Attention. Attention. Due to extreme weather conditions moving across a major portion of the country, a state of emergency has been declared. We are sorry to inform you that all outbound and inbound flights at Tampa International except in-state commuter flights have been canceled, indefinitely. Major hub airports from California to Las Vegas have already been closed, and the storm with accompanying high winds, sleet, rain, and snow is moving at a rapid pace. Within several hours this massive spring storm is expected to affect airports in three-fourths of the country. Weather officials are not certain the storm will touch down here, but flights in and out of Tampa are already being affected by other delays. We are urging all travelers to make alternate plans. Due to the seriousness and the severity of the storm, we are recommending you seek alternate shelter. It is unlikely the airlines will be able to help you with accommodations. For any assistance, please seek out an airport professional. Thank you.*"

Nan's cell phone has barely come out of the water when the announcement concludes. It's as if the entire airport has come to a complete stop. For one minute, and then another, the sound of silence is breathtaking. No screaming babies, petulant old people, moving luggage carts, bickering husbands and wives.

No banter, either, in the women's restroom across from the Jose Cuervo Tequileria.

The phone is still dripping. Nan looks at it, turns it over, then throws it onto the tile floor and stomps on it with the heel of her right shoe, which is nothing more than a small dagger. She pounds the phone until it comes apart and little pieces of metal are sliding under stalls, past the stall doors and in between Cathy's, Patti's, and Holly's feet.

No one stops her.

She bashes the phone until the floor is littered with springs and phone guts, until the black mechanical link to her everyday salvation has been murdered.

"This just totally pisses me off!" Nan shouts.

"We can see that," Patti adds. "I may be speaking out of turn, Nan, but I think we are all pretty pissed off. All that work for nothing and now we're stranded at the airport."

"It's not for nothing. We did something. We got the damn phone out of the toilet and we didn't have to call a man for help, and smashing it made me feel good for a second, so that's okay. It's okay with *me*." Nan glares, clearly still on the verge.

"Yes, but now what?" Margo asks as they hear the noise level in the hall begin to pick up.

The restroom brigade is quiet again.

The thought of one more hour, another day, even twenty more minutes in this terminal makes them all feel as if they have food poisoning.

"Well, shit. Just shit," Nan rages, and stamps her foot one more time. "Let's do something, for crissakes."

"Like what?" Holly asks timidly. She's wishing she had grabbed some aspirins out of her suitcase.

"Give me your phone," Nan demands, looking at Cathy.

But Cathy holds on to it with a river of fear in her eyes. She looks down at some of the little pieces of what was once Nan's iPhone and shudders.

"Give it!" Nan barks. Cathy gives it.

Just then there is a push against the restroom door and Margo gets shoved off balance. Holly and Patti rush to keep the door shut.

"Hold them back," Nan orders. "Listen, women. I'll call the hotel I was staying at. There's a convention starting but I know my suite is not filled, because they offered me a great deal to stay longer, and it's a hell of a suite. Let's all go there. Let's pool our resources. We can't stay here with all these people or at some trashy motel near the airport. Are you in?"

The other four women realize that in less than ten minutes a couple thousand people are going to be trying to get hotel rooms throughout Tampa. They all know that the last half hour in the restroom has been a sometimes hilarious, if not occasionally frightening, interlude. They also know that if it's a toss-up between a night in a five-star hotel with a couple of high-strung women with control issues who dress nice, or a night alone in a fleabag hotel—well, it's still sort of a toss-up.

Then Nan shouts, "It's a luxury suite, girls. There's an indoor pool. Restaurants. Twenty-four-hour room service. *IT'S ON THE BEACH.*"

That decides it.

Nan finishes dialing. She gets the suite reserved while motioning impatiently for them to close up their bags and grab their purses.

Then, just before Nan Telvid leaves the restroom, leading an Ohio hairdresser, a mom with three teenagers, some kind of elderly hot mama singer, and an overly sexy woman who claims to know Nan's husband somehow and works for a hamburger palace, she kicks the toilet one more time, flushes it, then runs like hell.

two

H olly looks into the rearview mirror seconds after Cathy wheels the last available vehicle for rent at the airport out toward the exit. She sees a swarm of automobiles behind them that is almost as frightening as their negotiations to get the mini-van had been.

"Oh, my gosh," she exclaims, rolling down her window to get the full effect. "It looks like some kind of mass exodus or something."

Unfortunately Cathy also turns around to look, somehow forgetting she has rearview mirrors, and two minutes from blast-off, horns are honking and the women are almost in their first—of what could be many—accidents.

"What the hell are you doing," Nan screams at Cathy. "If you can't drive, pull over. I'll drive!"

Cathy laughs. It's a fake laugh but it's a laugh. "Drive? You can't even keep your phone in your pocket."

In the backseat, Patti, Margo, and Holly exchange sideways glances. "This adventure to the hotel," they say without speaking, "may be a huge mistake."

Considering everyone but Holly almost physically assaulted the shy young man who was bombarded with car rental requests the minute people began flocking from the terminal, this St. Petersburg Beach adventure could result in long prison terms for some of them.

By the time Nan was done browbeating him into giving them a vehicle he was trying to save for a reservation, the terrified young man was inches from tears. Holly almost grabbed her carry-on and ran, but when she turned to look at the other people fighting for cars she decided it was worth the chance. She got in the mini-van.

Now, with Cathy maneuvering the Chrysler as if she had flunked her speed-driving license test, Holly questions her own sanity. She wonders what in the world she is doing in the back-seat of a car with a mess of women who appear not just danger-ous but who should, from what she has seen thus far, also be on serious medication.

Or maybe they are on medication but not enough.

This thought could be a bullet ricocheting from one woman to the next. At first glance, none of them look crazy. Considering the circumstances, even Nan flipping someone the bird out the window, Cathy swerving like a drunk, Margo sucking on a Toot-sie Pop, Patti forcefully gripping the front headrest, and Holly moving her head like a wild duck, might very well appear normal.

There is no way to know that the five women in the swerving blue Chrysler van heading toward I-275 are total strangers. Almost total strangers, Holly reminds herself. Cathy supposedly knows Nan's husband but she doesn't know Nan beyond the twenty-eight-minute interlude with the toilet and thirty minutes before that at the bar.

"Are we crazy to be doing this?" Holly asks in her sweet, but terribly quiet voice. Which is the exact same thing the other four women are thinking.

"Probably," Patti admits. "At this point I'm just hoping we live until we get past the airport entrance."

Before Cathy can open her mouth, Margo whips the red sucker out of her mouth and suggests they each say something about themselves. She scoots forward, yanking her seatbelt off her shoulder, and starts telling a story about a friend of hers who stopped for gas once near Memphis and ended up spending a week with a nun who was standing in the parking lot and needed a ride.

Patti turns sideways in amazement but before she can say what is on her mind, Cathy, who should simply not be driving, stuns them yet again.

"I get it. We're like the mile-high club. You know—where you meet someone you don't know, maybe don't even know their name, and then, well, you know, *do* it in the bathroom or some-thing, and then that's it. You never see them again. Anyone ever done that?"

This comment confirms a few things, at least for Patti, who silences everyone by saying that screwing someone you do *not* know in a tiny bathroom is *not* like spending time with a nun who needed a ride. Or driving off into the sunset with a mess of stranded women who just met randomly over a toilet. What Patti does not say is that she's thinking of asking to be dropped off at the nearest hospital so she can have her head examined.

"Well, you know what I mean," Cathy, who is clearly proud of her half-exposed breasts, says as if everyone does. "It's just random. Like us."

"It's different with women, I think," Holly shares innocently. "I mean, I can't imagine any of you hurting me, you know? I wouldn't be in this car with four men, three men, or two men."

"One man?" Cathy just has to ask.

"One really hard-up man," Holly says this time, actually blushing.

"Oh, come on," Patti says, pushing Holly with her elbow. "You're adorable."

Holly doesn't respond, and it's surprisingly Nan who says she's pretty sure four men would not have cordoned off the restroom and helped her without thinking they would get something in return.

Nan's philosophy of life and of men is probably tainted by the professional demands of a career that has turned south with the economy so many times it lost its way. But as Nan goes on and on about men and how they can never be trusted, Margo leans over the seat and points out Nan's wedding ring.

Nan laughs. No one is quite sure why.

She's married and has a son, she says. And she includes her husband and her son in her missive about men being takers and not givers.

"I don't feel that way about men," Cathy disagrees, hurtling the van around a bright yellow Volkswagen. "You just have to accept that they feel different and are wired in ways that are totally opposite of the ways we're wired. I imagine most men would not even bother trying to save the phone, especially if it wasn't theirs."

"Well, you may be wired differently than most women," Nan

retorts. "You and I may wear the same kind of shoes, but I mean, really, does that mean we are the same kind of woman?"

"At least in the foot area," Cathy says, with a smile. "I just think I like men more than you do. That's all."

Nan looks out her window without replying.

Margo is not ready to let go of the conversation. "So how does Cathy know your husband?" she pipes up.

Nan doesn't move her head. Cathy remains quiet until the silence demands a response.

"It was one of those convention things," Cathy says quickly. "We do events sometimes when we're trying to lure in new franchise investors."

"Is your husband in investments too?" Margo is not the only one who wants to know the answer to this question.

"He was," Nan mumbles into her window. "Was" meaning up until three weeks ago, when he was let go, which really means he was fired.

Could this possibly explain Nan's nasty temper and her willingness to argue, smash things, and organize groups of women to temporarily abandon the tried-and-true patterns of life?

Margo leans even farther forward, pats Nan on the arm as if she is an old dog, and tells her she, Margo, has been living with one income for a long time. Not to worry. Things will work out.

Patti is thinking this might be a good time to jump out the window. Cathy, she decides, clearly has some kind of sexual disorder. Holly has no self-esteem and keeps rubbing her damn head. Nan is an angry, man-hating bitch. Margo is peacekeeper of the year. Patti's beginning to think it may have been better to sleep in the hallway outside the restroom where they all met.

When she turns to look at Margo, she's wondering what her kind of life must be like. A life Patti never had. An apparent stay-at-home mom. A husband who picks up his lunch bag every day, kisses her good-bye, and most likely comes home to roast beef and stories from the kids. They probably have two frigging dogs, a huge yard, and Margo organizes the neighborhood summer barbecues, knits, and goes to church twice a week.

Patti decides to find out for sure.

"What about you?" she asks Margo. "The story about the nun is enlightening but it doesn't say much about you. We know you came here to visit your parents but I'm guessing you don't usually fly around the country and hook up with utter strangers."

Margo falls back into her seat, flips her seatbelt back around her shoulder, and tries very hard to look excited about the question.

"This is actually the first time I've been away alone in seven years," Margo admits. "It wasn't exactly a joy-filled week, but my parents had this bright idea to move to Florida and I needed to check up on them."

"The kids?" Nan prompts. She is so relieved not to be talking about her husband, her work, or her jackass son, she'd pay Margo to talk non-stop about her brats until they got to the hotel.

"Our kids are great, even on the hard days. Some parts of child raising, as you know, Nan, are not that easy. Does anyone else have kids?"

Everyone keeps shifting the conversation away from themselves so quickly, it's as if talking is a hot potato that is being thrown up and back, from the front seat to the backseat. Patti is determined to get more than a routine answer out of Margo.

She solicits a very quick "no" answer from Cathy, Holly, and herself about the kids question and then once again asks Margo about the other parts of her life.

"It's kids mostly," Margo finally admits, shrugging. "I work in the school nurse's office about twenty hours a week. It's something semi-mellow until my kids go off to college. I suppose if you drew a picture of a typical stay-at-home mom it would look like me."

"You are definitely too thin to look typical," Cathy says matter-of-factly. "My two sisters are in your same boat and they look like human garbage cans."

Holly wonders what Cathy would look like with a large sock pulled over her face. She is trying to recall if she knows or has ever met anyone as brassy and sexually orientated in her entire life. Cathy has flirted with at least a dozen men. And to think that less than two hours ago she was eating a sub sandwich and wondering who her first appointment would be with in the morning.

"Oh, hell's bells," Holly suddenly shrieks.

Everyone else says, "What?" at the same moment.

"I forgot to call in to work to let them know I can't make it tomorrow."

"You're not the boss?" Nan asks, astounded that someone with such great hair didn't run the place.

"Hardly."

The women listen as Holly plugs in some phone numbers and begins talking to a woman named Grace on the other end of the line. In the front seat, Nan mouths the word *"Grace"* and raises her eyebrows so that Cathy notices. Cathy mouths back the word *"Ohio."* They have no idea that Patti can see everything and is restraining herself from slapping them both upside the head.

This while Holly starts trying to explain to Grace where she is and what she's doing because of the travel and airport mess.

"I met them in the bathroom when we tried to get Nan's phone out of the toilet.... No, the phone just fell in there and we all tried to help her. Well, sort of. They're all women.... No. A little bit, but, look, it was this or sleep next to the water fountain

until we can leave. Stop worrying. Well, I don't think it's as crazy as it sounds.... Who cares if you would never do this? I'm doing it. Don't worry, for crying out loud. Watch the weather. The storm might make it to Ohio. I'll call you tomorrow."

Holly hangs up and realizes it does sound crazy. It sounds insanely crazy.

"I have to ask again. Are we all nuts? Maybe we should have stayed at the airport...." Holly falters and then she pops several aspirins from her purse in her mouth and dry-swallows them.

Patti reaches over and pats her hand, which is exactly what Margo would do if she were sitting there.

"Of course it's crazy, darling," Patti agrees with a smile. "That's what makes it all so delicious. I've been doing things like this my entire life and I'm much, much older than you are and still alive. And although I've never been in a situation quite like this, I've been in some doozies."

All four women wonder what a *doozy* would be for someone the likes of Patti. They each imagine her life in separate ways, stringing what little they know of her and her life in a short line. What they don't know seems more important. Last name. Town of origin. Number of men besides the plumber who have paraded through her life. The sound of her voice when she's wearing one of those sequin-adorned dresses. What chances she has missed. Why her face closes when anyone talks about children. Why a woman like Cathy irritates her so much. Where, besides the grace of age, she got her self-assuredness.

Patti wonders too. She wonders which window each one of these four strangers would dive out of if she shared even a handful of her doozies. When she strings the extraordinary events into her own line it seems as if a mess of can-can girls have sprung to life. Older surely than her four female companions, Patti would bet money right now that she could outdoozy them five-to-one—

with sexy-looking Cathy, for sure, coming in right behind her. Cathy even winked at someone old enough to be her grandfather while they were walking to get the van.

"Tell us," Holly finally begs, halting everyone's meandering minds.

Patti laughs and first tells Holly aspirins are going to chew a hole right through her stomach. "Start doing that when you are eighty, sweetheart. Seriously."

"Tell us," Holly says again, totally ignoring the aspirin advice.

Holly, of all people, might be the first one out a window. She seems sweet and young and Patti now wonders the exact same thing everyone else has been wondering, *Who are these women? Who are they really?* Beyond names and professions and all the other insane and inane things people seem to measure one another by during the once-over at cocktail parties, office gatherings, and parent-teacher meetings, Patti senses a wealth of variety in her new comrades that could end up being a doozy itself.

And if she did share a story, which one would it be? Could she grab something remarkable that these women would understand from her large life bag? Would Holly, Margo, Nan, or Cathy think her memorable life moments—those lovely instances of place and time and people—grand enough for them? Could she even pick one out of all the living her sixty-three years have given her?

"Darling," Patti finally tells Holly, "let's keep the doozies for later. I'd either startle the living hell out of you or bore you to tears. How about we get back to the basics, like last names, where we live, and if we prefer bikinis or those absolutely horrid thongs that make you look like you have rear ends twice as big as they really are."

"What if we wear both of them at the same time?" This from Margo, who Patti is certain wears sensible Jockey cotton.

"Then I'd say you are well protected," Patti shoots back.

"I bet you're like a dragon onstage," Nan says, laughing as she gestures frantically to Cathy to take the beach exit. "This is your idea, so why don't you start? Interview yourself for us, okay?"

And so this unlikely and potentially volatile combination of stranded travelers avoid their worries and concerns. Each woman gets one minute to say something about herself as if they are at a bridal shower. Shoe size. Favorite cookie. High school mascot. Drink of choice.

Holly, however, is distracted. If they can't get along in a short car ride, how are they going to make it through the space-challenged hours at a hotel? This is one time when listening to her mother about strangers would probably have paid off. How in God's name can she get herself out of this situation?

Patti goes first. She talks slowly on purpose so she won't have to say much. She'd so much rather listen. But she also knows once they hear her last name, she won't have to say anything else revealing.

"My last name is Nuttycombe," she says flatly. And no one has ever heard of a Nuttycombe.

"Is that your stage name?" Cathy asks this in total astonishment.

"No. I use Patti C. That's it. Sweet and simple."

"Was it made up or something?" Margo guesses.

"It's English. A mess of Nuttycombes came over from England, brought their red hair with them, and then apparently stopped having babies. There are not many of us."

Holly leans over, and, without asking, bravely moves her fingers through Patti's hair quickly and instinctively, checking for red roots.

"I've been covering up the gray for so long any signs of red have long since vanished." Patti laughs, lightly touching Holly's hand.

Margo has totally blown the one-minute rule. Just as Patti suspected, her last name would throw them off the track.

"There's like one minute left until we get there," Margo, the timekeeper, says. "Last names at least. Shout them out."

Even though Margo's voice and actions have the edge of an irritating ex-cheerleader, the women oblige. This is, after all, much easier than shutting down a busy restroom. It's Margo Engelstrom, Cathy Girard, Nan Telvid, and Holly Blandeen, who all quickly agree they do not have names as great as Patti.

As they turn into the palm tree–lined driveway of a five-star Rivera, Holly pulls her eyes away from a glimpse of the white sand beach and astonishes herself by saying, "Well, I hope we get to finish this meet-and-greet in more detail so I can sleep tonight knowing no one in here is an ax murderer."

There's a brief shifting of eyes. Patti coughs into her hand so her face is covered; Margo pops another sucker into her mouth; Cathy swerves to miss an elderly man on a three-wheel bicycle; Nan turns to look sharply at Holly as if *she* may be the ax murderer; and the car finally glides to a stop at the hotel entrance.

"See, no one died," Cathy barks as she gets out, slamming her door like a five-year-old.

"Not yet," Patti remarks sweetly as they all help the bell captain pile bags on a cart.

When they swoop into the hotel lobby, with everyone but Nan making quick calls to family members, it is crowded with men and women registering for the convention of the week. This irritates everyone but Patti and Holly, who lag behind Margo, Cathy, and Nan, who are elbowing their way toward the registration desk. Holly and Patti bond over their shared love of people watching as they shuffle behind Cathy and Nan.

Patti and Holly whisper about inappropriate clothing, the shifty-looking guys in tacky polyester suits planted at each door, how absolutely disgusting it is to see a man wearing socks and sandals at the same time. "Doesn't anyone love those men?" Patti asks this as they finally stop and just look around. Then Holly spots a woman at the conference registration desk who looks like she has never had her hair professionally styled, and when Holly makes a lunge for her half-jokingly, with her fingers twitching, Patti pulls her back and acts as if she is going to spank her.

Margo sees the pair of them standing in the center of the grand lobby laughing like best friends and gives them the evil eye just as a tall man walks out of seemingly nowhere, stands in front of Holly, and says, "Hi, Holly."

Holly looks up at the newcomer blankly as something hot moves across the top of her hairline and her temples start throbbing. She has absolutely no idea who he is. He's the kind of average-looking guy who might blend in a crowd but he has gorgeous dark eyes and Holly can see right away that his hair has extreme potential.

"Do I know you?" Holly asks this just as a woman walks past the man, grabs his arm, and pulls him away.

"Wait!" Holly calls, but the man shrugs and moves away.

When she turns back, Patti has moved to the far side of the lobby and is posed like Vanna White next to a sign. She motions to Holly with her index finger and Holly moves toward her, not just totally confused, but dazed as well. How did the mystery man know her name?

"Before you ask the next question, read this." Patti's pointing to a welcome sign close to the front desk.

Before Holly can even take a look, however, Margo, Cathy, and Nan move in front of her and block the sign. Patti tries to push them out of the way and explains that some man just walked up to Holly who she claims not to know, addressed her by name, and then walked away.

"What in the hell are you talking about?" Cathy barely gets this out when Holly pushes her aside so she can read the sign.

Welcome Para-Psychic Professionals.

Everyone looks at it.

Gypsies? Card readers? Psychics? Intuitives? Who in the hell are Para-Psychic Professionals?

Margo says she knows. She tells the other four women that a bunch of teachers were talking about it just before she left home. One of the teachers where she works has an uncle whose neighbor is involved in something psychic that sounded strange but really isn't so strange when you stop to think about it. Margo explains that there are ghost whisperer kinds of people. They can see and hear things. They might, for example, know Holly's name, what she likes to eat for lunch, or, not unlike on the popular television show *Medium,* what could happen to her if she turns left when she crosses the street instead of right.

"That's who's staying here with us?" Nan asks this as if she's been ordered to sleep with a busload of lepers.

"They are regular people, really, with gifts," Margo assures her. "Anyway, that's what I was led to believe."

"Oh, come on!" Cathy seethes, grabbing her carry-on. "These nutcases could be using their secret powers to rob banks and look under our clothes, for God's sake. You people watch too much television."

Margo is insulted, and poor Holly has not moved.

"What if he really knows me? Or knows something about me?" she asks wretchedly, without taking her eyes off the welcome sign.

"He looked like a nice fellow," Patti reassures her. Then she takes Holly by the arm and picks up her bag, sets it in Holly's hand, spins her around, and points her in the direction of the elevator. "We're obviously stuck here, sweetie. I suggest you just forget about him."

But Nan cannot let go of the psychic angle either. She peppers Holly with questions as they ride up to their room on the sixth floor. Patti longs to slap Nan so she will shut up, and is worried that she might actually do it. She'd already wanted to smack a couple of them in the car and is praying that this whacko hotel adventure will be very short-lived.

Everyone is momentarily saved from the verbal, and possibly physical, assaults, when the door finally opens on the sixth floor. Nan turns left, the rest of the women follow, and they walk into their hotel room.

None of these women are from Florida. Four of them live in places where winter claims the most days. Places where it often snows in April and people cry in the morning when they open the window and see yet another gray skyline. Cities that literally rejoice when the temperature jumps past thirty or forty degrees. Towns where wool is always in high fashion. In Milwaukee, where Margo lives, it's not uncommon to see people walking toward the grocery store in shorts the moment it's one degree past forty-three. In San Jose, where Patti leaves her bag when she's not traveling, the California sun is often obscured by car exhaust, fog, and smog, and clouds that have a tendency to move in and never leave. Cathy's hometown of Denver is a freezing snow bowl that often closes freeways.

Paradise for each one of these women is suddenly right outside the long balcony that caresses the three sides of their lovely suite.

One after another they drop their bags and rush toward the balcony. Nan flings open the huge patio doors, moves her hand across her body, and without saying a word invites each one of them to take a look. She can't help herself and says, "Told you so," as everyone rushes past her.

The view is a postcard look at the Gulf. Seagulls are soaring. The white sands of St. Pete Beach fan out so far it's impossible to see either end of it, even if you lean dangerously over the side of the balcony. The outdoor pool just below is shimmering. Despite the storm warnings, the sky is Caribbean blue. The contrast between the quiet beauty of the hotel and the chaotic mess at the airport almost blinds them.

It's suddenly impossible for any of them to even imagine that a wild storm has caused them to stumble and fall into this slice of non-reality. There isn't a cloud in the sky. The breeze is so slight it's almost non-existent. How could a storm possibly be hammering the rest of the world?

The glorious view, a full kitchen, wet-bar, living room, two bedrooms, and a pullout couch also make some of them feel a little guilty. Schedules, families, and life responsibilities that are outlined on phones, in notebooks, right at the tip of each one of their minds, overtake them like a plane-stopping tempest.

And the women scatter before one of them says or does something to once again set off a bickering procession.

There are suddenly meetings to cancel, kids to talk to, an agent who needs to reschedule a booking, husbands who need not drive to the airport, lost connections that must be put on hold, plans times five that can no longer drift. The extraordinary view may offer a hint of paradise but it is, after all, only a view. Each woman has an almost desperate need to be alone.

It is a good hour later when the aroma of pizza lures everyone back to the kitchen. Patti had broken into the bar so she could have her nightly dose of wine, or medicine, as she prefers to call it. Then she'd used her one phone call to order three large pizzas.

But the sixty minutes apart might as well have been a year. When the five women converge again they have already stepped back into the shoes of distrust, short tempers, longing for what they thought they were supposed to be flying toward. And the cold reality that what they were really headed for was this particular mix of women.

There's Cathy and her brazen sexiness. She's managed to change into a pair of shorts that people in the olden days called underwear. She's beautiful in that harsh, too-much-makeup kind of way that people either find irresistible or nauseating. She has long blond hair, blue eyes, great legs, and a personality that at times seems like the sharp edge of a new knife. Nan could be her shorter, dark-haired, brown-eyed distant cousin. The *smart* cousin. The girl who got her business degree and an MBA, stormed into the world of finance, and used her high heels to not just look taller but to also keep handy in case she needed to gouge out eyes... or attack toilets. Holly is a woman waiting to happen. She's a subtle, dark-skinned beauty with hazel eyes, extra weight in all the wrong places, some weird aspirin addiction, a voice that needs to turn up its volume, and a personality that needs a shove down a long hill to get kick-started. Poor Margo looks like a sweet but often beaten and extremely thin doggie. Even though she's essentially managing a small company—three kids, a husband, volunteering, and who knows what in the hell else—something terribly big is missing. She appears to be a size 0, constantly pulls at her own blond hair, and moves her fingers as if she's always craving a cigarette. Her skin is flawless.

Patti takes one look at the four women marching into the suite's kitchen and immediately suggests they eat the pizza with steak knives in case someone feels compelled to stab the woman next to her.

"You all look like you have just been drafted," she says,

handing out succulent slices. "May I suggest a lovely scotch, chardonnay, vodka? Or better yet, one of each to accompany your sad meal?"

"Is there beer?" Margo's already dipping her head into the refrigerator. "I think I've had pizza and beer every Friday night for the past ten years. Pizza on Sunday is something new."

"Why not really mix it up and have wine?" Cathy says this while lining up three mini-bottles of vodka, which she intends to pour into a tall glass. "I mean, live it up."

"You seem to be doing enough of that for the rest of us," Nan fires. "I mean, really Cathy, can you just ease off for a few minutes? Not everyone lives the high life like you do."

"I was kidding," Cathy says, clearly mystified that her remarks are not universally accepted. She's also hurt. Why do women always take what she says the wrong way? She's just trying to make herself a martini without vermouth, trying to get Margo the mommy to let go a little bit, trying to blend in with a group of women she doesn't know, probably doesn't even want to know. And she's definitely thinking of her missed connections—not just in this room but at the next airport and the one after that.

Patti is about to slip out onto the patio when Holly, clearly unraveling, announces with more than a hint of panic that the storm is going to make her miss four of her biggest clients tomorrow. It's how she lives. How she pays her rent. There's no executive husband. Yes, she's one of those dumb-asses who has to live from paycheck to paycheck, but there it is. One missed day isn't so much, but two, maybe three? It's a disaster.

"What is *this*?" Holly's waving a beer bottle around in a fashion that startles everyone. "A *five dollar* beer? I mean, really. I buy a six-pack for less than that with a flipping coupon. My share of this room is like a week's worth of my house payment."

Patti sighs. She obviously can't sneak off to eat her pizza in glorious solitude on the balcony now. She might miss something.

"I'm right there with ya," Margo admits to Holly. "A pair of cheap tennis shoes for a teenager is about half my food budget for a week. I really don't know what I was thinking about when I said I could come here. I'm sorry. My husband freaked. I've been in the bathroom for thirty minutes trying to see if there's enough money in the damn checking account to stay even one night."

Outside the wind picks up, but the women do not even notice that the blinds near a half-opened window are shaking. It's gotten pitch-dark and the tide has swept in to swallow most of the beach. The moon has long since disappeared.

Without warning, the differences between the women have grown longer, deeper, crueler. Most of them know it was a mistake to have left the airport, to not be in a fifty-dollar-a-night hotel, to be with women they would most likely never befriend, or have the chance to befriend. Maybe sleeping in a chair in the damn airport wouldn't be so bad after all. Could what they are doing be any more ridiculous?

Patti is thinking of a song. Something in the back of her mind that she heard a long time ago that makes her feel sad. A longing that she cannot put into words. All her life, songs have floated through her, ignited her feelings, and brought back memories that she cannot always identify. Tonight's song is old. Patti has to stop herself from humming it out loud, so instead she squeezes past Margo and sits on the couch. She also struggles not to say she's barely a step ahead of the others financially. It's cheap wine for her, unless some old bald guy at the bar starts to buy.

Nan softens just a bit when Margo finishes speaking.

"Oh, forget about it," Nan says quietly. "My company will

probably pay for the whole damn thing. I'll make up the difference if they don't. It's the least I can do for women who helped
me save my phone."

"We didn't actually save it," Cathy reminds her, clearly unhappy about the phone's demise. "You smashed it."

Nan suddenly has yet another surge of violence that she can
barely contain. The phone is obviously a touchy subject. Or
maybe Cathy is a touchy subject. Patti quickly steps in before
someone commits a crime. She orders everyone to sit down in the
living room.

Patti's order somehow takes about half an inch off of an anxiety level that could launch three space shuttles.

At first.

Cathy breaks open the mini-bar and buys a round of drinks.
Beer, wine, scotch, vodka, and whatever else the women can
reach. And for a moment they forget about missing connections,
the difference between Miller Lite and really good French wine,
hanging out at the airport bar, or eating a whole bag of greasy
potato chips while slumped in a plastic chair. Margo stops texting her kids. Holly temporarily lets go of the idea that Cathy
would be almost beautiful if her hair was just three inches shorter
in the back. Patti moves on to a sweeter song. Even Nan relaxes
her jawline.

The women try very hard to talk without irritating one another. Patti has an uneasy feeling this truce can't last long. They
drink, toast fast-food pizza, and the alcohol temporarily helps
them forget about their myriad differences.

Cathy's strong martinis have made her the positive life of the
party and she loves the attention. She's dipped into her purse,
grabbed out her hairbrush—which Holly thinks needs to be
thrown away—and is using it as a make-believe microphone.

"Let's do this right," she commands, flourishing the brush. "Intro time, ladies."

Patti itches to throw her down when the hairbrush is dipped into her face. But she plays along, imagining this is what summer camp must have been like for the rest of them. It was surely not something she ever got to do.

"I'm a well-worn sixty-three," she begins. "I've been singing my entire life and have always been three steps away from being in the right place at the right time. Never married. And that's about all you are going to get out of me tonight."

Patti pushes the brush toward Holly while Cathy grabs her own glass for a refill. Holly shrugs, says very softly that she's obviously single, and reveals that if she had to say much more about her life she'd probably start crying. She's not about to tell this gang of half-testy women her deepest secret.

Cathy for once has the good sense to keep quiet and Nan tells Holly that's just fine because they know enough about her. Margo says kids, school, the dogs, her workaholic husband, and her parents pretty much say it all. Then they all fall silent, staring at their emptying glasses and the two remaining slices of pizza. Apparently, no one is much in a sharing mood. Maybe they are all just tired.

The peaceful interlude heads south, however, when Nan grabs the brush and tries to interview Cathy.

"Tell us about those little events you host to lure in new customers," Nan asks, looking directly into Cathy's eyes.

"What?" Cathy is taken aback by the bossiness of Nan's tone.

"Or maybe you should tell us about all those husbands you mentioned," Nan fires again.

Patti now knows for sure this must be what summer camp for adolescents is like. Before Cathy or Nan can say another word, she grabs the brush, hands it to Holly, and looks first at Nan and then at Cathy. "Should I say, 'Take it outside'?"

"I was just having fun," Nan lies.

"Look, we are sharing bedrooms and space. We should all just lighten up, okay?" Patti advises. She's imagining how quiet the corridors of the airport must be right now. Then she narrows her eyes at Nan and Cathy. "Are you two sure you do not know each other?"

Before either can answer, Margo's cell phone starts ringing, and she's so relieved to leave the room, she trips when she turns to walk away. This gives everyone else a good three seconds, all the time they need, to call themselves idiots for having agreed to this stupid adventure.

Nan uses Margo's absence as an excuse to leave and make some phone calls. She retreats to the back bedroom to use the bedroom phone. Holly murmurs that her head hurts from worrying. She's wondering if she can sneak some more aspirin without Patti noticing and commenting on it. Cathy saunters back to the bar. Patti says, "This party appears to be over," and asks Holly, as the least offensive woman in the immediate area, to help her pull out the sofa bed. They don't say a word as the bed pops open, Holly salutes her, and disappears.

Everyone withdraws into her own separate world. The suite has quickly become littered with empty glasses, bottles, clothing, and an unspoken thought that everyone needs to shut the hell up and get some sleep before someone actually commits a felony.

When the lights are finally dimmed, there is only the soft chatter of women speaking into phones, women who are hoping that no one within earshot will hear them. And not one of the five women notices that a piece of paper has been quietly slipped under their hotel suite door with the word *Emergency* boldly written across the top.

three

he April moon has appeared in the gloom and wedged itself into a tiny opening between a long line of clouds that sag lower by the minute. It is the darkest hour of evening.

And inside the best suite at the St. Pete's Rivera there are two empty beds.

Margo's rollaway bed, tucked into the corner of Nan's room, and Patti's better-than-expected pullout couch have not been touched. Holly, in spite of her misgivings, is sleeping like a baby. After downing four beers and making the horrid mistake of calling her mother to tell her where she was, Holly finally hung up, had one more beer, shouted to the phone, "I am *not* going to be killed in my sleep!" and then prayed to God that she would still be alive in the morning.

Nan spent so much time on the bedroom phone the receiver

got hot. "No one uses hotel phones anymore," Cathy snarled as she tripped over Holly and fell into her own bed after she called to remind Housekeeping to make certain the mini-bar was restocked the following day.

Both Nan and Cathy joined Holly in the land of drunken dreams very quickly after they fell into the sheets. But not before Cathy realized she had forgotten to take her cell phone charger out of the last hotel wall and Nan laughed so hard about her misfortune that she fell off her chair.

A perpetual bad sleeper, Patti pretended to be trying to sleep as everyone else sloshed around to their beds. She did doze off and then woke up, jerking herself awake as if someone had frightened her. She would swear with one hand on top of a Barbra Streisand album that she woke up when she heard one of the women arguing in her sleep. Patti—a woman who can easily handle bar drunks, a wild crowd, and rejection—isn't quite sure she wants to handle the women she now happens to be living with. Or that she even likes them.

Patti has gotten used to the up-and-down sleeping routines that have plagued her relentlessly for the past forty years. She's tried everything, including Cathy's drinking remedy, but nothing works. She's finally managed to convince herself she will not die from lack of sleep.

Rolling over and tucking the fat, lavender-scented pillow under her head, Patti looks outside. The door to the balcony is open and the shades are dancing when she decides to listen to the waves from the balcony. Surely that will be a much better sound than the ticking of the stove clock.

That's where she finds Margo, sitting on the floor, arms laced in between the metal balcony poles, her feet dangling off the edge. For a moment Patti's tempted just to back up and hope Margo has not heard her. She wants another confrontation or sullen woman in her face like she wants another delayed airplane. But the richly damp night air seduces her.

"Couldn't sleep either?" Patti asks this quietly and walks toward Margo, who is smoking a cigarette.

Margo doesn't answer, which is not what Patti was hoping for when she took this risk. Damn.

"Is that why you are so thin?" she wants to know, pointing to the cigarette.

"Part of the reason, I suppose." Margo shrugs without bothering to look at Patti. Then she says it could be because she doesn't eat well, she's busy all of the time, and after spending a week with her mother, who constantly told her she's "got a nervous condition" because she can never sit still, that could be her newest reason as well.

Patti starts to laugh loudly and then remembers the other women are sleeping; she claps her hand over her mouth, and struggles to sit on the floor and dangle her feet like Margo.

"This is the kind of shit that makes me feel old," she grumbles, groaning as she grabs a cushion to sit on without bothering to ask if she can invade Margo's space. "I am pretty sure wearing high heels onstage for fifty years didn't do much to help my legs, ankles, and feet either."

"You look fabulous," Margo exclaims, which is such a nice thing to say that Patti is startled. She hasn't heard many positive exchanges from these women. "I would never have guessed you are sixty-three. My mother isn't that much older than you and she looks like Phyllis Diller on a really bad day."

"That's what living with a man will do to you."

Margo glances at her, gives her a half smile, and looks as if she wants to say, "I know." Instead, she takes a very long drag on the cigarette and blows it out so slowly Patti thinks she must be pulling smoke from her toes.

"Rotten habit," Margo admits when she's finished. "I'm sorry. Does the smoke bother you?"

"Actually, I was thinking of bumming one from you."

"You smoke?"

"Well, it's mostly secondhand smoke from the bars and people I know, but sometimes, when I see someone like you smoking as if it's the best thing they have ever tasted, I just have to have one."

"Your voice?"

"Some jackasses think it helps. But really, when you think about it, it's like sucking in a bag of chemicals. What the hell, though. Light me up."

Soon there are two tiny red dots on the balcony, beacons in the midst of a very dark night. The beach is deserted and the waves seem to get higher and louder each time they push toward shore. Both women are silent for a while, until Margo talks about the hypnotic sound of waves and water. She's got one of those white noise sound machines in her bedroom but her husband almost always turns it off. Sleep comes in spurts. It's coffee all day long, cigarettes when the kids are not around, and then an occasional energy drink to help her stay on her feet the rest of the day.

Patti is surprised by Margo's confession. She's sensed a level of unhappiness or confusion in Margo since the moment she saw her fidgeting in the airport restroom; now she decides to ask her why she can't sleep. Getting personal is always a risk but she asks her anyway.

Margo hesitates. What to say?

When she closes her eyes and leans her head against the railing she pictures each one of her children sleeping. Justin, the oldest, at seventeen will be on his stomach, covers on the floor, feet hanging on either side of his bed, in spite of the fact that she's told him a million times stomach sleeping will screw up his back.

The girls sleep like little dolls even though her second-oldest child, Meggie, would rather die than know her mother sneaks in to watch her sleep. She's a not-so-lovely fifteen and right now hates everyone who has her same last name. Alyssia, thirteen, still curls around her big stuffed dog. Margo watches her the most. She's convinced she will be able to see the very moment when her baby crosses over from being just that to a not-so-little girl.

When she finally speaks, Margo doesn't answer Patti's question.

"I thought it was like this for everyone, especially after kids came," Margo shares, shrugging. "I guess I've never thought about it too much. I'm just not a sleeper."

"That's what you think?" Patti asks the question delicately. Maybe this too-thin woman with early worry lines around her eyes has really never thought about why she sleeps so badly. There's no reason why she would lie to Patti.

"What else could it be? I mean, my brain is always flying around in there and I'm afraid I'm going to miss something, because I juggle lots of stuff."

Patti desperately wants to ask Margo if she is happy. Happy the way people who do not have families always think people who have families are. Happy the way people who never started out not to have a family but ended up without one think they could have been happy if things had just been different.

What would it be like to have two daughters and a son to call when you're stranded far from home, instead of an aging booking agent? What would it be like to have a couple of grandkids drive to pick you up at the airport and then spend a week with you fixing the back fence, taking the dog for a walk, and just keeping you company? A husband? A real man who made a commitment and stayed around for however long the relationship might last. Someone to care past the first few nights, past the false glamour of being with the woman singer. School lunches, family vacations, visits to see the relatives, parent-teacher conferences, the girls getting their periods, first dates, family squabbles, and making up after them.

"You know what," Patti says, finally blowing out her last, long-held trail of smoke and with it a long-held longing. "I've always been jealous of women like you. Women who have drawings from kids and notes and copies of report cards on their refrigerator doors."

"You're kidding me, right?"

"No, I'm totally serious. I have a sister. When I was younger I would go to visit her whenever I was singing near her city and I'd actually steal the things off her refrigerator. I still have some of them. One is just this little note her son wrote her the first day of school—this must have been like thirty years ago—which said, *Don't be sad mama.*"

Margo immediately reaches for another cigarette. Patti grabs another cigarette too. If her damn knees didn't hurt so bad she'd get up and get them both another drink.

"You know what, though," Patti continues. "I'm old enough to know that we all want what we don't have. My sister eventually got divorced. The cute little boy who wrote the note ended up in drug rehab. But I still have that note. One thing lasted."

"It's not always bad," Margo shares, addressing Patti and her own experiences as well.

"Tell me."

"You know, when we first decided to stay here and not hang out at the airport, I was freaking," Margo confides. "I mean, really, what were we thinking? Don't you think this is a little ... well, screwy?"

"Honey, in my world everything is screwy. But yes, I think we are all a little nuts."

Margo looks away and takes a small chance. She says she knows worlds are different. She knows that her single friends want to get married and half her married friends want to be single. No one knows what it's actually like until you get there. It's hard work. Marriage and kids and balancing everything that comes with that damned piece of paper you signed at the altar. *And you get so tired.*

"You just don't take the time to think about it," Margo continues. "It's like there's no time left for anything but the next day and doing it all over again."

Even in the dark Margo looks exhausted. Her shoulders sag and she lets both arms drop through the railing openings. And then she rolls her head and Patti can hear the bones crack.

"What about now?" Patti asks this gently. Margo looks as if she could slide right off the balcony.

"Well, I could stay right here for about twelve years, I think," Margo answers, turning slowly to face Patti. "I mean, Nan and Cathy are driving me crazy and Holly really needs to get a backbone, but hey, it's sort of like being at home. Some days everyone and everything pisses me off. No offense or anything but what were we thinking?"

"Maybe this airport closure is some kind of weird gift so we can see how much we can endure."

"I don't want you to get the wrong idea about my life, you know?" Margo says quickly. "I mean, it's not all bad, but I feel like I've lost my car keys, my original road map, pretty much everything else some days."

But then.

Then Alyssia will curl up in her lap. Justin will actually be affectionate for three seconds in a row. Meggie will not act like a total ass when her mother won't buy her something at the mall.

"It didn't start out this way," Margo says. "It's been so damn long now, I sometimes have a hard time remembering what I thought this part of my life would be like. My husband is a guy. A guy's guy. If someone asked me if he's a bad father I couldn't say he is. A bad husband? Not really. It's just..."

Margo trails off, then suddenly stops talking. She can't believe she's said as much as she already has. Patti doesn't need to hear the rest. The rest of the story is written all over Margo's face. And it's a story that Patti could recite for her.

Things were different when they married. They were... equal. Maybe Margo and her husband were in college together and he finished and Margo did too but then he went to work and Margo stayed home. While she stayed home, her friends got jobs and went on to get their advanced degrees and some of them moved to places much, much farther than Milwaukee, Wisconsin. One baby came and pretty soon Margo had a hard time remembering what she dreamed of being the first day of college. Then her husband got a promotion and he worked longer hours and Margo found a few friends in a children's play group who also could not remember what they once wanted to be when they grew up. There were more babies and school and becoming a chauffeur and a maid without ever thinking twice about it. There were books to read so one did not have to think hard. There was the smoking on the back porch so the kids could not see. There was the exercise plan that never lasted long because of the smoking. And of course right after the last baby the not-sleeping business started. And the woman Margo used to recognize, the one she would smile at in the mirror, the one who was still excited when everyone was home at the same time and safe and sound, and who once threw a pumpkin pie at her husband when he said dinner was horrid—that woman had gotten so thin she was disappearing.

Patti makes up Margo's story without saying a word and is busted when Margo complains that she's been doing all the talking.

"Your life is probably a lot more exciting than mine." Margo curls her legs underneath her, leans back on her elbows. She's done talking about things she doesn't even like to think about, let alone say out loud, especially to a woman she barely knows.

This interesting insight has plagued Patti for almost fifty years. Here's what she knows for sure: People always want what they don't have. People always think someone else has more money than they actually do. Margo is one unhappy mama. And everyone thinks it's absolutely glamorous, exciting, thrilling, and wonderful to be a singer.

They don't want to hear about the shitty pay and hours. They don't want to hear the three thousand stories about drunk, groping men, asshole agents, long bus rides, and hotel rooms that should have been gutted twenty years ago. They don't want to know about the hundreds of lonely nights, the lost chances to hit the main stage, how every time another teenager with big tits and a voice that should never be let out of the bathroom makes it huge it's almost impossible not to stalk her and say, *"It should have been me, you little brat."* If you speak of never being able to retire, how the veins in your legs throb as if knives are being plunged into your calves, how you had to barter for a Pap smear—about the price you paid to be a singer—they back away and think you are insane.

Patti doesn't think Margo needs to hear that right now. She doesn't need to hear any of the other horrible parts about her life either. So instead she reveals the one thing that supports the heavy center of her soul.

"It's true that you often have to give something up to get

something else," Patti explains, turning away and looking out toward waves that are crashing much louder than they were when they started talking. "But when I start singing, when I am standing up there, and I connect to that place inside me that is a river of notes and lyrics, everything else falls away and I know for however long it takes me to sing a song that I am standing in bliss."

Margo lifts up her left hand and lets it fall softly for just a few seconds onto Patti's arm in a surprising gesture of affection. Then she smiles. It's an unspoken thank-you for sharing something so personal, for opening up a small door, for letting her off the hook by not asking if she's really happy. And considering the local emotional climate, physical affection is also a bit of a risk.

"I'm sure lots of people never think their life is going to end up the way it does, but..."

Patti trails off for a moment because she knows if she says what is coming next she may have to own up to it, believe in it, maybe even live it herself.

"What?" Margo is almost begging.

"It's easy to think nothing can or will ever change and then what happens is that is exactly what happens," Patti shares, digging deep. "The real truth is that anything and everything is possible. Hell, I sing about it all the time. I usually have a hard time believing the songs that come out of my own mouth."

Margo is suddenly angry at herself for opening up a slice of her life, her real life, to a woman she has known for less than a day. So she leans away, shifts her weight as far from Patti as she can without standing up and walking away. It's as if she has drawn a curtain, hung up a *Closed* sign, signaled the final play of the big game.

Patti turns away too. She's just as glad to be done talking.

She's already started wondering what in the holy hell these women are going to do besides drink, smoke, argue, and avoid serious discussions for the next few days.

In many ways, she decides, what is happening is no different from all the other times she has languished in hotel rooms—*waiting.* Waiting for the next call, for a knock at the door from the right person, a phone call from someone who didn't want something but had something to give. Here, beachfront or no beachfront, Patti thinks of herself as the older referee in a female tango that could be a lovely waltz if any of them, herself included, could just slip on the correct shoes.

She laughs silently at the thought that Margo sees her as attractive and younger-looking than she really is. She has only genes to thank for her tight skin, a figure that has not expanded, great teeth, expert experience with fabulous makeup, and an attitude that usually distracts everyone from what Patti considers her many shortcomings.

If they only knew how impatient she's become with life and the people in it; how she sees grown men and women slumping through one day after another without even one song to savor; how the thought of intimacy—on any level—almost paralyzes her; how being onstage, acting out an obligatory persona, has carried over to the rest of her life; how laughing and turning away has become easier than asking the next question, pushing into emotions, or embracing a relationship.

The uncomfortable silence widens. Both women sit without speaking, counting the crashing waves, each one wondering who is going to hang it up first and exit the balcony.

Patti finally surrenders. She groans with a half laugh as she gets up and warns Margo that something weird happens when you reach fifty because you suddenly can feel every bone in your body.

"My knees feel like broken sponges," Patti admits.

"That's what my mom says."

"How old is your mother?"

"She's sixty-five, or maybe sixty-four. I forget."

"I'm old enough to be your mother."

Now Margo laughs.

"You sure as hell could not be my mother," Margo exclaims. "She's one of those women who was always old. Never young."

"Well, this non-mother thinks you should go to bed. Who knows what time the wild ones will get up and start bothering us again."

And Margo jumps up, says a simple, "Good night, then," and quickly turns and walks through the living room and into the bedroom she is sharing with Nan.

A few minutes later, Patti hears Nan's bedroom door close just as she steps into the bathroom and turns on the shower, guessing that everyone else is passed out and will not hear her.

What she doesn't see or hear is Margo grabbing the keys to the van, her own purse, and then quietly slipping out the door. And in the dark entryway Margo steps over the emergency notice without noticing it as she makes her escape and dashes for the elevator.

four

omewhere between nightfall, climbing into bed no matter how late it was, and the beginning of a new day, all of the women have checked in to their real lives.

The chatter on the phones when everyone was preparing to sleep was a concert of explanations, message gathering, connecting with home and work, and in Margo's case—a marathon logistics discussion with each one of her children and her husband. Margo also checked on her parents who were unconcerned about the storm and more worried about shuffleboard.

Throw it all together and the chorus of canceled meetings, the desire to hear a familiar voice, and the unknown results of the spring storm that is snowing in one state, blowing wind in another, then pausing to confuse weathermen in-between, and the end result was a very large question mark.

The last mechanical device to go off in every room was the television. The last station to go off in every room was the Weather Channel. And what a storm the five women were watching.

Call it global warming, or a freak of nature, but after a series of near calamities at airports and freeways across the nation the year before from another storm, everyone was being overly cautious.

No one even knew if the storm would move fast enough to actually hit Florida but officials were taking no chances. Airports were closed and because every major airport affected so many others, the ripple effect was massive.

The quick phone calls home had turned into long discussions bordering on panic about everything from soccer practice to re-booking a singing gig at a small tavern.

How bizarre that outside of the windows there was still a hefty breeze but no sign of the carnage they had seen on the television. But each of the women knows about travel and weather and sitting in an airport bar in one sunny city while the destination airport is on lockdown.

So when morning came, restless dreams of life back home with familiar beds, sounds, and people presented a kind of waking delirium. Are the kids still in bed? Did the paper come? Did I miss the alarm? Where in the heck am I?

Patti wakes up and cannot remember where she is. She's turned sideways on a sofa bed, nothing under or around her feels familiar, and when she opens her eyes she is looking at a blank fifty-three-inch television set that she's certain would never fit in her tiny apartment.

Then she smells food. Real food. Bacon, eggs, maybe even something baking in the oven. And the unmistakable fabulous perfume of really good coffee.

Without moving she yells to anyone who might hear, "Am I in heaven?"

"I cannot believe you slept through me cooking breakfast."

Patti rolls over, scoots her rear end onto the middle of her surprisingly comfortable bed, and when she decides to turn right she sees Margo standing in the kitchen with something that looks like yet another cigarette sticking out of her mouth.

Before she dares to say anything, Patti gropes for something on the end table and when she lifts herself up again on one elbow she has on a pair of huge black-rimmed glasses that would make Elton John jealous.

"Oh my God." Margo laughs so loudly that her Tootsie Pop, not a cigarette, falls out of her mouth and drops to the floor.

"What in the hell is so funny? Haven't you ever seen an old lady wearing glasses she bought from the drugstore twenty years ago?"

"No. Not even my mom wears glasses like that."

"Wait a minute." Patti drops her head, fluffs her hair, and when she looks up again Margo says, "Wow."

Patti tips her head to the left, raises her left hand in a "ta-da, there you go" kind of movement, and gets Margo to agree that the big glasses look *very* cool once Patti's hair is rearranged. Patti has not yet commented on the spare white sheet Margo has tied under her armpits that makes her look like someone from a reality show who has been forced to dress like a ghost.

"Do you wear contacts?" Margo asks her.

"No. I had one of the first eye correction surgeries years before Lasik was popular and back when you were probably still in diapers. For some insane reason it takes my eyes a while to wake up in the morning. Like right now, for example, it looks like you are standing in the kitchen, cooking, eating your morning sucker, and wearing a white sheet."

"Those big old glasses work real well," Margo agrees, shaking her sucker at Patti. "You were snoring when I started cooking, by the way. Were you tired, or what?"

"It was all the stimulating balcony conversation," she retorts, half sarcastically. "It wore me right out."

Truth be told, it would take Patti all week to remember when she had last slept that hard. She is still shaking her head and trying to wake up—not just her eyes, but everything else as well—when Holly and Nan come stumbling down the hall as if the smell of food is a leash.

Holly has on two-piece Mickey Mouse pj's that make her look about three times bigger than she is; Nan is right behind her and decked out in red silk boxers and a lacy white top that appears rather honeymoonish.

"Where did all of this food come from?" Holly closes her eyes, and inhales as if she's just taken her first breath.

"I went to the store last night after you were all in bed. I couldn't sleep. And I'm used to cooking, so I thought, what the heck."

Patti stands up and looks directly at Margo. Margo does anything but look directly at Patti. And Patti is mystified. *How did she get out of here and back in without me hearing or seeing her? Did I pass out? Did someone drug me? Who closed the drapes? How in God's name could I not hear someone cooking breakfast almost in the same room?*

Realizing there must be more to the story, Patti decides to remain quiet but she wonders if Margo could have gone someplace besides grocery shopping at one a.m. The hotel bar? Some guy she met while visiting her parents? Maybe there was someone waiting to drink gin with her at the airport bar. It seems odd that shopping would be this important. *Whatever,* Patti finally decides, throwing up her hands and traipsing to the bathroom while Holly and Nan swarm around the kitchen stealing food and hovering to see what is going to emerge from the oven. Both women are also extremely thirsty.

"Are you a little hungover?" Nan asks Holly, which also distracts Margo, allowing her to steal a slice of bacon.

"I'm dying," Holly shares. "But it's a good kind of dying. I think I kinda had fun last night."

"Yes, well, fun and drinking a lot usually go hand in hand."

It's as if no one can remember that if there had been a gun in the living room last night someone might have gotten shot.

Cathy comes out of the other bedroom just in time to hear Nan's last sentence. She stops, and starts telling a story almost as bizarre as the one she came up with yesterday, the one about the mile high club.

"I know this is hard to believe, but a very long time ago I was in Montana at a bar—"

"So far I'm not surprised," Nan remarks, cutting off Cathy.

"Shut up," Cathy fires back.

"Ouch." Margo frowns. "*Shut up* is like a swearword in my house. I forbid it."

"Then it's a good thing this isn't your house," Cathy grumbles.

Holly gently intercedes and asks them all to be quiet so Cathy can finish her story, which so far makes absolutely no sense. Not that anything has made much sense. Each one of them has spent more than a few minutes since they hopped into the van to go to the hotel wondering if staying at the airport might have been easier. What woman in her right mind just says "yes" like that in an airport restroom? Wouldn't trying to sleep in a plastic bubble chair be better than worrying about who is going to flip out next? Who cares if they are at a beachfront oasis if it's impossible to enjoy even thirty seconds of peace and tranquillity? Isn't hell five women shut up in a luxury hotel suite?

Cathy starts talking as if she's expected everyone to pause and give her their full attention. Apparently she was once on a road trip with a college roommate. They stopped at a cowboy bar near Bozeman, Montana, and started dancing with two very real cowboys.

At this point in the story Patti has come out of the bathroom, minus her Elton John glasses, and is standing with her hands on her hips, listening. What she sees is Cathy wearing what appear to be pink running shorts, a bright yellow jogging bra, an electric blue crop top that is covering up a good two inches of her torso, and holding a pair of tennis shoes that must be state of the art, because they are a color Patti does not even recognize.

The audience staring at her doesn't so much look mesmerized by Cathy's story as stunned. It's as if this is the first time they have ever seen Cathy, who appears as if she's going running and just popped out of the bedroom to tell a story on her way to the track. Patti wonders if she could fit through the bathroom window, jump onto the balcony below, and get on the next bus out of town.

"So, we drank, like, so much beer and honest to God, there was a band playing and halfway through the night a fight broke out and this guy was stabbed and everyone just kept dancing." Cathy stops for a moment to drop her shoes and sit on the couch to put them on. "I looked down and people just kicked sawdust over the blood that was on the floor and the worst part is coming."

No one says anything.

Everyone is trying to imagine Cathy in Montana. Cathy dancing with a cowboy at a bar where people stab one another.

Cathy making it out of the bar alive. Cathy being a senior manager at a company and conducting a meeting where she has to connect sentences and dots and stay organized.

"Cathy, finish the story." Holly, of all people, has appointed herself in charge of keeping Cathy on track.

"Oh. So the night goes on and on and finally my cowboy date slumps into his chair and I say to him, 'I bet you didn't think you'd have this much fun tonight.' And he wiped his mouth on his sleeve, like they do in the movies, for crying out loud, and he says, 'Yeah. I also didn't think I'd drink a case of beer and get drunk.' "

No one moves or says a word.

Finally Holly walks around the side of the counter. She gets it. Holly—who spends fifty-plus hours a week listening to women talk about high school sweethearts they cannot forget, the way their husbands piss them off, ungrateful siblings and children, trips to the Bahamas and wine country, Oprah's weight, recipes for tortes and chili, and revealing tales of personal habits, mistakes, longings, and passions that would make most people blush—understands how Cathy's mind works.

When she speaks as the new interpreter for the women from Tampa's Airside A restroom, it is an astonishing relief. "So every time you hear someone say something about drinking and having a good time it takes you back to that dangerous night where that guy got drunk?"

Holly asks this question even though she already knows the answer. This beautician can apparently pop in and out of minds as if she is a seasoned clinical psychologist.

Cathy stands up, slaps her legs, says, "Yes, it does," and begins stretching as Margo turns to open the oven and exposes an egg dish that looks like a painting.

Patti is afraid to move. She wishes she had some kind of a

video camera because she's certain she is going to want to re-member these conversations, these women, what might possibly happen next. This thought collides with a song she thinks is per-fect, "Strangers in the Night," which she starts humming as she begins walking toward the kitchen, where everyone is staring at the homemade egg dish as if the shape of the Blessed Virgin has miraculously become embedded in its top.

Even Cathy has stopped moving to take a look, and Margo explains that it's a kind of low-fat Eggbeater's veggie dish that she invented when she had to make something and didn't know if anyone was a vegetarian.

"Anyone here a non-meat-eater?" Margo turns to ask this question as everyone but Cathy swipes a piece of sausage or bacon from the counter.

"I eat fish, but that's it." Cathy stretches while she says this and suddenly Nan's eyes focus on the shoes, the shorts, the top Cathy is wearing, and away from the food.

Before Nan can start speaking, however, a mild electric charge ricochets through the kitchen. It's like the cold breeze from a ghost. Like the hard-to-breathe feeling three seconds be-fore it rains so hard the trees bend almost in half. Like that giant pause right before you realize you have sent the most horrid e-mail to the wrong person.

"Are you going out?" Nan asks. Cathy has one leg up on a chair and is stretching out her hamstrings.

"I can't eat first thing in the morning, especially when I have a slight hangover. I have to go for a run or I will go out of my mind. And I thought I could see if there's a phone store near here to get a charger."

Holly has a sausage in her mouth and a piece of bacon in her hand.

Margo has popped another sucker into her mouth.

Patti is poised with a fork to be the first one into the egg dish.

Nan who has just slathered her toast with raspberry jam slaps one hand on the counter, drops the toast, swallows, and takes four steps so she is standing right in front of Cathy.

"You can't go for a run." Nan says this with a hint of bewilderment and anger.

"Why not? Are you crazy?"

"I'm serious. We are all supposed to have breakfast together and talk. You are going to ruin everything."

"Nan, what in the hell are you talking about?"

"Look at us." Nan gestures with both arms like a bird trying to take off. "We have this chance to hide away for a few days. We can step out of our routines, find out, for once, more about who is sleeping in the same room with us. We are always so busy. Instead of being pissed off about being stranded here, we could actually do something positive."

Cathy continues to stretch throughout Nan's explanation. Nan goes on to say that although she knows just a little bit about every woman in the room she can guess that they all need something she calls "a time of grace." A brief, sweet period of time when they can rejoice about phones being lost, canceled meetings, no carpooling, whatever in the hell they would usually be doing.

"Margo, you probably cook all the time, don't you?"

Margo immediately says yes to Nan's question, then adds that she loves to cook.

"Don't you want a break, though?" Nan asks this question of everyone.

"Not really," Cathy answers. "And you can't tell me what to do and what not to do, Nan. Even if you are trying to ask me in a sort of nice way. You just seem so angry. Maybe you should take your own advice and just take a break from that yourself for a few days."

"I'm not angry," Nan responds quickly. But her voice is just a few decibels louder.

Cathy backs up and puts her hand on the door.

It is an electrifying moment. Every woman stands frozen and thinks about where they would be, where they should be if they were not standing in a hotel kitchen arguing with women they barely know.

They would all already have miles under their feet, minutes zipped from their cell phones, problems solved, and new problems waiting. And that, at this moment, seems easier than what they are doing.

How bizarre to be at a luxury hotel with a gift of time and chance and to be wondering, maybe even missing, the lives they often dream of abandoning—schedules, places, responsibilities, and the all-too-seductive face of familiarity.

The light on the porch no one ever remembers to turn off. The scents of last night's dinner still hanging above the stove. Two stained wineglasses on the bed stand. Fingerprints on every window in the house. Cold feet against warm thighs. The phone message that can never be erased.

Cathy moves first, breaking the silence, bringing them all back to the Rivera.

"Just save me some of those lovely looking veggie eggs, Margo," she calls as she pulls open the door, looks down, and finally sees the sheet of paper that has been lying unnoticed for hours.

She leans over, picks it up, slams it facedown on the counter, salutes Nan as if she is the general, and closes the door.

Holly wonders, if she told them all she thinks she's dying,

would everyone stop fighting and taking out their anger on one another. If she told them that she knows she wouldn't be lying. Even though the one doctor she has bothered to see told her there is nothing wrong with her, Holly knows something is not right. How can those weird feelings in her head be anything but a flipping brain tumor? But she's vowed to keep her funky headache feelings to herself with this group of whack-jobs. Even Patti, who so far seems the sanest, would probably laugh at her, she's certain.

While Holly ponders her mortality, Margo seizes charge, orders Holly to find some plates and set the table. Nan shifts the food from the counter to the small kitchen table. Patti fills coffee cups and then starts another pot, because she's pretty sure they may be drinking coffee for a long time. And no one is saying a word.

Nan turns on the television in the adjoining living room after she sets the food on the table. Maybe there has been a miracle and the airport will be open before the coffee cools.

But no matter what channel she turns on, the same red notice is riding across the bottom of the screen. *Unusual late spring storm still causing travel problems throughout the country.*

So much for that miracle. Nan switches off the television and marches back to breakfast.

If these women could be back at the airport eating Twinkies from a vending machine and washing up in the water fountain instead of standing in this lovely kitchen, every single one of them would leave now. These half strangers may as well be total strangers. Cathy is out running on the beach and the rest of them can't even say what's on their minds. Until Patti, once again, decides to push forward another inch. She just can't help herself.

She asks Margo how she was able to get out of the suite last night without making any noise.

"It was easy," Margo says with a wink. "I just acted like I did when I was sixteen and sneaking around my parents' house. You were in the shower when I left and asleep when I got back."

"I can't believe I didn't hear you, though. I'm a really light sleeper." *When I can sleep,* she thinks glumly, but doesn't say.

"I made a mess of phone calls from the lobby too," Margo announces while setting the egg casserole on the table.

"In the middle of the night?"

"I know people who don't sleep either," she retorts, ordering everyone to eat.

Patti can't imagine who Margo knows beyond a second- or third-shift worker who would be up at what she guesses must have been close to three a.m., but she lets it pass, even though she wonders if Margo is lying through her teeth; she is too ravenous to worry about it. And if she doesn't hurry there won't be a thing left to eat. Her testy roommates are eating like little piggies.

Eating has always been the connective social tissue in all of their lives. Nan has used her nightly cheese-and-cracker and cocktail routine to try to keep herself sane. Not that her husband has noticed, but it's also been a way to attempt to lure him into an occasional conversation. Holly grew up in a family that solved everything from a car accident to the death of the family dog by eating meals that would feed an entire city block for a week. Margo really does love to cook. She's been secretly keeping track of her gastronomical inventions and has this great idea to make each of her kids a cookbook for college, and life beyond, when they leave the nest. Cathy might not admit it if she was not out running, but she's always loved to use an expensive meal, two or three bottles of wine, and her bare foot under the table to help her get the guy sitting across from her to fall like a boulder. Patti counts fabulous meals with wonderful friends she has met all over the world as the times she holds dearest.

And if ever a bring-them-together experience was needed, it is right this moment. Everyone is on edge. Holly is constantly rubbing her temples as if she is about to get a headache or she's desperate to remember something. Margo cannot stop jiggling her left leg, which makes half the table shake. Nan is clearly totally pissed off at Cathy, who isn't there, and Patti keeps thinking about that bathroom window exit and the size of her own rear end.

The women gingerly attempt to ignore the tension by simply talking about what they're eating. How controversial can food be? There are six vegetables, a secret sauce, Eggbeaters, cottage cheese, and a subtle hint of fresh spices in this egg dish that has all of them moaning. They guess everything from basil and cinnamon to parsley and ginger. Margo will not tell them. "Secret recipes are my trademark," she does reveal, clearly happy that they love her food. And Patti can only wonder silently how long it took the cook to find an all-night grocery store with exotic spices.

They all eat so much they almost forget to save something for Cathy. Nan takes in a breath and is the one who puts the last slice of the egg dish onto a plate and shoves it toward the middle of the table.

"Thanks, Margo, I think that cured my slight hangover," Holly says, getting up to grab the new pot of coffee and refill cups. "I'm pretty sure I don't want to start drinking again for just a little while. But what else is anyone interested in doing today?"

There is another uneasy pause when instead of answering Holly's question, Patti chokes noisily on her eggs. As if anyone wants to do a social activity together when they can barely share a meal! Is there something wrong with this harebrained hairdresser? Patti glares at Holly, wipes her mouth, and starts to say something, but it's Margo who takes the bait.

"Part of me kind of likes Nan's idea about doing things we would never normally do," Margo declares. And then she adds firmly, "Unless it's cooking, of course. I'd have to keep doing that."

"Or running, I guess." Nan says this with a shrug.

"Are we not in a tropical paradise? Let's embrace that beach I see out the window."

This from Patti, who has suddenly switched the song in her mind from "Strangers in the Night" to "Let's Take a Chance on Love," lest she be the sour apple in this basket. She shockingly wonders out loud what it would be like to go up in one of those kite things people hang on behind a boat.

"It's called parasailing," Nan tells her. "I've never tried it because once when I was on vacation in Mexico, I saw some poor guy get splashed right into the side of a very tall beachfront hotel."

"So much for my great idea," Patti mutters, already defeated.

"I did it once on one of those wild Florida college trips a very long time ago," Holly shares. "I had to go two drinks over my limit to get into the harness. And when I came down the boat dragged me forever and my entire bathing suit came off."

This sets off a round of laughter that is such a relief, everyone physically relaxes. Legs uncross, hands stop clenching cups. Margo puts down the fork she has been tapping on the table and Patti has a fleeting hope for this sordid group of females.

Holly told them it was back in the day when she still wore two-piece suits, and she stayed in the water until the boat guys gave her three shots of tequila, held up a towel, and promised not to look when she got out of the water.

"Of course, they looked," she says indignantly before anyone can ask her. "By then I really didn't care, but I swear they dragged me on purpose."

"Then everyone agrees that parasailing is out for this afternoon?"

Nan asks this with a straight face and gets a unanimous "yes." She reminds them that they all came to Florida to work or for parental responsibilities—maybe being stranded here, they might actually do something they would not normally do.

And what she does not say is that so many parts of her world seem to be collapsing that she does not want to do one thing that reminds her of the life she has beyond the doors of this lovely, two-bedroom, full-kitchen suite with twenty-four-hour room service. The absent son. The equally absent and now unemployed husband. The tightrope she is teetering across every single day in her own merciless and often-hated job. The ass kissing she has to do on a daily basis that is turning her into a vile and angry woman. A woman who might not even be able to step out of her own high heels long enough to realize she's ruined her damn feet.

"I'm just so happy not to be wiping snot off some sick kid's face or driving someone someplace, I'd be happy building a sand castle and starting up the drinking again." Margo toasts them all with her cup of coffee.

"I've never been deep-sea fishing," Holly laments, thinking as she does so that this is one more thing she should do before her brain tumor explodes. She always cries when someone dies young in a movie, but she never thought it would happen to her. She battles back tears.

"I'm not sure we should let you anywhere near a boat," Patti tells her. "Anyway, fishing sounds like too much work to me. We'd have to get dressed. Walk to the dock. Sit down again. The thought of it all is absolutely exhausting."

"When was the last time anyone buried someone in the sand?"

This from Nan, who is thinking of paying someone to bury

her and dig her back up again in a couple of weeks. Or maybe in a year.

This brings a chorus of remembering. Everyone has a ton of beach and sand stories. Everyone except Patti.

"People think California is one huge beach," she explains, when Holly asks. "First of all, I live in a big city. It's forty minutes to the nearest beach and when you get there the thousands of people who live in your city are there too. It's not the Beach Boys kind of thing most people dream about."

"You never went to the beach?" Ohio Holly actually dreams about California beaches and touring wineries and driving through golden hills with a perfumed breeze blowing through her hair. "Not even when you were little?"

"My childhood was not one I care to remember," Patti says honestly. "Let me just assure you that it did not include trips to the beach and bouncing on my daddy's lap."

The way Patti says this makes it clear that this part of her story is over. She actually looks like she may never speak again.

Holly looks at Nan, who is doing everything to try not to look at anyone. Margo has picked up the fork again and is bouncing it on the table. Patti thinks she is tapping out some old Simon and Garfunkel song that Patti only sings when the crowd is really drunk.

"Maybe Nan's first idea wasn't so bad after all," Holly says in a whisper. "Doing nothing might be the way to go. I work pretty hard, but I'm also really good at doing nothing on the one day a week I do have off."

What she doesn't say is that way they can each do what they want, no one has to be forced to say anything personal about their lives, and she can keep her secrets locked away right next to her aspirin.

"If all else fails we can always go downstairs to the convention and have our fortunes read," Nan decides.

"Like I wanna know my fortune," Holly mumbles, and sips her coffee, wondering if she would ever have the nerve to hop in the elevator and go find the guy who knew her name. And wondering right after that if she would ever have the nerve to tell these women her real story.

Patti rolls her eyes as the first line from "Tracks of My Tears" bulldozes into her mind. "People say I'm the life of the party 'cause I tell a joke or two..." She shifts in her chair, clears her throat, and is about to suggest they all just put away the damn coffee and start doing shots when they hear someone stumble outside the door and then a series of very loud knocks.

Nan jumps up and pulls open the door. Cathy slides into the room, looking as if she has just gone swimming in her clothes.

"What happened?" Nan exclaims as Margo runs for a towel.

"Have you not bothered to look outside in the last twenty minutes?"

Everyone turns toward the windows.

Holly gets up, spills her juice, almost takes out Patti with her left elbow, pulls back the drapes, and opens the sliding glass doors. She exposes a world that makes everyone but Cathy gasp.

"Oh my good Lord."

Holly sees lawn chairs blowing across the beach. Three people are screaming and running toward the hotel entrance. The waves are massive and rain is coming down in sheets the size of huge garage doors.

"I was on my way back, just a few blocks down the beach, and this storm came out of nowhere." Cathy has dried off her face and hair and is standing with the towel wrapped around her shoulders. "I can't believe none of you heard it."

The other four women are silent, still stunned by the fury outside the sanctuary of their suite.

"We've been talking and eating and no one bothered to open the drapes," Margo explains at last, feebly. "I've never seen a hurricane or anything, but that looks scary as hell to me."

"I heard sirens too," Cathy tells them, shaking her head at their obliviousness. "I don't know what that means but I'm not going back out there. I need to hop in the shower. The temperature dropped like twenty degrees in five minutes."

At that moment, one of the suite phones rings and Patti instinctively leans over to pick it up. Patti is shaking her head. She doesn't say a word until the call is almost finished, then she says, "Thank you," and hangs up.

"What?" Nan impatiently asks before Patti can begin speaking.

"Just when you think things are looking up a little, the hotel management calls with startling news. You know that big-ass storm that brought us to this hotel? Well, it has unexpectedly twisted south. We are being advised not to leave the hotel for any reason. We are also being advised that if we do leave, we do so at great risk and the hotel accepts no responsibility."

Patti stops to take a breath, and to simply irritate cranky Nan a little bit. Then she tells them that they are also to be reminded that the hotel has three restaurants, a luxurious lobby, an Olympic-size indoor swimming pool, and a staff eager to serve them if they need help in any way, shape, or form.

Nan quickly turns the television back on and what they see when she turns on a local station is pretty much what she sees when she stares out the suite window. Howling wind. Crashing waves. Sand snaking across beaches that no longer look like a slice of sugar-white paradise.

Florida, the TV weatherman informs them, is now under a severe attack from Mother Nature. The spring storm has arrived.

"Holy shit." Margo speaks for all of them as she drops to her knees in front of the television set. "I hope you enjoyed your run on the beach, Cathy. Because it looks like we are now going to be on hotel lockdown."

"You've got to be kidding me!" Nan is glaring at the television, and imagining, exactly as the other four women are, how absolutely horrid it is going to be if they are indeed trapped inside the suite and hotel with one another.

Patti croons, "*Stormy weather...*"

Margo is the only one who smiles. Holly looks panicky.

"Do you think we're safe?" Holly asks this innocently, not realizing that Patti was thinking the same thing.

"It doesn't look very safe out there," Cathy shares. "It's months before hurricane season but it's clear that doesn't mean anything. This is a freak storm. I cannot frigging believe this is happening to me."

"To *you*?" Nan exclaims, and stares at Cathy as if she has lost her mind. "You are not alone in this room. We are *all* stuck here."

Margo gets up and walks back into the kitchen, half wondering how many heads she could fit into the oven at one time. She feels as if she's back at home listening to her kids squabble about who has to take out the damn garbage. She also can't wait to see what happens next.

"You know, girls, even though this sucks, it's kind of exciting." This from Patti. A screen bangs against a window and everyone jumps.

"If someone could just tell me that we are safe in here I would feel better," Holly pleads.

"Well, it depends," Patti tells her. "If we can't figure out how to spend the next however many days we are going to be trapped together in this hotel, you might be safer outside."

"That's not nice," Cathy tells Patti, who shrugs.

This is when Margo chooses to pick up the spatula and slap it against the counter. The noise sounds like a small handgun going off inside a coffee can.

"Jezus." Patti almost falls out of her chair.

Before Margo can move into her mother role another inch and tell them all to shut up, she exhales, looks down, and sees the pink sheet of paper that Cathy had placed on the counter hours ago. She sees the word *EMERGENCY* and snaps, "What the hell is this?"

"It was under the door," Cathy explains, going in search of another towel. "I didn't look at it," she says over her shoulder. "I just set it over there when I left, you know, when Nan was yelling at me."

"I wasn't yelling," Nan lies.

"Stop it," Margo commands and begins reading.

Her eyes get larger as they descend down the page.

"What?"

"Read it."

"What in the hell is wrong now?"

"Out loud. Read it now, please."

First Margo turns the paper around so they can see the large bold word on the top. Then she starts:

"Please be advised that it has come to our attention that a series of sexual assaults have been occurring for the past several weeks in this area, including on the hotel grounds. We have reason to believe that the person or persons involved have criminal records, are dangerous, and they will use deadly force. Please be careful. Also, please do not hesitate to come

down to see us if you notice anything suspicious. We are
hosting a twenty-four-hour booth inside the convention hall.
We have information not available to anyone else. Please take
this warning seriously."

The moment Margo hesitates, Holly starts wailing. Margo
has to shout to get her to stop, and says she isn't finished.

"Don't you want to know who put this under the door?"

"It would have to be the hotel management," Nan assures
them.

"No." Margo shakes her head. "It's signed by the people at
that convention downstairs. The psychics who are all over the
place."

"You have got to be kidding!" Patti says this in a way that
surprises everyone but Margo. As far as they know Patti has not
appeared to be startled by anything.

"Listen," Margo says, grimly. "I told you these people were
for real. I know things about them. We have to take them seriously."

"This is absolutely unbelievable," Nan snarls. "First my
phone. Then the damn stupid storm. Now a bunch of nutcase
fortune-tellers telling us we need to hide under our beds. I feel
like I'm in a flipping movie, for God's sake."

"A nightmare movie," Cathy adds. "And it's a show you
bought the tickets for, sweetheart."

Holly can feel herself trembling. It's as if a bulldozer's roam-
ing around inside her head. She stands up, grabs the paper out of
Margo's hand, reads it, then looks up.

Her face matches the color of the ketchup bottle on the table,
and when she finally manages to speak it's obvious she is seconds
away from bursting into tears.

"Something is just absolutely *wrong* with all of this," she insists. "These damn people know something. That guy *knew* me. I don't care what you say, Nan, I am scared half to death."

Before anyone can reassure her, the wind yanks the screen out of the patio door, throws it against the railing; when it bounces off the balcony, it sounds very much as if the world is coming to an end.

five

Holly is not sure she will ever come out of the bathroom. During tornado season in Ohio she's always taken great comfort in lying in the bathtub. She has just placed several towels in the bottom of the super-large soaking tub with whirlpool jets, rolled up the extra washcloths for a pillow, and she's sipping on a mini-bottle of scotch, which tastes like the smell of the burning garbage dump in the small town where she grew up.

Tornadoes, she knows, are not like sudden spring storms off the Gulf, but all she can ever remember seeing on the television set after big Midwestern storms were untouched bathtubs lying all over cornfields.

Her father, an overly cautious long-haul truck driver, always made his family stand in doorways, lie under the basement steps, or fling themselves into ditches anytime the sky darkened. He also told them you could survive any storm by lying in a bathtub.

Holly thought she was over it all. Over being anxious and worried and wondering if the sky would fall and collapse the walls. Over hanging on to that long string she always reached for when she wasn't sure about something. Over pulling on it so tightly that it was always breaking like a thin thread. Over letting anyone and anything push her into lying in the bathtub.

But the storm. The guy who knows her name. The rapist and would-be murderer running loose just outside the suite door. Her knowledge that her life is going to end too soon, when the brain tumor messing up her mind finally bursts. And four women who could qualify for a bitching marathon have driven her to crawling into this bathtub, because she thinks it's the only place she will be safe.

Even in the bathtub she can hear them out in the living room, still arguing viciously about things they have no control over, the argument that drove her into the bathroom in the first place. They like, she believes, to have control over everything that touches them. Well, who doesn't? Except this fierce combination of powerful personalities is akin to constantly holding a lit match under your left foot.

Holly is not alone in her bad-men, weather-induced, mind-reading-psycho-tracking-psychics paranoia. All of the women, even Patti, are on edge.

Before Holly had gotten into the tub, and when they were all still in the kitchen, Patti had scrambled out of her chair and gone over to see if there was any damage from the flying screen and had not come back to the table. She was standing silently by the window and the others, especially Holly, did not know if she was mesmerized by the storm, terrified by the idea of some predator lurking around the hotel, or just sick of being in the same room with them.

Margo finally went over to stand next to her and asked if she was okay.

"I'm fine," Patti replied, turning slowly back toward the other women and following Margo to the counter, where everyone was gathered.

"Don't leave us now, Patti," Nan had begged half-jokingly. "We're counting on you to be our mom."

"Me?" Patti snorted and raised her eyebrows. "Margo's the mom. Not me."

"Oh, you know what I mean," Nan said, poking Patti with a stirring spoon. "You seem to take everything in stride."

"Girls, if you only knew." And what she didn't say is, "You'd die if I told you everything."

Patti did tell them that at her age she's been around the block enough times to have botched up more than a few things. Relationships, chances, you name it. And a lot of what she's messed up, and what's been messed up for her, centers around men.

"This idiot running around raping women, maybe killing them, is frightful enough," she shared. "Just add this man, or men, to my long list of every other male jackass I've known. Sometimes it just gets to me."

"Well, sweet Jesus," Margo murmured. "Not to mention the fact that the possibility of being raped is terrifying. I, for one, am grateful every day of my life that testosterone is not my dominant hormone."

"I've always embraced my estrogen," Patti said quietly. "It's a lovely hormone that defines women and if men had just a little bit more of it, the world might be a better place. Maybe estrogen defense is what is keeping us safe right now. Maybe the power of all of our various estrogen levels will provide a protective barrier from the forces of nature and evil. That doesn't mean we are not scared to death."

The women were all stunned for a moment because Patti's admission was so emotional. No one had ever thought of estrogen that way before and no one would have guessed that Patti could be so revealing.

This is when Holly started to get even more worried than she already was. If Patti, a woman she perceived as the kind of chick who secretly carried a concealed weapon, slapped men upside the head on a regular basis, and had probably finished more than a few bar fights was frightened, where did that leave *her*?

Holly had tried very hard to weigh the good and bad parts of her present situation compared to the good and bad parts of being alone in a really crappy hotel or sitting on a plastic chair in the airport for endless days. She was really uncertain which option made more sense. And that guy who knew her name... She was working very hard to convince herself that it was simply a lucky guess. After all, hadn't people been telling her since she was a little girl that she looks like her name? "Oh you look so sweet" or "Your big red cheeks look just like those red berries."

This made her vow to never, *ever* name a child, if she ever had one, something like Holly just because she was born in December and had glowing red cheeks.

Nan had said they all sounded more than a bit down on men. Not that she could blame them, she continued. Considering her world is constantly dipped in the midst of devious men, she had to agree that most of the black marks on her own checklist were caused by the actions of men.

Everyone was thinking about that bit of female wisdom when Cathy, who had been eavesdropping on their conversation while she changed out of her drenched running clothes and into a lovely pair of tight yellow capris and a matching low-cut top, walked back into the kitchen.

"Can we lighten up here? Come on girls. Enough with the male-bashing, for crying out loud. It's such a cliché. What are we—college kids? Yuck."

That stung. And it managed to get everyone moving in a different direction. (Except Holly. She was so jumpy she could barely breathe.) Patti immediately clapped her hands and ordered everyone to help Margo clean up the breakfast dishes. Margo refused to totally relinquish her dominant kitchen position and told the others where to put each plate in the dishwasher. Cathy, of course, sat and watched while she ate the last of the secret egg dish.

But then they were finished.

They were finished and the wind was still blowing, the rain was slashing down, the planes were still not flying, no one had notified them that a violent killer had been captured, and there was a stretch of time that suddenly seemed like an eternity for five women who were not as strange to one another as they were less than twenty-four hours ago. But strangers still in so many ways.

It was as if the storm had brought with it a set of invisible curtains that had been strung between the women, making it impossible for them to see one another. See one another in the ways women see one another at the beginning of new friendships. At that point when you want to know everything about her; when you want to see photos of her kids and her husband and the house where she lives; when you want to ask her if she is happy— *really* happy—and not get just that chirpy, seemingly mandatory response people give when they really don't care aymore and they know you never did; when you want to lie down on her sofa, wineglass in hand, and talk for hours and hours about whatever pops into your head because you know however horrid, or silly, rude, or absolutely ridiculous it is, she won't care and she will listen; when you want to confess an inappropriate thought, feeling, or action, like the time last week when you came across the phone number of the man who propositioned you five years ago at the conference in Dallas and how you suddenly really wanted to call him; when you also want to confess that you did not rip up his phone number but stuck it back inside your old address book, where it remains at this very moment; when dreams that have been floating loose and unformed take a certain shape because you have met someone who you know will not laugh when you tell her that you want to join a women's ice hockey league, kayak down the Mississippi River, or—honest to God—take a cake-decorating class after you come back from a solo wine-tasting trip to the vineyards of Provence.

When the dishes were done, and nothing beyond that had changed, what happened next is what drove Holly to the bathtub. It was Nan turned program director who came up with something that made Holly feel as if the only place she could be momentarily safe was in the bathtub.

Nan suggested a trip to the small boutique in the lobby to look at clothes. She especially thought it would be fun to try on bathing suits, even if they couldn't use them right at the moment.

Nan's idea might not have gone anywhere if it had been a sunny day and they could walk on the beach, go try the piña coladas at the tiki bar, had the desire to have their fortunes read in the lobby, or go out stalking a serial rapist.

Patti would rather stick a pin in her eye than try on a damn bathing suit. Cathy, who probably wears a bikini when she goes grocery shopping, thought it was a terrific notion. Margo, who had just told her children for the fifth time that she is perfectly safe, even though it now looks as if Florida is blowing itself to Cuba, thought anything would be better than watching the screens blow away. However, Holly thought it would be more fun and probably safer to go swimming in the ocean.

Before anyone could say another word, Holly strode across to the mini-bar, grabbed the tiny bottle of scotch that was sitting on the first shelf, and walked out of the room.

Into the tub she went. And that is where she is now lying.

Patti at once immediately assumes the role of mother without realizing it. She looks from one woman to the other, and then she strides toward the bathroom door and raps on it, firmly.

"Holly?"

"I'm in here, Patti. There's no escape hatch."

"Are you okay?"

"I'm as okay as a fat woman can be who has just been asked to try on a bikini during a raging storm when a killer is on the loose and we are all trapped inside a suite we can't afford to pay for."

"Oh, hell, Holly. Most of that may be true, but you are *not* fat."

"Patti, I'm not blind. I'm from Ohio, but that does not mean I'm a dumb-ass."

"No one said you're a dumb-ass. I think we're all a little high-strung about our situation."

Holly wouldn't mind if Patti came in and sat on the toilet and talked to her for a while. But then she'd have to get up and unlock the door.

"Look, I just want a little time alone," she half whispers wearily. Her head hurts. "You all go on down. I'll be fine."

"Do you think an old woman like me *wants* to try on bathing suits?"

Holly starts to laugh. Patti doesn't seem old to her. Old is someone who doesn't swear, sing, travel, laugh, drink, live. Patti appears to be living with her declining estrogen levels perfectly.

"Just go. I'm okay."

"Are you sure?"

"I have a few calls to make too."

Patti knows Holly is lying, but she decides to give her the space she seems to need.

While Patti has been talking through the door to Holly, Nan, Cathy, and Margo have paused to make quick phone calls home, and to the trailer park. They want to reassure and be reassured.

Patti is desperately trying to think of the words for some kind of death-march, funeral-type of song, but she's so distracted, absolutely nothing pops into her mind. This rarely happens and it's disconcerting. She walks down the hall toward the kitchen, humming a series of notes that do not form a known melody. The stress of dealing with these crazy broads is getting to her; maybe she needs to go lock herself in the other bathroom.

Holly hears the door close when the other women leave and is already having second thoughts. She gags down the rest of the scotch and decides that even if the other four are acting like seventh-grade girls, there is strength in numbers. She puts away the towels, decides to throw on some lipstick, leans in to add a little more makeup, and then studies herself in the full-length bathroom mirror before she runs to try and catch the other women.

At first she sees the same Holly that everyone always sees. A short, slightly overweight, brown-haired, green-eyed young woman who has great hair and *potential*.

"Fuck potential."

Holly, who under normal circumstances hates to swear, puts her nose inches from the mirror and peers into her own eyes, frowning. Way back behind the missteps, mistakes, and misgivings she sees in them, she thinks she can see a glimmer of the woman she wants to be. She's a sassy, wild, no-holds-barred kind of woman who, naked, would have taken a fifth of scotch into the bathtub and filled it up with bubbles while singing a dirty song. *If only*. If only she could be a woman who would believe it when a doctor told her there was nothing wrong with her head, and who wouldn't be too frightened to get a second opinion.

"What in the heck is wrong with me?"

Holly pulls away from the mirror, throws the remaining scotch into the sink, and walks out of the suite so fast she doesn't take her purse or a key to the room. She lunges for the elevator button, thinking that if she hurries she can catch up to the women quickly, and act like she really meant to go with them all along.

Thankfully, the elevator comes right away and she rushes inside, presses the ground-floor button, and only then realizes that there is already a man in the elevator. And it's not just any man—it's the man she encountered in the lobby, the one who called her by name.

As the elevator descends, Holly can feel her stomach climbing toward her throat. Her heartbeat accelerates as he turns and says, "Hi, Holly. Some storm, isn't it?"

Holly squeezes her eyes shut and focuses on breathing. She's suddenly convinced he's not talking about the weather, but the tempest in her soul. She tries very hard to be a new woman, but when she swallows, she tastes nothing but fear and dread.

"Hi," she finally manages to answer. She forces herself to open her eyes.

He looks nice. Nice in that kind of gentle-lines-around-the-face, half-smile, blue-eyes, dark-hair kind of way. Dang. He's kind of handsome.

"How do you know my name?" Where this not especially polite question comes from, Holly has no clue, but she's thanking her usually hidden inner-strong woman.

"You'll just have to trust that I do," he says, shrugging.

"So I suppose you can read my mind now?"

"It doesn't always work that way. We're not kooks, you know. You could probably read my mind if you tried hard enough."

Wow. This sounds like a very unique pickup line. Holly isn't sure if she should be terrified or acknowledge her confusion. Maybe she should even be flattered, she thinks.

She decides to change the subject. "How's the convention?"

"Okay, so far. We have a lot going on. I hope you and your friends read the note we put under your door."

"That's serious? It's not a joke? There's really someone running around out there?" Holly wants to affirm her feelings.

"Might be more than one someone. It's for real. We are serious professionals. People get the wrong idea about intuitives, Holly. They think we smoke long cigarettes, use a crystal ball, and paint our fingernails."

Holly can't help herself. She looks down at his nails. He laughs and holds up his hands. Nice nails. No wedding ring. Being this close to him makes her feel a bit woozy. Did he cast a spell on her? What is happening?

"I don't suppose you'd have a drink with a strange psychic who has nice nails?"

Holly is so relieved when the elevator door opens she almost starts to weep. She smiles without parting her lips and has to force herself not to run across the lobby into the boutique. She steps out of the elevator resolutely. When she turns and sees him standing there, watching her with his head tipped to the right so that he looks like one of the questions he never got to ask, she realizes that although he knew her name, she hadn't even bothered to ask him his.

Holly moves forward, heart thumping, bursts into the small shop across from the registration desk, and it's immediately obvious that staying in the elevator would have been a much better choice. The shop looks like a scene from an early Goldie Hawn movie.

Nan, Margo, and Cathy are in various stages of undress. Patti is ransacking a display case filled with pink, orange, and lime green Florida T-shirts, and it looks as if the one dressing room is occupied. This must be why Cathy has a hot-pink bathing suit on over her clothes.

"Hey, Holly, find a suit," Nan orders, as if Holly had been there all along.

"No. Thank you," Holly says firmly.

"Make that two no-thank-yous," Patti adds. "It's like a madhouse around here with all the people trapped in the hotel."

Cathy, Margo, and Nan join them by the T-shirts and Holly can't help herself. She blurts out the story of the man in the elevator and then, trembling a little, waits for someone to say something.

"Did you get his name?" This from Cathy, who, thank God, has finally slipped off the bikini that was making her look like a misplaced trick-or-treater.

"No," Holly admits softly.

"The whole thing about him knowing your name is a bit odd." This comes, surprisingly, from Nan.

"It wouldn't hurt to go have a drink with him," Cathy suggests. "You were already drinking in the bathtub and everything here is pretty damn public. It's not like you could find a dark corner to sneak off to together. There are bored people *everywhere*."

Who are these women? Could it have been little more than twenty-four hours ago when they were total strangers who ended up together in a women's toilet? How did this happen? *How in the hell did we all get from a stupid cell phone mishap to this very expensive gift shop, which is the last place in the world I want to be?* Holly longs to be back in the bathtub.

Before she can open her mouth, however, Margo's cell phone rings. She grabs it as if it is on fire. The phone has a loud bleeping ring that sounds like a Code Blue at a hospital. And all the women turn to look at her.

"I've never heard a ring like that," Patti says first.

Margo looks flustered. She tells them she has to take the call and then without sharing who's calling, she walks into the lobby, sits down at a table, answers the phone, and starts taking notes.

"At least she has a phone that will ring," Cathy laments. "Mine is about to die and there isn't a phone charger in sight."

"Probably her husband," Nan guesses. "Or maybe someone from school. She's the nurse there too, isn't that what she said?"

"She could be the Queen of Sheba, for all we really know. Even moms can lie."

Patti says this, and then adds that the lobby, boutique, the entire damn hotel, except for their suite, is no better than being at the airport.

"It's about as relaxing down here as a surgical waiting room," she adds testily, as five teenagers bump into her on their way to the cashier. "There must be a thousand people stranded here with us. And let's not forget all those psychics."

"They should have seen this coming." Cathy laughs, parading past with her skimpy bikini dangling from her arm.

Nan looks absolutely frazzled. From the bewildered, hopeless, and frustrated look on her face, Holly fears she could blow at any moment.

Which is exactly what happens next.

First she turns very slowly around in a circle, eyeballing everyone who has seemingly disrupted her shopping plans. Two unsuspecting gum-snapping, halter-top-wearing girls who have shoved their way into the small store and are pawing through the bathing suit sale racks become her first victims.

"Hey!" Nan snaps.

Unfortunately, the girls ignore her.

"I'm talking to you," Nan says, louder, walking right up to them.

"So?" This from the short blonde who does not even bother to look up and has no idea what she is up against.

"Let me explain," Nan begins, a little louder and now an inch from the blonde's face. "You shoved past my friends without bothering to say 'Excuse me.' In my world, that's rude and ignorant behavior. In your shallow little world it might be just fine, but I'm here to tell you it is not."

Both girls stop chewing their gum but keep their hands on the discounted bathing suits. There is a crackling pause, not unlike the silent moment before a tornado, tsunami, or hurricane is about to touch down.

Patti and Holly begin moving forward, determined to act like human shields, but it's too late.

The blonde laughs, snaps her gum, and says, "You are not my mother, lady. Get over yourself."

Nan sets her hands on either side of the girl and although she doesn't touch her, the placement of her hands pins the girl against the swim suit rack. This finally gets her to stop laughing.

"Nan." Patti says her name firmly, as if she is trying to talk her out of a coma or off a ledge.

Without saying a word, Nan backs up.

The girl steps away, eyes wide and a little scared, and this time Patti cannot help herself. She says, "Wait just a moment, young lady," and doesn't even realize she sounds exactly like her own mother.

"What?" The girl really does need to be whacked upside the head, but there has been more than enough drama for one day—one week, maybe an entire year.

Is there really any way to tell this bratty product of overindulgence what someone should have told her years ago? She's what, maybe fifteen or sixteen, and trying hard to look like she's thirty. The kind of girl who had her first manicure before she was ten, gets to go to Florida on spring break and stay at a very expensive and lovely hotel, and probably has her father or mother's credit card in her back pocket. Her glossy lips curl in a sneer.

Patti realizes that saving children one at a time like this is useless, but for some unknown reason, maybe just to keep Nan from having to go to jail, she has already committed to saying something.

What saves Patti from slapping the girl are the opening lyrics to "What Kind of Fool Am I." When she thinks of the song, it's not love that drives her to speak, but her own folly for being right where she is at this very moment.

"Listen, you little smart-ass," Patti snarls through her teeth. "You don't own these goddamn bathing suits. You don't own the world. You pushed your way over here. You are rude and you have absolutely no manners. This is probably the fault of your parents. But you are not a ten-year-old, so you need to take responsibility for your actions. So get the hell out of here. And when someone who is obviously older than you are says something, you better start listening."

When the girl slithers away without saying another word, Patti makes believe she is washing off her hands and then asks Nan if there is anything else she needs out of the damn hotel store. Margo is still on the phone and taking notes as if she is working on a novel, and Holly wishes she'd stayed in the bathtub.

Unfazed, Nan says, "Yes."

She orders—not asks—each one of them to pick out a swimming suit even if they may never wear it.

"I'm paying for it. At this point, what the hell. I'll probably be broke in a week and this will give me something to remember."

There is no time to ask Nan why she believes she's going to be destitute. She's obviously got a great job—she may be one of the few employees left in the United States who still has a corporate credit card. But suddenly getting everyone out of this store is more important than asking questions.

The only person who really wants a bathing suit is Cathy. She still has the hot pink bikini on her arm. Holly, Patti, and Margo could care less. Patti is starting to get a headache. This usually occurs when she has a menopause flashback or a fruit tree is blooming. But boutique hotel stress could be ushering in an entire new era of allergic reactions.

"I'll get a suit if you promise we can all go back to the room and stay there," Patti not so much asks as demands. "We do not belong out in public right now. The bathing suits are a lovely idea but I'm certain we won't need them. But..."

Patti almost bites her own tongue in half to keep herself from saying, "But if it will keep you from flipping out yet again, harming someone, or causing us all even more anguish, worry, and stress, go right ahead, Nan—you can buy us the whole damn hotel."

Holly has also figured out they all need to get out of the small store and back behind a locked door. She's grabbed a bathing suit that may fit her in a few months if she has liposuction, and she's also snatched one that looks like it's a fairly good match for Margo, who is so totally lost in her phone conversation that she's missed the entire bathing-suit showdown.

Holly watches Nan throw down her credit card in front of the cashier and imagines what it would be like to have Nan for a client. Would she spill her guts? When her head was inside of a plastic bag, under the faucet, being frosted like a cake, or sitting quietly under her razor-sharp scissors, would she reveal whatever is making her act like someone who unfortunately just let her medication prescription lapse?

Unhappiness is so easy to spot. Holly can see it in herself when she looks into the mirror or when she looks at a strange woman. Laugh lines descending a little too far. A dark cloud filming the color of the eyes. A light shadow that flutters like a silhouette when someone moves. Nan has these attributes times ten.

Until this very moment Holly has never wondered if anyone else sees people the way she sees them. Or if anyone sees her in that same way. But the guy she met on the elevator seemed to know more about her than he revealed. When they walk past Margo, toss her a little plastic bag with her bathing suit, and get into the elevator, Holly feels suddenly as if she is transparent and others can see right through her.

The four women all ride in silence up to their floor. Margo styas behind, still on the phone. When they get out, Nan tells Patti she appreciates her backing her up.

"There's little shits everywhere," Patti says, meaning both Nan and the teenage girls as she winks at Holly.

"Thanks for the new bathing suit," Cathy says, searching for her room key. "Not that we'll get to use them. Have you looked outside lately?"

"There's an indoor pool." This from Holly, who tells them she loves to swim, loves simply being in or near the water, almost as much as she loves to cut hair.

"You'd be crazy to go down there and swim," Patti says. "The pool is probably more crowded than the damn lobby. The safest place in the entire hotel seems to be our room. And even that's risky."

They all manage to laugh as Cathy pushes the door open and they enter a room that looks nothing like the one they left less than an hour ago. The wind has shattered the huge sliding glass door leading to the balcony. The lamps have been tipped over, the television is on its side, there is a torrent of water pouring into the room. The place looks like the *Titanic* went down in it. Glass is everywhere.

"Oh my God!"

Cathy has tiptoed across the shattered glass to try to see if there is a way to keep out the driving rain.

"We need to call someone right away," she says, backing up. "The whole suite will flood. Look at that rain—it's just pouring in."

Nan already has her hand on the phone and is dialing when Holly asks if the others think it was the wind or maybe...just maybe...someone trying to break into the room.

"The door was locked. I made sure it closed all the way," Cathy reminds her. "I mean, I suppose someone could have thrown a rock or something through the slider but I don't see anything."

Holly tells them she heard the door click when she left also.

"It's terribly easy to break into a hotel room," Patti tells them, surveying the scene from just a few feet inside the doorway. "I could break into any room in this hotel in three seconds."

"Well, that's reassuring," Cathy snaps. "Now we can worry about that along with everything else we have to worry about."

"Let's check the other rooms," Holly suggests, no longer that thrilled to be back inside the suite. "We need to look around to see if anything was touched or taken." She doesn't know why she feels such urgency, but she knows she can feel her heartbeat in her throat.

Patti doesn't bother to move while Cathy and Holly check the rooms and Nan begins arguing with someone on the phone and then very fiercely slams down the receiver.

"They won't move us," she informs Patti. "The entire hotel is filled. They'll send up a maintenance crew when they can."

Cathy and Holly agree that it doesn't look as if anyone has been in their rooms or taken anything from their bags. And that includes the maid, as the suite hasn't been cleaned. Patti and Nan check their suitcases too. Everything appears to be in place.

"What about Margo's things?"

"Margo is apparently taking down the whole history of the world over the telephone," Patti answers. "We won't know until she gets back."

Cathy has picked up extra sheets and blankets from the bathroom shelf and begins throwing them against the wall near the window to soak up some water. Holly starts to help her and then abruptly stops.

"I suppose someone could have been watching the room," she blurts out. "If someone has been watching us, they would have known when we were all out of the room."

Nan offers a reasonable explanation.

"This loose cannon of a person the psychics are so freaked about is apparently after flesh, not our wallets. I'm putting my money, what's left of it anyway, on the storm. For heaven's sake, just look out the window."

A cluster of birds fly past, bucking the wind as if they are in a rodeo. Holly's tempted to put her hand out the broken window to catch one. When she does, she feels cold rain biting into her skin as if someone is sticking pins into her. And she is almost certain she sees someone—a dark figure—run like hell the moment he sees her standing there.

six

*T*he maintenance crew are a man and a woman who look, at first glance, like a tag-team wrestling duo. They have on matching blue and white striped hotel shirts. Their sleeves are rolled up to expose two sets of substantial biceps. The woman has a white-blond ponytail that is looped with something that looks like twine, and her partner has a 1960's flat-top cut that could be used for a spare plate.

The hair distracts and saves Holly. She's edged away from the window and even as she's trying to slow her heartbeat, trying to decide if what she thinks she saw is really what she saw, trying to keep from screaming, she cannot help but be distracted by the hair.

It's an amazement of retroness that she has not seen, even in Aberdeen, Ohio, since her beauty school days when she pored over photos from old styling books. Holly backs herself close to the wall and pushes her hands against it so she won't rush over and mess with the ponytail.

She tries to catch Patti's eyes, thinking she too will be noticing the hair. But Patti is sitting on the far end of the couch, away from the window, and for some reason she looks worse than Holly feels.

Cathy is doing a rather remarkable job of keeping the room from washing out to sea. Nan glances at her and wonders if Cathy has had to work her way up from the bottom at her Wendy's job. For some reason she finds it hard to believe that Cathy once wiped up fryer grease, smelled like grilled onions at the end of her shift, or had to clean orange soda from a sticky floor. But there she is on her hands and knees sliding around tables and mopping like a pro.

The unspoken details of all of their lives force Nan to wonder why a silent elephant isn't sitting on the kitchen counter, smoking a cigarette and drinking a beer while watching all of the action.

Her own life has been increasingly filled with *Selective Sharing*. If the letters *SS* didn't stand for a couple of other horrid things she'd have them tattooed to the top of her left hand. It always amazes her how a woman can paint a picture of herself using whatever she decides to provide from her own vast palette of life.

You can explain the scar above your left eye by saying you fell off of your bike when you were twenty-eight. Twenty-eight! Imagine that. Just turning the corner and thinking about work when you leaned a little bit too far and hit a small patch of gravel. All this is true, of course. It is also true that you were riding bikes with your husband. Arguing so fiercely that passing cars were slowing down to make certain everything was okay.

Arguing and wondering how in the hell your life had taken you to this road, to this person, to this moment. Arguing until he became so angry that he fell behind just enough so he could kick your rear tire and send you flying into a tree that most likely would not kill you but would give you a scar to lie about or *Selectively Share* the rest of your life.

You could, in fact, *Selectively Share* every single aspect of your life. Almost everyone does it. Correct details are not necessary. Not necessary because everyone forms an opinion very quickly about what they see. The clothes. The shoes. The hair. The title on the business card. So few people bother or care enough to ask the important questions. When was the last time you laughed so hard you peed in your pants? Do you ever wish that you could just lie down at work in the receptionist's office in your ratty T-shirt and running shorts and tell everyone to fuck off? Your son, the one you rarely see, does it break your heart to have this distance between you and him? When your mother died so suddenly, were you sad or secretly relieved?

The unspoken reasons for *Selective Sharing* could cripple the world. Or maybe make it better. Nan watches Cathy struggle to her feet with wet towels that are apparently headed for a wringing out in the kitchen sink. She figures the revelations behind Cathy's *Selective Sharing* might possibly halt public transportation for twelve years.

Who knows? Who knew? And the mistress of *Selective Sharing* moves forward.

"Do you two have names?" Nan asks this as she holds open the door and the maintenance workers pull in a cart filled with pipes and tools.

"I'm Bridget," the woman states. "Head mechanical engineer. Graduated from Cornell and headed toward the sun. This is

Terry. He's my almost-able assistant. Sometimes if he's good we let him use a screwdriver and a drill on the same day."

Nan steps back as Terry brings in a large piece of plywood from the hall in case they need it to cover a broken window. Without hesitating he then starts to drag in what looks like a new balcony door.

"Help," he asks gently.

Bridget pulls the door inside the room, then tells the women they are in luck because this is the last spare slider they have in the entire hotel.

"Luck, my ass," Patti says. "The only lucky thing that could happen to us is if we get out of here alive."

Margo chooses this moment to return. Her face explodes with surprise as she walks into the room and sees a scene that looks like a staged play about a construction project gone bad.

"The slider broke," Nan explains simply. "But you should go check to see if anything was stolen from your suitcase. We're not sure if it was the storm or if someone got into the suite."

Bridget jumps right in and says it doesn't appear to her as if anyone tried to get into the suite. The door lock was not tampered with when she checked it coming in and the damage is probably from the storm. There are, she tells them, problems throughout the hotel.

"This is Florida," she asserts. "This happens all the time. This early spring storm is a bit dicey, but it's nothing that unusual for Florida. These storms blow in from the bay fairly often."

"That's a lovely corporate response," Patti fires back. "But the truth is, there is some criminal running around and it is possible he could have broken in here. You know as well as I do that those new, supposedly foolproof, magnetic keys are about as safe as jumping off this building without a parachute."

Bridget tells Terry to set the plywood against the counter because they won't need it to fix the broken slider. Then she proceeds to tell Patti that she can understand the uncertainty surrounding the shattered slider, but the hotel has no proof or knowledge about a would-be crime.

Margo moves her hand like a game show hostess and points out that there's a roomful of women who have a right to be frightened if someone evil is lurking in the lobby.

"Did you get a note under your door?"

"Of course we did. We're also women. Note or no note, we are not foolish enough to think that there *isn't* a man lurking everywhere we go."

"Listen," Bridget says calmly, "the hotel did not have anything to do with the notes. As far as we are concerned, the hotel is safe. Even from the storm."

"I think those psychic people put those notes around so that people would come down and pay money to have their palms read. Or whatever they do." This from Terry, who has started to take out the broken slider casing.

"Just because they're psychics doesn't mean they're goofy," Margo retorts. "I haven't even seen any tambourines or crystal balls down there."

"Ma'am," Bridget says, looking at Margo. "Why don't you go check out your room? Nothing appears to be amiss here except the shattered slider. We have an explanation for that. But go check. Go on."

All of the women, even big-as-life Bridget, realize the only way anyone will know for sure is if the psychics actually catch someone. Or if someone is attacked. Or if there's a boulder lying near the balcony that someone threw through the glass. Or if the guy walks in, throws down his guns, knives, hatchets, and other sharp instruments of death and confesses to whatever it is he has done.

"Let's get the slider fixed." Bridget claps her hands together, smiles, and would probably then push Terry off the balcony for lying about what the psychics know if there wasn't a witness. "This storm has everyone on edge and it has us hopping."

"Have any other sliders or windows popped open and broken like this?"

Patti is not going to let this brazen woman get off so easily. Of course windows and doors can blow open or break in a storm, but this is one pretty damn big hunk of glass. It is, in fact, a sliding glass porch door. Corporate yammering be damned. Patti is furious. It's not the hotel's fault that there's a storm, or that their planes were grounded, but if there is someone dangerous lurking, the hotel management, and not psychics at a convention, should be the ones slipping warnings under the doors.

Patti could probably qualify as a hotel CEO. She's stayed in so many of them she can identify specific hotels by sheets, towels, television brands, the number of bed bugs, and the color of the tablecloths in their dining rooms. She knows any and everything that happens at hotels.

Bridget and Terry get the new slider placed with the one they thought to bring with them, but something isn't working quite right. Holly is tempted to offer them a beer.

"I'm not going to lie to you and I am not going to needlessly worry you either. We've had some minor damage on the main outdoor patio," Bridget reports. "There's flooding in the lower level. Tree branches are down. But to the best of my knowledge this is the only sliding glass door that has broken."

Margo says then that it doesn't appear as if anyone has been in her room besides Nan. She can tell by the footprints in the carpeting, even though the maid has not been up to the suite yet. Nothing has been touched. Her carry-on is in exactly the same position as when she left it, and the windows, which overlook the balcony, are still locked.

"Everything seems okay. But we sure could use some clean towels."

"The maids are running behind and some of them couldn't make it in because of the weather. If you can pass on a full-service clean and just need towels or sheets, we can discount the rooms. And because of this window mess, we are going to give each of you a free room-service meal. Believe me, we'd seat you downstairs but it would be like eating outside right this second. It's so busy you'd be pushed around like a palm tree in this wind."

Then Bridget whips out a raincoat that was around her waist, tugs up the hood, and disappears out into the driving rain on the balcony, with a drill in her hand. Terry puts on a pair of leather gloves and begins picking out the glass that's stuck to what's left of the slider frame.

Patti can't resist.

"Come on, Terry. Wouldn't you be a little nervous, if you were us? I mean, it's like we could be sitting ducks here."

Terry looks up to make certain Bridget is out of earshot. He hesitates, turning to drop pieces of glass into one of his orange plastic buckets.

"Those people downstairs are probably not just fortune-tellers," he admits reluctantly. "I'm thinking you're safer in this suite with one another than with them, you know? My aunt was into that stuff and it was spooky how often she was right."

Cathy snorts. She avoids the eyes of the other women when she tells him that even if a spaceship filled with evil aliens landed that might be safer than being in this room.

"You don't look too dangerous," he remarks, glancing at her, smiling, and then moving back to his slider assignment.

"Honey, let me tell you, five women trapped in a hotel room with a stocked liquor bar, high spirits, and nothing but time equals one hell of a dangerous situation."

And then she winks at him. Is it a real wink? Is she blinking? Is Cathy flirting? If there is a man in the room, can she not go thirty seconds without being the center of attention?

Nan is assessing this situation from the perfect angle directly behind Cathy, from which she can also see Mr. Handyman taking an occasional side glance at Cathy. She's got Cathy pegged now. She's a hopeless, man-hungry, never-satisfied super bitch who will one day look in the mirror and decide that she'd better start having plastic surgery ASAP.

Because Cathy's entire persona—minus whatever human resources skills she has managed to accrue over the years—depends on her tight ass, high tits, and that damn blond hair that men still stupidly equate with sexiness. So Cathy will focus on those areas first.

After that it will be endless. She will hang on for years because she's got the bones for it. Cathy would actually look even more beautiful if she didn't wear so much makeup or dress as if she's on her way to a strip club job interview.

Nan has often wondered how this happens to some women. Does their mother put a mirror in their crib when they are babies? Do they learn how to flip their hair and show their legs while they still wear diapers? Is it a daddy thing? Did they always hear someone telling them how beautiful they were when they looked most like Dolly Parton? Did no one ever go up to such women when they had on skanky shorts, a filthy T-shirt, unshaved legs, and hair that hadn't been driven into a holding pattern by a blow dryer and tell them in all seriousness that they looked awesome?

Nan would love to start a gambling pool to see if Cathy wears makeup when she swims, but she guesses she will never be able to find that out. And why in the hell she lets it get to her is a mystery she should probably address. Something that goes beyond Cathy's appearance and behavior pisses her off. Maybe it's just some back-to-basic primal bitch-against-bitch woman thing that some people think only happens to macho men who love to shove one another around. In reality, men and women, it appears, are equally prone to cat and dog fights.

Nan finally distracts herself by searching for the hotel menus and asking if anyone else is as starved as she is. Somehow several hours have passed and it's been a long time since they have eaten.

Bridget shakes off her raincoat and comes back inside just as Cathy advises the women that the bar is in dire need of restocking.

"Did you girls have a party last night?"

"We've been having one great big party since we met," Patti says sarcastically.

Looking around the room Bridget smartly decides not to ask these women anything about how they know one another. But she does manage to rescue them in one way.

"Let me take care of that," she tells them. "I'll get sheets, towels, and even some full bottles of liquor and wine up here if you promise to forgive us and the weather for the window mess. And for not having a maid on hand to finish cleaning up. Is that an okay deal?"

"It's just water," Holly says agreeably, thinking that some wine might help her forget about what she did or didn't see when she went to the window. "Can Terry get the slider in?"

"He should be done in ten minutes. I'm going to go take care of your things and try not to feel hurt because you didn't invite me to stay."

"It's not as fun as it looks," Nan says grimly.

"All righty, then," Bridget responds, smart enough not to ask any more questions. "Call us if anything else comes flying through your window."

Everyone quickly agrees that food will be a wonderful diversion from reality, which is a miracle, considering the level of bickering that has been going on. The five women, driven by hunger, somehow decide on a variety of dishes to order and have a potluck dinner. When Margo volunteers to once again manage the kitchen, Cathy remembers to ask her what the big phone call was all about.

"Nan bought you a bathing suit and you didn't look at it because it looked like you were busy taking down someone's life history."

"Just kids and family stuff," Margo says, shrugging.

"Must be serious if you were taking notes," Patti states, wondering what in the hell Margo could be lying about. More important, why would she be lying? This group of tainted and tart women will most likely never see or talk to one another again. So why lie about what she's up to?

"When you are juggling schedules and have three kids and do what I do, you almost need an assistant," Margo explains, avoiding Patti's eyes.

Really.

Manic Margo seems competent enough to be able to juggle more than a few things at once. Patti decides that if people think her life is nothing but sipping champagne out of crystal glasses and jetting off to the next B Class venue then it's possible they think she doesn't have a clue about raising kids, managing schedules, and living the way someone like Margo must live.

Terry announces he's finished his slider installation project and Cathy tells him that he is dripping all over the floor, when there is a knock at the door. Someone who looks as if he is ten years old, and probably is, hands off towels, sheets, and a box of bar booze that is received as if the kid is distributing sacred relics.

And Terry is smart enough to forget about Cathy, pack up his tools, and get out of the suite before someone cuts him up and puts him inside the microwave. The tension, snide remarks, glares, and deep sighs concern him almost as much as the raging storm and all the lies about the snafus of the hotel his partner told during the past thirty minutes.

The drinks do offer a distraction from the unanswered questions about the broken slider and the psychics as Terry slips out the door and glasses are filled. Holly phones room service and calls in a rather elaborate and detailed food order. While they're waiting, there's a once-over-lightly to sop up what is left of the slider mess, and a seemingly constant round of text messages.

"What is with you people and this constant communication thing?" Patti asks as Margo lights a pair of candles for the table that she found under the sink.

"It's addictive and pathetic," Holly admits, slamming her phone shut after texting her mom yet again that she is okay. "It's almost as if we're all afraid to be alone for five minutes."

This brilliant observation causes everyone to stop for a moment. In the world of twittering, in-your-face-and-space constant social networking, who has time to actually do anything, be someone, go anywhere so that they can report about it every fifteen seconds?

Whatever happened to handwritten thank you notes, Margo demands. People are so addicted to letting people whom they've barely spoken to, most likely have never met, and probably wouldn't like if they did meet them, know what they are doing. It's turned modern forms of communication into a joke.

Surprisingly, Nan gets into this conversation full throttle. Possibly because she is no longer the owner of a cell phone and has been borrowing everyone's phone and grabbing the suite phone to stay in touch with whomever it is she's staying in touch with.

"I have to say that twenty-nine hours without my phone has made me realize how much I use it," she shares while checking for ice cubes. "I find myself spending so much time looking for the phone that I don't have—you know, checking my pockets, looking on the counter—that I wonder what I could be doing instead."

"Text messaging is what's doing me in." Holly says that her friends text so much that it's like they never have any real conversations anymore.

"When we get together, it's like we talk the way we text. 'Hey. Yo. U ok. Dude.' I suppose linguistic experts are all thinking about jumping off a bridge."

Cathy tells them about when she started to travel, having been promoted after working locally for many years. She said she had a cell phone and a computer but wasn't prepared for how they affected communications with strangers, the people you would normally sit next to on an airplane, or in a waiting room.

"I remember walking through the airport and thinking how weird it was," she said. "People used to talk to one another, you know. Now they're plugged into their laptops, leaning against walls and talking on their phones. Everything has changed. I like to think of myself as a friendly kind of gal and when I first noticed it, it was sort of a shock to me. But now I guess I do the same thing with my phone and laptop."

"Honey, *friendly* seems to be your middle name," Patti tells Cathy. "I guess you just can't help yourself."

Coming from Patti, Cathy doesn't take offense to a remark that is clearly meant to be a little sarcastic. Nan was not the only one who'd seen her interacting with Terry.

As the women teeter on the brink of an actual non-bickering, non-confrontational conversation, the food arrives. The potluck feast is spread out on the table. Holly pulls in a chair from the bedroom so everyone can sit around the table, Patti makes certain they get really tall glasses of water, and Holly remarks, laughing, that they look like one big happy family.

There is a wild dash for food before anyone has a chance to respond, or maybe knock Holly off her chair. Margo has arranged the food on several platters and in bowls so that everyone can have a little bit of everything. It's a feast that includes a broiled captain's platter; cream sauce over a Southwest pasta salad that has the largest shrimp any of them have ever seen; old-fashioned barbecue chicken and a mountain of extra wings to go with it; potatoes baked, mashed, and fried; a Caesar salad with real anchovies; a tofu bowl with sesame vegetables; and hot bread which smells like heaven. Margo has decided to hold back the six desserts until after they have annihilated everything else.

The women eat as if they are ravenous, with appetites accelerated by the wine, and for a blessed fifteen or twenty minutes not one argument erupts. If someone walked in unannounced and didn't know better, they might actually think these five women were having a good time. Cathy and Nan are exchanging lovely compliments about the dinner, which is being consumed at such a rapid pace that Margo gets up even before the last dish can be licked clean and sets an assortment of cakes, pies, and tarts on the table. The women stare at the sweets as if a naked dancing man had just been carried into the room.

Holly excuses herself for a moment to use the restroom and hurries back so she won't miss dessert. Before she sits down, Patti asks her to quickly check the Weather Channel. Nothing has changed. The screen is alive with dancing arrows that show the storm is still in high-intensity mode.

"...*and Central and Northern Florida continue to be hit with high winds, driving rain, and low temperatures as this freak spring storm collides with the higher water temperatures sweeping into the Gulf.*"

"Dang," Holly says, pointing to the rain driving against the window. "Not a thing has changed."

Then there is incentive for more drinks when Margo assures them that, in her world, red wine is made for drinking with something sweet. Cathy becomes almost joyous at this news, takes the biggest pour, and announces she's suddenly having so much fun she doesn't even care if her phone has nearly gone dead.

Holly looks up. Her plate is holding nothing but a short trail of luscious chocolate crumbs. The desserts are so good that she is tempted to pick up the plate and lick it. When she says this out loud, Nan laughs so hard that she starts choking.

"That reminds me of the time when I was a senior in college. I moved off-campus and rented a room above the garage from this beautiful older woman who loved having someone coming and going. She was a fashion designer and always looked as if she was about to run off and be in a runway show herself. We became fast and lifelong friends. Anyway, the reason I am laughing is because one day I was eating dinner out of the pots I had cooked in. My friend walked in from work, sat down, picked up a pan, started eating, and said she'd wanted to do that her entire life. We ended up putting ice cream on plates and licking it off because she'd always wanted to do that too."

Nan shares this story, something personal, something lovely, something funny, without realizing how intimate it is.

"We could maybe pass for sisters or something right now," Holly jokes as she sees everyone on the same page for the first time since they decided to flee the airport and come to the hotel. "Adopted sisters, of course."

"There's a joke in my family about that," Cathy tells them. "Every time someone is acting like an ass we say they're adopted, so it's an explanation for their behavior."

"Who has a real sister?" Holly suddenly has to know this. The answers are not much of a surprise. Patti had two brothers who are both now dead and only one sister . . . that she knows of, considering her father was a philandering womanizer she freely admits hating. Margo has two sisters. One here. One there. Everyone is busy. Cathy has two sisters and was a surprise and understandably a very pampered oops baby. Nan has one sister. Sometimes they are friends and sometimes not.

And Holly?

Holly has three terribly successful, lovely, and very married sisters who can't believe anyone can breathe without being in the same situation. She's turned into their project, which has taken a bit of a toll on her relationship with them. It's hard to consider someone a friend when you feel like a class project.

"They probably just want you to be as happy as they are," Patti responds with a very wide smirk. "Tell us, are they happy?"

"*Happiness* has turned into a very vague word for me," Holly responds, still longing to lick her plate. "What would make me really happy right now is to lick my plate like Nan's friend did."

"I have to say that I've been thinking the same thing," Margo shares. "I mean, does anyone even *order* dessert anymore? My God. We're worried that if we use the wrong toothpick we're going to get heart disease, cancer, bad arteries, or grow fangs."

With that, Margo picks up her plate and starts licking.

Nan immediately grabs the few remaining slices of dessert, tops off the wineglasses and plops them on everyone's individual plates as if she has been their server all evening. Then she announces, "No forks!" and claps her hands together bossily like she's directing a scene from a play.

"What the hell," Patti says, encouraging them all to eat without silverware. "Maybe this is how the swine flu started. People just got tired of waiting for the fork to get to their mouths."

Although it might look like a group activity at first glance, the plate licking quickly turns into a totally singular event. It's not unlike a marathon, a horse race, or a singles tennis match. There's no doubt that if one woman had more crumbs than the next, there would be a spontaneous fistfight that could turn deadly. And there's something else. Something none of the women can stop to acknowledge or recognize. A silent shifting of energy that loops around each one of them—touching faces, hands, arms, legs—in a dance of sameness.

Before anyone gets a chance to say anything, be embarrassed, acknowledge the surge of sisterlike energy, wish they had not eaten a piece of cherry pie, raspberry cream pastry, apple strudel, or something that looks like a piece of jewelry made out of dark chocolate, Cathy's cell phone rings and then totally shuts down. Three seconds later it sounds like Margo receives two text messages in a row. Then Holly's phone beeps.

Patti wishes she had not swallowed her last piece of cake so she could spit it out across the table like a spoiled baby.

"We are right back where we started," she exclaims, dropping her plate onto the table and not caring if it breaks, which it thankfully does not. "The damn cell phones."

Everyone is a bit woozy from the sugar rush and the unexpected sharing of emotions and family ties.

Holly and Margo set their phones down on the table without looking at their messages. Cathy's phone shows no signs of life. There is a pause as if they are waiting for Patti to say something else, and it's a pause Patti welcomes because she's struggling to come up with what she should say or do next.

Something randomly comes to her from a place that she will later think was simply fueled and encouraged by one of the psychics sending her a secret message through the air vents. First she internally hums the melody to "You Are My Sunshine." Then she tells a story.

Happy childhood memories are few for Patti. But she had a grandmother who was her soulful and often physical salvation. Her grandmother loved to write notes and letters and cards. When Patti was a little girl, often abandoned at Grandma's house for days and weeks, her grandmother would take her along to look for special paper—something to write her notes on. They would spend hours going to the little shops, card stores, old-fashioned stationery stores so that her grandmother could find the perfect piece of paper.

"I suppose it was a fetish of sorts," Patti tells the other women. "My grandmother would close her eyes, put her right hand—always her right hand—on the papers, and ask me to lead her, as if I were a seeing eye dog, down the rows and rows of paper."

Patti would always slow down by her favorite colors. Pastels that reminded her of sunsets, the Christmas morning when someone was not fighting and she got up moments before dawn to see the sun rising above the white hills and then held on to that image for days because she was the only one who remembered Santa Claus was supposed to come.

And her grandmother (did she really close her eyes?) would always pick a color that Patti loved.

"When I watched her write, it was the closest I think I have ever felt to something other people call a sacred moment. It was... sensuous. Touching the paper as she put down intimate words was very personal for her. And I think, what is personal now? Text messages? A hundred phone calls? Announcing to the whole world that you are going to get in your car and go pick up a pizza? I mean, *really*."

The women are quiet, and even plate licking has disappeared from their minds. And Patti is so taken by her own story she seizes the moment. She also realizes that they are all an inch from getting drunk yet again and it's now or never.

"Let's all put our cell phones away for a day and see what happens," she says as if she is still in the middle of her grandmother story. "We have the suite phone for emergencies. We are surely not going anywhere. The weatherman just told us nothing is changing yet. Really. What the heck? Only three of us have phones that work anyway."

Not waiting for someone to come up with some stupid-ass work or family excuse, Patti walks to the kitchen, opens the drawer next to the dishwasher. Then she raises her own phone, turns it off, and drops it with a *clunk* into the drawer. She holds out her left hand, palm up, in a lovely welcoming gesture.

Margo throws her phone to Patti without even getting up, as if she is relieved to be getting it out of her hands. Holly passes her phone to Margo, who throws it to Patti. Cathy gives her phone a very long and loud kiss, gets up slowly, walks to the kitchen, and as Patti slips it into the drawer, she says, "Bye-bye, useless weapons that keep us apart."

Perhaps if this mismatched bunch of stranded female travelers were not high on sugar, half-loopy from a surge of carbs and alcohol, and partly terrified that they will either get blown out to sea or be kidnapped, they would see the phone surrender as insane as moving into a hotel suite with a bunch of strangers.

Later, Patti slips all of the phones into her suitcase. She's certain someone will be jonesing for their phone the moment they remember someone they should have called, and try to cheat. And if she could cheat herself and call a bookie, she'd bet that the suddenly mysterious Margo would be the first one to steal back her phone.

seven

*I*t takes Holly over an hour to convince herself she will not die if she sneaks out of the suite and tries to break in to the swimming pool in the middle of the night.

Normally, hotel swimming pools want you out of the water at ten o'clock. Normally, people stay in their rooms in the middle of the night so they can sleep. Normally, a grown woman would not feel as if she has to sneak around like she did her entire last year of high school, when there was a party every night for almost nine months. Normally, this same grown woman would not quietly take off her ridiculous-looking pajamas, slip on a brand-new bathing suit, and then cover it up with shorts and a T-shirt while she is still under the sheets, so the woman in the other bed will not see her in a bathing suit—even though the other woman is most likely sleeping.

But there is absolutely nothing normal about anything Holly has done or is about to do. In fact, pretty much everything that has happened since she ran into this bunch of wise-ass, fast-talking, hard-drinking occasionally insecure and kind women of the world in a public restroom at an international airport is so far from normal, Holly is fearful she may not find her way back from it all.

Which may not necessarily be a bad thing.

Holly cannot sleep even though she has consumed copious amounts of wine and...oh, yes, there was also the brandy that someone, maybe Margo, passed around so they could all sample it. Somehow the glass ended up in Holly's hand and she had to finish it.

The hours immediately following dinner were almost fun. Not that anyone will be able to remember too much. There will be hangovers and hopefully Nan will rescind her verbalized threat to throw them all out on the wet streets so she can be alone. Maybe if they talked about what they thought had happened, what they thought had been talked about, what they thought caused the last argument of the evening between Cathy and Nan, they could put together some portion of reality.

As it was, things went from *really* fun to kind of fun, then quickly to just plain *horrid*. That's what Holly remembers as she listens to make certain Cathy's breathing is regular and signals some deep-sleeping action. Just before she's about to slip out of bed, Cathy turns onto her side, and Holly, who desperately wants to be alone, isn't sure if Cathy is sound asleep.

Damn it. Holly lies like a brick, waiting for Cathy to snore. She wonders how her suitemates went from the lovely dinner to a wild card game that was like poker—but with some bizarre rules—that Patti said is played by tons of musicians around the world every night after they warm up and wait till showtime, then to an argument, between Cathy and Nan, which sent them all running for cover.

What was with those two? And what were they arguing about? Nan wondered if Cathy flirts with dead men, too? Cathy yelled back that Nan is jealous? Jealous of what? Simple female feline nastiness? Hormones gone wild? Higher cleavage? What in the hell?

Holly had thought the entire thing was sort of a joke until Nan stood up and made a move for Cathy's arm. Cathy stepped back. Margo and Patti shot to their feet like referees. Holly had been kind of hoping someone would throw a glass but then she realized Cathy was not going to waste the good vodka they were drinking and neither was Nan. These two chicks needed to drink. They also needed a boxing ring.

Nan had finally stomped off to her room. Cathy had stomped off to her room. Margo and Patti had gone outside to smoke and immediately raced back inside because they were so tipsy they had forgottten they were in the middle of a raging storm. After that everyone simply, or not so simply, had slammed or crept off to bed.

And even though she is terrified of the storm, the guy who knows her name, and the apparent criminal who is running loose, Holly knows she has to get some space. These women are driving her nuts. Maybe crazier than she already is.

And there is this gnawing feeling, some hidden voice whispering to her, "Get up," as if something or maybe even someone is waiting to reveal itself to her. The uneasiness of this feeling is not unusual. It's something that comes to her often. Sometimes she ignores it. Sometimes she listens. She knows it is the tumor growing in her brain as if it has been fertilized. She has never told a soul about this and she's certainly not about to tell any of these insane women.

And that's why, at one in the morning, she is desperate to get into the swimming pool and do some laps. The water, and maybe just one more aspirin, will surely help her push away the thread of uneasiness that is tapping against the inside of her forehead. And traipsing through the halls and lobby might be safer, even at this hour, than wondering after last night's outburst if someone is going to flip out and smother her with a pillow while she is sleeping.

So Holly slips super cautiously out of bed, magically finds her sandals, and walks on eggshells through the living room, past Patti, who is really snoring. And then she is in the semi-lit hall. And then in the elevator. And her heart is pounding so thunderously at the top of her throat, it feels as if her teeth are about to shatter.

Luckily, the lobby desk attendant has her back turned so she doesn't see her slip into the unlocked swimming pool corridor, and the pool area is blessedly empty. Holly feels her way around the room, guided by a pool light that gives the space a sinister look. And even though it's apparent that no one else is in the room, she looks all around before slipping off her shorts and T-shirt and lowering herself into the pool.

The warm water quickly unleashes a cascade of memories that are as confusing as they are comforting.

How did sneaking out of a hotel room as a grown woman become such a big deal? When did covering up her body become a part-time job?

Crap.

Holly kicks up her heels and is elated to see that she can still float aimlessly, even though the center of her weight has shifted from her chest to her frigging hips and stomach. When she was a little girl her aunt taught her the joys of floating on her back with her arms tucked under her head. It's one of the sweetest memories from her childhood. They were at her aunt's lake house, miles and miles from the city, and her auntie would kneel in the shallow water, prop Holly up, whisper encouragement, and hold her in the gentle waves for what seemed like hours, until Holly realized her aunt was no longer touching her.

And she was floating.

Somewhere between the time she dropped out of college and finished her internship as a beautician, floating turned into drowning. Somewhere Holly had disappeared into someone else's life and was living like a shadow.

Sometimes she thought it was because her college and high school friends had started dismissing her because she didn't want to finish college and knew instead that she had a passion and talent for something they considered frivolous. Even as they were addicted to their own hairdressers and salon experiences.

Her parents had been so disappointed. Her sisters had been startled because they had finished college. And as the expectations of others for her began to drop like bowling pins, Holly herself realized she was taking a step backward. She ate. Then she ate some more. When friends called, she started saying no to their social invitations. When she moved out of her parents' house after she'd built up her own list of devoted clients, her routines suddenly became addictive and unchanging. And then, of course, there was the past three years, living with the constant fear that her head might explode at any moment.

Wiggling around in the water, listening to the womblike pool sounds, Holly suspected that what happened to her, had happened to lots of other women too. Sometimes family expectations and pressures can freeze you right where you stand.

What the hell.

Even Patti seems younger and filled with more life than Holly does. Now, as she bobs in the water, Holly promises herself that she is going to start swimming again, daily. She is going to see if she can find the pieces of her life that she let drop like loose tangles of string to be vacuumed up and never seen again. Maybe she will even embrace her estrogen like Patti has. And while she rotates, so she can glide back the entire length of the pool, she is just starting to imagine what the new Holly will be like.

Slimmer. More spontaneous. Bolder.

Then something dark crosses in front of her. It is the long slender shadow of a person, moving slowly, walking down the left side of the pool.

Oh my God.

Keep swimming? Scream for help? Drop to the bottom?

Holly panics, drops her feet to the pool bottom, and scoots down so that she is eye level with the top of the water. All of this makes a rather large amount of noise.

"Holly, it's me—Cathy. Don't freak out."

"Shit, Cathy! You scared the living hell out of me!"

"I'm sorry. I heard you leave and I followed you. I couldn't sleep either. I wasn't sure where you were going but I saw you take your bathing suit to bed with you earlier."

"Yeah, well, some people have stuffed dogs. I like to sleep with bathing suits. And I could swear you were snoring when I left."

Cathy sits on the edge of the pool, dangles her feet, says she has never snored in her life, and tells Holly to keep swimming.

"I'll be your lifeguard," she says. "I didn't mean for you to stop or anything. I was having a hard time sleeping too. It's not like we can go for a walk on the beach."

So much for being alone for an hour.

Holly doesn't say anything. It doesn't really matter. Cathy obviously wants to talk.

"It was brave of you to come down here. This whole hotel is starting to give me the creeps."

Holly drifts in a circle twice, abandons her floating, and treads water not far from where Cathy is sitting. And Cathy just sits and stares down into the water. Holly's water. Holly's pool. Holly's alone time.

If she really is going to start being bold, Holly decides this would be a great time to do it.

"What in the world is up with you and Nan? You two fight like sisters who hate each other. You say you've never met but there's something just odd about the way you two keep going at each other."

When Cathy looks up from the water, Holly can see the whites of her eyes. Her face turns almost spooky Halloweenish because of the way the light from the pool is reflecting on it.

And Cathy hesitates. As if she is struggling to decide something.

"You can trust me," Holly shares impulsively. "I've got so many secrets bouncing inside of me I feel like I could explode sometimes."

"I suppose you do. Every time I go into a salon, I hear women letting it rip. Hairdressers must be like bartenders."

"You know, they even have a class on it now in beauty school. They bring in psychologists and teach us the art of fine listening. I actually love that part of the job."

"You're sweet, Holly. Honest."

Holly, who is used to being criticized, feels a little flutter of fear. "But?"

"But nothing. Except I'd really love to do a little makeover on you."

"Ouch."

"I think you are more attractive than you realize."

"And I think you are trying to change the subject."

Holly isn't even sure she wants to hear what Cathy might be thinking. She's pretty certain she herself is in no mood to share her innermost, deepest thoughts with this blond bombshell from hamburger world.

But being bold has its consequences. Holly loves to listen, so she prods Cathy again. She promises to treat what Cathy says as Salon Sacred. Then she not-so-boldly moves so that her entire body is underwater except for her head, so Cathy will not see her in her bathing suit. Initial bold moves do have their limits.

Cathy starts speaking and creates a kind of rhythm with her feet moving in slow circles in the water as she admits that her life is a mess and there are reasons why there is friction between her and Nan—friction between Cathy and lots of other women.

"I've been married three times."

"I think that fact has already been revealed."

"Well, I've been unfaithful to every single one of my husbands."

This is a moment when floating all alone in this shadowy, silent place would be so lovely. Holly would gently lift up her feet, slide her hands behind her head once again, and produce very tiny foot movements that could conceivably keep her floating for weeks.

Maybe Patti or Margo would come down and drop food and water into her mouth. The storm would stop. The desperate killer would leap off the building roof and the handsome stranger would be a man from her university biology class who has been in love with her for years.

But being the nice girl that she is, Holly does not float away from Cathy's confessions. Instead, she continues her bold streak and asks, "Why were you unfaithful?"

"I suppose that's something I need to stop and ask myself one of these days."

"For some people there are religious and moral implications that are related to sleeping around. Some people, so I am told, have a huge sex drive. Some people are just insecure—"

Before Holly can finish, Cathy cuts her off.

"Why do *you* think I was unfaithful?"

"I barely know you, Cathy. I mean, really, I'd need to find out more about you and then, in the end, isn't it just a judgment call? It must be bothering you or you wouldn't be on edge like this. Look...do you really want me to tell you what I think? Or to be kind and gentle?"

"Tell me the truth. I'm a big girl."

Oh shit.

"You do flirt all of the time. At the airport. In the lobby. I don't know if it's just the way you are or if you need the attention. My friends and I have a theory about women who are married more than twice, though."

"What is it?"

"We think it means you are a lesbian."

Cathy laughs so long that Holly has to tell her to be quiet so a security guard won't come in and throw them both out.

"I'm certain I'm not a lesbian because, believe me, I've tried. It just works better for me with men."

Go figure. Cathy? This is why it's impossible to totally judge a woman or a man by their hair, Holly thinks. The last wild-looking guy who sat in Holly's chair was a Mormon, for crying out loud. So a Barbie doll like Cathy definitely could be more open to sexual experimentation than she looks.

"There goes that theory," Holly says, splashing her hands on top of the water.

Holly has to ask about the latest husband, Number Three. She has him pictured as an older man who fills up the bird feeders, cooks dinner every night, and spends the afternoon down at the VFW sipping light beer and playing cards with the guys. But she's wrong again.

"He's a little older than I am. He's handsome. Very busy, like I am, because he coaches football at a college outside Denver. I don't know why I flirt and can't stay married. Maybe it's my wayward traveling lifestyle. I'm gone a lot."

"That's an excuse," Holly tells her bluntly. She's also starting to wonder how long she can stay in the pool before she begins to get cold from lack of movement. If Cathy keeps on talking, Holly realizes, she may have to get out of the pool in front of her.

Shit.

"It's worse than what you think it is."

Worse? Could Cathy be the malevolent hotel stalker? A liar who really has the hots for fat hairdressers? On the run from a hamburger scam?

"Cathy, get real. Look at you. You're beautiful. Successful. Confident. There's just this one area of your life that needs a little attention."

"I can't swim," Cathy says suddenly, to Holly's astonishment.

"That's it? The thing that's worse than infidelity?" she blurts out.

"No. But how many people my age do you know who've never learned how to swim?"

"Still, I'm pretty sure that's not why you flirt all the time and are unfaithful."

"Could you maybe just show me one thing? Like floating or

that litle kicking thing that you were doing when I came in and scared you half to death."

This is definitely not how Holly imagined her quiet time. Holly can't help herself. She has to be nice and she orders Cathy to step into the pool and reveals that she's a former high school lifeguard and swimming teacher. But it's been a while.

"I've got on shorts and a swimming suit top—"

"Perfect attire for a late night swim. Get in and walk over to me."

Holly tells Cathy that not knowing how to swim is sort of ridiculous, which is not the comforting discussion Cathy is hoping she'd get.

"I'm not picking on you. It's just that where I live everyone swims in lakes and rivers. I swear people are hopping in the water twenty minutes after the ice melts. That might be a regional thing, though."

"You'd think the way I like to expose myself I'd be in the water all of the time."

The joke erases the tension separating these two women who would most likely never even speak if they hadn't met in the airport restroom.

Holly dips into her long-ago lifeguard persona and quickly assesses Cathy's water abilities, which are non-existent, and then gently walks her from one side of the pool to the next. She simply wants Cathy to be comfortable in the water.

And all Cathy wants to do is float.

"Can you hold me up so I can float like you were when I came in?"

This request is near sacrilegious. Floating, Holly believes, is a rite of passage. It's a gift from a beloved relative. It's a step into a world of lightness and relief. It's a family secret that is passed down from one generation to the next. It's the one thing that

Holly can always go back to that never changes, that never lets her down no matter what she looks like or how much she weighs.

Can she suddenly pull back from her aqua nirvana and just show Cathy how to float?

Shit.

Holly makes believe that Cathy is that one little girl with pale-blond hair her last summer of teaching who was so afraid of the water that she had to be carried into the pool. Nothing bad had ever happened to the girl but her fear of water had accelerated as she'd grown older, and suddenly she was ten and so terrified of anything wet that it was ruining her life.

Cathy becomes a little girl in Holly's mind and scared too.

And one of the many lovely things about water is its ability to make everyone the same. Wet. Light. Clean. Free. It's a baptism every second. And because of that Holly manages to place her hands under the small of Cathy's back and lift her up. She speaks gently, knowing Cathy's fear, and sensing a long-held inability to let go. She directs Cathy's hands and feet, leans close to Cathy's ear, promises her that she will not let her go unless she asks to be let go.

Cathy bobs her head back and forth and feels the gentle pressure of Holly's fingers on her skin. Something magical is happening to her in the water. Suddenly, time or place has no meaning. She embraces the swirling sounds of rushing water.

Holly can feel Cathy's body creeping toward that secret place of release where she can finally relax in the water. She pushes Cathy forward an inch and then another inch so that she can gradually let go of her, ever so lightly, like her auntie did, so that it seems as if someone is still holding her up.

And even as she releases her, Holly keeps her hands just an inch or so under her in case Cathy panics or stops gently moving her feet and starts to sink.

It is hard to do this for a long period of time. Holly is starting to feel the effects of no sleep, booze, the pressures of survival, and fear. Somehow this is transmitted to Cathy, when Holly's hands start moving. Cathy jerks upward and is shocked to realize she has been floating by herself.

"I've got you. I've got you."

Cathy is back in Holly's arms even though they have never really left shallow water.

"That was amazing, Holly. I felt absolutely peaceful. It was as if something left me and I was so light."

"The magic of water."

"I wish I could remember why I have been so frightened of it all these years.

"Holly," Cathy exclaims, "just thank you. That was so nice . . . and I never even told you the worst thing."

Shit.

Holly decides to just ask what in the world the worst thing could possibly be. Cathy obviously needs to go to confession. Holly is suddenly determined to try to remain bold as long as possible, just to see how it feels. So she tells Cathy to tell her the worst.

Cathy doesn't even flinch when she says it, the last thing that Holly might have imagined, because Holly's mind does not even work that way. Something that, after hearing it, makes perfect sense.

"One of the guys I'm having an affair with is Nan's husband."

Shit. Shit. Shit. Shit. Shit.

Holly has really actually sort-of never wanted to kill someone. But she thinks for a very brief moment how easy it would be for her to drown Cathy. She is a marriage-breaking slut. She could use the weight she hates on her own body to push Cathy under and hold her down so that, just like in all those drowning movies she'd showed to students about two hundred times, Cathy would go down slowly until the air in her lungs was empty and she would end up on the pool floor.

"I see," she manages to say as she drops Cathy's feet, and keeps her hand on her arm like a good lifeguard until Cathy reaches the first step.

"Nan doesn't know for sure. About her husband. That's what I think anyway. And she's fishing. But women usually know something, you know?"

If Holly could scream now, this is what she would say:

"No, I do not know. What the fuck is wrong with you? Nan is a sister by default. We are all sisters. Can you not just leave your hands off of one man just one time? You are not right. And why the holy hell did you pick me to tell? Me? Could you not just go to the bar and tell the waiter cleaning the tables? I was just starting to like you. Now I want to gouge your eyes out and run screaming from the pool."

When Holly doesn't say anything, Cathy asks her if she hates her.

"*Hate* is a strong word, Cathy," Holly explains, dropping into the deep water so she can get away from Cathy. "What you did with Nan's husband is...I don't know how to say this, it's distasteful. I know Nan now. Maybe if I didn't know her or something. Come on, Cathy. Think about it. You agreed to stay with us knowing you slept with Nan's husband. It's dishonest and tacky."

"Do you think I should just tell her?"

"I am certain that would not be a good idea," Holly says firmly. "She's already a bit...edgy."

"Even though she probably knows?"

"She probably knows something is happening or has happened, but how would she know it was you? And maybe there is more than one person her husband is having an affair with. Nan does not seem like the happiest girl in the world. Their marriage must be on the rocks."

Shit and more shit.

"I mean, it's not like it's a real regular thing or anything like that," Cathy confesses. "It was a two-night stand during that convention and then he called me when he was in Denver, before he lost his job. And..."

Holly knows for sure she doesn't want to know anything else about this affair, the one before it, after it, or anything else about Cathy's ridiculous, messy sex life. Or any part of her life at all.

When she dives under the water she is pretty sure Cathy is still talking. When she comes up, after holding her breath for so long her lungs ache, Cathy is standing on the steps with a towel, and she isn't finished.

"Get up here," Cathy says.

"Why?"

"You showed me how to float. I want to show you something."

"Are you going to show me how to flirt or something?"

"Very funny. Just come here."

Shit.

Holly is so trapped it's not even funny. She's so out of her element she's swearing to herself. What is going on? She could take all the *shits* she has said in the past twenty years and put them in the palm of her hand. Now she is swearing like a commando and has to get out of the pool in a bathing suit in front of Cathy. Even in the dark, even with this making-believe-she-is-bold business, she does not want to do this. She does not want to get out of the water.

"Listen, I shouldn't have told you everything. It's my problem, not yours. I'm sorry. Just forget about it. I'm not an ass all of the time."

Holly feels like she's a little kid playing in her front yard and Cathy has just pulled up in her car to offer her some candy. She'd rather be hit by the car than take the candy. But Cathy looks utterly pathetic standing there in the shadowy half light, dripping wet and trying to be nice despite the fact she's a lying adulterer.

Holly walks out of the pool so fast she's almost certain Cathy doesn't see anything. She hastily grabs her towel, tucks it under her armpits, around her breasts. She waits.

"I can make you everything on the Wendy's menu or I can show you the most excellent way to stretch before you walk or run, which is what you should start doing."

Then, without waiting, Cathy does a series of leg stretches, back stretches, and arm stretches that she says could change Holly's life.

"The flirting would help too," Holly tries to joke when Cathy is finished and tells her to try it. "Thanks for showing me. I'll remember and I will start to walk. Maybe I'll be running by Christmas."

When they plod across the lobby, where several groups have gathered with their drinks from the bar, and get into the elevator, Cathy turns to Holly and apologizes again for talking too much, for revealing so much. And even though Holly hates herself for bothering to listen, she takes another chance.

"I think someone is watching our room. I think I saw him when I looked out the broken slider."

Why she tells this to Cathy she doesn't know. Maybe it's lack of sleep, or maybe it's because Cathy shared something with her. Maybe she's just a half-drunken, paranoid, dying fool.

"Are you sure?"

"You saw what it was like out there. But I'm almost certain."

Cathy doesn't believe her. Holly can tell by the way she moves her hand and dismisses her without asking any more questions.

Double shit.

"Well, Holly, we're safe now. That's all that matters. Don't worry, sweetie."

This condescending remark is almost as disconcerting as the man they now see is standing in front of their suite door. He's got a stack of papers in his hand and he's about to slip one under their door. A geeky-looking, terribly short, bald man.

Their presence startles him. The poor guy drops all of his papers. Holly bends, picks one up, unlocks and opens the door, slams the unread paper on the counter. She walks into her room, Cathy trailing behind her.

And then she climbs into bed, still wearing her wet bathing suit, clutching her aspirin bottle that she took out of her purse, and feeling about as bold as a kitten trapped under a rear tire of a roaring dump truck.

eight

When Patti rolls over for the second morning in a row and discovers she's not so much slept as passed out again, she doesn't even care that it's also the second morning in a row that she has a mild hangover.

A swirl of activity in the nearby kitchen has jolted her awake. Nan and Margo are trying to whisper as they stand with the refrigerator door open, and Holly and Cathy have just tiptoed into the kitchen dressed bizarrely in various pieces of bathing suit attire.

Their serious attempts to maintain at least partial silence work well enough for Patti to hear the pounding rain and fierce winds that hammer the hotel.

"Did we go to bed ten minutes ago, or what?" Patti half shouts from her pullout bed, startling the other women, who thought she was still sound asleep.

"It's almost ten o'clock," Margo shares, turning back to look at the nearly empty refrigerator shelves. "And what's with the light sleeper disguise? Were you lying to me when we talked on the porch?"

"Honey, I normally do not get shit-faced every night and stay up so damn late," Patti explains. "It's nice to see that all of you are still alive. No one apparently walked in their sleep and accidentally put a plastic bag around their roommate's head."

"Very funny," Nan says.

"I thought of suffocating each of you all night," Holly said. "I'm trying to change my image. I decided maybe a prison stint would boost my ratings if I whacked some women in a hotel."

Patti is surprised to hear Holly talk this way even though she knows the younger woman is kidding. She rises up on one elbow and sees that Holly is not smiling.

"Why are you two in bathing suits, or parts of bathing suits? Did I miss a pool party?"

Holly looks at Cathy. Cathy looks at Holly. Neither one of them speak.

"What? Somebody talk to me."

Cathy still isn't talking. She's slipped behind Nan and Margo, who are now looking inside the refrigerator as if they are waiting for it to speak. Holly walks over and sits down on the edge of Patti's bed. She's got bags under her eyes, and her hair, usually close to perfect, is sticking up in the back and the sides. "We call that hospital head where I come from," Patti tells Holly.

"I feel like I need a hospital. I'm not used to this drinking and nightlife. Or all these spontaneous cat fights," Holly adds, groaning.

"All right. What happened?" Patti wants to know.

"I went swimming. Cathy followed me. I suppose that's a good thing, considering who might have been lurking in the hall."

"I must have really passed out. Sweet hell. I usually never sleep like this. I cannot believe I didn't hear you leave or come in."

Holly has more to say. This is so obvious that Patti almost asks her to go for a walk. Then she remembers there is no place to walk. And that she's suddenly in dire need of a visit to the bathroom. And part of her isn't sure she wants to know any more than she already does. Living with these four strangers is like living in a soap opera.

Nan slams the refrigerator door, and announces that if they don't get some groceries soon, they're all going to perish.

"We can either start drinking again, share three pieces of left-over bread, order some high-carb, overpriced meal from the kitchen downstairs, or I can risk my life and run to the market so we won't starve."

Food, Patti thinks, is the least of their problems.

Besides Holly's hospital head, partial bathing suit, bags-under-the-eyes sulking demeanor; Patti's own uncombed hair and wrinkled clothes; and Cathy's interesting bathing attire, it's painfully clear everyone needs not only food, but a shower, and maybe some kind of relationship mediator. The lovely plate-licking air of the previous night has been totally sucked out of the suite.

Even Cathy hasn't bothered to put on anything sexy yet. From a distance it's possible to think that she may not have even washed her face before she went to bed.

Considering how Nan sulked off to bed, it's no shock that she hasn't showered, either, and is wearing the same thing she had on last night. Her T-shirt is soiled from some of the pasta, she's got her hair in a ponytail that has the skin of her face pulled so tight it looks like her nose is about to pop off, and her dark blue shorts are pulled up so high it's a wonder she can breathe.

Margo and Nan must have gone into the bedroom, slammed the door, and fallen into bed just like Patti. Margo apparently had swiped her son's Grateful Dead T-shirt as she was packing and then grabbed her oldest daughter's shorts to round off her outfit. She's a wrinkled mish-mosh and seems to be freaking out, maybe because she's out of candy and there is only enough coffee left for one pot.

Patti tiptoes to the bathroom, where she hopes to get out of her own pajamas—not that she remembers even putting them on—take a shower, and perhaps reenter the land of the living, which may or may not include any of her suitemates.

Such angst. Such pettiness. And such a fascinating cocktail of personalities has her humming old Joni Mitchell songs before she's managed to lock herself in the bathroom, turn on the fan, and escape whatever might explode in the kitchen.

What explodes is a simultaneous verbal collision of Nan announcing she's going outside in search of food, weather be damned, and Cathy suddenly remembering that a guy was standing at their door last night to deliver what she assumes was another scary warning.

They talk over each other until Holly jumps up, clearly agitated, stalks over to the counter, and picks up the paper she'd slapped down when she came in from the swimming party. She pulls up her elastic-waisted shorts that are covering the bottom half of her suit, and snaps the elastic so that it sounds like a firecracker exploding.

She does not bother to wince when the thick elastic snaps back into place, even though it clearly must hurt like hell. Instead, Holly silently reads the piece of paper and makes it known by the way she stands with her feet apart, arms flexed, paper at eye level, that everyone else better shut the hell up for just a few minutes.

She finishes. Rolls her eyes. Turns the paper over. Keeps reading. Drops her arms. Looks up. And then says, "Ready?"

Everyone nods. Speaking does not seem like a choice.

"*A big thank-you to everyone who has come to visit us in the conference room,*" Holly reads aloud. "*Some of your information has been of great value. We continue to work very intently on this case and we want to caution guests to remain careful. Female guests especially need to take precautions. We believe it is wise to stay in pairs. And contrary to what some might think, we really are just ordinary people with extraordinary gifts. If we have any news we will let you know. Please consider us as friends. And please, if you have any information, see anything out of the ordinary—come see us.*"

When Holly finishes she looks up and catches Cathy's eye; Cathy interprets this as a signal to begin speaking.

"Thank God I followed you last night, Holly," she says loudly. "Anything could have happened to you. Do you think the guy you saw out of the window is the creep they're warning us about?"

Holly suddenly wishes she had drowned Cathy when she had the chance. She'd told her about the man she thinks she saw from the balcony window in confidence. Does this woman have *no* boundaries?

Nan and Margo are staring at Holly as if she's just transformed into a goat. This is the moment when Patti sticks her wet head, wrapped in a towel, out of the bathroom doorway because she has heard raised voices.

"Now what?" she asks innocently, wondering what discussion she's now missed.

"Apparently Miss Holly here spotted someone lurking outside just after we found the broken sliding glass door," Nan explains. "And, oh yes—the fortune-tellers have left us another note about the killers running around at this lovely five-star hotel."

Patti slams the door, ducks back into the bathroom. Three minutes later, she comes out with one towel around her head and one around her body.

"Holly, what's going on? Why didn't you tell us about this man? We could be in real danger."

If this is what being bold gets you, Holly is ready to fall back three steps, eat a bag of carbohydrates, spend the rest of her life as a celibate hairstylist. She makes a solemn vow to never ever use a public restroom again. What if the guy was a mirage?

"Okay. Here's what happened. I went to the broken slider while you were all cleaning up the broken glass and I thought I saw someone. Maybe a man. Maybe not. He was standing down there and looking up at our window. But it was storming. It was raining. I wasn't sure. I mean, how could I be certain? And I didn't want to alarm anyone. You already all think I'm a baby, for God's sake."

Margo suddenly goes pale and announces she has to go into the bedroom and make a phone call.

Nan throws her hands up as Margo brushes past her in a "I have no idea" gesture that gives Holly a second to steady herself and everyone else the same second to wonder if there really was a guy lurking out there and if he had something to do with their broken window.

"She's probably calling her kids," Patti tells the others as Margo closes the bedroom door. "But, Holly, really, what if there *was* a guy out there?"

"Look, I felt comfortable enough to go down to the pool, so how threatened could I have felt? And you know that when you're stressed or emotional you tend to see things that might not exist." Holly's trying very hard to convince herself that is exactly what happened. "Do you really want me to go down to the lobby and tell those people about this man I may or may not have seen? Maybe I was just tired. Maybe it was the beer or whatever we were drinking, were about to drink, or had already consumed. Come on, guys. We're all getting paranoid."

"For good reason, it seems," Cathy exclaims. "I mean, these psychics might seem a little odd, but something is apparently going on."

Patti is afraid to get dressed because she might miss something. A small pool of water has formed around her feet. She wraps the towel around her breasts a bit tighter and then steps forward so she is closer to the action.

Now that she's finally starting to shake off her mild hangover, Patti's also realized that they all appear to get along much better when they're drinking. Of course that didn't end up so well last night but for a while anyway, it was almost fun. If she still didn't have a slight headache she'd drop her towel and pour them all a drink.

Instead, inching forward, Patti is trying hard to remember the lyrics to "Highway to Hell." Her little highway is the small stretch of carpeting that runs from the living room into the kitchen.

"Girls, girls, girls." Patti sounds like a nun trying to get the attention of an unruly math class. "Everyone take a deep breath, good God."

No one is about to take a deep breath, except maybe Margo, whose muffled phone discussion seems to be going on and on. Nan and Cathy actually seem to be agreeing, which is an astounding coincidence, and Holly looks like she's about to melt into tears, which would be just about perfect right now.

"Listen, Patti, I think Holly should have said something about what she saw," Cathy insists. "We would have listened. It's true we're kind of loud and obnoxious, but really, we're all in this together."

Right.

Holly wishes she could jump out the window. Maybe jump out the window holding Cathy's hand. Maybe this seeing-things mess really does mean something is wrong with her.

"What if I went down there now and made a fool out of myself?"

Patti doesn't care that she's standing half-naked in the kitchen. She pretty much stopped caring about non-singing-related appearances a long time ago. She remembers hitting the lovely age of fifty as if it were a gift carried on the wings of sweet golden-haired angels. It helped that she still looked years younger than people expected someone her age to look, but she has a theory about it all that she calls the "I-don't-give-a-damn" philosophy, which she'd love to tattoo on Holly's left hand.

Basically, it's the lovely license to be who you have always been all along—only without the makeup, butt-hugging underwear, skin-tight nylons, clothes that leave nothing to the imagination, hair that's teased until it surrenders, and whatever else happens to be the style of the decade, month, or day.

Patti looks intensely at Holly. She wishes she could transmit everything she knows and has learned, mostly the hard way, right into Holly's barely-been-tapped brain. Holly probably had seen someone down there. Was it the bad guy? A tourist trying to get a great video clip for YouTube? A groundskeeper looking for lost garbage can lids? And if Holly bothered to go down to the psychics now, or then, what good would it really do?

These are the things that a woman of age can assess and decide so quickly it's hardly worth mentioning. Patti's hesitation level is so low she could probably interview every man within a three-mile radius and correctly pick out instantly the good, the bad, and the really bad.

"It's okay," she says, reassuring Holly. "If the psychics are as good as they say they are, and they probably are, you didn't do anything wrong. They should be all over it by now."

Before Cathy can respond, Margo comes flying out of the bedroom. She looks at Nan as if no one else exists, and asks if they are going now to get groceries. She says she's sick of talking to her kids, is starving, and doesn't mind risking her life to venture into the storm if Nan still wants to go.

So the two women dress quickly and no one tries to stop them. If they could all shut up for more than three seconds their growling stomachs would give Patti the beat to a new song. When Margo turns to go back for her purse, Nan grabs her and says she's buying, not to worry.

"You already bought the bathing suits. And are paying for the room," Margo argues.

"You've got to spend it while you have it," Nan fires back. Then she orders everyone else to back away from their wallets.

"This part of living with strangers I could get used to." Cathy laughs as Margo and Nan go out the door and head for a wind-and-rain-blown world so wild Patti has to wonder if they will ever see them again.

Margo admits on the way down in the elevator that she needs a candy fix, otherwise she'd never try to make it across the street where she saw a store the first night she ventured out. And "across the street" really means down about a half block, which will also mean they will get drenched, possibly float into the storm sewer, or mistakenly get picked up by a van headed toward Margo's parents' trailer park community.

When the elevator door opens it looks like an entire football stadium has been evacuated into the lobby. Everyone is aimlessly milling about looking for something to do, because there is obviously no place to go.

Nan nudges her way through the crowd and is trying to convince the bewildered-looking doorman to let her borrow two umbrellas, while Margo scans the mob scene. She is appalled by how many parents are simply letting their children run wild throughout the first floor of the hotel. This irresponsible behavior has been driving Margo crazy since she became a mother.

She's always thought that there are places for adults, there are places for children. There are also places for adults and children, and all of those places are not the same. She was once tossed out of a restaurant when she brazenly walked up to a woman whose two-year-old was throwing food onto the table of an elderly couple who were obviously trying to have a quiet, intimate dinner. First she scooped up all the food the darling baby had flung onto the floor, the table, and onto the unhappy man's suit jacket. The she dumped it on the mother's plate.

It was probably the way she said, "There's a McDonald's down the street," or the way she made certain the returned food ruined the mother's dinner, that got her physically tossed out, but she felt she had proved an important point.

The lobby-based herd of uncontrolled children makes her shudder and then eagerly slip under one of two umbrellas that probably cost Nan at least a twenty-dollar bill. Going outside is a dance of total dare. Neither Nan nor Margo can recall seeing or feeling rain this hard ever before. The places on their bodies that are not covered by the umbrellas are being pelted by rain that feels like torrents of needles being stuck into their arms and legs, where the umbrellas don't cover them.

"Jesus," Nan curses as they weave around puddles the size of small lakes until they miraculously make it across the street without drowning.

That's where Margo learns it isn't just the food Nan is after, but something you cannot eat. Margo is elated to be inside the tiny neighborhood grocery store. She immediately grabs a cart and excitedly turns to ask Nan what they should buy, and this is when she discovers Nan frantically looking from left to right as if she's lost or trying to find something.

"I need a pay phone."

"A pay phone?"

"I need to make a very urgent call. I tried to get someone's cell phone out of the drawer but that damn Patti must have hidden them. I can't believe we let her take the phones. Talk about being hypnotized by the moment. It's stupid."

"You could have gone into the bedroom. The phone in it works, for crying out loud."

"I need more privacy than that."

"Nan, go look for a phone," Margo advises, because it's clear Nan *really* needs a phone. "I'll shop, but I'm not sure there are any pay phones left in this entire country."

Nan turns without hesitation and Margo, who loves to grocery shop almost as much as she loves to cook, discovers that she's in the middle of a food-buying frenzy. Because of the storm, the small store is jammed, with mostly elderly people, who appear to be purchasing everything but the shelving and light fixtures.

What she can't figure out is how the hell they all got to the store. She's heard Florida car insurance is some of the most expensive in the world; maybe that's because these people drive around in tempests to buy groceries.

When Margo reaches into the meat cooler for a package of fresh chicken, an elderly man behind her swoops in and grabs it.

"Excuse me, sir," she reprimands him, trying to get the chicken back. "You just took this right out of my hand."

The man feigns shock, snatches the chicken back without saying a word, and dashes down the aisle.

Before someone else can accost her, Margo quickly locates a huge beef roast and then begins dashing through the aisles as if she's a contestant on a television game show who has only a few moments to fill her cart.

This is how she bumps into Nan.

Nan is standing in the middle of the canned goods aisle, or what is left of the canned goods anyway, and has both hands on an elderly woman's grocery cart. She is trying to convince the obviously terrified woman to let her use her cell phone. Margo wants to intercede immediately but the conversation is so hilarious that she can't move.

"Really, I'm a nice person," Nan pleads.

"Nice people do not grab other people's shopping carts."

"I could stand right here and make a call. It would just take a minute. I won't steal your phone."

"Dear, please let go of my cart."

"I'll pay you." Nan is starting to whimper. "I dropped my phone in the toilet."

Margo can tell the older woman is in fear for her life. Before she can call for help, Margo steps forward. She puts her hand on Nan's arm, nods sympathetically toward the older woman, and gently says, "Nan, honey, let's go."

Margo smiles and then pushes Nan back. "She's not been well. This storm has wrecked her nerves. She's not used to this kind of weather."

"Maybe she could use your phone, then," the woman suggests, a little sharply. "The stories you hear nowadays. There are troubled people everywhere. Nowhere is safe, is it? It's frightening what people will do."

Margo is certain that if she tells this stranger her phone has been taken away from her by a torch singer she barely knows, a woman she met in a public restroom and who she is now temporarily living with, she would sound as nuts as Nan.

Thankfully the woman moves on. Margo is tempted to run after her to offer her the roast for her trouble. She decides to keep it in case she has to whack Nan in the head with it so she'll stop accosting old ladies.

"Nan, get a grip."

"What? What did I do that was so awful?"

"You scared her, for pity's sake. What's wrong with you? You're not making sense. Why didn't you just ask Patti to use a phone back at the hotel?"

"I was trying to cooperate for once," Nan admits. "Patti is so nice and besides, she's right. Phones rule our lives. But I really need to make two calls. It's important."

"Then find a pay phone," Margo says firmly. "Don't run around scaring people. You're acting like a crackhead."

"Let me look up front. Get your candy and whatever else we need. I'll meet you by the cash registers."

"Do not talk to strangers. Do not beg anyone for their phone. You can call from the lobby if it's that important."

No one is ever going to believe her. Margo is certain that for the rest of her life when she tells someone about meeting these chicks over an airport toilet, about the wild storm, the five-star hotel room, the paranoid palm readers in the lobby, frenzied shopping in a monsoon, or saving an accosted grandma near the string beans, people are going to look at her as if someone else has entered her body.

And who in the hell would blame them?

The entire scenario sounds absolutely ridiculous, if not downright hilarious. As Margo scurries toward the candy aisle she imagines what she might be doing right this moment if her plane had not been grounded. She laughs out loud when she realizes she might very well be shopping for groceries at home.

The same elderly woman Nan had been bothering happens to be in the candy aisle and catches Margo laughing at nothing. The woman stops abruptly, looks Margo in the eye, then wheels her cart around so fast it almost tips over.

Looking and acting crazy is usually something her children are in charge of, and Margo, who knows for certain her children are doing just fine without her, relishes the chance to step out of her old shoes and move in a new direction.

She scoops up several bags of candy and skates through the store selecting a variety of food that most people would never imagine combining to make a four-star meal. Cereal, sausage, eggs, taco shells, potatoes, a frozen pie, two six-packs of beer, the last three bottles of wine, and three boxes of macaroni and cheese are all she figures she can carry back to the hotel.

When she discovers Nan lurking around the cash register, Margo decides to also grab a mess of junk food and get out of the store before something else happens, even though she'd kind of like to stay. In some ways it might be safer than to be in the suite with those four women. But they must be starving.

Nan, to her credit, has scrounged a box of pancake mix, some cheese, vegetables, cookies, a bag of potato chips. And an antiquated cell phone that she is hugging to her chest like a newborn baby.

"Look," she yells in elation when Margo motions for her to get in line so they can check out. "It's got fifteen minutes on it and then you put it in this bag and send it back."

Nan slips Margo her credit card without the checker seeing it, whispers that she should simply sign the bill, runs the cell phone through the scanner, and tells Margo she will meet her under the canopy outside.

"I just lost a bet because of that dang phone," the checker snarls. "We've had that thing in here for three years and it's so expensive we didn't think anyone would ever buy it."

"She lost her phone. I lost my phone."

Margo wants to tell the whole story to the checker but she decides it would be ludicrous to explain any further. She waves her hand in a "forget it" kind of way, asks to have the groceries double-bagged, and then slips outside under the huge green canopy where the rain continues to flood the streets. Nan is apparently talking to her husband.

And it isn't pretty.

"I have to do it," Nan is not so much saying as shouting.

Margo splashes noisily through the puddles so Nan knows she is standing there. Nan turns, mouths "just a few minutes," then turns back and resumes yelling.

"If you move the money now it is going to look bad and it won't matter if they go through the records and see it was all done legally!" Nan shouts into the phone. "You've heard of guilt by association. This is how it works in the world you once inhabited, you asshole. I cannot hold the pieces together any longer."

Margo is trying to disappear. If she could slip back into the store, dash across the street, make herself invisible, she would do it. But the bag boy dropped the groceries around her feet when she checked out and she's trapped.

It sounds like Nan's life is about to burst. Margo can't help herself. She leans closer.

"We've been over this and you know that I can no longer live with the guilt of knowing what you did, John."

John.

John is Nan's husband. She mentioned him somewhere between the airport and the grocery store. Margo is certain of this and it doesn't take much to figure out what they are talking about. John has lost his job. Investment bankers have been proven to be mostly crooked for several years now. The banking world has miraculously recovered but some slimy dogs still have not been captured. Could this be part of Nan's constant angst? And if this is her second phone call, who could she possibly have called first?

Margo longs to interrupt. She wishes she could grab the phone and do something, say something, to rescue Nan. She would do it. She really would. But she realizes that some things have to play themselves out. It's not time. Not yet. Nan needs to rescue herself this time.

When the phone finally dies in mid-sentence Margo is relieved. Nan turns and Margo is surprised to see that she doesn't look furious. She looks frightened.

Margo tries to apologize. "I'm sorry. I heard most of the call—there isn't anyplace else to go...."

"Oh hell. I *wanted* you to hear, Margo. Everything I am and own and know is about to be shattered."

Margo really didn't imagine this. She's worried about the meat and eggs and beer getting too warm. She's worried that Cathy may have pinned Holly against the door and is making her go talk to the psychics. She's worried that Patti is filling up drink glasses with ice. She's worried that her parents will find out she lied when she called to tell them she is home safe, and will come find her and make her go back to the trailer park even though she knows they are fine. She's worried that her life is changing and moving in ways that may have startled her even a day ago. But she was not worried about self-assured Nan who convinced a group of women strangers to share a suite.

"What can I do?" Margo manages to say this as the rain pounds even harder.

Nan bends to pick up some of the groceries, looks at her, and just smiles. "Let's go," she says.

The dash back to the hotel is not unlike dancing through the center of a waterfall with a bag of rocks attached to each arm. Somehow they manage, and when they are safely inside the elevator Nan says a series of sentences so rapidly that Margo can barely understand her.

"I have information about insider trading and bad banking deals and men who are living as if they have not ruined people's lives and the world owes them because they look nice in hand-stitched suits and I have been keeping secrets for so long that I feel as if my insides are rotten and I can no longer live like this and I have no idea who to call or what to do and my husband is a fucking asshole who should probably be in jail and I think he is having an affair probably with someone I know and my son never calls and this storm and the planes not leaving and the phone in the john and pretty much everything that has happened to keep me from going home is wonderful."

Just as she finishes, the elevator door opens, and who should be standing outside of it but Cathy. And right behind her is Patti, who, thankfully, is no longer wearing just two towels.

"Geez, we were coming to find you two," Cathy squeals. "We thought the bad guy got you or something."

Nan glances sideways at Margo. Margo glances sideways at Nan, and they have no choice but to shut the hell up and get out of the elevator.

When they get back into the suite, set down the groceries, and have three seconds to look up, what they see is either a mirage or a makeshift beauty salon that has suddenly materialized in the center of suite 6502 at the St. Pete's Beach Rivera.

"We're going to do makeovers," Holly happily informs the astonished and soaking-wet women as she rummages through her purse and pulls out yet another hairbrush. "Go get all your makeup, hair stuff, anything you can, and start thinking about what you want to look like."

Look like? How about who you want to be, where you want to be, what you don't want to be?

nine

No one wants to wait for a roast to cook. The stranded women in the sixth-floor suite are so hungry they could eat all of Holly's hair products. This is why Margo orders everyone, yet again, to clear the kitchen so she can create magic with the groceries that Nan has just helped her haul from the store.

Margo is also hoping that she can fry Nan's secret along with the eggs and sausage and pancakes. Does Nan expect her to shut up and forget what she heard or does she want Margo to say something? While she throws groceries around the kitchen she can't help but wonder if Nan's quick thinking in the airport restroom was really a long-thought-out plan to give herself time to escape or figure out a way to keep her husband and possibly herself out of prison. She's so glad for the distraction of cooking that she's considering letting Holly give her a mohawk.

And she knows if she can keep busy that it will be her salvation. If she can focus on the pancakes then she won't risk getting involved any more than she already is, or say something she maybe should not say, or grab Nan by the neck and ask her why she didn't pick someone else to hear her confession.

The moment Cathy hears the meat begin to sizzle she decides that no decent breakfast—or lunch-and-breakfast, in their case—should begin without being preceded by Bloody Marys.

She rummages through the remains of their liquor supply and announces that she is going to make a quick bar run so that she can get some mix. There's surprisingly enough vodka left, which is either going to be a really good thing or a really bad thing.

Nan is so distracted she doesn't even bother to make a snide comment about Cathy wanting to go to the bar for mix most likely so she can keep up her flirting statistics. When Margo looks up and sees Nan staring out the newly replaced sliding door window, while Patti and Holly rearrange furniture so they can all sit at the little table, she figures it will be just a matter of time before Nan spills her secrets. She's hoping Nan shares her real problem before she does.

Margo imagines the burden of what Nan knows, and what she must do, like a huge weight that has her pinned in place. While Margo continues to cook, and Patti and Holly keep them updated on the weather—no change—she cooks and tries hard to do just that.

By the time Cathy gets back, Margo has finished cooking, and the entire suite smells like a pancake house on a Sunday morning.

"What is it about bacon?" Cathy asks, as she sets down a full bottle of thick red drink mix and several wine bottles she has managed to carry unaided. "I have other vegetarian friends who eat nothing but tofu. Then the minute they get a whiff of bacon they eat half a pound."

"It's the grease," Patti explains. "The smell of grease. And the taste of grease. I doubt if there is a person alive who does not equate the smell of frying bacon with some lovely childhood memory. That is true unless you are me and your father threw the bacon grease on your mother every other day, when he wasn't throwing it on you."

"That's a lovely story," Nan snaps.

"Sorry," Patti says, although she is not. "Are you okay, Nan?"

"I'm fine," Nan snaps again.

Margo, who stopped breathing when Patti told her horrid bacon story, will pretty much do anything at this moment to distract herself from Nan's professional and personal problems. She quickly thinks of her own story.

"My mother kept a little porcelain dish right on the stove where she put all the bacon drippings," she shares. "She would make eggs, and pretty much anything else she could cook in that grease, and to this day I'm sad that health aficionados discovered fat can kill us."

"It's not going to stop me from eating as much bacon as I can," Holly admits.

Cathy starts mixing up drinks for everyone and at the last minute they all decide they have had enough drinking and the Bloody Marys become virgins and the meal miraculously begins without any fresh arguments.

Outside, frequent cracks of thunder make them all jump. It's something no one can get used to, and perhaps the missing vodka is necessary self-medication. Patti keeps telling them the weather report and the storm-to-beat-all-storms is apparently not even close to surrendering. Half the airports in the country remain closed and weather experts are predicting the entire thing is going to go down in history books as a record breaker.

"Has anyone ever been trapped by a storm for this long?" Holly asks this as she grabs more bacon. "I got the last piece," she adds triumphantly, and everyone laughs.

"Storms always seemed bigger and stronger and longer when I was a kid, but that might just be because I was little, not so strong, and when you are younger your sense of time is about as tall as you are. Everything seemed like forever when I was a kid," Patti admits. "Enough of the storm. Right now, you girls go scoot. I'm going to clean up. Margo, as a thank-you for a terrific breakfast, you should get the first makeover."

Margo doesn't argue because what she loves is the cooking—not the cleaning. Then Holly asks both Nan and Margo to bring out any hair products, makeup, or beauty do-dads they might have brought along. Which has them alone in the bedroom for a few moments.

Damn it.

Nan will not say a word. She won't even look at Margo. Margo knows how to address unspoken deeds and emotions. She's got kids. She has experience using subversive tactics to pry out secret information. Once she got her son to admit that he and his best friend had taken two beers out of the refrigerator by simply making believe she couldn't remember what beer tasted like. She wants to know if she is supposed to comfort Nan or spill the beans.

"Nan," she says, softly. "Are you okay?"

"I can't believe I told you," Nan whispers as she picks up her cosmetics bag. "This is stupid. Makeovers? My whole life is fucking falling apart—nothing can make it over!"

Nan grabs her little blue plastic case, a hairbrush, and slams out of the room.

Damn it.

Margo is convincing herself that Nan wants her to say something or do something to try to help. Why else would she have let her hear the conversation?

By the time Margo finds her one tube of lipstick, her daughter's used hair gel, and a tweezers, Nan has inserted herself ahead of everyone in Holly's makeshift salon chair, Cathy has poured everyone fragrant coffee, and Patti is almost finished with the kitchen cleanup. There's nothing to do but wait for an emotional meltdown, or another window to blow out.

Holly has taken a cushion off the couch and set it on top of one side chair so she doesn't have to bend while she works on everyone's hair. She's pulled a side table over, lined up bottles and lotions and a variety of hair products that would put even a small salon to shame. Her own suitcase was loaded with products she picked up at her Florida convention, and it doesn't take long to see that she's clearly in her element.

She orders Nan to go wet her hair, takes a huge sip of her coffee, and prepares like she's about to perform surgery. The moment Nan gets back, Holly asks her if she can cut her hair.

"Anything you want," Nan responds with a wave of her hand. "Can you change my face and give me five inches more height too?"

"Yes on the face. No on the height. Now sit down and be quiet."

Patti is leaning on the kitchen counter, watching the action and wondering when someone will lob an insult. She is trying hard to remember the last time she was with a group of women for so much time, in such close proximity. A time when there was so much going on—spoken and unspoken.

Holly is suddenly totally in her element. She's sorting through products, mashing her fingers around in Nan's curls, and it looks to Patti as if she's deep in thought about matters that may go way beyond hair. Holly isn't acting like a terrified young puppy and Patti suddenly has the feeling that Holly knows more than she lets on.

On the other hand, Margo looks terrified for some reason. She's tapping her foot, looking out the window, at Nan, back to the window, and then into her glass like she is waiting for a message to pop out of the lovely liquid.

And Cathy is busying herself with making more ice cubes, checking the level of the remaining vodka, in case they decide to ditch the virgins, and worrying out loud about whether or not they will be able to get more drinks out of Bridget and her ever-able assistant. She is the only one interested in anything but coffee.

Patti starts humming, "Love Is a Many-Splendored Thing" to herself as Holly's scissors begin to snap and the distance between all of them seems to grow longer instead of shorter. It's as if something or someone unseen is pulling them all backward, holding them in place, not allowing them to break free from whatever it is that has them treading water.

Marionettes, Patti decides. That's what everyone has become. Pulled in directions by strings that will not let them really be present, to really lean into one another, to feel the full force of this fiercely female gathering. Is it too difficult, too hard, and just too unsettling to let go of those damned strings for even a short period of time?

Patti has done large performances where women sometimes bond so quickly it's almost frightening. There's hugging and laughter and cheek kissing going on so fast it's just like a drunken family reunion. And this may be the first time Patti admits that she likes it when that happens. She loves seeing the women throw back their heads, embrace one another, dip into their deepest bag of secrets so quickly you'd think they were on their way to purgatory. Even as she's kept most of her secrets locked up in a place so deep and dark she wonders if she could find her way back to them. And what would that do? And what would Patti do if she crawled back that far? Could she do it? Could she step out of her lounge-singer persona long enough to play her own game of truth-or-dare?

Patti honestly doesn't know.

Her careful observations are halted when Nan declines a makeup application, bends to look at her clipped hair in the mirror, and actually smiles and announces she loves it.

"It looks great," Margo manages to say, resting her constantly tapping foot for a few seconds. "It's amazing how tapering it like that in the front totally opened up her face."

"Good eye, Margo," Holly congratulates her and then gives her the "come here" gesture with her pointer finger.

"Me?" Margo eagerly says as she jumps up and asks Cathy if she can stop playing with the bottles and make more coffee and pour them some water.

"I'll be the afternoon waitress," Cathy agrees, turning to grab glasses. And then filling them with water. She hands one to Margo.

"It's a dream come true for you." Nan smirks.

"Nan," Margo scolds. "Knock it off. You've been sniping at Cathy since we got here. Enough already."

Nan glares at Margo, who is still standing with her hand on the recently filled water glass. The moment Nan and Margo make eye contact, Margo lifts her glass to her lips, tips back her head, gulps down the entire glass as if she is dying of thirst, holds it out, and says, "Refill, please."

No one moves. Not even Cathy.

Margo gets her own refill and walks slowly over toward Holly, who gestures with her open hand toward the seat. Margo sits.

"I want the deluxe. Haircut. Makeup. Do whatever in the hell you want to me."

Everyone is beyond thrilled that it is neither Margo nor Nan who will be holding the scissors. Holly first walks around Margo as if she is admiring a Renaissance painting. Then she places her hand on Margo's chin, tips it back, moves her fingers through Margo's hair, then steps back.

This is when something in the room unexpectedly shifts yet again. For Nan speaks now, with a voice that is new. It's softer, slow, unsure.

"I'm sorry, Cathy," she says. And when she drops her head she does not see Holly and Margo exchanging a quick glance.

"That's okay," Cathy answers.

"No," Nan says quickly. "I've been a total bitch. There's something I need to talk about, something I need help with, something that I have to address right now."

Margo so wishes she was drinking wine instead of water. But when she raises her glass and starts tipping it, Holly pulls her arm down. Reluctantly Margo takes this as a signal that she should probably say something.

"Nan," Margo mutters, "can I help?"

"Just kick-start me."

Which is what Margo does. She reminds everyone that Nan's husband has recently lost his job and that Nan is in investments and has been riding out the last storm of financial problems thinking that everything is fine with her business. But then, well, this is where Nan has to take over because Margo's information, picked up at the grocery store, is sketchy at best—what with the rain hitting the canopy, and grocery carts skidding on the sidewalk, and her own inability to hear through the back side of someone's head.

And Margo craves a cigarette so badly she's considering eating one just so she can get a little nicotine into her system. Right about now she'd rather be wrestling with her three kids, half the members of the high-school soccer team and their overbearing mothers, and the twelve other rather huge items that are on her to-do list.

Nan starts slowly. She isn't sure what to say. Patti and Cathy have filled up their glass and cups so far they have to walk slowly toward the end of the couch that still has a cushion on it so they will not spill their drinks. Holly is dauntless. She's listening intently but she is still managing to create magic with Margo's hair. She must appear much as she looks when she is working at the salon.

Nan's story starts out small but it's apparent that it is going to grow quite large before she gets to the end. This is when Patti so badly wants to do something she often does at the start of new gigs. She talks about how wonderful it is to be there and tells a story about new places and mentions *The Sound of Music*. Then she sings, "The hills are alive . . . and it's rather frightening." She so wants to do that now, but Nan is in such distress; Margo is clearly trying to prod her along as she bends her head so Holly can move around to get at the nape of her neck, and Patti's just not sure anyone would get it.

So she lets it pass, crosses her legs, and holds on to her water as if it is the weight that is keeping her exactly where she needs to be.

Nan's story is amazing and scandalous. She met her husband while they were working at competing firms. They dated. Fell in love. Married. And, yes, she was pregnant at the time, but, no, that is not why they married.

Nan's greatest regret is that she always put her work, her job, her career, in front of her son. He was always second and apparently he knew it. They are estranged—but she is getting ahead of herself. Her son is the hardest part. The rest be damned. Her husband especially be damned.

The world changed and banking changed but investments did not change and Nan's husband was caught with his pants down. Nan had never seen him like that before. He hadn't told her that he was selling his soul and Nan was so busy bumping her head against the glass ceiling that she didn't see it happening. She was outpacing him. He was falling behind in his contracts and contacts, and he saw Nan blazing a trail that left him in the dust. He was embarrassed and lazy and so he turned into a criminal.

"I trusted him," she says haltingly. "There was no way I would ever have guessed that he was sneaking into my briefcase, removing records, and gaining access to my accounts."

"Sweet hell," Patti says out loud, without even realizing she's speaking.

"That's putting it mildly," Nan says forcefully.

"You mean he was snooping into your trades and whatever else you had in your briefcase or on your computer and then sending out a notice to his people?" Cathy asks.

"Yes," Nan replies.

"That son-of-a-bitch," Patti snarls while taking a gulp of her water.

"There's more."

"More?" Cathy says.

Margo is afraid to breathe. This is not what she imagined when she stood outside the grocery store and sort of eavesdropped. It's worse than she imagined and it's apparently about to go even beyond that.

"What I have recently discovered is that some of my investors who caught on to what my husband was doing decided to join with him and create a kind of double scam," Nan explains. "It's a complicated dance that involves a mess of people and transactions and illegal activity and includes so much money it makes my heart shudder."

"Well, Jesus H., girl," Patti exclaims. "What are you doing about it?"

"Just drinking this glass of water Cathy handed me, wishing I had the guts to have confronted the people I came to Florida to meet, and praying that this storm never ends so I don't ever have to leave."

Margo can't stand it any longer. She lifts up her head slowly so she is certain Holly does not have scissors pointed close to any major veins and asks Nan a very important question.

"Did you do anything wrong?"

"I married him."

"Besides that."

"No. I didn't know until recently that he was stealing shit out of my briefcase. I never knew. From day one, we talked about privacy and keeping our professional lives separate. I had no idea."

"Did you keep records of your transactions and communications with your own clients?"

Margo suddenly does not sound like a housewife from Wisconsin. But no one wants to stop this conversation to ask her if she's been watching back-to-back episodes of *Law and Order*.

"Down to the second. I'm guessing even my husband doesn't know about the security system my company installed to track every single entry into our system and into every account."

Cathy whimpers just a little bit because she's apparently had an affair with an animal, and gets up to grab not one but two bottles of wine. The bartender pours herself a drink and then sets the bottles on the coffee table in front of Nan, goes back for some glasses, waves her hand in a "help yourselves" kind of motion in case anyone decides to switch to wine, and then slumps back into her chair.

"Sweet," Margo says, a little wide-eyed but sticking to her water.

Patti would be singing "Joy to the World" if she knew these women better. Instead, she waits like everyone else, because Margo is apparently the stay-at-home-financial-mother-wizard of the decade.

"The math teachers at school are always talking about this kind of thing and I know there is someone who can help you," Margo begins explaining thoughtfully. "Remember when Obama took office? And remember how the banks were belly-up? How they started all these new watchdog bureaus? Well, there's a number you can call. Kind of like the money-minded sister of the FBI or something."

Or something.

Holly cannot take her eyes off Margo. She feels like she is standing on air and there's a tiny sensation, like the fingers of ants, pushing against her eardrums. She shakes her hand quickly to try and dislodge the sensations, but when they remain, she wishes she had time right now to think about what they are, why they are happening, what caused her to feel as if she could walk on water. It's the tumor, she knows. Who else feels this way except people who have a deadly mass sitting on their temporal lobes? To hell with the MRI she'd had and the doctor who tried to get her into counseling. Please pass more aspirins and get the coffin ready.

Margo looks around the room and sees that everyone is staring at her in wonderment. Obviously, they have not spent much time in teacher lounges.

"I'm serious," she says, jumping up. "There's a fairly new watchdog regulatory bureau that works independently of the Securities and Exchange Commission. They hold hands with the FBI. One of the teachers has a brother who works for them, I swear to God."

"She's right," Nan says. "I don't know why I didn't think of this. Well, I do know. I'm scared out of my mind."

"Who has a laptop?" Margo asks.

Cathy backs away from her waitressing duties to get her computer, while Margo explains the intricacies of a teacher's lounge. It's like an encyclopedia of knowledge, she shares. There are lots of people, each of whom knows a little bit about one thing, and when you throw it all together it's like sitting in the middle of a live Google search.

Plus, so many of the teachers are always planning what they are going to do when they retire with their supposedly secure pensions. And in her school, several teachers happen to be commodities, trading, investments, and banking geeks, who could probably secure several cabinet positions with the federal government.

This is what she tells them as she works on the computer. And it takes her less than five minutes to prove it by locating a government website that would have taken any of the rest of them a good hour to find.

Nan feels like an idiot for not remembering about the government agency.

"It's not something you would automatically think about when you're under stress," Holly tells her. "I mean, really, you just decided to do this. I have no idea what I would do in the middle of some kind of hair scam."

"Now what?" Nan asks.

"There's a number to call. I'm guessing that if you call and explain everything, they will want to move on this very fast, before any more damage is done."

"What kind of school do you work at again?" Nan tries hard to joke. "Is it one of those federal prisons where all the big shots go who finally got caught after years living the high life?"

Holly has paused her scissors and is looking over Margo's shoulder. She nods her head up and down in agreement, as if she is the quality-control assistant. Then she tells Nan to take down the phone number while she twirls Margo's hair with one hand.

Nan writes down the number and then freezes.

"What?" If it was her, Cathy knows, she'd already be dialing.

"Are you sure they're not going to arrest me or something?" Nan begs Margo.

"Documentation is everything."

"I have it."

"Want me to call?"

"Give me a few minutes."

Cathy notices Nan's glass is lacking about two ounces of water. She rushes over to fill it and then stands at attention as if she is Nan's private sommelier.

Holly does some random plucking to Margo's eyebrows with the edge of the scissors and wishes she had the guts to say to Cathy, "Pouring her a drink is the least you can do, you little tramp." But she doesn't.

There's really no reason for Cathy to confess to Nan what an unfaithful, husband-raiding lowlife she is right now. It might turn out to be the message that finally pushes Nan over the edge, and she's already leaning in that direction anyway. The chances of Nan staying with a man who clearly did not care if he ruined her professional *or* personal life seem slim to none. Even though other women stick with losers all of the time, Nan doesn't seem like the type, Holly decides.

Nan is more like a woman who was crossed and then double-crossed. A woman who trusted her husband and then became blind, deaf, and almost dumb when she discovered how she had been betrayed.

Margo recognizes a place in herself that might allow her to shoot her husband if the same thing happened to her. If there weren't a gun lying around, she thinks she could take him with the carving knife she keeps next to the barbecue tools in her kitchen. For a while she had a penchant for archery when her son was taking it in gym class and she organized an after-school school-employee archery night that fairly drove her wild with excitement. She was unbeatable, and for months had African Queen movielike dreams where she was shooting at snakes and alligators with her trusty bow and arrow. She isn't a poison or hit-and-run kind of gal, but Margo clearly knows that physical violence isn't beyond her. And she thinks she may not be the only woman in the room with these same kinds of feelings.

Being a law-abiding, moral citizen of the world sucks. Margo and her supply of Tootsie Pops from the store would have been a hit in the Wild West. She decides she could turn Nan, Holly, Patti, and Cathy into a wild, ass-kicking female hit squad in about three hours if she had the right tools.

For now it will have to be the phone call and her zippy new eyebrows and twisted hair.

Holly motions for Patti to get into the chair next when Nan jumps up, announces that she's going to go into the bedroom to make her call, gets halfway there, and then comes back to get a wineglass and fill it.

When the door closes, Holly admits that if anything else exciting happens she may wet her pants and not be able to finish the last two haircuts. Aberdeen, Ohio, may as well be in the middle of Russia. Right this moment, life is pretty darn exciting.

Patti distracts her by asking for some specific hair work. She wants "barely a trim" because she is sick of having stylists take off way too much every time she goes to a salon. And she wouldn't mind a little layering, she adds.

"Aren't you demanding," Holly says, laughing. "Forget about the hair. I'd love to be listening in on Nan's conversation."

"I'm stunned," Cathy admits. "I mean, her husband seems like a stand-up, professional kind of guy."

"Oh, Cathy," seethes Margo. "He's a crook." *And more,* she thinks.

"But how do you know that when you, like, just meet someone? I can usually tell after a while, but some people, you don't know right away."

"Well," Patti answers, "some people simply have bad energy. You can simply tell. It's not always the sleazy-looking guys with bad shoes. It's often the best-dressed guy who has sort of a cosmic non-smell."

"I know what you mean," Holly says, back to her hair fluffing. "There's something to this psychic stuff. I don't know why I didn't think about this earlier, but my aunt was always finding lost dogs and wallets. And she could pick out a sleazeball from a mile away."

Nan is in the bedroom for a very long time and talk of sleazeballs begins to fade as Patti's hair is slowly transformed. This is a feat in itself, considering Patti already has lovely hair. Holly is clearly a miracle worker.

It's almost as if Holly is a hair fortune-teller. Cathy cannot recall ever having seen any of her dozens of spa, hair, and salon attendants working with such fierce and obviously affectionate talent. Holly has probably never watched herself work and doesn't even know that she falls into a kind of mesmerized rhythm.

Cathy nudges Margo and points at Holly, who is clearly in the "hair almighty zone," and when Patti catches them looking she demands, "What?"

"Holly is in a hair trance," Cathy shares.

"Is this good or bad?" Patti wants to know as she widens her eyes in fake fright.

"Good. Your hair was fine before, but, wow, Holly is a magician."

Holly isn't even listening. She's off in hairland and it's only when Nan reenters the living room that she puts down her scissors.

Everyone turns to look at Nan.

"Oh my God."

When Nan says this it's not as a prayer or a sign of fright, but as a measure of her relief. Even though she looks as if she's just been dragged behind a cement mixer.

"You were right about everything so far," she tells Margo. "I'm not sure if I should feel relieved or frightened half to death. Cathy, I need more wine."

Cathy obliges and then Nan launches into the conversation she had with the secret government agent—or whoever in the hell he is—for the past thirty minutes. He said he was taping the conversation, asked about her documentation, wanted names, yelled to someone to start a background check on Nan Telvid even while he continued to grill her, and by the time they were finished he totally believed everything she told him.

"They have an amazing network, it seems, and access to everything," Nan tells the women.

"Now what?" Margo wants to know.

"I have no idea how they're going to do this, but they're sending someone now to meet with me."

"Right now? In *this*?" Patti cannot imagine anyone being able to drive through the tidal waves of heavy rainfall.

"Yes. Apparently it's important to them. He's coming from Tampa. His name is Bret. Maybe he's arriving in a boat, for crying out loud."

"These guys can get anywhere," Margo informs her. "My friend at school says we'd faint if we saw the inner operations of these government organizations."

Nan also tells them that time is of the essence. Because she is still in Florida, where some of the key players are living and working, and she just saw them, they need to move fast.

"I told these asshole friends of my husband who have been trading illegally that I was worried, but I didn't say I was going to turn them in or anything because, well, to be honest, I had no clue what to do," she confesses. "Mr. Bret assured me these creeps were probably already moving money and throwing dirt over their tracks."

Holly looks stunned. "Just when I thought we had hit our excitement peak, this happens."

Patti tells Nan to sit down, to breathe. She finishes her own drink, motions for Cathy to fill her glass, and then walks over to look approvingly at her new haircut in the huge mirror hanging by the door.

"Girls, I have something to say." Patti turns from the mirror to face them.

Patti looks absolutely serious. The suspense is so thick it's impossible to breathe.

"As long as we are all telling secrets and being honest, I think you should know that I killed a man."

ten

*T*here is nothing like the smell of a cooking hunk of meat seasoned with some kind of magic sauce to slow the pulses of four women who have just found out that they are sharing a suite with a murderer.

Margo is the first to spring from her seat after Patti's surprising announcement. She knows that food can settle people down, bring them together, or give them something to do so they don't faint. No one else is moving.

Holly longed to run to the bathroom and climb into the tub, like she did when everyone was leaving to try on bathing suits. But she stayed where she was.

Patti really doesn't know what to say after she's shared her own deepest secret. It has been so long since she has even mentioned the word *murder* that she has no idea what to say next.

For years and years Patti has been singing, "Please release me, let me go..." whenever thoughts of what happened all those years ago parade through her mind. She's struggling to keep herself from singing out loud as if she's just been introduced onstage and it's time for her first number.

Why now, for the love of God? Why tell a bunch of disgruntled, stranded, mismatched women, when so many crises have already been launched that it will be a miracle if anyone can even breathe after this latest announcement? Why dig up the whole damn mess? Why share such an intimate story when intimacy beyond shouting and arguing has been close to non-existent with these women, who met on a blind date in a public restroom? What in the hell has possessed her, Patti Nuttycombe, to pick this particular moment to expel a long-held truth that she has worked feverishly to suppress for so many years she may not even be able to count them up?

After Patti told them, she had a sudden moment of physical relief. Her heartbeat slowed and there was a slight tug at the back of her head as if something had fallen out and she could now move in a direction that just moments before had been blocked. She had an almost unstoppable urge to drop her glass and let her hands flop to her sides.

And she hated herself.

She hated herself for revealing in those few words who she had been and what she had done, because now she had to tell the entire story. She had to explain everything and waltz them back to her beginnings and show them a world she was certain none of them had ever seen except in magazines or made-for-TV movies.

Patti Nuttycombe had to be honest and open and for the first time in many years there was not a song she could hide behind.

For a brief moment she thought of simply lying. She could

make up a story or tell them she just said that to throw them off, and to keep Nan calm until the big government cheese showed up. This idea passed quickly, because she knew they wouldn't buy it. These women might be a brick or two short of a load, but they were far from being ignorant. They all had their own stuff—issues and people and lively events that you might think would throw them off a trail made hot by a woman confessing she had once killed someone. But underneath all of that shit, and most of it was shit, there was a substance in them. When it was all broken up and sifted, it was likely, Patti knew, that she would end up being the biggest nutcase in the group.

She quickly reasoned that her connection with these sometimes likable females would last about as long as the storm. The front would lift, airports would crank it up, she'd give them back their damn cell phones. And within twenty-four or thirty-six hours, they'd all be where they started. They'd never see one another again.

But there was something else. Something the strong and seldom shy Patti could not identify. It was something beyond the alcohol and the storm and Nan's close-encounter-of-the-criminal-kind that encouraged her to speak up. That is why she hesitated. Because Patti hates not knowing the reason why.

And that is what made Margo jump up and begin talking about food, before Patti could figure out how to start in on her murder tale, before Nan fell over, before Cathy wet her pants, and before Holly said something stupid like, "You have got to be frigging kidding me!"

Thank every goddess dead and alive for the blessed roast that Margo had managed to paw out of the bin at the grocery store now drowning in the rain.

"Listen," Margo announces. "Let me get that roast and set up for the next meal while we regroup for a minute. Some of us happen to be drinking again and we're going to need to put something in our stomachs besides melted ice cubes and booze. Nan's got an important meeting coming up, and it sounds as if Patti might want to tell us a very long story."

"And Cathy needs to get her hair done," Holly adds, with a small tremor in her voice.

"There you go," Margo agrees. "Patti, sit. Cathy, tend to the drinks. Let me throw that meat in the oven and well—Patti, if you want to fill in the blanks then I'm pretty sure we are going to be all ears."

"We've got a plan, then," Patti manages to say, and for a short while there is another welcome silence.

Holly is relieved to have a distraction. She wants to get Cathy into position in her chair and away from her wineglass for five minutes. She's been eyeing Cathy's split ends since the moment they met and she's betting the bank that her hair has been slaughtered by hair coloring and improper cutting techniques for a very long time.

The wedge of silence while the roast is prepared and Holly plays with Cathy's hair is exhausting. Nan's dilemma and the pending details of Patti's involvement in a murder—a murder for God's sake!—have made the spring storm seem like a windy fall morning. If anyone has a notion to grab a suitcase and run, this would be the perfect moment. But no one is moving. Because where is there to go?

Patti imagines what each woman might be thinking as they squirm and wiggle and do everything they can to avoid looking at one another. She's walked into the bathroom to look into her own eyes and have a quiet moment before she begins telling a story that has lain dormant for . . . how many years now? Thirty-five? Thirty-six?

It has been a very long time. And yet when she closes her eyes to regain her emotional balance, she can recall details from that time and event in such perfect precision that she startles herself.

"Oh my," Patti whispers, putting her hands on the top of her breasts so that the simple weight of her fingertips helps her slow her breathing. "What am I doing?"

There are some things she will not tell these women. She will not share how all the years of silence have taken a toll on her heart and soul. She won't tell Nan, Cathy, Holly, and Margo how she lies awake so often and imagines what her life might have been like if she could have forgotten, if that moment and all the moments that led up to it had never existed. She's already passed up the chance to tell them how she took those drawings her sister's children sent her, and held them against her heart. How she sometimes put them under her pillow, wondering what it would be like to have her own son or daughter.

She already knows it will be impossible for her to describe what the word *terror* feels like when you are living inside of it. There is no way to know if any of these women would do what she had done. Could they? And once they did, what would they feel? Relief? Anger? Sorrow? Happiness to be finally free?

There were so many years of second-guessing and vowing to herself that she would never bring it up.

"Damn it," she seethes. "It must be the drinking."

Patti closes her eyes and then opens them again and knows there are many things she will not tell them. She is not the only one wondering how in holy hell they have veered off of their original flight and life plans the last few days. The entire scenario is almost unbelievable. Even though there is silence in the living room and kitchen—minus the sounds of chopping vegetables— they are all thinking and wondering the same thing. "Who did Patti kill?"

Cathy finally breaks the spell while her hair is under the

expert hands of Holly. She whispers, "What do you think she did?"

"She said she killed a man. She was pretty clear about that," Nan replies, unable to hide her own nervousness. She's moved from the couch, to the kitchen, back to the couch. She is now standing by the window watching the rain, which has not slowed for even one minute.

"I'm sure there's an explanation that does not include intentional murder or she'd be in jail," Holly decides. "She's not a bad woman. I can tell."

"How?" Cathy demands, a little snidely. "Does her hair tell you stories?"

To Holly's own surprise, she doesn't hesitate. She says yes. She thinks it's the hair, and other things too. The way Patti reaches out to people. The sparkle in her eyes. Her easy way when there is a crisis, like when Nan dropped her phone in the toilet, or when Patti knew Holly was embarrassed about the bathing-suit adventure.

"It's like with those psychics," she shares. "Come on. Don't you have *feelings* about some people?"

Nan looks at Cathy, and neither one says anything.

"Not *those* kind of feelings," Holly says, without even seeing the two women exchange glances.

Margo jumps in and says, Of course. That's how people fall in love or know when their kids have screwed up—or to turn left that one time when they always turn right, and end up avoiding an accident.

"You just know some things," Margo agrees. "Patti's not a bad person. Sometimes bad things happen. That's what I know. I'll be shocked if her story is one of intentional murder. Speaking for myself, there are several men I have wanted to murder over the course of my lifetime."

"Put my name on that list," Nan agrees. "I mean, really. At this particular moment I'm pretty sure I'd commit a crime if my husband and I were in the same room and there was a weapon within arm's reach."

Patti can hear the women talking. If she stayed in the bathroom until the roast was done, at least two hours, they'd probably figure out she was trying to avoid them and sooner or later they would come drag her out of the bathroom.

She bravely opens the bathroom door, shakes her head to clear her mind, and then not so much walks as struts into the living room. There is another awkward moment of silence.

Then Holly looks up and smiles and Patti thinks this hair wiz is a remarkable woman, and probably the only person who does not know it.

"Sit down, Patti," Holly suggests so politely that Patti almost sits right on the floor. "Cathy would get you a drink but if she moves I'd end up cutting her hair so short she will never be able to leave this suite."

Margo is already halfway across the kitchen with a new bottle of wine, a bowl of potato chips, and some thinly sliced cheese that Nan must have found when she was stalking a pay phone.

No one is quite sure what the proper etiquette is when you're listening to a murder confession. Do you eat the chips? Do you just have cheese? Can you put the cheese on the chip? Would it be improper to simply drink as much and as fast as you can before you pass out?

Patti senses that everyone is about as uneasy as she is. Even though she is afraid she may gag, she takes some cheese, chews it slowly, has a long sip of wine, and decides it's now or never.

"I suppose you are all dying, pardon the pun, to hear my story," she begins. "It's not as mysterious as you've probably been imagining. Mostly it's tragic and sad...and it's something I haven't spoken about in a very long time."

"Why not?" Holly asks, deciding to sit down right in the middle of Cathy's haircut so she can listen.

"It was traumatic. Life changing. And I suppose I convinced myself that if I didn't talk about it, then it didn't happen."

And, she continued, what do you say? How do you talk about it and bring it up, and more important, why would you? It was always easier to walk away from what had happened, and who she had become because of what she did.

Patti begins her story way before the killing. And just before she launches into it she realizes it has been so long since she's spoken of anything but the present that it will be a miracle if she can remember how to speak of the past in a way that makes sense. Unearthing the past is the one thing Patti Nuttycombe has not rehearsed.

She starts slowly and travels back more than fifty years so the women will know where she came from, how she lived, why it was impossible for her not to do what she did. And where she came from was a 1950's and '60's world on the rough side of the tracks in a town where you were lucky if you had a pair of shoes that only one or two siblings had worn before you.

It was as if verbal and physical violence was inherited like blue eyes and blond hair or a set of teeth that would be perfect if only there were not tiny spaces in between all the front teeth. *Survival* is the one word Patti can think of to describe her life until she graduated from high school and left.

If you breathed wrong, you were smacked. If you moved wrong, you were smacked. If you ate too much, you were smacked. Mother was smacked. Two brothers and one sister were smacked. Laughter was something that was so foreign it was almost a shock when the explosion of joy was heard at school or in the neighbor's yard. The entire family jerked in fear if there was a loud noise, if a door slammed, when they heard the car pull into the driveway.

And all Patti wanted to do was sing.

Leaving was the easiest thing she ever did. A note for her mother wrapped up in a kitchen towel so her father, who would never touch a towel, would not find it, was the only clue she left before she disappeared.

And disappear she did.

It was 1965 and the world was changing so rapidly that to blink was to miss a decade. First it was New York. Hostels and street singing and washing dishes and never once thinking that going home was an option. Because there was no home. There was not a light on in the kitchen and an oven warming sweet rolls and someone to wait up for her on the front steps.

Three years slid by so quickly it took Patti another year to realize that there was a fair chance she was not going to make it on Broadway or Off Broadway or anywhere near Broadway. People were so transient that it was close to impossible to develop friendships, any kind of long-term relationships, a love that lasted more than a few months. In some ways she may as well have never left home. There were always waitressing and bartending jobs. There was an occasional chance to sing ... and then there was this guy.

A guy with promises and the title "agent" and Patti eagerly signed a paper and sold her soul to the devil without even realizing what she had done. She had small gigs, but there was never any money. The devil agent said there were expenses and that he would eventually make her a star but it would take time. And there were the drugs and the men who offered to pay her to do other things beyond sing and all the while Patti kept hearing the melody of a song that so desperately needed words that never came.

There were endless nights of worry and so few moments of artistic joy that Patti felt as if she was going backward so quickly there might never be a way for her to recover. And there were all those things she'd done that made her hate herself.

"I suppose I was stupid," she admits to the four women, who are listening, mesmerized. "I did the drugs and I did the men and after a particularly brutal evening that I could barely recall, when I woke up in a room I did not recognize, with bruises all over my arms, blood crusted in my hair, and not a song anywhere near my heart, I realized if I did not leave I would probably die."

While she has been speaking no one has moved. Cathy has not even bothered to take a sip of wine or look at her hair, and the scissors in Holly's hand have been still so long, Holly's hand is about to cramp up from gripping them so hard.

"This sounds like a Janis Joplin biopic," Nan whispers. "Jesus, Patti."

"If only." Patti sighs. "I was about to get even more stupid."

"It was the late sixties, you probably went to California along with thousands of other hippies," Margo suggests. "You may have run into my three aunts, two uncles, and half of the rest of the family."

"I did go to California, but it wasn't so I could lie on the beach naked and smoke dope all day," Patti shares. "I went to Los Angeles. The second I left New York on a dirty old Grey-hound bus, I swear to God I started hearing music again."

"What do you mean?" Holly asks, thinking she may already know the answer.

"Before I moved to New York I thought in music. Everything was a song. I'd see something or someone and a song would pop into my head. In New York, it was as if someone had strangled

my ability to create. I suppose I was so busy worrying about sur-
viving that there wasn't an ounce of energy left to create or be
creative. My singing must have sounded absolutely horrid
toward the end."

The women have so many questions it would seem like a fir-
ing squad to Patti if they asked everything they wanted to ask. So
instead, for once, they pause without question. Patti's story is far
from over.

Patti tells them everything you can imagine about a cross-
country bus trip in the late 1960's is true. She was surprised Peter
Fonda didn't try to ride his motorcycle up the bus aisle. That's
about the only thing that didn't happen on her four-day trip. One
passenger had a heart attack. She was propositioned so many
times by both men and women that she lost count. The bus driver
threw up on the windshield, the toilet broke three times. And that
was just in the first two days.

Los Angeles was warmer than New York City, of course. But
that's it. Simply warmer. It was just as harsh and cruel. The people just as rotten and the agents just as insane and crooked as
they were back East. But when the music in your head is alive and
loud, what choice do you have?

Patti stayed with a friend until she got work at yet another
club, found yet another agent, and fell yet again into the same life
she had before. She did get singing work. The music scene in Los
Angles was flourishing. As were the seedy jazz clubs that needed
young, good-looking singers so men would come in and sit at the
bar. And the men came, one especially.

He followed her from club to club and seemed to know
everyone. He surely wanted to know Patti, but Patti didn't want
to know him. He was pushy and frightening and he said he
"knew people."

"I was starting to get a small following, just what you need to get noticed in the music world," Patti recalled. "I was working enough that I finally had my own apartment. It was really just one and a half rooms but it was mine. I had this feeling that I was so close, so close to everything that I had always wanted."

Patti knew that success was a crap shoot. She knew that she had given up a lot to get close to the front of the stage. She'd never been in love, the kind of love she sang about night after night. The few friends she had made in New York, who had lived through the drug-crazed nights and days of what really could only be called dumb-ass debauchery and the stupidity of youth, were either in rehab or trying to remember how to put on their shoes. Her birth family was a fast-fading memory. She had sent occasional messages to her mother to let her know she was alive and singing, but she'd never once included a return address, and as far as she knew no one ever bothered to try to find her. It would be years before she contacted her older sister again. She was twenty-eight and there was no going back.

The stalking and harassment started out slowly. The man who was following her from club to club was not ordinary. Patti never knew for sure, but she suspected he had connections that gave him access not just to places, but also to people and the money they had. It was as if everyone was afraid to say no to him.

Everyone but Patti.

He kept following her. She was careful not to give out her address, to drive home the long way, to never be alone when she left the club. But his connections were much grander than her ability to dodge him. One night he pinned her against her car. He somehow got her phone number and left her messages that forced her to sleep under her bed with a knife in her hand. She remembered her father and how no one ever tried to stop him because they were always so afraid.

And she bought a gun.

It was her agent who betrayed her and gave out her address. Once he had it, the locked doors and bolted windows did not stop this man. She sometimes wished she had simply invited him in, taken off her clothes, and laid down on the old linoleum floor. Instead, she shot him three times.

The gun slipped into her hand so quickly the first time he hit her, and that was his mistake. He did not know that her father had hit her the same way, with the back of his hand moving across her entire face so that there would be a welt that looked like a long burn mark and blood from where his ring had cut into her thin facial skin. He did not know that for years and years Patti and her sister would lie awake at night and think of ways to kill their own father. He did not know that when Patti purchased her gun from a man behind the gas station, she already had no doubt she would use it if her own life was threatened. He didn't know that she never put it away and that it was on the counter when he pushed himself through the cheap front door and the three locks he knew would not hold against his weight.

The neighbors were the ones who called the police, because Patti could not stop screaming at him, even after she shot him. She had to force herself not to empty the remaining four bullets into his face. She hated him and she never once hated herself not before, during, or after.

"Sweet mother of God." Nan whistles. "What happened next?"

"This isn't a movie trailer, Nan," Margo scolds. "This really happened."

"It sounds like a movie, for crying out loud. I'm just asking."

"Girls," Holly says like a mom, "let Patti finish."

"It's okay. It does sound surreal, but I assure you, it all happened."

She had been smart enough to call the police several times earlier. There were reports on file. A neighbor saw him break down the door. The unregistered gun was a bit of a problem, but it was the seventies and thankfully the man she killed had a bit of a record. There were no charges. But the publicity was a nightmare, and she lost all her bookings.

Patti had been performing under a name she had made up in New York, Caroline Dean. She simply changed Patricia to Patti C., and for the first time in her life someone really helped her.

A female detective helped her relocate to Northern California. She hooked her up with a real agent, and, although by then Patti was pushing thirty and had missed whatever big chance she might have had, she could still make a living doing what she called "offshore gigs."

"And I've lived happily ever after," she concluded.

Where to start? The women know immediately that Patti has not told them everything. How could she? The lines of truth and reality always become blurred by time. Days and nights begin covering themselves in ways that challenge the memory, make the easy seem easier and the hard maybe not so bad. Patti knows this better than any of the women, because she is older. She holds the wisdom-of-age-and-experience card in the palm of her hand and likes to think that she has long since passed the point of regret and wondering what might have been.

But being with these women, and their tangle of personalities and problems, has ignited her in a way she'd believed was no longer possible. Suddenly she has so much she would like to say to these relative strangers about life and chances and love and moving on and pulling the trigger of your own life without the pressures of others' expectations and the always-present possibility of horrid failure.

But Patti is also exhausted. Unearthing the saddest, most horrific event of her life has made her light-headed. During the past two days she's also felt as if she's been living on the edge of a pre-, peri-, and post-menopausal cesspool. Being around these women has been like an adolescent hormonal outbreak and she's not certain it's going to slow down anytime soon. One of these women could blow at any moment.

Patti's not sure if she wants to open her wounds any deeper. How much do they really need to know?

It's Margo, who has quickly turned into the guiding light of this mass of femaleness, who is seemingly the most perceptive. "Patti, did this mess with the attacker running around here trigger some old memories for you?"

"Yes. I've been living a relatively safe life, I think anyway, for a long time. But, you know, it's like just taking a walk in an unfamiliar city and not even being aware you are on the most crime-infested street in town. Sometimes ignorance really is bliss."

"I always worry about lurking men," Nan confesses. "Women are forever moving targets. Really, how many times do you hear of women jumping on men just because they see one?"

Everyone laughs as the mental image of a group of marauding women jumping men from behind bushes and garbage cans parades through the living room.

Margo confesses that as the mother of daughters she is constantly terrified that something evil, sexual, or horrid is going to happen to them.

"I know it's not fair, and probably sexist, but I don't worry about the same thing with my son," she shares. "I know boys can be molested just like girls but it's surely not as common, and my son has a different set of skills."

"If I had a daughter I'd arm her with everything from Mace to a rifle and take her to a self-defense class twice a day," Cathy tells them. "I've been harassed a few times myself but nothing like what happened to you, Patti."

It would seem more than possible that Cathy, the tease, would have pissed off more than a few men. And it also makes sense to give girls, daughters, nieces, granddaughters the same lessons of physical survival that boys seem to be outfitted with from the beginning. Patti has to ask who else has been affected by the unwanted physical advances of men.

And it's everyone.

Holly ran from her boyfriend's car when he tried to force her to have sex. Nan's been the target of unwanted sexual advances, some of them close to violent, so many times she has stopped counting. Margo admits that an old boyfriend showed up several years ago and her husband had to threaten him to get him to leave. Cathy tells them the worst thing that ever happened was when she was almost twenty, on a road trip with college friends, and she gave out her address to a guy she met at the beach.

"He just showed up one day with his duffel bag, and a pair of silky red underpants for me, and assumed he was going to move in," she recalled. "I was so scared, because I really didn't know him. My brothers came to toss him out, but I swear to God I did not sleep easy for a year after that."

"At least you didn't kill someone," Patti says softly.

"I think we have all wanted to," Margo asserts. "It's something we are all capable of, don't you think?"

"Without a doubt," Nan says, without hesitation. "If it's me or them, it sure as hell is not going to be me."

When Holly begins working on Cathy's hair again, all of the women think about life-changing moments. If the stalker had not entered Patti's life, would she be a recording star now, with her own Las Vegas show and appearances on *Ellen* and *Oprah*? Would the suitcase she lugs around be filled with designer clothes instead of the knockoffs she buys at secondhand stores all over the Bay area?

There's been missed chances, lost loves, wrong turns...and what good it does to sit around and bring it all up is suddenly way beyond Patti. If she could, she'd slap herself right now so hard she'd leave a mark on her face.

It's obvious that the women are all wandering around inside of their own minds. The damn distance between all of them that seemed to vanish when Patti shared her story has reappeared. It's as if they are all terrified to let go of something, a rope, chain, very long string which leaves them unable to embrace one another in the way women usually embrace during these wild, unscheduled, spontaneous moments of life.

. Perhaps it's the convergence of heat and cold and rain and wind that has whipped them all into an emotional frenzy. Patti doesn't know, and she's certain from the serious looks on the faces of her suite comrades that they haven't even bothered to think about it.

Whatever.

She slaps her hands on the top of her thighs as a kind of grand finale just as Holly finishes with Cathy's hair. The haircut's a change just as subtle as the others—a little shorter here, texture there, nothing too startling. The change in the women's emotional levels is equally as subtle.

Everyone has pulled back.

It's as if they are realizing that even with what they now know about one another, they may as well be in a room with perfect strangers.

A murder. A financial mess that will most likely end up on the front page. What other secrets could possibly be lying under all those new hairdos?

A very loud knock on the door interrupts everyone's fearful thoughts. The women all turn at once as a man's voice booms, "I'm here to talk with Nan Telvid. Please open the door."

Which is exactly what Nan does.

eleven

The roast and vegetables prove to be a wonderful diversion. The moment Nan leaves, gently shutting the door, all eyes and stomachs are focused on the kitchen.

It's a wonder half the hotel has not shown up at the suite, because the smell of slow-roasting meat is driving *them* all insane. Margo has managed to create yet another masterpiece that smells so delicious even vegetarian Cathy is thinking about taking a bite.

"How long has it been since you had real meat?" Holly asks this question innocently, and Patti is glad that Nan is not there to make a snide sexual comment.

Margo raises her eyebrows at Patti anyway, but Cathy is either oblivious or decides to ignore the question.

"Since college," she shares. "At first I just went vegetarian because all the girls on my floor were doing it, but then I realized how much better I felt, and I never went back."

"I would die without hamburger and steak," Holly admits. "You'd think I could look in the mirror and figure it out. But I tell myself lean meat is okay, even if it's on a bun."

"Taste is relative in all things," Cathy says, getting up to turn on the television set. "I feel the same way about a soy burger, men who have a touch of gray in their hair, and a fabulous cabernet."

Patti is not saying a word. She may as well have melted into the carpeting. Holly looks at her while Cathy fishes for an updated weather report and Margo whacks vegetables around in a metal bowl.

Holly never really paid much attention to her perceptions about people beyond the cursory once-over-lightly first glance. It's as if she's always just known who people are by that initial glimpse. And people, especially clients, have a tendency to reveal themselves very quickly once they say something, or don't say something.

But she was surprised by Patti's murder confession. *Really surprised.* And she thinks Patti was wrong to say she had murdered a man. The guy actually murdered himself, for good God. He was asking for it with every single horrid thing he did. Patti didn't *murder* him, she *killed* him.

Buried down, under layers of thick skin, backstage dust, and the hazy film left by all those years of singing while people blew smoke in her face, Holly sees someone no one else can see. Patti C., or Caroline, or whoever in the hell she is, is a woman who's living, but also counting up her losses. She's wondering for the first time in a long time what it might have been like if everything had been different. What if she had killed her father instead of that bastard who stalked her? What if her mother had killed her father, or at the very least, taken them all away from him? What if she had made it in New York and sung on Broadway and had a chance to appear in a major movie? What if she had let someone—and there were most likely a lot of someones—sweep her off her feet, marry her, and lead her to a house she could fill with friends and laughter? What if there had been babies, and friendships with women that edged out everything? What if there had been a friend who came over to play cards and then spent the night and took her for that test at the hospital—because she shouldn't be driving after one of those damn things, no matter what the doctor tells you? And maybe, in a different life, there could have been something as simple as a green lawn dotted with flower beds and a light always on in the living room window.

Back in Ohio, outside Columbus, where Holly grew up, she witnessed years of auntie-sister love. Her mother had five sisters and her father often joked—well, maybe he wasn't joking—that the six of them should just get their own damn house and he would move into an apartment and call when he wanted to visit.

It was such a glorious way to grow up, with excessive birthday gifts, someone besides her mother to talk with about her periods and sex, a place to stay when she was being a snotty teenager, and with such glorious examples of female friendship that Holly was sometimes hard-pressed to find girlfriends who measured up.

She decides Patti would have been a great hands-on auntie instead of drifting so far from her sister's life. And she's certain, absolutely certain, that Patti would have loved being one, could still love being one, and thinks about being one more than she has ever dared to share.

"Why are you staring at me?"

"I'm thinking of adopting you, Patti," Holly tells her.

"What? Is there an opening for a murderer in your salon?"

"You are not a murderer, Patti. You shot someone. *Killed*

him. You could sing to my customers and I'd get bigger tips and then I would introduce you to my single uncle. He'd adore you."

"Jesus," Patti fake-whimpers. "That's just what I need. One more old fart who wants me to take off my dress while I sing, 'Anchors Away.'"

This bravado is exactly what Holly was thinking about. Most of the time, especially if something emotional about her dips onto the screen of life, Patti diffuses it with humor. She's pretty damn good at it.

And well, just *shit.*

Maybe this whole way of looking at and thinking she "sees" people is what sets Holly apart in a way that makes her just about as close to odd as you can get. At twenty-four, really, shouldn't she be down doing shots in the hotel bar with the psychics and all the weather-trapped salesmen? This is the kind of stuff that makes her head feel light and swirling and drives her to take her aspirin, which she tells people is simply a miracle drug that is good for her arteries. Holly is a big fat liar too.

Here she is, teasing hair, evaluating the psyche of a confessed murderer, and worrying about Nan, who, *sweet Jesus,* left with a government agent, without taking her precious cell phone.

"Hey, guys," Holly asks feverishly, forgetting she was thinking about sharing the news of her brain tumor with these women, "did anyone get a look at that guy's credentials?"

Everyone freezes.

"It happened so fast, and she slipped out the door. I never thought to even ask to look at his credentials," Patti shares. "I think his name is Bret."

"He probably took her to a mental hospital," Cathy decides. "Did you see the look on his face when Nan was trying to explain how we all ended up in this hotel suite together?"

It had been a mixture of astonishment and disbelief. Bret was a tall, brown-haired man, who most likely has been thoroughly trained to show no emotion. He had dark eyes, shaded by eyebrows that Holly desperately wanted to trim. It was all she could do not to run up to him with her razor-sharp trimming scissors.

Beyond that, he looked like a television version of a secret agent. He had on a long black trench coat, wing-tipped shoes, a button-down, white-collared shirt, and Patti convinced herself immediately that the umbrella he had leaned against the door was really a machine gun.

Nan had politely introduced them, but before Bret could even get out one word, Cathy started talking.

"How in the holy name of hell did you get here in this storm?"

Not that the storm mattered to them anymore. It had become a backdrop to so much drama that the constant sounds of thunder cracking over the ocean, the monsoonlike rain, the wind pounding against the sides of the building so fiercely that they could actually feel it pushing through the small cracks in the windows, and waves rolling in so fast there was a constant splashing sound, which reminded all of them of someone throwing one barrel of water after another off the side of a very tall building were secondary.

Bret appeared totally disarmed by Cathy, her question, and by the ten eyes that were staring at him.

"Weather doesn't stop us," he explained nervously. "We train for this type of thing."

Nan turned quickly to look at Cathy, hoping that for once she would shut up and realize this was one occasion where flirting was inappropriate. And this quick pause helped the agent regain his composure.

"How do you all know one another?" he had asked.

It was a simple and necessary question, which launched five separate laughs.

"Did I say something funny?"

Bret was not so much disarmed as bewildered this time.

"Let me try to explain," Nan said, swallowing hard and then turning away from everyone else so she would not be able to see them and start laughing again.

While Nan told him, the other women tried to imagine what the phone-in-the-toilet-stranded-at-the-airport story must sound like even to someone who deals with nutcases on a daily basis. They listened to the retelling of the story and watched Bret's face, and then noticed how he turned to look at each one of them as the tale unfolded.

He obviously had no idea what to say, and Margo was thinking that whoever trained him or wrote the manual needed to get in touch with them as quickly as possible to prepare the next line of Bret-like agents, or whatever he was, to deal with the Nans, Cathys, Pattis, Hollys, and Margos of the world—women who fed off of one another and seemed to grow bolder and occasionally stronger when in one another's company.

Bret, who was remarkably resilient, stood his ground and then repeated the entire story back to them in a shortened version, without stopping, as if he couldn't believe what he had just heard.

"So you dropped your phone in the toilet and all these women were in the restroom and they tried to help you, and then the airport closed and you decided to all get in a car and come to this hotel?"

It made sense to them, but when they looked at poor Bret, in his dripping trench coat, they could clearly see that this must be a female-male thing. Bret, what with being Mr. Undercover and all, would probably never help some guy fish his phone out of the toilet, unless financial espionage was involved. Actually, just the thought of putting their hands in the men's toilet at the airport is enough to give the women the shakes.

Most men are so homophobic, they are afraid to look in the mirror in public restrooms. To think that they would all gather round a toilet, talk a bit, and then decide to drive off in a rented car toward a beach hotel seems so beyond possible that more giggling and snorting amongst the women ensues.

"I know it sounds nuts," Nan had finally admitted. "But we are women. Women do these kinds of things. It's not a big deal. It just made sense. We thought it might be fun." The women knew Nan was lying. Fun had not been at the top of any of their lists. It was more like survival.

Fun?

Bret seemed to get a little irritated when the women attempted to stifle yet another laugh.

"None of you know one another?"

"Not really," Cathy told him.

"And how many of you know why I am here?"

"Well, we all know," Holly told him. "We talk. We're trying to help Nan."

Bret inhaled as if he needed extra air in his lungs to keep standing.

"Please do not speak about this to anyone else until I have a chance to talk with Nan," he ordered. "It's easy to pick up a phone and just talk to people, but please, I am asking you, keep this quiet until we can help Nan too."

Without saying a word or snorting yet again, the women silently agreed that telling Bret that Patti had taken away their cell phones as if she were their concerned den mother would not be a good idea.

And then he had touched Nan on the arm and without another word led her out of the room. The door closed, and they disappeared.

The roast is almost done when they really start worrying.

The aroma is making them all a little insane, but they are also not convinced that Nan has left with the right man. Patti freely admits that they would not be feeling so horrid if she had not taken away their cell phones. But to her surprise they brush this off as a mere coincidence. The phones, they all agree, are a necessary plague.

"Nan's a big girl," Margo reminds them as she opens the oven to remove the roast. "I mean, really, who else would just show up like that and start asking questions? I'm sure he was who he said he was."

"Apparently there are wild men running around all over the place," Holly fires back. "I hate to sound like a scaredy-cat, but at this point I wouldn't be shocked if the phones were tapped and Bret is from the mafia or something."

"Oh, sit down," Margo orders. "You are starting to sound like my girls on a stormy night."

"What does that mean?"

"It means that you are thinking too much," Margo responds. "Kids have terrific imaginations. A tree banging against the side of a house is a plastic dinosaur that has sprung to life. The old refrigerator grinding away in the garage is a bunch of al-Qaeda spies breaking in to carry them away—"

"I get it, Margo," Holly says, cutting her off. "I admit I still have to pull the closet door shut before I go to sleep. I'm just saying there are things going on around here that we do not know about."

Margo is exasperated. Nothing Bret said or did made her feel as if some evil person jumped the agent in the hall on the way to their room, switched clothes and identities with him, and then locked him in a closet. She'd love to launch into a wonderful verbal epistle about not being afraid. It's a key theme in her life, even as she sometimes has to lie about her own direction, and tries, sometimes desperately, to impart this type of wisdom to her own daughters.

It's not that her son isn't afraid. He's had his moments and he will have them again. Right now her girls—one tiptoeing in the fast lane of teenagerhood and the other still sleeping with her blankie and thirteen stuffed animals—are the most fearful.

Balancing their emotional needs with the reality of chance and risk has always been a huge challenge for Margo. She likes to think she is not fearful. She likes to think that all the years she spent with her military-minded father have not left her in an emotionless void. He all but made them line up and salute each morning and did ridiculous things like throw them into the deepest part of the lake to see if they could swim. There was the counterbalance her mother provided. Even though she was barely over five feet tall and thinner than the candy-loving Margo, she could stop their father in his tracks with a single look. They were a classic case of opposites attracting. Her mother would crawl into bed with Margo when the spring storms circled, still holds her hand when she's not telling her what to do, and seems to be getting bolder as she gets older.

Margo has tried to walk the same line as her mother with her own children, even as she sometimes leans more toward her father's emotional makeup. On any given day, one or all of her children hate her for brief moments and tell her she should be in the Army herself. This is her sign that she must be doing a good job.

Right now she'd like to marshal in a squad of troops to scan the entire hotel and let everyone know that they are safe. But there is a glimmer of uncertainty in her own heart and veins. She knows that anything is possible, but she'd also like a thirty-minute break from the constant worrying so this group of very different women can share a meal like normal people. She'd also like to go around and hug each one of them, even Cathy, and let them know there is safety in numbers.

If only.

If only she could lean forward just a little bit more. If only there was not an unapproachable sign hanging around everyone's neck. If only the fear was not so palpable and she, and everyone else, could just be honest. If only they were not suspended in time like this, and if only this life pause had been a planned and perfect choice. If only there were not so many mini-dramas occurring at the exact same moment.

It's as if they have been thrust into the middle of a made-for-television movie and the director keeps changing her mind about the outcome. Margo has no idea what kind of ending she would choose for this absolutely emotionally diverse group of women. Someone flings herself off the balcony? A lovely group hug and the exchange of addresses and phone numbers? Reserving the room for the same time next year? A drunken brawl in the lobby with the psychics?

Good Lord.

Margo realizes she's probably thinking the exact same thing at this moment as Cathy, Patti, and Holly. They've been together for hours and hours, but there is still a level of distrust that has shaded everything. For good reason.

Holly is probably best suited for the group hug and openness that usually occurs when women gather like this. She's young, perhaps not as tainted with life's woes and worries as the rest of them. And maybe her secrets and misgivings, beyond the ones that are so terribly obvious, have not yet driven themselves through her skin to pop out on the surface of her life.

Twenty-four. It's hard for Margo to remember the fifteen years that have passed since she was Holly's age. Her career was unfolding then in brilliant waves that continued long after she married and had a succession of babies. Amazingly, she can't recall hesitating about her direction. There was always something going on, always a goal, always a challenge, and never a heart-stopping moment that derailed her for longer than a few days. Maybe it was the military mentality her father gave her. *Never say die. Walk through the storms. Showing pain is a symbol of weakness.*

As she pulls out the roast, Margo can only wonder what her own children will remember if they are trapped in a hotel room with a wasp nest of strangers.

"Damn!" she shouts.

"You okay?" Cathy calls, as she finishes setting the table.

"A little burn."

"Stick your hand in the freezer for a minute," Cathy advises. "I read someplace that it, like, shocks your system into healing really fast once you take it out."

"Seriously?"

"Seriously."

Margo decides to let go of some of her own fear, sticks her hand in the freezer without more questions, and then starts laughing.

"What?"

"Agent Bret should see this. He'd think we'd all run out of medication."

"I can't even imagine what we must look or sound like to outsiders," Cathy shares as she puts bread on the table.

"So we are all insiders?"

"Absolutely."

Well.

Cathy has just leaned in a little bit, and this makes Margo smile. Patti has been listening too and she's humming "Everything

Is Beautiful." Holly is still studying everyone's hair so she won't think about Bret and Nan.

But she can't help herself.

"I'm terrified for Nan," Holly admits.

"Sit first. Then we will talk." This from Margo, who is pointing to the table. "We need to eat."

Such a mother, they all think. But they do not disobey.

For the first few minutes everyone is so ravenous, no one speaks. The roast has been seasoned with some of Margo's magic sauce. How she did it with what she purchased at the small grocery store and what she found in the cabinets no one knows. And they don't really care. They sound like wine sommeliers trying to decipher the nuances of a lively bottle of label-less wine someone pulled from the back of an old closet.

Smokey. Garlic-scented. Lemon pepper. A hint of rosemary. Lively first bite. Smells like fall and burning leaves.

Margo thinks they are hysterical. She cooks from memory. Throwing in everything she can find. Rarely using recipes. Sucking on her candy and thinking about everything but the preparation of food.

The women of suite 6502 devour bread, meat, vegetables, and several glasses of wine, and are totally lost in the joyous inhalation of food, for exactly twenty-three minutes. Then it's back to Nan. And to worrying. And to a series of "what if's," which end up making them all feel foolish, unsafe, a little angry, and unsure about what to do next.

Patti insists that they should have asked for some kind of identification. Margo disagrees. Who the hell else but a government agent would know who they are and that they are in the suite and that Nan holds information that could probably get her killed?

"That sounds lovely, but remember, we are surrounded by a

mess of psychics," Holly blurts out. "I mean, if they really can read minds, they can figure out anything."

"That doesn't make sense," Cathy says.

"Well, what if the person they are looking for is one of them?"

"I never thought of that," Cathy admits. "But wouldn't they know that too?"

"Hells bells, I have no clue," Holly almost shouts. "I am just saying that anything is possible, including Bret not being Bret. I just can't believe we didn't ask to see his card or badge or whatever he has to prove he is who he says he is."

Patti is looking beyond glum. "I should have never taken away the phones," she admits. "It hasn't really changed anything anyway."

"What does that mean?" Margo thinks Patti is being too hard on herself.

"First of all, we wouldn't be sitting here worrying ourselves to death about Nan's safety. We could just call her and find out if she's okay."

"For God's sake, don't beat yourself up about this," Cathy admonishes. "Look at us. We wouldn't even be having this conversation if our BlackBerrys and iPhones were beeping next to our plates."

"But, still, after everything I've been through, I can't believe we let her go off like that," Patti tells them.

Margo throws up her hands. In her house this is the universal symbol for *"Knock it off and listen to me or you are going to be in deep shit."* Surprisingly the gesture works with grown-ups too.

"Nan is a big girl," she says. "Don't you think she can take care of herself?"

Everyone stops to think, because when Margo is in her

mother mode it's almost as if their own mothers are speaking to them. Disobeying is not an option. And of course Nan is a big girl who can take care of herself, but these are extraordinary circumstances. In a week, if they all make it out alive, it will be a miracle if anyone actually believes what they all have to say about their time after being stranded at the Tampa airport.

And what if it was one of them leaving with Bret? What if they were standing in a dark corner, or a secluded back room, being interviewed by a man wearing a wet trench coat who appeared miraculously in the middle of a raging monsoon? What would they want? Backup? An escort?

Patti wonders out loud what Margo has actually been thinking for quite some time. And it's as if everyone has suddenly been nailed in place.

"Nan met the people she's turning in. That's the reason she came to Florida," she says, talking softly, as if she is really just thinking out loud. "What if she told them what she was worried about? What if she said she was concerned and that she might turn them in? What if she told her husband and he alerted them?"

"Damn," Margo says. "I've thought about that too. I mean, really, not to get anyone any more riled up than they already are, but it's just way too easy to track people these days."

Holly wants to know if anyone thinks Nan would have told her husband where she is staying, who she is staying with, and what room they are in.

"Why wouldn't she?" Cathy asks this quickly, and Holly looks at her and almost says something. The not-saying-something makes her heart accelerate.

"Margo, you heard her on the phone outside the grocery store. What do you think?"

Margo's thinking could fill up an oil tanker. She decides to be as honest as she can be at this particular moment. What she thinks and tells them is that Nan will probably get rid of her husband just as soon as she gets rid of her job, the criminals she has been working with, and as much of her past as she can.

Once the now-frightened Nan discovers the lovely and complete joy of letting go and moving on, they may never see her again. She may not even come back to the room. There's a good chance she might be hitchhiking down the highway at this very moment in the pouring rain, toward the freeway.

But she's also under stress and stress makes people do strange things. She, like everyone, lives a life that is adorned in patterns. She's used to telling her husband where she is and what she's doing and what hotel she's staying at and maybe even what room she has charged to her credit card. And if it's "their" credit card and she used it instead of her business card all he has to do is log into their account and, bingo, she's staying at the Rivera in St. Pete's Beach. After that it's as if everyone he tells has a key to their door.

"So he could know?" Patti has to ask even though she already knows the answer.

"Yes."

Damn.

This is when everyone spontaneously gets up, the dishes are cleared, the empty wineglasses are set aside for the first time without refilling, and there is a wedge of silence in the room that could level a football stadium.

There's also a rising level of anxiety mixed with anger that feels like a hot and very unsettling gust of wind. It's as if someone has opened a huge window that lets in so much thick, muggy air it may be impossible to keep standing.

They look like the posed actresses in a movie. Margo is slumped as if she is praying. Holly is resting her forearms on the lip of the counter like she is about to lean over. Patti has her hands braced right next to Holly and she has such a fierce look on her face, it seems she might fall over if even one finger shifts. Cathy's hands are at her side, one leg is forward and bumping into the counter for support so she can steady herself.

They clearly have no idea how statuesque they look. How confused. How ready. How anxious.

"We have to do something."

Patti moves first. She drops her hands and starts snapping her fingers and tapping her feet. All she can hear is the *West Side Story* gang snapping their fingers and getting ready to rumble.

"What's with the clicking?" Cathy asks this even as she begins tapping her right foot in rhythm.

"Do the names Natalie Wood and Rita Moreno mean anything to you?"

"There's a dim light going on in my head, but not really."

"I've got it," Margo says, as she begins snapping her fingers.

"What?" Holly does not want to feel left out of this.

"*West Side Story*, 1961, fabulous music and a rumble." Patti then reveals her secret life where songs parade through her mind and where people, places, and things call to mind a specific melody, and where she sometimes has to struggle to speak instead of sing.

"This is what goes on in your mind?" Cathy is shaking her head but still tapping.

"Yes, but I'm serious, and what we have to do is pretty damn serious too," Patti insists. "We have to do something. We have to get the hell out of this hotel room and go see if Nan is being tied to a chair in a conference room or something."

The snapping stops. There is nothing funny about what could happen to Nan.

"We can't just run down there without a plan," Holly asserts. "If something is going on, we'd make it worse."

"Weapons," Margo says without hesitation. "Everyone, find something."

"Shit," Cathy seethes. "I used to always carry a knife. It was one I had from Girl Scout camp years ago, and once I forgot to take it out of my purse at the airport. The guy who took it just smiled at me as if he had a new treasure. I miss those knife-carrying days."

"Look around," Margo orders. "It doesn't have to be a sawed-off shotgun, for God's sake."

The next ten minutes are a bizarre mix of frantic hunting, second thoughts, and grumbling, as the sounds of drawers opening, doors slamming, and suitcases being savaged echo throughout the suite. The women have scattered and the unmistakable roar of the wild ocean pounding in the background is like an urgent drumroll.

The conversational lull gives them all a chance to not simply hunt for weapons but to ponder what in the holy hell they are about to do. And how this came to be.

Really.

How does a plane ride lead to this? How did four women with unconnected links end up in an intimate dance of survival while acting as saviors? How in the world will they ever explain to anyone they know and love what is apparently about to happen?

The questions linger for the ten minutes it takes for the women to rummage through their bags, the kitchen drawers, and the bathroom for something they could use as a weapon.

When they meet again in the kitchen, the gathering place of all gathering places, they look like suburban warriors.

Holly is holding a steel comb with a pointed tip. Patti and Margo have both selected knives from the kitchen, which are a little dull but could still draw blood. Cathy has emerged from her room with a large and very solid can of hair spray, which she asserts cannot just bruise but also maim.

"I know this can works because I've used it on someone before," she shares as they all gather by the door. "It's almost as good as a .38 special."

"Do we have a plan?" Margo cannot believe they are going to run aimlessly through the hotel with sharp objects.

"We can figure it out in the elevator," Patti tells her with more than a hint of urgency in her voice. "We should have left an hour ago."

It's well into the heart of the night when the women brace themselves, throw back their shoulders, ignore what sounds like a constant rumble of thunder, and move out of the suite.

And when they file from the room, soldiers ready for battle, they totally forget once again to ask for their cell phones. Moments after they close the suite door, before they have even reached the elevator, the wild buzzing ring from Margo's cell phone rattles the entire kitchen, where Patti has moved the phones back to the drawer from her suitcase and secretly stashed them behind the silverware. It was easy to do when everyone was asleep.

And it's a call Margo definitely should not have missed.

twelve

The inside of the elevator feels like a fast-warming oven the minute the door closes and the women position themselves like bodyguards in the four corners of the metal, tomblike structure.

They are so nervous there is no small talk, even though they have absolutely no idea what is going to happen next or what they are even going to do once the elevator reaches the ground floor.

And Margo wants a cigarette so badly she could lick the floor where it looks as if someone has dropped an illegal no-smoking-indoors pile of ashes. She would love to slip behind a door, a chair—anything—light up, and then disappear into the haze of her own smoke. But there's no time for that as the elevator jerks into motion after Cathy pushes the button that will help get them down to the lobby.

Cathy *thinks* she presses the correct button.

When the door flies open three stories later, the women step forward without realizing they are on the wrong floor. They look like a commando unit about to storm a prison. Three startled men about to get on the elevator step back and unsuccessfully try to stifle a variety of fright-induced sounds. This is when the women realize how they must look. They have been so focused it never dawned on them someone else might get on the elevator.

They retreat almost in unison, left foot, right foot, left foot, and leave the men cowering in the hall with their hands covering their faces.

Patti is the first to speak. "We must look positively frightening."

"Isn't that a good thing?" Holly now wants people to be afraid of her. She's nourishing a rush of testosterone that feels like a slap across her face.

"Of course," Cathy assures her, "but we should take a minute and think about this. We look like a mob about to lynch someone, for crying out loud."

Cathy leans over and hits the STOP button. It bumps to a stop and then jerks as if it still wants to keep going.

"That's comforting," Holly lies. "The way things have been going in Florida, we could end up being stuck in this elevator for three years."

"Look at us," Cathy commands, ignoring Holly's comment. "We look like we just escaped from prison ourselves but at least our new haircuts look good. I think it might be a good idea to conceal our weapons. Well, maybe you can conceal your weapons. I don't think I can hide this rather large can of hair spray in my bra."

Everyone turns toward the mirror on the back of the elevator when Cathy circles her finger without saying a word. They quickly agree that two knives, a large can, and a comb that looks

like a bayonet are not the most perfect accessories for a middle-
of-the-night outing in a busy hotel.

The women spend the next few minutes trying to conceal the
knives and comb in their pockets, down the sides of their waist-
bands, and in between their bras and shirts. They quickly discover that knives, even semi-dull ones, and very sharp combs do
not belong next to any area of the body that bends.

"This is stupid," Patti admits.

"We still have to do it," Margo says.

"Of course we do," Patti fires back. "It's just that we should
have grabbed some stuff, towels maybe, to carry this stuff in."

"Maybe we should take a breath," Holly advises. "It's sometimes best just to take a second and put the ends together."

For two cents Holly would now be glad to run back upstairs
and climb into the bathtub again, but her testosterone and estrogen are jogging through her bloodstream. And she had no idea
how powerful it would feel to hold her long-tailed comb like a
knife. She's never even thought of using a comb as a weapon, beyond the attacks she makes on a regular basis on horrid hair.

She liked it that the guys who'd been wanting to get on the elevator looked terrified. And she liked it when Cathy circled her
finger and all four of them turned around and realized they
looked like total badasses when they saw themselves in the mirror. She doesn't even realize that she hasn't needed an aspirin for
hours.

"We are wasting precious time," Margo warns. "Let's just
get the hell down there, try to be discreet until we find something
lying around like a newspaper to cover up these weapons, and go
find out if Nan is okay."

Without waiting for anyone to answer, Margo leans over and
releases the STOP button. The elevator springs back to life with a
huge jerk that throws them all off balance.

Patti would love to have a song come into her head right now. Something lively, like the theme from the old television show *Cagney and Lacey,* which she misses as if it just went off the air last week. Hell, even a little number from *Gunsmoke* might be the ticket at this particular moment. But there isn't a song blossoming within earshot. The damn hotel doesn't even have canned music piped into the elevator. Music should be everywhere.

Cathy is in a mental and physical position she never could have imagined just a week ago, or a few days ago, or the last time she saw Nan's husband. The one thing that has totally been bothering her since she met Nan at the bar and they started talking was an eerie and lingering feeling that Nan *knows* he's been cheating, maybe even knows with whom.

But how in the hell could she? Cathy's certain Nan's husband, who actually text-messaged her as she was sitting at the airport bar, with his very own wife, would never say a word. *Really.* The guy was so far beyond his own rear end and neck in trouble that he'd be a total fool to say anything about Cathy. And if there was a Cathy, there is a good chance there is also another somebody or a couple of other somebodys too.

And then there's Nan. And Cathy supposedly ready to pounce on someone to save Nan. If such a thing is even happening or possible. Cathy is realizing that she has gone along with this adventure without thinking much about what could or might happen beyond the physical risk. She has no clue what to do or say if Nan does know about her unfaithful husband and what Cathy has done with him. What will she do if Nan decides to bring it up? Even if Nan does, which seems unlikely considering everything else on her overflowing plate, what difference would it make? It's not like these women will picket outside of a Wendy's.

Cathy sneaks a quick glance at Holly, then Patti, then Margo. They are focused. Ready. Two knives and one very large comb are poised for action.

Damn.

Cathy wonders if she put out her hand if she could feel the invisible wall that she always imagined separates her from these women, from all women. When did she start building the wall? Who showed her how to place the bricks so they are staggered and the wall can grow higher and higher without worry about external support?

External support. Make that external female support. Something Cathy has neglected and ignored for so much of her life that remembering longtime female relationships is a struggle. Surely Nan, Margo, Holly—even wandering Patti the Murderess most likely has female connections with fans, that sister she speaks with, maybe a neighbor, women around her neighborhood and at the stores she frequents.

There have been so few moments when Cathy has bothered to think about what she might have missed, what she might have given away by placing her soul in all things almost totally male. This soft and fast-moving moment is as uncomfortable to her as almost anything hard she has ever done. And yet there is a glimpse, a small yearning, of what life might be like for women like this.

Women who have girlfriends.

Women who without a single question will grab a knife from the kitchen counter and run into harm's way to try to save a woman they barely know. Women who have a sacred spot inside of their own hearts for a woman they love who is a constant reminder of loyalty, honesty, all the good things that can come into your life. Women who have someone who understands the pace of their moods, their list of regrets and longings, the reasons why they let go of some things and cling to others. Women who know that the call will always be answered without hesitation. Women who can at any given moment fill the hollow pit of loneliness that sometimes cripples them. All of this and so much more, because of that one thing: *She is a woman, like me.*

How simple and lovely that must be for them. Cathy thinks of this as the elevator glides through the last two floors. She thinks about having someone to call, a woman—not one of the many men—who would simply come because she called. She thinks about drinking tea the first night the snow falls in late fall and then walking toward sunset with a friend. She thinks about missed baby showers and how long she had to think, especially before her third wedding, about who would stand up next to her in the ceremony and call her "friend." She thinks about all the mistakes, the choices to go with a him instead of a her, the women who were waiting on the other side of town for the man she was with, how ridiculously easy it was for her to get whomever she ever wanted just because of how she looked.

Cathy is not ashamed by all of this, but a yearning, a longing for something that she might still one day be able to have, grabs her by the throat when she is staring at the other women in the elevator and makes her feel weak and hungry. Before she has a chance to address it, to acknowledge what might be happening, the elevator bell rings and the door starts to open.

And, without thinking, Cathy leans over to press the HOLD button and the door closes. It's as if something unseen has moved into her body to give her a chance to do something, to see something she has never seen before. The elevator door tries to open but it's as if a magnetic force is holding it, just barely, so that Cathy can say something.

But she releases the chance. She says "Oops" instead and then pushes the button again, so that the door opens and she loses what ground she may have covered by simply thinking about female friendship. As the door flies open, she shuts whatever it was that was opening inside of herself. She waves it off as an offshoot of a brief moment of fear.

"You okay?" Holly, of course, is the one to notice that Cathy is off balance.

Cathy looks into Holly's eyes. They are filled with a pure light that makes them seem iridescent—green turning into blue turning into soft brown, and all the colors mingling and then disappearing into a place that is gentle and kind. Cathy knows that if she leaned over she might be able to see right through to the end of the rainbow.

"It's just the elevator," Cathy lies. "The jerking drives me nuts."

"Sure," Holly says, lightly touching Cathy on the shoulder. "It's the equilibrium thing. I understand."

Cathy looks away and as the door opens the women are shocked to see that even though it's way past midnight, the lobby is still littered with people. The bar is hopping, which now that they think about it, makes perfect sense. What else is there to do when you are trapped at a hotel in the middle of the Storm of the Century? Obviously not many other guests have been squatting in their rooms, wishing they had packed a shotgun, or rendezvousing with men in dark trench coats who came in a military tank to see them, or however in the hell Bret managed to drive through a wall of water.

The women look at one another, their eyes darting back and forth, until Patti indicates that they move by tilting her head and they shuffle to the back side of the large lobby. She hands over her knife to Holly, tells them to wait a second, and walks as if she knows where she is going toward the bar.

When she comes back a few moments later she is carrying three linen napkins that work perfectly as secret knife holders. And she has another idea.

"It's like Grand Central Station on New Year's Eve here, but I think we can find her if we split up," she tells them.

"Split up?" Holly prays Patti is joking.

"We've already wasted enough time. She's been gone for several hours. We need to spread out, and meet back here in like fifteen minutes or so."

This is when Cathy and Margo instinctively reach for their cell phones at the same time. It's a habit. A modern-day pushing-up-the-glasses kind of physical response, which could be likened to farmers hoisting up their pants as if they have forgotten their suspenders.

"Son-of-a-bitch," Cathy moans. "We forgot to take the damn phones again."

Holly smiles.

"What?" Margo looks at Holly as if she's lost her mind.

"First of all, we don't have one another's numbers programmed into our phones. Second of all, if we call 911 the cops might never get through this damn storm. Although I have to admit, a phone does offer a small bit of comfort."

"We are still wasting time," Patti says. "Yes, we should have the phones, and Holly, you are being very brave, but can we please start looking?"

Cathy is the one who really wishes they had their phones. She'd speed-dial half of the United States and men from twenty directions would come riding in on horses.

Maybe.

Now there is no choice. If anyone wanted to turn and run, they'd be sleeping in the hall. It would be like treason. If Nan really did need help and they went upstairs to watch a movie, how could they ever look themselves in the face again and see anything but the features of a rotten coward?

So again there really is no choice, and while they devise a plan to scour as much of the first level of the hotel as possible, Cathy, Margo, Patti, and Holly have an unspoken connected thought:

"This is one of those things that you will remember the rest of your life. When it is over, you will not even believe that you were able to do it. When you try to explain it to friends, people you love, someone at the grocery store, they will look at you as if you should be taking a pile of small white pills every morning. It will be a series of moments that may change everything you know and think about yourself and your abilities. And if you do not do this, if you back away, if you cannot do this one thing that seems rather simple, you may regret it the rest of your life...or you may simply live to tell everyone else what happened to the other three women who went running from the lobby with a weapon tucked into a napkin."

They all go. They leave with pumping hearts and a clear vision of what could possibly be happening at this particular moment if Bret is indeed a prophet from hell. They leave clutching a weapon in their hands, with a lively vision in their heads of Nan's face the moment she looks up, sees them, and knows she is rescued.

They also leave much slower than when they arrived.

And they scatter as if they are following a memorized road map. Margo starts with the bathrooms and has an immediate plan to accidentally waltz into the men's room, slip into the sacred back room behind the check-in counter, and then blend into the lobby crowd and see if anything weird occurs.

Patti, without hesitation, rolls into the bar, where she is

stunned to see a lovely stage, which immediately makes her heart ache, but she is all about the business of finding Nan. She is going to look as if she has arranged to meet someone, and walk through the entire bar, restaurant, and back area. She will listen at closed doors and then move down the outside entryway to make certain there are no loud, Nan-like whimpers coming from behind sealed doors.

Cathy skids up and down the halls leading to the small conference rooms and employee areas. She's decided to use her can of hair spray a number of ways, including blunt force, spraying it in eyes, or simply telling whoever questions her that she borrowed the spray from the spunky engineer and wants to give it back.

Holly turns into the main conference and convention area, a huge part of the hotel with its own catering wing and capabilities for everything from movie screenings to live music productions. It's where the psychics are camping, and she intends to parade through the booths, then walk as fast as possible to the back of the main room so she can peek into all the side areas, and then conversationally engage some of the wise mind readers, who may have seen someone dragging Nan down the hallway by her hair.

Even though it's now past one a.m., there are still people walking through the lines of psychic exhibits. Holly guesses they are non-barflies and are sick of ordering movies in their rooms. There is also an outside chance they are seriously interested in psychics and the world they create and live in.

She sees nothing unusual. Even the few people with badges—psychics themselves, probably—look like store clerks and business people. No throat slashers, men dragging chains, women adorned in witch hats or with glass eyes and smelling of incense are anywhere in sight.

Holly moves toward the back of the hall, where she discovers a series of small unlocked rooms, soft lights, coffeepots steaming, fresh trays of fruit and breads waiting to be devoured. Nothing is out of place and the few people sitting in the back areas are engrossed in what appear to be very serious discussions.

When Holly turns to walk through the exhibits one last time, she isn't certain if she is feeling relieved or just plain happy. She almost wishes she could pull up a chair and talk to one of those psychics. Maybe ask them how they think, how they know, what they see when they do whatever it is they do to slip inside someone else's beautiful mind.

Through the other doors and hallways she can sense that Cathy, Margo, and Patti are busy assessing the same kinds of things. Looking at people who might know something. Stepping into empty rooms. Turning on lights in dark places. Challenging a locked door.

And this gives her a feeling of security, as bizarre as it might seem, if she really started to think about it. But for now she eases into her walk back toward the center of the convention hall. The crowd has thinned in just the five minutes or so it took her to walk through the other rooms and she drifts toward the table by the door, which was crowded when she arrived. It's the table to talk to someone, especially if you know anything about the alleged bad guys running around the hotel.

When the last person leaves the table and the view clears, Holly has to stifle a large cry, lest she drop her hidden weapon, when she sees the man who had claimed to know her, sitting behind the table.

Damn.

She is so trapped she may as well be on the wrong end of a drug bust, but she doesn't flinch. She walks forward and he smiles and says, "I was wondering when you would show up."

Holly loves the feeling of holding the comb as a weapon and

not as a hair-fixing instrument. This mind reader can say whatever he wants—although, he's about as threatening as a piece of birthday cake.

"Well," he says, as if he's waiting for her to ask him out to prom.

"Do you have a name?"

"My friends call me Duffy."

"What do people who aren't your friends call you?"

"Charles."

"Hi, Duffy."

Holly knows she doesn't have much time. All the women are due back in the lobby, unless they are on their way to a trauma center, in five minutes. But there is something tantalizingly mysterious about this Duffy guy. And something else. Something that feels like a plate of rocks being set on Holly's chest.

"Do you know things about me?" She asks this question as Duffy gets up and leans in toward her across the table.

"Sure I do. You are gorgeous and smart and you change people's lives by making them look better and sometimes you are really scared—"

Holly holds up her hand to stop him. She remembers a skit one of her cousins used to do when they had their Fourth of July family picnic. The kids would set up their own show, with singing and acting, and this one obviously talented cousin was always throwing a shirt or towel over his head and making believe he could tell fortunes.

"*I can see you will soon be eating a hamburger. One day, maybe even today, you will drive down a long highway and come to a stop sign. Young children will soon ask you for many favors. Soon you may need to use the restroom.*"

Her mind-reading psychic relative was amazingly funny and now Holly thinks that this Duffy man could tell so much about her by simply doing what her cousin did? All anyone has to do is look at her, for God's sake, with her hidden comb, lovely hair, and the slight shadow of terror in her eyes. But he knew her name. Could he guess that?

"What?" he asks innocently.

"I'm a walking open book, for God's sake, Mr. Duffy. Tell me something no one would know just by looking at me."

She is trying to remember if she had on her convention name tag when she first entered the hotel.

"Are you sure?" He asks this as he leans forward just another inch. He is now so close to her, she can feel his breath on her face.

"What the hell," she responds, clutching her hidden comb.

After he says, "You live in Ohio and come from a wonderful and very married family," Holly starts to fade away. Even though she can hear the rain pounding on the slanted tin roof, and the muffled voices of the people still in the hall, and this Duffy guy talking, she *needs* to go outside. It's her head thing happening, the blessed tumor, and this time it has taken over her entire body.

"I'm sorry. I have to leave now," she says.

Duffy looks stricken. "Are you okay?"

"I just feel like I need to get out there and check something."

Duffy's eyes widen as if they have been suddenly replaced by buffet platters.

"You have to go, then. Hurry," he urges.

Holly turns, and suddenly he touches her arm. "You must be cautious. If you'd like, I will follow."

Holly cannot bring herself to say, "Are you serious?" because her need to get outside is an overwhelming physical desire. She simply pulls away without answering and begins walking, although she wants to run, toward the back entrance. The entrance that fans out toward the beach and an empty and very wet outdoor restaurant, where it is pouring, thundering, and lightning non-stop.

And as she walks it's as if nothing else exists. Not even Duffy, who is desperately trying to keep up. Not even the three people behind the check-in counter who are throwing pencils at one another because no one has checked in or out of the hotel for days and they are obviously bored. Not even the groups of people who are coming out of the bar. Not even the lone security guard who is so obviously flirting with three girls whose combined age is probably only a hair over forty.

But three people do exist for her, and they see her and know that she also exists, even if she does not actually see them at the moment.

Patti, Cathy, and Margo are loping from the ground-floor corners of the hotel and their self-assigned patrol duties. They see Holly at almost the exact same moment, from different locations. And it at first does not look like Holly. It's a woman dressed like her, but walking as if her rear end has a fire urging her forward. She is leaning forward as if her own feet cannot move fast enough to get her where in the hell she wants to go.

It's odd. She looks odd. Almost...possessed.

There is a moment of confused hesitation for the other women following her as Holly pushes through the back door and emerges into a world of wicked weather, which physically assaults her the instant she steps into its cruel arms.

What in the hell is she doing? Where is she going?

Holly's behavior, as she walks faster into the darkness, is so bizarre to Margo, Cathy, and Patti, they actually stop and think for a moment to try to answer all the questions about her behavior that have paralyzed them.

Then they see the guy. Holly's guy. The one who knows her name and found her in the elevator and who keeps inviting her to come see him. He's a psychic, and holy shit, it looks as if he's stalking her.

Margo would love to fly just now. She is the farthest back, and she desperately wishes she had the ability to leap tall buildings and jump on the man following Holly. *Her Holly.* Within seconds she has managed to move her candy-fueled, very thin legs so fast, she's pushing past Patti and Cathy, who plunge into the storm directly on her heels.

It's impossible to see anything. The outdoor lights from the hotel appear to be swirling in the rain. The water is distorting everything, and the farther they move forward, the harder it becomes to see.

"Do you see her?" Patti is frantic. For Holly and the man following her have disappeared.

"Should I go alert someone?" Cathy is pretty certain a can of hair spray will not help very much at this moment.

Margo stops suddenly. She turns to face Cathy.

"Go to the desk. Tell them it's an emergency. Call 911 and then give them this code number: Say 1652. And then say it's *Status Gold.*"

Patti, Cathy, and Margo cannot see one another's faces, but if they could there would be a bewildered look on Cathy's face that is beyond dazed and confused.

"Go!" Margo commands in a voice that does not leave room for questions. "And hurry."

Cathy turns. She runs back through the rain into the hotel; Patti stands frozen behind Margo, who is bending her head into the wind and searching into the darkness. Patti has no idea how Margo can see anything. She feels like they are standing on the bow of a huge ship that is about to go under.

Margo starts moving again and Patti whips her head back and forth searching for Nan, searching for Holly, *her Holly.*

Where in the hell did they go?

Margo's instincts tell her to follow the side of the building, walk around the pool, and look behind the outdoor restaurant. She starts walking and within a few seconds she begins to run and there is no way Patti can keep up. Margo is fast for such a skinny babe. When Margo loops around the pool she turns, just in time to see Holly, with the man close on her heels, turn the corner. She decides to go in the opposite direction. She'll cut them off from the front. Plus, she is much, much faster than Holly and Mr. Psychic.

Patti steps it up and closes the gap between her and Margo and prays to God she does not slip on a lost beach towel, a tossed plastic cup, or a flying beach chair. Every few seconds the wind takes a break and the hotel's outdoor lights illuminate the entire area.

Margo slows as she comes to the corner of the pool building and Patti finally catches up. Margo crouches, looks both ways, and when Patti glances over her shoulder, she sees Holly on the other side of the building and it looks as if the psychic has his hands on her waist. Maybe he does. Maybe it's just the wobbling shadows. But why isn't Margo moving? Why is she not screaming and pulling out her knife to stab the guy in the back?

Before Patti has a chance to ask her these very important questions, Margo springs out into the darkness as if she has just been shot from a cannon. In three seconds, she vanishes. Patti looks right, and sees that Holly is not moving. She is looking off into the same black hole that swallowed up Margo. And then Holly too starts to run forward, with the psychic not far behind.

Oh my God.

Patti starts walking forward as if she is blind, shuffling her feet, waving her hands in front of her, wondering how in the hell Margo can see in the dark. What she herself sees next almost drops her to her knees.

Margo is literally flying through the air and is about to land on top of a man twice her size, who has Nan pinned against the railing that leads out to the beach.

Holy shit.

Patti rushes forward, drops the damn napkin covering her knife, and has absolutely no idea what to do next. The man on top of Nan is taken totally by surprise. Nan pops out from underneath him, just as Holly leaps out of the darkness and Mr. Psychic draws a gun.

Not that Margo needs the guy with the gun. In four seconds she has managed to wrestle the bad guy, who is not Agent Bret, to the ground. She has his hands pinned behind his back, her bony knee braced right down the center of his spine, and as she reaches her hand out to Mr. Psychic, he tosses her some handcuffs.

And then Margo says, "FBI. You are under arrest. Now stand up, you sorry piece of dog shit."

And Patti has all she can do not to fall over right on top of the sorry piece of dog shit, who is whimpering like a hungry baby.

thirteen

The cell phones, returned to their nest next to the knives, forks, and spoons, start buzzing as if they are part of a timed production just a few minutes past ten a.m. and the noise just about gives Patti, who is passed out on her pullout bed, a heart attack.

"What the hell!" she shouts, rising up and instinctively groping for the knife, which has now become like a third hand.

It takes her a few seconds to not just remember who she is, and where she is, but what is causing the commotion. She has half a notion to gather all the phones, open the window, and throw them out into the storm. Except when she listens for a moment, the sounds of rain and wind and cracking thunder have diminished, turned into something barely audible.

Could the storm possibly be ending? Might they all escape? Has anyone died or been attacked during the past, what, maybe six hours since most of them fell into bed exhausted, relieved, frightened, and totally confused?

Patti swings her feet to the floor and admires the scratches on her legs and lower arms from running in the dark and bumping into bushes and trees and lawn furniture. She shakes her head, and for some odd reason she thinks about Carmen Miranda, the infamous singer and dancer who bounced through the forties with a basket of fruit on her head and made everyone feel as if they were in the Caribbean. A dashing rumba beat starts pounding through her mind and Patti hums along as she gets up to look out the window.

When she pulls back the heavy curtains and pushes her nose against the windowpane there is a world of change in front of her. It is still raining, but lightly. The swirling angry clouds have spread out, and to the south Patti is astounded to see a small patch of blue sky.

"Apparently we are not going to drown in Florida," she says thankfully, and then turns to see why in the world the cell phones were all being texted to death.

Damn cell phones.

Patti realizes now that it really would not have mattered if she had never bothered to take them away. What could she have possibly been thinking? After what happened last night, she feels as if she's been sharing rooms, time, and space with a lynch party of strangers, and she's pretty sure she doesn't even know the half of it.

Margo is apparently an undercover agent, for the love of God. Holly has been possessed by some kind of spirit that evidently helps her find bad guys, and she was mumbling something about a brain tumor. Nan could end up in prison. Cathy has been whimpering about some big secret she is dying to tell everyone.

And all Patti wants is a cup of coffee and for a live band to start playing outside the window.

By the time the police showed up last night, Nan had been examined and had then stubbornly refused to be transported to a hospital for further tests. Margo had disappeared with Mr. Psychic. Holly could not stop crying, and went on about her aspirins and how she feels as if something isn't right in her head and how she's dying of a flipping brain tumor. Patti listened to Holly sob out her story of feeling "different" and a mess of other ridiculous things that were surely not symptoms of a brain tumor.

"Honey," Patti said, feeling for once grateful that she wasn't a mother, "the chances of you having a tumor are very small. I think you worry too much. In this group especially, I'm pretty certain we all feel odd. We sure as hell act odd."

"Something is wrong with me," Holly almost shouted. "I know they can't always find tumors, especially if they are small, and I'm positive I have one."

"Even more reason, then, to dance naked every chance you get, and live, Holly," Patti had retorted.

Holly shook her head, whimpered a bit longer, and Patti finally decided the best thing to do was shut up and let Holly believe she has a brain tumor. What in the hell else could happen? Brain tumors, guns, crooks, government agents, people leaping through the dark like trained circus performers. Patti was beginning to think she was having a doozy—in her world that means something beyond memorable. That was not on her Florida agenda.

It was almost five a.m. when everyone but Margo stumbled into bed and collapsed. Patti cannot even remember if she heard Margo come in, and right now she's not sure she cares.

She thought she had a great story to tell when she confessed that she once killed a man. Obviously, for this group, that's a drop in the bucket.

Before she can open the kitchen drawer to see what's causing all the ruckus, Cathy comes staggering into the kitchen. It looks like she fell off a moving truck.

"What was that buzzing?"

"I think it was one, or more, of the cell phones. Don't take this personally, Cathy, but you look like hell."

"Well, geez, Patti, last night was not like going to a movie premiere or something. I still don't know what happened with Nan. Did you talk to her? Is it true Margo is, like, some kind of super cop or something? And does poor Holly really have a brain tumor? Christ! I keep thinking it might have been better to sleep in the hallway outside the airport bar."

Patti finds herself agreeing with Cathy. That's something positive at least, for crying out loud.

"Cathy, why did you keep saying you have to talk to Nan? You said it about three hundred times after the cops left."

"I did?"

"I'm exaggerating, but you said it a lot. Please tell me you're not her long-lost sister or a Russian spy or anything. I'm not sure I can take any more excitement."

"Oh, forget about it. It's nothing like that. Really."

Patti can tell Cathy is lying, by the way she keeps dropping her eyes. Even normal people who are not secret agents know some basic things about human behavior, for God's sake. Before Patti can call her on whatever her secret might be, Cathy distracts both of them by asking, with a slighly pitiful and desperate voice, if there is any coffee left.

Patti is quietly relieved. She's gone out on a limb far enough for this group of broads. She's longing for the relative quiet of her tiny apartment, a reprieve from the drama of living in close proximity with more women than she has ever lived with at one time in her entire life. *Distract me with coffee. Please. Hurry.* Which is exactly what happens.

And they forget about the cell phones yet again.

As they make coffee and rumble around the kitchen, they both realize that there are still dozens of unanswered questions. Holly dropped into bed last night like a bomb, Cathy tells Patti. She just rolled over, pushed herself close to the wall, and was asleep, or acted like she was asleep, before Cathy could even ask her a single burning hot question.

It was the same way with Nan, who'd come into the suite, gone to the bathroom, and never said a word. Margo, secret agent number whatever in the hell she is, has not been heard from since they saw her under a horde of red spotlights, talking with her hands as if everyone who surrounded her was deaf.

"Is she even here?"

"I passed out myself," Patti admits. "I don't remember hearing her come in."

Patti totally understands why no one wanted to talk after they were set free by detectives, and other people flashing badges, after Margo waved them off and said she would fill them in later.

Cathy and Patti exchange silent glances, put down the coffeepot and cups, and quietly tiptoe down the hall, past the bathroom, and to Nan and Margo's room. The door is closed.

"Can you open it quietly?" Patti mouths to Cathy.

Cathy nods and turns the doorknob so slowly that Patti thinks it will take her a week to get the damn door open. But Cathy's obviously done this before. When the door opens in absolute silence, they can see Nan sleeping like a baby, and Margo on her back, also sleeping, but probably not like a baby, because everyone knows secret agents are always half-awake.

Back in the kitchen they finish making the coffee and Patti

remembers to share the good news about the blue sky while they wait for someone else to wake up and tell them what the hell has gone on and is going to happen next.

"Do you think Holly has a brain tumor?" Cathy asks this while they both lean into the counter and wish the coffeepot would work faster.

"Hell no. Don't you ever get an ache or pain and think you have bone cancer?"

Cathy nods.

"She's young. She'll figure this out."

"But what if it's true? She pops those aspirins and she always says her head feels funny."

"She doesn't have a tumor," Patti assures Cathy, but wondering if maybe there really might be a chance.

Before the water can finish riding through the coffee, and before they can finish their brain cancer discussion, both women jump a good two inches as Margo's phone starts ringing so loudly, the entire counter shakes. They know it's Margo's phone because it has the same distinctive and terribly obnoxious ring her phone had the day they were buying bathing suits.

Patti yanks open the drawer and answers the phone, just to make it stop. "Hello?" she snarls.

"Margo?" A man on the other end clearly does not recognize Patti's voice.

"Just a moment."

Patti shakes her head, looks at Cathy, and then heads down the hallway, praying to God she won't get shot when she wakes up Margo, who most likely has a gun concealed under her pillow.

And as she pushes the door open, not as quietly as Cathy had, she decides that this would be a bad time to laugh, but that is exactly what her body is telling her to do as the theme song from one of the way-too-many James Bond movies rises up inside of her.

The FBI, the psychics, the storm, phones with obnoxious rings, her murder confession, Nan's apparent abduction... Sweet Jesus, when you add it all up, it seems as if someone on drugs tried really hard to write a bad movie script. Except everything is not make-believe. And the real reason Patti longs to laugh is because she has not had this much fun in a very long time.

But to admit that would be to admit so many other things lost and forgotten. So many things that never happened, that went missing in all the years of waiting, hiding behind a microphone, searching for quiet places, when her heart truly could have used a bit more gunfire, barking phones, and women gone wild.

This is why she is smiling when she leans over Margo, says, "A mean-sounding man is waiting to talk to you on your magic spy phone," and then quickly steps back in case Margo wakes up swinging or—better yet—shooting.

Margo rises as if there is a rope attached to her forehead. She turns sideways, looks as if she has just been caught sneaking in a window after curfew by her mother, and groggily demands, "Seriously?"

"Yep. The cell phones are in the kitchen. It's that mystery ring you told us was your kids."

"I had to lie, for hell's sake."

"Sure."

Margo throws her legs to the floor. "I can't believe I didn't hear the phone. I must be tapped out. I've never missed one of their calls. Ever."

"You're tired. You provided quite the show last night. I bet you've killed more men than I have."

Margo glares at Patti as if her eyes were gun barrels. Patti almost ducks, but then steps aside as Margo stalks past her, wearing a T-shirt and a lovely pair of black bikini underwear. If this is standard FBI attire, Patti is thinking of signing up.

She cannot wait to hear what happens next. She follows Margo into the kitchen, where Margo grabs the phone, does not bother to turn her back, and simply barks, "Margo Engelstrom here," into the receiver.

She crosses her arms with the phone cradled between her neck and chin, in classic pissed-off "I'm not really listening to you" mode, while Cathy lovingly holds the first cup of hot coffee as if it is a religious relic. Now Margo is closing her eyes, and finally she speaks.

"You have got to be shitting me."

She says the exact same thing again two seconds later.

When she slams her phone shut, and then throws it back inside the silverware drawer rather than slip it into her pocket, both Cathy and Patti jump.

"I have to go downstairs for a while and talk to some people," Margo tells them flatly. "I can't force the four of you to stay in the room until I get back, but I'm asking that you stay inside until I can figure a few things out."

"So, we're not, like, under arrest or anything?" Cathy asks half-seriously.

"No. It's not like that. Just some, ah, complications."

"Whatever." This from Patti, who wishes she could send along a tape recorder when Margo leaves. "When you come back will you promise to tell us who you really are and what's going on?"

Margo looks up, nods yes distractedly, and then walks down the hall with such force the table rattles.

"I think she's pissed about something," Cathy observes meekly. "She probably had, like, two hours of sleep."

"It's more than just lack of sleep," Patti answers as Margo runs to get dressed, then marches past, slamming the suite door as she leaves without saying a word.

The slamming door wakes up Holly, who staggers into the

kitchen to join them, then Nan arrives. They both look like hell. Worse than hell.

Holly obviously slept in her clothes, and her hair looks like a bird's nest. She has bags under her eyes, both knees are scraped from one of the times she fell when running in the dark, and there is a huge glob of dried-up mud on her right arm.

And Nan could be her twin. She looks like a walking grass stain. Her hair, clothes, everything, are just as messed up as Holly's. Except for one difference. One horrible, terrible difference. There are nasty finger marks, which will most likely turn into ugly bruises, around her neck. It looks as if she is wearing a red necklace, until you get really close and can actually see the imprints of fingers.

His fingers.

Sweet Jesus.

"Girls," Patti says, rushing protectively toward them. "Coffee? Showers? The morning special? How are you two?"

Holly and Nan utter the word *coffee* at the same moment, and Cathy all but throws down her cup so she can take care of them. She then says that Margo just got called to go to some kind of important meeting and that she, Cathy, will make them something to eat, before or after they shower...if they want.

After wishing just minutes ago that she had never met these women, Patti finds herself gripped with compassion. She suddenly wants to clean them off, feed them, make sure they are okay. She can't imagine feeling any other way, which is almost upsetting to her, and Cathy must feel the same way, because she volunteered to cook—which should be interesting if it actually happens.

"Does anyone need something else?" Patti asks, hovering over them like a mother or a best friend.

"Nan." Cathy obviously cannot stand not knowing and

jumps right in. "Can you tell us what happened? We don't know anything. Are you okay?"

"That son-of-a-bitch," Nan answers. Then she looks at Patti. "I can understand why you would want to kill someone."

Patti is not the kind of woman who cries at movies or when she reads emotional books or even when an acquaintance dies. She's sheltered her emotions behind songs and long skirts and a smile that she's used as if it were a large tarp. But Nan's confession fills her eyes with tears.

"Can you tell us?" she whispers to Nan, sitting so that she will not fall over.

Nan leans back in her chair, rolls her neck in a small circle, sets her coffee on the table. And then tells them.

Agent Bret was who he said he was. He'd taken her to a private hotel room, where two other people, a man and a woman, were waiting with tape recorders, a computer, and a video camera—and yes, she did ask to see credentials, and everything seemed in order.

She'd wondered about making certain there was an attorney there more than she'd wondered about her own physical safety, but she realized she had nothing to hide, nothing to worry about, because she hadn't done anything wrong—except maybe wait too long to call someone.

Before they started, however, she had her own list of questions. The agents answered what they could, and that meant they said very little. But she found out that they had also been tracking her husband, his clients—the clients Nan would be turning in to the agents. They also had been tracking her, which meant they knew she had done nothing illegal.

Then there were two hours of questions and Nan accessing her accounts via their computer and her sharing with them that she had everything backed up and hard copies of documents in a safe place. Considering other messed-up cases they had worked, they were astounded and thrilled that she had kept such detailed records. And the good news, before all the bad news, is that as soon as these people, her husband included, were arrested, she would be eligible for a percentage of whatever the government recovered from all of the illegal accounts. This financial incentive had clearly helped the government recover millions of dollars from scandals just like Nan's husband's mess.

"Maybe we could open up a salon-slash-espionage-slash-cabaret-singer-slash-hamburger-place with the money," Holly suggested, trying to give Nan a chance to take a breath. "I'm kidding, but really, it sounds like once you get through this, there's a new life for you."

Cathy turns away and Holly is praying to God that she does not pick this moment to clear her own plate of the piles of guilt that must have gotten even deeper during the past twelve hours. Thankfully, Patti asks Nan to finish the story.

And Nan is so far away from thinking about what will *really* happen when this part is over and she has to face the music of her husband and the clients and who the hell knows what and whom else, she is absolutely relieved to keep talking.

"I could tell right away that they were deep into this investigation, because they knew things I don't think anyone else knows but me," she shared. "These clients I turned in have been working with people in foreign countries. The kind of foreign countries where lots of bad people live."

"That could mean New York or Idaho, for crying out loud," Cathy says, totally aware of the fact that those are states and not countries. "Are you talking North Korea, Iran, Cuba?"

"It may as well be Florida, considering what we've been

through," Holly shares, momentarily forgetting about her brain tumor. "This part of the country has turned out to be pretty foreign to me. I feel like I'm in *The Wizard of Oz* or something."

No one asks Holly how she knew to go look outside and why Mr. Psychic was following her as if he was a bad stalker. But then, Nan is not even close to being finished.

She tells them that her interviewers brought in food, fed her coffee, and had her go over so many papers that her head spun. They had video surveillance of her meeting John's and her clients in Florida and close-ups that made her want to run and get Botox injections.

"Sweet hell," Patti exclaims. "I imagine we are supposed to feel good that they were catching the bad guys, but doesn't a part of you feel a little violated, Nan?"

"What do you mean?"

"Like, what if you were blowing your nose or had to pull your slip down or use the restroom, and they were always filming you?"

"I don't wear slips."

"You know what I mean," Patti says, clearly agitated. "Is there a way to know exactly how closely they have been watching you? I mean, maybe they saw us wrestling in the restroom at the airport, for crying out loud."

It's surprisingly Cathy who puts her hand on Patti as if to say, "Take a breath, honey. Everything is okay." And her touch, the warmth of her fingers, brings Patti back down to an earth she has seldom left.

"Sorry," Patti apologizes. "I'm one of those people who freaked out about Homeland Security and now it's invaded my entire life. I'm always a little bit torn between being pissed off and totally frightened."

Nan says at this point she really doesn't give a damn. She's just glad to be alive. They can film her picking her nose naked, for all she cares.

"So what happened? How did this attacker find you?"

"It was a fluke, I guess. It got later and later and they finally ran out of things to ask me and I really didn't have anything else to say. I'm sure more things will come up, but seriously, I was frigging exhausted."

What happened next was supposed to be easy and simple. Nan sat quietly while the agents packed up all their documents and equipment. During the long hours, the only thing they hadn't done was tattoo her or sew a secret transmitter under the skin of her left arm. At the end, she was exhausted, but also a little high from the adrenaline rush that had started the moment she decided it was time to come clean and turn everyone in.

Agent Bret set up a follow-up meeting in three days in Chicago. He said he would be contacting her before then and that it would be best if she simply called in sick, made up an excuse, feigned anything to keep from going in to work. He all but ordered her to do it.

By the time they left the room and got into the elevator, Nan was so wired from coffee and emotion she felt as if she could fly.

"It was a relief to have told them everything, almost as if I had just gotten really good news," she shared. "So the elevator went down to the lobby. We were talking and it didn't occur to me that I should be going up and not down. At the last minute Bret asked if I wanted to be walked back to my room and I said no."

"It was late," Cathy says.

"But there were people still out, as you know," Nan says. "I got out and watched Bret and the other two leave and then I started back toward the elevator, but I thought just one breath of fresh air, that's all I wanted, and so I walked toward the back doors, and that's when this prick came up behind me and said he had a gun."

Shit.

Everything from that point, Nan told the mesmerized women, was fuzzy. It was as if someone else was there—she was watching it all happen from a distance.

Patti wants to stop Nan right there. She wants to tell her that she knows exactly what it felt like to be suspended like that. To wish that you could be anywhere but there and to especially wish that you had put a flame thrower in your purse. To wish that he might die. To wonder if anyone will come to save you. To realize you might die.

Patti forces her mind to stop so that she can listen to the rest of Nan's story, which is not unlike her story but not exactly the same either.

"He kept saying things in my ear that made no sense," Nan continues. "It was so rainy and cold and windy outside that even though he was pressed up against me and I could feel that damn gun, his words kept flying away into the storm."

She caught *"going to"* and *"you will like it"* and *"they will be"* and *"never should have"* and as he shoved her forward, all she could think was that he was going to hurt her, rape her, probably kill her.

"The funny part is that I never actually saw him," she says, as if she's trying to recall anything memorable about him beyond his husky voice, the feel of his gun against her back, and the way he kept pushing her.

At first she thought he was taking her someplace. That he had a plan. But as they stumbled outside, and he fell, and then she fell, and he realized that the storm was as fierce as he was trying to be, she knew he had no plan and was a total whacko.

And then he hit her. He hit her once and threw her down and

he hit her again. Then he put his hands around her neck. And Nan was just about to go ballistic and fling sand in his eyes before he murdered her, when Margo flew out of nowhere and took him out.

"It was amazing," she said, closing her eyes to capture the moment.

"We thought so too," Patti agrees. "Margo's such a tiny thing. Who would have thought?"

"How bizarre that you were meeting with FBI people and Margo is an FBI agent or something and they leave and then this happens." Holly says what everyone else is also thinking.

"Is she really an agent?" Cathy wonders out loud.

"She said FBI, and everyone who came after that seemed to know who she is, but, really, I don't know anything more than you," Nan admits. "At least they caught the guy the notes warned us about."

"And you helped with that," Cathy reminded her.

Patti turns to look at Holly. Holly knows what's coming next.

"That psychic guy," Patti says lightly. "Who is he?"

Holly is just about to say something, when there is a knock at the door. No one moves. The second knock is louder and, as if on cue, she hears Mr. Psychic say, "Holly, it's Duffy, the psychic. Can you open the door?"

Still no one moves.

"Is he a psychic who carries handcuffs or an FBI agent who poses as a psychic?" Cathy leans over to whisper.

"Maybe both," Holly whispers back, feeling her tumor spring to life.

"You mean you don't know?"

Mr. Psychic Duffy knocks again and asks her to open the door.

"Margo knows," Nan shares. "Open the damn door, Holly. He helped save my life."

"At least now we know he has a name. Duffy," Patti says as Holly opens the door. "That sounds like a lovely, safe name. Are you sure he's not a mechanic or something?"

Duffy wants Holly to go downstairs so he can talk to her and explain everything about the psychic world. Holly shrugs her shoulders, tells the women she'll be back in a little while, and leaves before Cathy or Patti can stop her.

"Margo asked us to stay in the room," Cathy shouts, and runs to reopen the door. By the time she gets there, and sticks her head out, the elevator door has already slid shut.

Patti throws up her hands and wonders what in the hell is going to happen next. Nan also raises her hands, as if to surrender, and heads into the bathroom to take a much-needed shower. Cathy starts rummaging through the refrigerator to find anything edible.

The cell phones again have been forgotten and the blue sky, which is getting closer by the hour, is nothing compared to everything else that is going on with the women in suite 6502.

By the time Nan emerges from the bathroom, looking one thousand percent better, Cathy and Patti have made another pot of coffee and found enough bread and eggs to make some French toast. The three women sit quietly and act about as normal as possible for women who have just survived a living nightmare.

Nan wants to say thank you. She wants to tell Cathy and Patti that she is grateful they came to look for her, but she's thinking it would be better for her to wait and thank them all at once so she doesn't have to go through the process twice. And she's afraid if she starts talking again, she might start crying. She can either cry or talk, not both. Absolutely not.

And she's not even sure what to say beyond "Thank you for saving my life. And for risking your own." After all, she hardly knows these women, is not even sure they like one another, and look what they'd done for her.

"Oh my gosh," Patti says, finally remembering, "the phones were buzzing like crazy and I forgot to check them, to give them back."

Before she can even get up, Margo pushes into the suite as if she has just jumped off a rocket. She slams the door shut, then goes to stand with her hands on her hips in front of the table. She looks about fifty degrees beyond pissed.

"Where's Holly?"

"She went to meet with Mr. Psychic Duffy. Well, that's what we call him," Patti explains.

"I thought I asked you not to leave the room," Margo almost shouts.

"We didn't," Cathy snarls back. "Holly did."

"Shit."

"What?" Nan asks, but really isn't sure she wants to know.

"The guy that was caught last night is not the guy *we* were looking for," Margo tells them. "I'm sorry, Nan. The other guy the psychics warned us about is still running around someplace. Actually, there's probably more than one guy too."

Nan drops her head onto the table as if her neck muscles have snapped. Margo sits down next to her, gently puts her left hand on top of Nan's head, asks for a cup of coffee, and to their astonishment, says, "I suppose you want to know who I really am."

fourteen

Patti thought no one could ever sing "What Kind of Fool Am I" like Frank Sinatra until that one lovely moment when she had a New Orleans gig and shared the stage for five minutes with Harry Connick Jr. while he blew the song and Sinatra out of the ballpark.

She had been singing at a small cabaret, and Connick, and his career, were just about to take off. It was a magical moment for her then, because she was hearing genius, but it was even more magical several years later when an autographed copy of his new CD and a lovely personal note showed up in her mailbox.

Harry, she thinks, would love this messed-up group of broads.

Really.

Patti feels like the fool the song talks about. Her little old murder is nothing compared to the tangled mess half of her roommates are in. She only feels a little betrayed by whatever it is Margo is going to tell them. Had any of their initial discussion on the balcony been real or true? Does Margo even have kids? Has she ever really even been inside a grade-school nurse's office?

Patti is exhausted. When she closes her eyes to try and silence the song that is moving through her, Patti visualizes herself on her worn-out couch in her one-bedroom apartment. Everything of importance that she owns can be loaded into the back of a small pickup truck in twenty minutes if she moves fast.

She loves the way she lives when she's not on the road. Quiet. Unassuming. Simple. The perfect way to recharge her batteries before the next gig. Her television set, the neighbor bumping into her walls, and the constant California traffic, with its honking horns and roaring engines, help her know she's alive.

That's what waits for her. And soon, when the flights resume, Patti knows she could step away from the table, not listen to whatever in the holy hell Margo is about to tell them. Maybe it will finally be the truth, maybe she will actually know who Margo is after this latest story . . . maybe an elephant will fly out of the refrigerator and some Army commandos will flip in through the windows, or a blind duck will follow Holly into the elevator and ask them what's to eat.

Someone definitely should have some of this on film. But, given the FBI was involved, that's probably happening anyway.

At this point, she thinks, Cathy and Nan must be feeling the same way, although their worlds are seemingly not as simple as Patti's. Nan's world as she knew it just a few days ago no longer exists. The devious schedule of meetings, liaisons, rendezvous, and secret gatherings that Cathy must hold together while also holding her own breath has been shattered. All because they have been held hostage by the weather.

Cathy, who has been unusually quiet, has ordered more coffee from room service and a mountain of sandwiches and anything else she could think of to keep them satisfied while they wait for Holly, and while Margo revs up to tell them her life story. One of her life stories.

Nan is wishing Margo would get to it already, because she's dying to ask several questions, the least of all being, "Should I be worried about losing my life?"

This question has been driving itself like a wild hammer from the back to the front of her head for so many hours, Nan thinks she may lose her mind before she loses her life.

"Does anyone have any aspirin or Tylenol?" she asks.

"I'll get something," Patti offers.

Cathy walks over, and, without asking, starts to massage Nan's neck, back, and shoulders.

Nan flinches. She's startled by the touch of human hands, even female hands, on her body. She feels violated and bruised emotionally as well as physically. It's not as if she's never been pushed around before, had someone try to exert physical force over her, or slam her to the ground. But this time Nan felt so helpless, helpless in a way that is still ricocheting through her. And because she hasn't processed it all, she isn't certain she wants anyone to touch her. Not yet.

But Cathy knows what she's doing, so Nan lets go just a little bit and something falls slowly from inside of her that she will later describe as a long string with hooks, gathering speed, collecting particles of dirt, sand, and rust, until her heart accelerates and she reaches her arms straight out in front of her across the table and begins to cry.

No one even notices at first. Nan is embarrassed but then she feels a slight popping in her chest and the string rotates in a circle around her heart, and then it is as if a dam has burst. There are tears everywhere. And when she remembers that Margo probably now has a gun and that these women ran through fifty-mile-per-hour winds from the powerful spring storm to rescue her and wouldn't hurt her, she makes a whimper that sounds like a small sneeze.

"Are you okay?" Cathy stops massaging her.

Nan lifts her head, wipes her nose on her arm, and all at once realizes that part of the reason she's crying is because she's angry. *Really angry.*

"He terrorized me," she confesses. "I'm not the kind of woman who wants to be helpless. He made me want to get a permit to carry a gun. I'm just so pissed that he made me feel that way."

"You have a right to be pissed," Margo, who has been sipping the last cup of coffee, reassures her. "Speaking purely as a woman, and not a law enforcement agent, it always pisses me off when I'm involved in cases like this. It's always men who do stupid shit like what Nan has been through. That's part of the reason I quit this damn business."

"You have a funny way of retiring, Margo," Patti reminds her, handing Nan some aspirin. "You must have been like a flame thrower when you were really working."

"Are you always this sarcastic?" Cathy asks, as if this is the first time she's realized Patti has a sharp tongue.

Patti feels as if she has just been slapped. She apologizes, which makes everyone turn and stare at her. It's been four days, but fearless and sure-footed Patti has not struck any of them as the kind of woman who would say "I'm sorry" so quickly. Is everyone having a meltdown? Cathy is being nice. Nan's sobbing. Patti apologized. And Margo is about to confess. God only knows what Holly and Mr. Duffy are up to.

"Really, I am sorry," Patti says, because it looks as if no one believes her. "We're all a little tired. Nan, are you sure you're okay?"

"It's just a little meltdown, Patti," Nan explains. "We've talked about men and girls and always worrying, but it's something that never goes away."

"We all wanted to bash the living hell out of that jerk," Patti says. "That's not much comfort, I know, but I've been where you are. We all have been there. Maybe that's why I'm cranky and sarcastic now."

Margo decides it's time to take control, something she is obviously pretty good at. Once the food arrives, and there is fresh coffee, she gently suggests they relax, and ask her anything they want once she is finished. Besides her secret life, she says, there is also the problem of the missing bad guy and what will happen to the man who assaulted Nan.

There's no hand-holding at this meeting. In fact, the women spread out at such great distances, Margo longs to order them to sit closer. It's not church, she almost says, but instead charges into her story.

And no, she's not going to wait for Holly, who is in her own briefing. "I'll let Holly tell you about her end of this when she gets back," she starts.

All eyes are on Nan as Cathy and Patti prepare to hear what Margo has to say.

It feels like a decade ago when the women first met in the bathroom, tried to save Nan's phone, and then had a wild notion to find shelter in a luxury suite while what surely must have been a world-record spring storm ripped through the country.

Ironically, the very thing that has kept them in Florida is now not even on the front page of their lives. To hell with the weather. They have much bigger things to discuss and then argue about.

Margo, apparently the mistress of tremendous focus, asks if she can tell her story in two phases. One as Margo the chick from the restroom and one as Margo the manslayer.

Everyone simply nods, too spellbound to speak.

The manslayer goes first.

The manslayer was recruited before she graduated from college because of her language, math, and analytical skills. Margo grew up speaking a bit of German and a bit of Polish and lots of Spanish and even though she was recruited for her intellectual skills, she blew everyone out of the water when she went to a pre-enlistment training weekend and her skinny little ass was over walls and under buildings as fast as a rocket, just like her father and brothers had taught her. They'd also taught her to shoot a gun, self-defense, and how to trap a beaver in late spring in the Wisconsin marshes, and how to track a deer when there was no snow. For her, learning how to keep a gun oiled had been better than home economics class.

After a not-so-short hiatus to do the mother thing, she couldn't stand being away from her government job. So she went back very part-time. And part-time wasn't the running-around-with-guns-and-handcuff stuff she did before the three kids popped out of her and temporarily changed the direction of her life. It was more like phone consulting, a few meetings, and maybe three trips a month, but not too far away, and never anything dangerous that might leave her children motherless.

She was still doing the carpool and school nurse gigs and everything else times twenty that a woman who has three kids does. Her working only part-time had allowed her husband to totally kick-start his career as an engineer in a small but growing company, and then Margo had suddenly moved into that restless period of married life and motherhood.

She tells this part of the story with her head down, fingers moving in circles across the tops of her knees, as if she's trying to steady herself.

This next phase of her life, she shares, is like standing on a tall platform that is raised above the present borders of your life. There's your husband's company and there's the high school and the middle school. Your friends' houses, the grocery store. You can see from your platform all the spots where you love to sit and smoke when no one is looking. The best store to buy candy in the entire Midwest. The park where your kids and your friends' kids have almost worn out the playground equipment. The corner bar where you sometimes meet with an available friend for an afternoon beer on those days when everything seems really, really hard.

And one day when you climb up onto that platform you decide to stand on your tiptoes. You stretch your calves and dare to look past everything that is yours. Even after all you've done with the guns and the babies and the trips to the emergency room and the bad men and women you have looked in the eye—the view is terrifying. It is terrifying because very quickly everything familiar disappears. It is just the slightest difference. Just a few inches from the world you thought you knew. But it's as if you blink twice and the world changes and the view . . . the view is frightening. There are the disappearing shadows of the almost-adult people who were once your babies. The grown friends of your children who are off to college and the Navy and Europe, who once slept under your family room table and went to the bathroom in the garden when they thought you were asleep. There's your parents, who used to live twenty minutes away, now playing shuffleboard next to a lovely swimming pool in Florida, and two of your friends who went back to school when their kids left home.

You look and look, and what you are looking for is yourself.

There is no one to make cookies for. No one needs a ride. The dog and cat have decided it's time to go to the animal cemetery. Your husband is at a conference in Boise, and your youngest child is at a sleepover and the other two are about to leave the nest, and suddenly, because you ignored all the warning signs, there is no map for you to follow but the one you had years ago.

And when you drop back down, you go find that map. The directions are so clear, it is as if you just have to breathe and walk forward and you will know what to do.

And that is what Margo did.

That is why the mom is turning back into the manslayer.

"I have been in the process of slowly getting back to speed on specific cases and training when I can, because I still have kids at home and I am not going to dump them for my career," she explains with quiet conviction. "I don't want to wish away any of my time with them, and they're terrific, and they're going to continue to be terrific. My husband is behind me, but once I stood on that platform and looked around at my life I had to follow my heart again."

The women are leaning forward, almost bent at the waist. Margo's story is so sincere and lovely it's now impossible for them to be angry at her for being a secret agent.

She tells them that everything else they know about her is true. She did come to Florida to check on her parents, before she took the next step and beefed up her hours at the mysterious secret agency she works for. She is moving forward, but she is still torn and a little afraid too. And just like almost every other woman in the world who has an ambitious heart, steely talents, children, and a husband, she wonders if it will all be okay.

"I still have some hard years left with the kids, but I have to move on this now or everything changes," she shares. "There are still unspoken rules in life, and I turn forty in seven months."

Forty.

That year is so far behind Patti that she thinks she would go blind straining her eyes if she turned back to look.

"So how did you get looped into whatever the devil is happening here?" Nan asks her most pressing question first.

"I mean, did you just, like, stumble into this case?" Nan asks, obviously exhausted. "And now you're telling me that the man who tried to do whatever it is he was trying to do to me is not the guy you were looking for?"

"Yes and no."

Patti has sat as quietly as someone like Patti can sit without interrupting with the three hundred questions she is dying to ask. *How can we trust you?* is right at the top of the list. Plus, she knows this is far from over, even if they all split up and never find out if the other bad guy gets caught. There are legal issues involved. There might be a trial. There will without question be lawyers and press coverage. The fear of all of that agitates Patti and throws her backward in time so fast she feels as if she's fallen and smacked her head on the sidewalk.

Margo explains that she's kept abreast on all the active cases in her department. Yes, she knew that there was something very active going on in the Tampa area and even though she was lost with elderly exercises when she was visiting her parents, she was still notified that an operation that she cannot even name for them was close to busting open.

And she also knew that there was another agent at the hotel.

"Mr. Psychic Duffy?" Cathy guesses.

"Is he the one whose calls have that weird ring?" Even Patti knows Margo's kids would program a horrid rap tune or a baby screaming as their signature ring tone.

"It's the agency tone," Margo tells them, revealing more than she wants to.

"How does Holly fit in to this?" Patti is dying to know.

"And why aren't there news people crawling all over this place after what happened last night?" Cathy asks.

Nan pales. She never thought about that.

"All these government agencies might seem like a dysfunctional mess, but we really do cooperate and work on the same page and the media doesn't know yet," Margo explains patiently. "Nan's securities and fraud case is high-profile, but we have this other ongoing case, which I swear to God I would love to tell you about. But I can't. Not until I get permission or the investigation is over."

"Must be dangerous," Nan says. "Just breathing around you is dangerous, Margo."

Cathy laughs, very softly.

"I know right now this is hard for you to imagine or accept, Nan," Margo says, "but in so many ways it's a good thing that you dropped your phone in the toilet and that this group of women were all there at the same time."

Patti stares at her. Cathy looks away. Nan smiles.

And Margo rolls her shoulders, and to their astonishment suggests that they all take a nap. She's not certain how much more she can tell them without getting into trouble. And the lack of sleep is making her emotional. Margo is afraid she might say too much.

And the word "nap" seems to do the trick. Naps for Margo, Nan, and Patti are normally about as likely as a three-week spa vacation in the South of France. Cathy has taken more than her share of afternoon naps at hotels throughout the country and several foreign countries as well. But that is not the kind of nap Margo is now suggesting.

It's obvious everyone is exhausted because no one has noticed, or commented on, the reappearance of the cell phones.

Patti has simply reached into the kitchen drawer and set them on the counter. The women don't even know they were in Patti's suitcase and that she moved them back to the kitchen after they went to bed.

Not so suddenly, Nan is weary way beyond the physical, mental, and emotional strain she has endured during the past twenty-four hours. She really does want to lie down on the table, have someone throw a sheet over her, and sleep for three weeks. She's not sure she has the strength to walk to her room. It's the kind of tired that can actually make people fall down if they aren't careful.

When she lets her eyes close for just a second, her head bobs back and she sees a swirl of color that is like a fast-moving parade. There are faces and voices and a mingling of everything that she has fallen into and out of since she left the airport. Or maybe long before that.

Maybe long before she got on the plane to come to Florida and knew that she was very close to never going back. She had this idea while she waited in the airport bar in Chicago that maybe she would simply disappear. People do it all the time. Sooner or later someone would come looking for her when they discovered the financial time bomb her husband and his clients had ignited. She had already made copies of documents and cleaned off her hard drive and all the other small, seemingly inconsequential things people do before they find the exit sign.

And she really was serious about disappearing. She'd had her now almost obligatory three drinks before boarding the plane and was about to sign her bill when a young man walked in who looked a lot like her son. She felt her heart fly right toward the roof of her mouth, which she quickly shut so it wouldn't go anywhere.

Nan's estrangement from her son was probably just as much

her husband's fault as her own. The bickering and professional competition was not a healthy environment for a child. And her failings—Nan thought of them as failings—as a mother always seemed to be dangling right in front of her. Mothers are supposed to know what to do, how to keep the chaos of life from spreading over into every moment of a child's life. That she had not been able to do that was the biggest regret of her life, and she had absolutely no idea what to do about it.

This is what kept her from running away: the faint but possible notion that she could one day find a way to make that up to her son.

Nan would love to pull Margo aside and ask her how in the hell she balances the dangers of motherhood with the dangers of stalking horrid criminals. Nan can remember days when she had a hard time brushing her teeth, turning on *Sesame Street,* dressing, dropping off her son at daycare, and then driving to work.

Couple her feelings of failing as a mother with her recent mess of a professional life, and Nan may be one of the few true depressed menopausal candidates for Prozac.

And there's Margo now staring at her cell phone and looking just as tired as Nan feels. Margo, Nan thinks, needs to perform a counseling session with her like she needs to round up another bad cowboy.

Cathy has turned on the television before everyone gets up to take their naps just as cell phones start beeping with incoming text messages.

"The storm is slowing down," she informs everyone. "Take a look."

The skies are clearing. Airports are gearing up. Flights should be back to normal by mid-morning. There will most likely be text messages alerting them to their approximate departure times, but the local station warns that everyone needs to be back at the airport by late morning tomorrow, because traveling is going to be a mess.

From the looks on their faces, Nan isn't certain this is good news. It should be good news. The girls should be jumping for joy. But they're not. Nan figures it's the exhaustion. Either that or they have grown very fond of hotel life, squabbling, wild night adventures, and consuming as much alcohol as possible.

"That's it," Nan decides, clapping her hands, and struggling to her feet. "Margo's right. Everyone gets a time-out. Now. Go sleep for a few hours and then we can have dinner, and maybe Margo will let us question her some more."

They do not argue.

Patti falls into her bed in the living room. Nan drags her feet down the hall right behind Margo, and they both drop like stones into their beds, without saying a word. Cathy leaves the bedroom door open just a crack so Holly will know it's okay to come inside, and slips into bed.

And when Holly does return an hour later, she is amazed—and more than a little befuddled—that the suite at first appears empty. She closes the door, walks forward, then notices Patti asleep on her pullout bed. She tiptoes down the hall, sees the closed door to Margo and Nan's room, and then peeks in to see that Cathy is either dead and not moving, or deeply, deeply asleep.

Darn it. Equally as exhausted as her suitemates, but eager to talk, Holly decides to sneak into her own room and flop into bed.

She has absolutely no idea how she is going to tell her suitemates what has just happened to her.

And no idea what in the world she is going to do about it.

fifteen

During the three hours and twenty-six minutes the women in suite 6502 are napping, the most delicious, beautiful, summerlike Florida weather descends onto the beaches right outside their closed windows.

The sun finally takes command, as it should, pushing back the last of the storm clouds. Within an hour, the temperature is a lovely eighty-three degrees, the sapphire blue waves are lapping sweetly against the golden sand, seagulls and pelicans are so relieved to be able to fly again, they are actually singing. And Patti Nuttycombe, Margo Engelstrom, Cathy Girard, Nan Telvid, and Holly Blandeen—to a woman—are snoring so loudly they couldn't hear a wave if one smacked them in the face.

This is what it was supposed to be like the past four days. The stranded women had all planned to sit on the beach, swim, drink copious amounts of rum-laced beach drinks and look at the legs of eager and very tan cabana boys.

They hadn't planned on bonding.

They hadn't planned on stalkers or monsters carrying weapons.

Cathy wakes up first and cannot remember where she is. She jerks awake and sees the white-speckled ceiling, a beige wall, the drooping sheets of another bed, and someone's foot dangling off the edge.

Shit.

It takes a few seconds for her to shake off that groggy, drunk feeling people have after they sleep when they should not be sleeping. It's as if she's just waking up the day after an all-nighter, in yet another hotel room, with yet another someone. And that feeling she knows too well of wanting to grab her clothes and run out the door.

But this time it is not like that. This time the stranger is Holly. Cathy does not want to run. She wants to stay. She wants to make sure everyone is okay, which may be the reason for her odd feeling, considering she is not known as the Queen of Comfort and Abiding Love.

It takes her a good five minutes to make sure she will be able to stand when she puts her feet on the floor. When she finally does, and hears her stomach growl as if she's just coming off a ten-day fast, she quietly slips past Holly, closes the door behind her, and moves toward the kitchen. She has to flip on a light in order to see the clock by the stove and is shocked to see that it is way past seven p.m. When she turns to look out the window, she sees the last burst of a sunset that was probably absolutely magnificent.

Shit.

She dials room service while she pulls open the fridge to

check on the beer and wine. If she's hungry, she knows her temporary roommates are going to be ravenous. While she waits for the food, Cathy decides to throw open all the windows and to step outside.

The balcony is dry and must have been sun-drenched for hours, because the cement floor is hot and, for the first time in days, dry. And the view is astounding. Cathy watches the sky bleeding dozens of shades of red and pink, and cannot move. She thinks she should go wake everyone up so they can see the sunset. But if she leaves, she will miss it.

And as she's trying to decide what to do, Holly comes stumbling toward her. Cathy stretches out her arms because she isn't certain Holly is even awake. Holly is rubbing her eyes, and Cathy thinks she may flip right over the side of the balcony if she keeps going.

"Wow," Holly exclaims. "It's absolutely beautiful. And I slept through most of it."

"A little bit is better than nothing," Cathy assures her. "I was going to go wake everyone up, but it would have all been over by the time I got everyone out here."

"Everyone else is still sleeping?"

"Looks that way. I'm starving, so I ordered some pizza and drinks."

Holly turns her head away from the beach, and then without thinking or asking if it's okay, sweeps her hand around Cathy's hair.

"What are you doing?"

"I thought I saw something," Holly says. "I'm sorry. Maybe it was just a wild loose hair."

"That's okay," Cathy says. "That's what women do, I guess."

When they tiptoe back inside, thinking Patti will still be

asleep, Patti is up and in the bathroom. Cathy decides they had better wake up Nan and Margo. If they sleep much longer, they will be up all night. After everyone staggers to the kitchen and the food arrives, there is a feeding frenzy around the table.

They've just attacked the pizza when Margo's phone rings. It's the not-so-pleasant ring of someone she must work with—a loud, shrill sound that not even Patti could turn into a song. Margo swears. Gulps down her slice and takes the phone into the bedroom.

And she stays there for a very long time.

Long enough for Patti to all but order Holly to start talking and fill in the space of time from the moment she left the suite until she returned and found them sleeping.

Long enough for Cathy to start staring at Nan again.

Long enough for Nan to realize again that her life as she knew it four days ago no longer exists.

Holly looks confused, weary, and wary. And she says she kind of wants to wait until Margo gets back, because she needs to make certain she's not losing her mind.

"She probably knows most of what you're going to tell us already," Nan says. "She's a government agent and she's just starting to get back into it full-time. She told us the whole story when you were out."

"So it's all for real?"

"What does that mean?" Cathy asks, finally taking her eyes off Nan.

"The agent stuff and the psychics working with them and Duffy being an agent and—"

Patti cuts her off by first putting out her hand and then simply asking her to start at the beginning. "We are just waking from comas, dear. Slow and from the beginning," she commands. "We don't want to miss a thing."

Patti doesn't know the name of the song she suddenly starts hearing inside her head, but it is something a marching band would play to get everyone revved up and excited. What else could happen? Maybe Holly was abducted by aliens on her way downstairs with Mr. Psychic. Patti's had so much weird excitement during the past four days, she's planning on checking her bank statements when she gets near a computer to see if she can retire early so she doesn't have to travel and run into strange women.

No one has really guessed what might have been going on with Holly, and what she tells them makes them all set down their glasses and bottles.

Apparently, Holly has the potential to be some kind of psychic genius. She tested out-of-orbit on some exam when she was a young girl and her parents had taken her to see a specialist, who asked them to enroll her in a special program for children who have certain gifts.

Gifts, meaning psychic ability that can be developed and used in positive ways as a child grows into an adult.

Duffy, Holly told them, had paperwork. Copies of the tests and the other exams that her parents allowed her to take, and then one final paper with a note in her mother's handwriting.

We want our daughter to have a normal childhood and life. There would be nothing normal about growing up as a human guinea pig and being dragged around from one scientist to another. We understand this may be for the good of society, but as parents we have decided to do what is best for our daughter.

When Margo walks back into the room, everyone else is so engrossed in Holly's fascinating story that no one notices her.

"So I didn't go into the special program," Holly tells them. "I didn't even know about how I'd scored on the tests. Or that someone was assigned to occasionally check on my progress in life." Or the hope they had expressed that one day she would address her innate psychic abilities herself, maybe talk to her parents, maybe reach out to someone else who had similar abilities.

Abilities such as knowing things without question and being able to touch someone and know things about them they have never told you or maybe anyone else. Abilities that went beyond simple kindness and understanding and listening. Abilities that allow you to look at the world and the people in it in ways that other people cannot. Abilities that stretch into the past and future so that you can sense actions, intent, secrets of the heart.

And the person who was assigned to check on her abilities was Mr. Psychic Duffy, who had almost fainted when she walked into the hotel three days ago. He'd been so stunned by her arrival that he'd made the horrid mistake of walking straight up to her and saying hello. And one of the things he admitted to her when they talked today was that he had studied her and her life so much he was, well, attracted to her.

This is when Margo stops Holly.

"That's not normal protocol, by the way," she explains. "Duffy should have passed your file off to someone else, but other things were going on, and Duffy is really aces, and then we were all stranded here anyway," she shares, rambling in a way that proves she is also on edge. "I can tell you that the government has used and continues to use psychics in special cases," Margo tells them. "They help in murder cases, espionage, locating lost babies, whatever might help someone. It's really just a coincidence that I am here and Holly is here when they are having a legitimate convention."

Holly looks at Margo and says she thinks there's more to it.

"I'm thinking they had the convention here because of something ongoing. Something the psychics tried to warn us about when we got here," she says.

"Did Duffy tell you that?" Margo snaps.

"Absolutely not. I just figured it out."

"Or maybe your psychic heart has finally been kick-started," Nan suggests. "Maybe you just know it because you know it."

Margo shrugs. "I suppose the secrecy doesn't matter anymore. Holly is right. Duffy's case has been active for two years and has affected lots of people, mostly women, and they thought they would have a convention here and see if they could crack the damn thing open."

"And one other thing that is like a miracle," Holly adds. "I think my brain tumor is really this psychic stuff. I may be cured."

"What brain tumor?" Nan asks, bewildered. Margo looks totally confused, because this is also the first time the brain tumor has been discussed in front of her.

"You weren't here when we talked about it," Holly tells Nan. "I convinced myself that I had a brain tumor because of these weird feelings I always have. It's been driving me crazy."

"So now you know there is nothing wrong with you, Holly," Patti says, smiling. "It's the start of your new life."

Holly tells them she has absolutely no idea what she is going to do with the information she has. It's all sort of hovering an inch or so above her, she says, and when she looks up to make sure she's not dreaming, all she sees is a descending cloud of indecision.

Duffy has offered to mentor her, and he wants her to come to Washington, D.C., to take part in a two-week program where she will meet with other men and women who are involved in helping people in the same way she could be.

"It totally explains my weird feelings," Holly says. "I sort of do this work already every single time someone sits in my chair, or I hear a phone ring before it actually does, or when I look at someone and can see something that I just always assumed other people can see too."

Cathy cannot bring herself to make eye contact with Holly. She's not the only one. All of the women, even Margo, are wondering exactly how astute Holly's gifts are. And what she can see now that she realizes she can see so much.

"You know, I almost went to the other restroom," Holly says suddenly, as if she did indeed read their minds.

"What?" All four of them say this at the same time.

"In the airport. I was going to go to the restroom on the other side of where I was supposed to board. But for some reason I walked toward the restroom you were in instead."

Silence.

"And if I hadn't, I would never have met you, and come to this hotel, and, well, you all know the rest. I'm just so thankful to all of you. To each one of you."

More silence.

It's as if someone has stuck an invisible vacuum under the door and sucked out all of the air. Holly could end up being the next great medium. She's young and smart. She's likable. And she hasn't even discovered half of the woman she can be. Holly's suitemates are witnessing a lovely transformation.

Margo, the manslayer, knows she should step up and say something. But she also knows that if Holly decides to follow her newly discovered path, it won't always be easy. It won't always be safe either. But it will give her something she has never had before. What could happen to Holly would be profound, exhilarating, and heart-wrenchingly challenging in ways that even Margo cannot explain.

Sometimes it's just better not to know things. It's easier to never get on top of that platform and stand on your tiptoes and see beyond the top of the trees and into tomorrow. It's sometimes easier to stay where you are and to stop thinking there is a better view if you climb higher. And if you stop and think about it, and look at your life, it is lovely and pure and fine just the way it is.

Isn't it?

So when Holly thanks them, Margo tries very hard to mingle her two selves. If she were simply being a mother, she would grab Holly and cradle her in her arms and say, "Oh, honey." She would then hold her tightly and whisper softly into her ear so that Holly would know everything will be all right, everything will be just fine. Instead she puts her hand on Holly's shoulder, brushes her lips across the wisps of Holly's sleep-mangled hair, which she would never do if she was simply Margo the manslayer, and says, "Holly, the pleasure has been all ours."

Patti jumps up without saying a word, grabs the wine, and starts to open it.

"Holly, do you know we're leaving in the morning?" Nan isn't sure, because of all the psychic excitement, if Holly knows their forced incarceration at the hotel is about to end.

"Right now, I'm not sure if that's good news or bad news," Holly says.

For a few moments there is nothing but the rustle of plates being pushed aside and corks popping and cardboard pizza boxes being folded so they can be stuck into the trash can. Patti pours wine into all of the glasses and then says it's time for a toast. And only Patti knows she is struggling to come up with something to say. These women have hit her right across the face and they don't even know it.

"To phones in the toilet," she finally says, raising her glass.

"To the phones!" everyone responds as they clink glasses and try not to make eye contact.

Again there is silence. Blessed silence, when five minds wander in five separate directions. The air turns almost electric with the stillness of it all. No one is moving and the glasses of wine are all paused just inches below lips that you would think have so much to say out loud. Because so much has happened.

If an outsider would happen to look in through the window, it would appear as if the women have all been turned to stone. In truth, none of them can actually figure out what they are supposed to be celebrating. Nan's confession? Margo's ability to kick the shit out of bad men? Holly's secret gifts coming to light? It's as if all the pieces of their lives have been tossed into the air and a once-in-a-lifetime wild breeze is keeping everything afloat.

Ironically, none of these women is thinking about what is going to happen tomorrow when they get to the airport, or when they get home and try to resume their lives, or what is left of their lives. Margo's family has already gotten used to these lapses in her communication. Patti's agent won't bother her until he needs money or somebody calls with a gig. Nan's husband is probably fleeing to Brazil. Cathy can't bring herself to think of the succession of calls, liaisons, cover-ups, and missed meetings she has to confront.

And Holly, she has tapped into some kind of new thought pattern that has her moving forward so fast it's a wonder she can keep her glass in her hand. It's as if she's finally been given permission to think the way she has been supposed to think all along. A faucet the size of a beer keg has been opened up inside of her and she hardly knows what to say or do first. Her mind has turned into a pinball machine the size of Texas and she's having a hard time keeping track of where the ball is headed next.

The silence is almost deafening and quickly becomes very uncomfortable. And even though the women could go downstairs to the lobby or walk on the beach or discover that the tiki bar has reopened and all of the drinks are free, no one even thinks of leaving the room.

Or speaking.

Or digging deep to say something meaningful and lovely about the past four days.

Or admitting that they are on overload and have no idea what should happen next.

Finally, when the stretch of silence turns awkward, Nan simply wonders out loud if there is enough wine to get them through the next couple of hours.

Patti turns slowly toward her and swears to God she hears a choir singing "Silent Night." Maybe it's because that's what Patti thinks she is longing for. A silent night. The lively hum of her about-to-die refrigerator. The man in the apartment next door coughing. The bark of the dog across the street that must have the largest German shepherd bladder in California, unless he has trained himself to pee in the toilet, because they rarely take the poor canine outside. Horns honking for absolutely no apparent reason on the busy street a block away.

And then Holly finally says it.

"Margo," she starts out slowly, "I think I know something."

Margo isn't really sure she wants to know what that something is, but they have come this far. It's a definite "what the hell" moment. And how could she ever restrain herself from asking, "What?"

"I think I know who you are looking for," Holly reveals.

"Really," Margo responds, but everyone else could have said the same thing because it's what they are all thinking.

Holy crap.

Holly starts to feel her heart accelerate. This is something that has happened to her before, but she's always dismissed it as some weird reaction to plastic, or hair spray, or, of course, the tumor. She couldn't keep silent now if someone held a gun to her head.

Patti wishes there was some popcorn. This is the best movie she has ever seen.

Holly sits back down. All of this is new. She's never just let her thoughts come to her without interrupting them. She's never had anyone—so many anyones—hang on her words like this. And believe her.

When she was a little girl, she always knew when people, even her parents, were lying. She knew when she was not invited to birthday parties, and when someone called everyone else to come over but not her. When she got older she always stopped herself from saying things like "Stay home tonight" when she knew a friend should do just that to remain safe, or "of course he is cheating." She'd wanted to tell about fifty people not to get married and she wanted to tell herself many things also.

And now she wants to tell Margo that the one man, the main man, that she and her colleagues are looking for is very close. He might even be in the hotel. Because he knows it is full and that lots of people are stranded here and it's prime for what he wants and needs to do.

Holly looks around and does not feel foolish for anything that she's said. But still, she needs a slice of reassurance. She needs that half manslayer, half mom thing from Margo again.

"It's okay if I just, you know, talk like this?" she asks, as if she is going to confession. "I think it might be important."

"It's okay, Holly," Margo reassures her.

That's not good enough for Holly. She looks first to Patti and then to Cathy and then Nan.

"Is this, like, too weird?"

"No," they all say at once.

And without even noticing it, they all raise a hand to that

universal spot where people of every place and purpose in the entire universe think that emotions live and grow.

Right over the heart.

Just to the right side of the left breast.

Near the spot where life pounds and pumps and keeps them all connected.

And then Holly tells them.

First she closes her eyes so she can describe what she is seeing, who she is seeing. What she sees crosses borders and involves so many, many people. There is darkness everywhere and money changing hands and she is trying so hard to see through the blind corners of her own mind.

Margo gently guides her. She tells her to look for faces. Right now the most important things to watch for are the faces.

And Holly sees several. Her descriptions are exactly what Margo is looking for, and Margo flips open her phone and shows Holly a series of photographs that she has stored in it.

"They're here," Holly reveals. "I know these people are all here."

"You're sure?"

"This is all new, you know," Holly admits. "But either I actually saw them when I was in the halls walking with Duffy or they are on their way or already here in a room or something. I think they have a room. Maybe more than one room."

Cathy cannot help herself. She must speak.

"But if these are the people everyone is looking for—well, the FBI is looking for anyway—wouldn't they stay away from the hotel?"

"Hotels are where they do most of their business," Margo responds. "Besides, only a few agents here know what they look like. That wouldn't stop them."

"What the hell are these bad people you keep talking about

involved in?" Patti wants to cut through everything and just find out what the big secret is all about.

Margo hates this part. Technically, it's her choice whether or not she wants to reveal details of the case.

And it's a case she simply fell into because she was staying at the Rivera where the operation is based. In her first phone call when they first arrived, Margo learned what was happening, and why the psychic convention was scheduled for the Rivera.

It's an ongoing investigation and it's of international scope. At this point knowing more about the actual case, and not just her newly recognized psychic powers, might help Holly. Revealing some details of the operation probably won't matter now and Margo feels she owes it to all of them. After all, these women ran through the storm to save Nan.

"It's an international slave market," she finally tells them. "There is a group of men who coerce women into everything from prostitution to drug running by promising them money and citizenship."

"Here? In this part of Florida?"

"It's perfect here because of the high tourist rate, boats can come and go at all hours of the day and night, and there are tons of immigrants who move here because of the climate and, well, because there are so many low-paying jobs."

She also tells them this operation is the largest one her unit, the FBI, and immigration officials have ever uncovered. It involves multiple managers and housing locations. Some of the women are forced to work at strip clubs and become prostitutes. They are guarded every hour of every day. Their handlers tell the women that they're "holding" their wages until the women earn enough to pay for their citizenship papers, but that day never comes.

"And there are houses where the women are kept, some of

them quite lovely from the outside, all up and down this side of Florida," Margo explains. "The only thing is, no one ever leaves. We think some of the women may have been murdered, but we can't confirm that because so many are illegal and there is no record of them."

"So, what are the mechanics of the scheme?" Nan asks. "The men in charge come to places like this and work the bars and businessmen and conventions and then keep moving?"

"Exactly. The ring leaders have so many women—and girls, I might add—working for them, and they can arrange it so the same girls never even go back to the same hotel."

"It sounds huge," Patti agrees. "It will come as no surprise that I've known a few pimps and bad guys in my time, but almost all of the women I knew were not coerced."

"This is not like that," Margo responds quietly. "It's horrible, and we are very close to shutting them down, but we have to do it all at once so no one escapes, and so we can keep these women and girls safe."

Holly's mouth has dropped open as if there is a weight sitting on top of her bottom lip. Duffy only talked about her psychic gifts, not actual cases.

"So this is the kind of stuff Duffy was talking about that people like him do to help?"

"Exactly," Margo tells her.

"But what if I'm wrong about the people I see or the feelings I have?"

"Sometimes that happens. Sometimes we go running blindly into the night when we get a tip from someone on the team."

"That's *our* job," Nan says, which makes everyone laugh and gives both Margo and Holly a chance to take a breath.

The mere thought of running around in the dark again gives them all, even Margo, the shivers. Last night was the first time in a while that she's chased bad men, and although she's secretly missed the dangerous aspects of her job, she's felt as if steering her children through life is about as dangerous as anything she's done with a gun in her hand.

"Now what?" Holly asks, while she shakes her head to see if the images of the men she has seen will disappear. They don't.

"If it's okay with you, I'd like us to go down right now and talk to Duffy so you can tell him exactly what you see and feel," Margo suggests, softly, when she really wants to yell it, because every moment is important. "It won't take long. The guys with the guns will be doing the hard part from here on in. Duffy will want more details. He will help you with that."

Holly knows it would be absolutely ridiculous to say no. She's already stepped so far out of her box, she figures it would be invisible if she turned around and tried to see it.

It's already close to ten p.m. when Margo and Holly wave from the door as if they are going out on a date and Margo promises to have her little protégé back within an hour at the most.

"We'll extend curfew just this once," Nan jokes. "But don't forget your phones, for crying out loud. Call if you're going to be late."

Both Margo and Holly laugh, turn away from the phones, and leave without taking them. Holly has no one to call and Margo can use Duffy's equipment.

Cathy hasn't said a word for a while. She has, however, managed to finish not just her wine but the glass Margo never drank and half of the glass Holly left behind.

Patti is about to ask her why, when, without warning, Cathy walks up to Nan and says, "Nan, I know this is probably totally out of line, and the worst possible thing you need to hear right now, but I just have to tell you this or I'm going to die."

Nan blinks twice and waits.

"I had an affair with your husband."

Patti almost chokes on the wine that is in her mouth, runs to the sink to spit it out, and then grabs the bottle sitting by the sink and drinks what is left without even putting it in a glass.

sixteen

One night away from a full moon and the white sand in front of the Rivera looks like a glimmering postcard. It is so bright that the day's legacy of footprints still lingers on the beach. Here and there brave—and most likely drunk—visitors stumble back where they came from after hours of celebrating the return of life as they know it.

Patti sits down very slowly on the balcony floor and dangles her feet like she did just days ago. It seems like years. Years and tears and dozens of other tangible and not-so-tangible things have passed around, through, and in her since that night.

And while she sorts them out, without much success, she looks at the long tendrils of moonlight and remembers the nights, so long ago now, when she would slip through the house with her siblings to escape their father.

Sometimes they would run for blocks to the end of the long street where they lived, to where there were no houses or lights, and where they would stop running under a moon like the one tonight.

Her sister always told her the moon rays were grace from God. God was up there, her sister was certain, and Patti loved to race through the streaming light, because she thought it would make her holy and pure and all her sins would be forgiven.

As if a child could have sins. How could that be? She's never stopped wondering this, and wondering why other people think it could be true, and she does all she can to resist the urge she always has on nights like this to run like a little girl through the lightness of the night.

How absolutely perfect to have such moonlight this night, especially when so many women in this suite have bared their souls. What a bonanza of emotional melodies! So many that Patti has been at a loss for a song to enter her mind since Cathy told Nan she'd had an affair with her husband and Nan started laughing.

Laughing!

Now that Patti is alone and has a chance to think about it, laughing was probably the perfect response. Really, after everything else that has happened to Nan during the past few days, knowing her husband is even more of a jerk than she thought he was is kind of a lovely gift.

Nan hadn't been shocked, or hurtful toward Cathy, though Cathy looked as if she was braced for it. Ready to have Nan slap her or scream or all the other things most other women would have done. But Nan didn't do that. She told Cathy she didn't really care anymore—and then she told them a hilarious story that went way back to her college days when her friends in business school would get frustrated with professors or stupid internships or the system in general. They would say, "Fuck 'em and feed 'em beans," Nan said calmly, and in a way that was not how many would respond if told the same thing.

"I hope you have beans, Cathy," Nan said, looking right at her. "And if you have any extra, please give me a can or two because I have lots of people who are going to need beans."

That was the beginning of a very long conversation that really did not include Patti. She listened, but her mind went traipsing off into her own world as the two other women discussed love and loss in a way that should have been recorded. Cathy first explained how she and Nan's husband had met and where they went and how many times it happened, in a singsong voice that sounded almost as if she had memorized a speech. And maybe she had.

Maybe Cathy had been thinking about what she was going to say for days and, finally, when it was so close to the end, she simply had to get it out. Maybe she was scared that she might be called to testify in about three years when Nan's husband went to trial with the rest of the crooks he associated with and his trail of infidelity and what she might or might not know about his business would finally be uncovered.

But it seemed as if she really wanted to clear the air. To say especially that one word, *sorry*. And this is when Patti thought for sure she would be roused by a song. But nothing came to her, which was an amazement in itself, and then Nan started to talk.

It was as if a moderator said, "All righty, then, Nan, now you go." And that's what Nan did. She detailed a marriage that had gone sour almost before it had ever begun, and all her assumed failings as a mother, and how she could have predicted almost everything that has happened—except maybe all these women in one spot and the bad people running around and Holly being a psychic whose brain tumor had turned into a psychic gift.

And Cathy just sat there and nodded. It was surreal. Patti kept pouring wine, wondering if either of them would even remember the conversation. She also wondered what they were really thinking. How lovely to have a tunnel right into their minds.

And hearts.

And then Holly and Margo came back and reported that Operation Rivera was now hitting full stride.

Margo couldn't tell them anything much beyond that, but, apparently, Holly had been sent out to sit in the hall numerous times while top-secret phone calls were made. In the end, Margo and her cohorts were certain Holly was right about this particular hotel and the men who were somewhere inside it selling the bodies of frightened young women.

Finally, it was well after one a.m. and Margo went into the bathroom, turned on the fan so no one would hear her, and made some phone calls to her office while Nan, Holly, and Cathy flopped into bed. Patti knew she would never be able to sleep. She was still searching for a song. And she was about as befuddled about her lack of success in doing that as she'd ever been about anything in her life.

That's why Margo found her on the balcony, feet dangling. Patti didn't hear her arrive, but was so happy to smell her cigarette smoke that she almost teared up.

"Want one?" Margo asked, joining her.

"I may eat it," Patti confessed, sticking out her hand.

"Sweet hell, it's beautiful out here," Margo exclaimed, as if it was the first time she had ever seen an almost full moon on the beach.

"Beats what we've been looking at, doesn't it?"

Margo is the kind of tired that makes people want to lie down wherever they are when it first hits them. In the center of the railroad tracks. In the middle of a parking garage. On top of the restaurant bar. Next to the microphone stand onstage. In the women's restroom right in front of the first stall.

Her eyes ache from lack of sleep, concentrating so hard, and chasing criminals. The long muscles in her legs and arms are quivering from the hours of focusing, and she's spent almost an entire day without candy.

She tells Patti that she thinks she's so tired because her heart hurts.

"Your heart hurts?"

"Yes. Doesn't your heart ever hurt?"

"You mean like a physical hurt?"

"Yes and no. Like someone you love or care for did something you cannot even fathom at the same moment you went jogging and are out of breath. So it hurts both ways."

Patti knows she is supposed to be honest now. She's supposed to say that she saw two hurting hearts the entire time Margo was gone with Holly. She's also supposed to be honest and say that her heart has hurt so much and continues to hurt so much, she doesn't even notice it anymore.

Instead, she takes a puff on the horrid cigarette and can actually feel her heart accelerate—so at least she knows she's alive. That kind of physical hurt makes lots of sense to her.

And then she asks Margo if she got a chance to see the Body Worlds exhibition that has been floating around the country from city to city for years. Margo has seen it and she also forced all three of her kids and her husband to see the exhibition, which is a marvelous modern educational display of bodies. Bodies preserved in all their anatomical glory so that visitors can see tendons, veins, the magnificent inner workings of a human being in a way that has never before been seen or shared except in medical laboratories.

"I was absolutely astounded by the heart," Patti shares quietly. "It's the size of a fist. So many possibilities. I walked through the exhibit by myself for hours and I kept imagining who belonged to the hearts I saw. Who had these hearts loved?"

"It's amazing how we always equate the heart with love," Margo agrees.

"I suppose most people get caught up in the mechanical workings of the body parts when they see something like that. But I couldn't get beyond the heart."

"I came away thinking the human body is an amazement of creation. It's like a whole world is there, right inside of every single body."

Patti hesitates. This would be when something like the lyrics from "Heart and Soul" would normally flood into her mind. Or maybe it would be a ridiculous love song about two people who meet, five minutes later fall in love, screw each other's brains out, break up, and then cry.

But instead she cannot get her mind off the heart.

She asks Margo if she thought about the actual people whose body she was seeing when she was viewing the exhibit. Margo admits that she was in manslayer form that day and looked at everything from a clinical perspective. Plus, she'd been busy moderating all the questions from her children.

"I cried," Patti confesses. "That's a pretty big deal for me. And then I kept wondering what my heart would look like if I had lived a different life."

"The physical heart? Or the one you wear on your sleeve?"

Patti turns for the first time since the two women have started talking and looks into Margo's eyes. "It's the same to me, I guess. That's what was so startling about the entire experience."

Margo resists the urge to reach over and put her arms around Patti. The older woman is outgoing and fun and seems generous enough, but the heart she is talking about does not have a *Come On In* sign on it.

This is not exactly the conversation she thought she would be having when she headed out onto the balcony for a smoke. Her hesitancy makes her think about her own heart. She's been so busy guarding the life and limbs of her three children, of the schoolkids at the health room where she works, and all the potential victims she tries to help and protect, there isn't much time left for anything else.

It's been a long, long time since she's thought about her own heart. And what would her kids and husband say about the status of her heart? Is she cold or warm? Do they see her as the kind of mom who snaps too quickly or is always easy and eager to listen? Has she done enough for them? For her friends? For her own parents?

Patti shakes her head as if that will help her return to the lost page in her mind where she usually resides. "Maybe I'm just tired. I mean, look at what we have all been through the past few days. Maybe I'm terrified that something else is going to happen before we get on the planes."

"Something else is always going to happen."

"You're right. I'm older than you are by a long shot. That's something most women figure out when they're pushing fifty. You got here early."

"So how is your heart right now?"

Patti shrugs. It's so light outside, Margo can see how often Patti hesitates before she answers a question, how she nervously flicks her cigarette ash. She lets Patti swallow what she has asked her and turns her head back to watch the waves repeating themselves over and over again.

There is something absolutely narcotic about swaying repetition. Waves. Flames from a fire. Dancers. Wind in the trees. Birds on the wing. Margo knows hypnosis springs from these kinds of moments and she also knows that it works. There's a mess of people on Duffy's side of the building who use the technique all of the time. She knows too if she looks at the waves much longer she's going to fall right off the balcony. It's going to take her more than a day to recover from something that started out as a visit to see her hilarious parents and ended up in massive mayhem.

"You don't have to answer me," she finally tells Patti.

"Well, I would answer you if I knew."

"Oh."

"I think maybe I should have been looking at the heart differently all these years. It's just that my vision from the stage has impaired me."

"That's why God invented bifocals."

"Yes, but you have to be willing to actually wear them."

Margo wonders if Patti, who could probably still win a college drinking contest, isn't a little tipsy. She and the other girls sloshed down almost all of the wine while Margo was gone with Holly. Couple that with lack of sleep, stress, anxiety, mostly crappy food, and whatever else everyone is carrying around that they have not yet revealed, and someone should call the paramedics.

But when she turns from the waves, Patti looks beyond sober. She's so serious she's even stopped flicking her ashes.

"I've spent a little time thinking about all of our hearts, and I've given them names."

"What?" This doesn't sound like Patti. Maybe the waves have already claimed her and she's in some kind of trance.

"Oh, hell, I know it sounds ridiculous and this is probably why I haven't been able to embrace a song tonight. But hearts— it's all I can think of."

Margo wishes there was more than half a bottle of wine left.

"Someone must have poisoned me," Patti continues flatly. "I can't believe I'm even talking to you about this."

"I'm a secret agent. Everything is safe with me."

It would be so easy for Patti to get up now and go back inside, because it's what's she's always done and it's what she would do if she wasn't flat-out exhausted. She feels as if she's done back-to-back shows in twelve cities. She looks behind her to make sure everyone else is in bed, and that's when she decides to hell with embarrassment. To hell with not thinking out loud. To hell with worrying that even Margo might think she's lost her last handful of marbles.

And so she turns her head back toward the waves and continues her discussion.

Nan, she starts out slowly, has a *Heart of Change*. Every single thing about Nan's life is about to move in a new direction, nothing will ever be the same and she couldn't stop any of it if she tried. She may even end up throwing away those fuck-me heels she was wearing the first time they all met in the restroom, and Patti isn't even sure if Nan will ever get a cell phone again.

Cathy's *Heart of Deception* glows in the dark, Patti says. She hops from bed to bed and man to man and wings her way through life as if she is hanging on to a swinging door. The person Cathy deceives the most, however, is Cathy. She's not totally emotionally ruthless; otherwise, she wouldn't have told Nan about her affair with Nan's husband. That was a gift, really. Any half notions Nan may have clung to about her marriage and her man were bowled into the gutter when Cathy came clean. The one thing no one can know is if she did it for herself or if she did it for Nan.

Margo wants to light up another cigarette but she's afraid she might miss a word. She hasn't bothered to think about what Patti will be saying about her heart. She's totally absorbed in what she is hearing from the untouchable torch singer from California.

Holly is so easy. Her *Heart of Hidden Joy* is on the verge of bursting, Patti says. Holly's not just sweet, kind, and perceptive—she's mature in ways only women who have solid foundations and introspective minds can be. This young woman has barely touched on all her lovely talents. Watch her work, touch someone's hair, actually think before she speaks, or place her hands against the deep white lines of someone's forehead, and you can almost feel how happy she is now that her brain tumor evaporated and how happy she is going to be.

Margo, who has been busy trying to keep everyone from getting killed, had no idea that Patti was being so contemplative.

"There are two hearts left, Patti. What about mine?"

"Sure you want to know?"

"Are you kidding me? This is better than any movie I've seen in the past five years."

"You carry a *Heart of Loss*."

Margo is stunned.

"Want me to explain?"

"Absolutely."

Patti tells Margo that she could almost be a *Heart of Change*, like Nan, but because she is going back to something she loves so much, other things will be lost. Schedules will change and her children will have to adjust and there will be loss in all of that. But especially there is the loss of her babies. They are growing and going and so the only thing that will be left of this part of their lives before they all become adults will be photographs. The ones Margo always carries in her wallet and the ones she carries in her heart.

Now Margo is astounded. Of course she has thought of all of

this. Every mother alive thinks about loss and change on a daily basis when she is not trying to keep her head, and a mess of other heads, above water. Every mother knows that it's not just her life that will be affected by her return to work. And Margo's secretly kept tabs on all the moments that she might miss. All the things, places, people, and moments that will soon be covered in what Patti tells her is her *Heart of Loss*.

Quiet afternoons when her youngest daughter comes home from school and lies on the couch with her head in Margo's lap. The way the damn refrigerator bangs open and closed constantly when everyone is home at the same time. Her husband's growl when he can't figure out something on the computer and a child helps him find a solution. Her middle child languishing in front of the bathroom mirror and forgetting that she left the door open, so that Margo can see her and be reminded of exactly how it feels to be in so much despair about a pimple. Phone calls when someone forgets something and needs her to find it. Those ridiculous and forever memorable nights when she makes everyone, herself and her husband included, put on their jammies, get in the car, and go out for ice cream at the last real drive-in for three hundred miles. That absolutely lovely feeling when everyone is home and safe and the doors are locked and the house is clean and for just a few hours there is the scent of calm happiness everywhere she turns.

All of that.

All of that and so much more will be lost, but not really. Margo knows there will be new mileposts. The kids will step up and see their mother not as just an occasional waitress, chauffeur, and someone who takes care of them, but as a solid, whole, real person of value. Her husband will stop working so damn much and will have to be home to drive his own children to games and all the other activities that happen after school. She'll have a chance to see if her harping and yelling all these years about everything from making a bed to being polite has done any good.

"It's okay, you know," she tells Patti, breaking away from her own chain of thoughts. "Hearts can turn around on a dime. I think I'm in a good place."

Patti smiles and for a brazen moment acts as if she is simply going to get up and walk away.

"You are *not* leaving." Margo says this with a little more force than she means to. Sometimes the manslayer and the mother collide.

"Why?"

"There's a heart we have not yet addressed," Margo reminds her.

"Oh, go on." Patti acts like she is going to push Margo off the balcony.

"I'm serious. You can't just sit there and go on and on about everyone else. You have a heart too, Patti. I've seen it."

"Damn. You caught me." Patti is trying hard to deflect these questions, and to avoid what she knows is coming next.

"Well?"

"You tell me."

This is so easy Margo cannot believe it. All the miles and songs and stories and the empty spaces Patti has seen seem to be so obvious. All the people Patti watched when they were not watching her. The letters she must have received from her special, moon-loving sister and the ache she surely felt at the tip of her uterus when she realized she was never ever going to have babies. The nights driving home alone because there was no one to pick her up at the airport. The pull just below her stomach when she saw a woman her age running in a terminal to greet her grandchildren. Her dresser top littered with not one family photograph.

Margo has had her own quiet moments these past few days, albeit not many, when she has had fleeting thoughts of each of the women's lives. Beyond the part of her life that requires instant assessment, it has not been hard for her to figure out what it must be like when each one of them turns off the light at night before she goes to sleep.

And Patti's life especially calls to her. Maybe that's why the two of them are awake smoking cigarettes hours before dawn and talking about matters of the heart.

"Are you sure you want to know?" Margo asks Patti.

"Are you teasing me? You used to be so serious when we first met."

"You are almost always onstage and in control, Patti. And yet sometimes I think I could push you over with a feather."

Patti's first reaction is, of course, to say something she might say onstage to some wiseass who has had three gin and tonics and has decided to join her on the stage. But for the first time in a very long time she is not only without a song but just about to be beaten at her own game.

"I'm not really teasing you, Patti. I bet it's been a long time since you talked to another woman like this, like a friend."

Patti cannot answer her. Her lips and her obviously exposed heart are suddenly frozen solid.

Margo has to tell her. No matter how much it might hurt. She has to do this.

Patti's *Heart of Loneliness* cannot be disguised by her stage jokes or the way she sometimes stands back and shakes her head.

It is the soft place of comfort that Patti chose after she killed that man, after she balled up the cruelty of her father, the abandonment she felt from her family, all the people—and especially men—who betrayed her. It is a thin cloak of solitude that Patti used as an excuse to never allow herself to love, to have her own family, to be bold enough to take that one step forward that would finally break the last of the chains all those people who really do not matter anymore have placed around her ankles.

Margo isn't finished and Patti wishes to hell she was and that she had never had the last two glasses of wine and smoked the cigarette and peeled off that one layer of her heart that has now allowed Margo to see who she really is.

"The songs too," Margo says. "You have used songs to hide behind, Patti. And that is why they have suddenly disappeared."

Damn.

And then one cloud moves in the sky, sneaking across the dark blue background like a wild hungry cat, and it thankfully hides the stunned face of Patti C.

"Touché," Patti mumbles, pulling herself up by the balcony bars, and then all but running back into the suite.

Margo sits on the balcony alone, dangling her feet, and suddenly misses her husband and children so desperately it feels as if the pit of her stomach and her *Heart of Loss* are on fire.

seventeen

THURSDAY MORNING

If unspoken thoughts were visible, none of the women in suite 6502 would be able to move. The doors, windows, halls—every possible exit— would be blocked so that they would all be forced to communicate.

No one is talking. Holly is whistling in the shower, and that's what wakes up Patti. She's been in bed a mere five hours and now she pulls up her tangled sheet and blanket so that her entire head is covered. Maybe if she doesn't have to look at anyone it will be as if she's in the hotel room all by herself. She can get up in a little while, shower, pack, and then run out the door to catch a ride to the airport.

If only.

Things are about the same for Nan and Cathy, who have declared an unspoken truce and smile at each other in that fake kind of way where people turn up the edges of their mouths and don't even bother to expose their teeth.

Margo has been on and off the phone so many times she just paces around holding the phone because she knows it's going to ring again very soon. Between her kids, who are having some kind of crisis in the kitchen back home, and her fellow manslayers, she's one busy gal.

Heaven forbid the women should share a cup of coffee and talk about anything serious and possibly lovely before they depart.

Like what Holly plans to do with her newly discovered gifts and the lively man who helped her uncover them.

Like Nan not bothering to freak out when she found out that Cathy and her husband have been having an affair.

Like Cathy being uncharacteristically honest and then quiet. *Really* quiet.

Like Patti not being able to address the truth behind her *Heart of Loneliness* and the sudden disappearance of all the songs that usually keep her afloat.

Like Margo's secret life and all the untold stories about danger and death they could be sharing.

Like the shape of the day ahead of them and the one after that and the following month, when these absolutely unbelievable days in suite 6502 will be nothing but a blur of memories.

And lost time.

Lost time when not one of the damn things they thought they might be doing in a beachfront suite in Florida at the beginning of spring happened. No long walks in the warm sand or swimming out into the waves. No drinks around the tiki bar or doing the limbo around a campfire just as the sun sets. No fishing or flying off into the blue sky with a parachute hooked to your back as a boat pulls you through the air at fifty miles per hour.

The weight of what happened, and what didn't happen these past four days, is like an anchor that has everyone but the humming Holly moving in slow motion. Holly's bathroom music is way too perky for everyone but Holly, and there's a silent standoff to see which woman is going to tell her to shut up first.

No one can summon the energy to speak, but Holly's noise does help Nan drop her feet to the floor and move as if she is on drugs from the bedroom to the kitchen. Her first bright idea of the day is to see if there is enough coffee left to fill up five cups before they have to leave for the airport. On her way across the living room, even moving like an old snail, she bumps into Patti's bed, and falls on top of her.

"Jesus," Patti shouts.

"Sorry! I'm so sorry," Nan says. "I looked down and stumbled or something."

"At least you aren't whistling."

"No shit."

"What in the world is she so damn happy about?"

"She's young," Nan decides, now sitting on the edge of Patti's bed. "And she's probably got the hots for Mr. What's His Name. I'd be happy too if my imaginary brain tumor dissolved. Or maybe she's just so deliriously happy to be getting out of here, she can't help but burst into melody."

Just then Holly sticks her towel-covered head around the corner, grins, and says, "I can hear every word you're saying, girls."

Patti tugs the covers so far over her head, her feet are sticking out the bottom. Nan sighs. She can't remember where she was headed or what she was going to do before she fell on top of Patti. What she does remember, after a night of turning so many times in her bed she may as well have been a yo-yo, is her last conversation with Cathy.

Goddamn Cathy.

Part of Nan wants to be grateful because while her husband was apparently busy with Cathy and God knows who else, he didn't have time to notice that his wife was busy downloading his files, so she could share them with government investigators when she was trapped in Florida.

The other part of her, the part that always went to the wall for her girlfriends, is absolutely astonished. Infidelity is infidelity. That Nan understands. She understands zippers that never close and women who can't resist the challenge, or the temptation. She gets that some people are not happy and do not know how to walk away cleanly and clearly. What she doesn't get is how Cathy could act so nice at the airport bar and pour Nan's wine for four days, and open up a little bit more each day. And then tell her this dreadful thing. Just blurt it out like that.

One thing that does give Nan a great amount of satisfaction is knowing that her husband was just another of many notches on Cathy's belt. Nan now finds him so unattractive she cannot imagine ever again having a physical relationship with him, or actually wanting to be in the same room with him. She doesn't even want to look him in the eye when he is arrested, or whatever in the hell will now happen when he's rounded up with the rest of the financial hoodlums.

Cathy comes stumbling out as a horrid image of her naked with John spills into Nan's mind, and she has an urge to get up and slap Cathy across the face. Instead, she sits on her hands and drops backward so she is lying across Patti's feet.

"Someone is bringing up some rolls and more coffee," Cathy tells them. "I figured we'd all need as much coffee as possible, and a little something to eat before the airport."

"Thank God," Patti mumbles under her blankets. "When it comes, just pour it down my throat."

Cathy smiles, walks into the kitchen, and finds enough small hotel packets of coffee to start one pot while they wait for room service. Then Holly bounces into the kitchen looking like she just emerged from a happy winter-long hibernation.

"Didn't anyone sleep?" Holly asks when her sunny greeting is met with a chorus of snarls and grunts. "And is Patti dead or are her feet hot?"

"Why?" Nan imagines they all look as if they were dragged behind a race car. "Are you doing one of your new hocus-pocus things?"

"That's not nice, Nan," Holly fires back. "You all look so tired, and for some strange reason I feel like I just slept about one hundred hours. It's amazing."

"Well, honey, I'm just real happy for you."

Patti kicks Nan on the shoulder in a "shut up" gesture and Cathy simply turns away. She knows Nan has more than a few reasons to be cranky.

Meanwhile, Margo is gesturing with her free hand while she listens on the phone. She looks as if she's trying to conduct an orchestra that is way out of control. Holly finally figures out that she wants them to turn on the television, and she riffles through a pile of Patti's clothes, stacks of hotel magazines, and the dishes on the coffee table to find the remote.

"Watch the news," Margo mouths.

Patti turns to face the television, rolling over with a very loud groan as Nan shifts her weight to one side so Patti's feet are resting on her lap. Cathy hands Holly a coffee cup. They both stand in front of the TV while Holly keeps clicking to find the morning news. Margo stands, hand on hip, ear to phone. She looks like a hired guard.

And if someone slipped in and saw this moment they would think it was almost tender. They would decide that these women were old college roommates, or half of a book club, or a family reunion, or any one of several intimate gatherings of female friends or relatives. For a moment, before anyone can speak again, before Holly asserts her new perky self or Nan is a wiseass or Patti grumbles or Cathy says something with a sexual connotation or Margo mentions something about one of her children, there is a hint of calm expectation.

What in the world are they looking for on the television? Another storm moving in? More delays at the airport? Nan's destroyed phone has flushed itself out into the ocean and been picked up by a group of tourists from Brazil who are out fishing? What could possibly happen that has not already happened to this sodden group of female storm survivors?

Margo clicks her phone shut the very moment Holly stumbles across the morning news on the *Today* show. There's the adorable Ann Curry rambling first about the blue skies and the resumption of air travel from Denver to Detroit to Dallas and as far south as Miami and all along the East Coast where the spring storm finally died. When she shows film of groups of people snoozing in lounge chairs, on airport floors, and even one guy snoring on top of a bar at an airport, a loud cackle snaps them all awake.

"That could have been us." Nan laughs for the first time in twenty-four hours.

"Think of the damage we could have caused if we had slept in that bar across from the airport restroom for all these nights," Holly joins in.

And then Ms. Curry gets to the next story, and all of them—except Margo, who must be used to this kind of news—inhale so loudly it sounds like a massive wail of sorrow.

"Here's an amazing story out of Florida. An undercover government operation that has been active for several years launched a nationwide sting operation late last night that resulted in the arrests of more than one hundred people. Sources tell us that this international ring was based in the Tampa Bay area and that its ringleaders held hundreds of illegal immigrant girls and women in captivity by promising them green cards, housing, and food in exchange for their services. These women were being held as virtual slaves who were guarded twenty-four hours a day, forced into work as prostitutes, and never allowed outside except when they were going to work."

Curry pauses and video footage of several beautiful beach-front homes is shown. Then the camera flashes toward a group of men in handcuffs being led from a beach house to a police van.

"Authorities say the women were shown these lovely rented homes, but once inside they were forced to sleep on filthy mattresses, were fed barely enough to keep them alive, and were often subjected to severe beatings if they asked questions or tried to escape.

"Here's Jim Shultz, a special lead investigator with the FBI. 'In my thirty years in this business I have never seen anything like this. These women were slaves. Their living conditions were not fit for animals. It took an immense amount of work and coordination to make simultaneous arrests across the country without tipping off any of these criminals.' "

When the camera pans back to Curry it looks as if she's on the edge of tears.

"Amazing. Absolutely amazing that such a terrible thing could happen to women in this day and age."

Holly snaps off the television. Everyone turns to look at Margo, who is smiling as if she's just won the lottery.

"That's the good part about what we do," she shares. "And just think, you all played a part in this. You girls saved a lot of lives this week."

"We didn't do anything," Patti protests, finally rising up on one elbow. "Holly did her psychic thing. That's about it."

"Oh, that's so not true," Margo insists. "Running around the hotel, chasing that guy out into the storm, hanging in here when you could have been down in the restaurant with the rest of the hotel guests. You were all terrific."

"Then why do I feel so damn depressed?" Cathy wants to know.

"It's all those women," Nan says quietly. "I can't stop thinking about what it was like for them to live like that, to be so terrified, to wonder if they would be killed."

Everyone imagines then. They imagine women from Mexico and Cuba and Honduras gathered like hungry, wild bees and pulled into the promise of a real life by men who had absolutely no intention of ever paying them, helping them, or setting them free.

Women lined up like criminals on thin mattresses that were picked out of trash Dumpsters. Women who had photographs of their babies sewn inside of their blouses and who doubted they would ever see them again. Women forced into life as sex slaves, who wanted only to one day have a house with curtains, a yard, maybe even a refrigerator.

Women who cried in the dark and then reached out a hand to dry the weeping eyes of the woman next to her. A sister. A cousin. A woman just like her.

And all of them together trembling through one night and then another and absolutely afraid to run, because where would they go?

"It's the perfect trap," Margo says. "Those women had no place else to go. If they left and went to the authorities, they would be doomed in another way. Most of them would be deported. So they form bonds with the other women. They became this insane family where every dream is lost and all they want to do is breathe and not die. It became all about survival."

"I keep thinking about them turning to look at the ocean they can never touch," Holly shares. "And look," she goes on, pointing toward the window, "it was happening right out there."

Margo is quiet. All of the men and women she has helped suddenly surge forward at once in her head, and her heart skips a beat. She tries to catch her breath, drops her phone, and rests her hands on the edge of the table.

Cathy notices and reaches out to steady her.

"What's wrong?"

Margo closes her eyes and tells them that when she first stepped back from this job her dreams were filled with all the people she kept thinking needed her. Faces of abused children and women on the run and elderly couples bilked out of their retirement money. She said it had almost made her crazy.

"I wouldn't sleep, it seemed like for days, and that's when I started with the candy thing and that led to the sneaking-a-cigarette thing and then I tried to get even more lost in the life I was living," she tells them. "Gradually, those faces were replaced by the faces of everyone I did help. Internet porn stings. A huge narcotics case where little girls were carrying dope for their daddies. There's a shitload of sorrow out there, and knowing you have the power to do something about it is sort of addicting."

"Addicting?" Patti finds this word interesting.

"Addicting as in, I have to keep helping because it's something I'm good at, but I'm certain my husband would prefer me to sell Mary Kay cosmetics or work as an attorney or a nurse."

"Can you excuse yourself from the dangerous parts?" Holly asks.

"Yes. Most of the time. It's kind of an agreement I have with my husband and my kids. I want to make sure the kids grow up before I throw myself in front of a bullet."

"You better put down the candy and beef it up a little bit," Patti quips. "Your skinny little ass could use a little more meat on its bones."

"True, but my skinny little ass is also a small target to hit."

"Bravo, sister." Patti applauds, swinging her feet to the floor, totally amazed that they are all having a little morning slumber party.

There's a knock at the door and the coffee and rolls arrive. Patti is glad for the distraction so she can use the bathroom, and because she was terrified that everyone was just about to start singing "Kumbaya" while holding hands and kissing one another on the cheek.

From in the bathroom she can hear them mumbling with joy as they chow down on the sweet rolls. These women. Friends? Roommates? Strangers in the night? Haphazard shipwrecked and stranded travelers? Patti paws through her sleep-deprived mind to try to remember where she would be today if things had been different, if the planes had not been grounded, if she had not gone into that restroom, if she had turned down the ride to the hotel and the sharing of the room.

"How pathetic," she says out loud, leaning in to look into her own eyes. Eyes that are red from lack of sleep, outlined in deep creases, and surrounded by eyelids that could stretch halfway to Texas. The eyes, she now believes, of a woman who is very, very tired of always thinking she has to respond with some kind of wiseacre joke.

How pathetic when she realizes that this is her day to do

wash and then spend thirty minutes, tops, cleaning her rat hole of an apartment. How frigging exciting is that? How pathetic that if she were not in this hotel, having survived a near heart attack, a freak storm, manic psychics, and a madman, she'd be slipping quarters into the washing machine in the apartment basement and stepping over her neighbor's rusty bucket of work tools.

Patti feels frozen. She doesn't know what to say, which is about as close to a miracle as she thinks she will ever get, but she has a tiny urge not to leave the hotel or part from the women eating sweet rolls in the next room. When and where this urge springs from, she does not know, but directly behind it is a joyous note. Just one note. A simple, beautiful, lovely *la,* and she lets it slide from her stomach, into her throat, until she sings it. And sings it very loudly.

In the kitchen the other women turn and stop chewing.

"What the hell?" Margo runs down the hall. "Patti? Patti? Are you okay?"

"I'm fine," she calls through the door, smiling at the reflection in the mirror of a sixty-something smiling woman. "It was a note. A music note."

"You scared the living hell out of us."

"I'm a soprano. Sorry."

"Guess you're happy about going home."

"Just trying to keep myself awake in here," Patti lies. "I really need that coffee."

"I know what you mean," Margo agrees, releasing the tension in her shoulders and wondering why they never asked Patti more about her singing. It's hard to tell by hearing one lousy *la* in a throaty, sexy voice, but a singing Patti probably knocks her audiences dead.

It seems like two years ago since Margo waltzed into the restroom and wanted to lie down on the floor, exhausted from her trailer park adventures and craving some much-needed non-stress-filled days.

Even with all the somewhat magical excitement created by Operation Rivera there is a huge slice of her that would've loved to have gone way beyond those first few days when they met over all that wine and some serious bantering.

One more day. Right here. Kicking up sand on the beach. Ordering in one more meal. Yanking unspoken thoughts and long-repressed feelings out of hiding. Telling these women how half the time she is scared to death when she is working on a case, even if she's simply sitting in her office. If there were more time, she'd tell Patti how right she is about her *Heart of Loss*. She'd confess how she has a constant nightmare that allows her to see her children growing into adult strangers right in front of her eyes. And an equally horrific nightmare that one day she turns to look at her husband and doesn't recognize him.

Just as she has half a notion to pound on the door and say those things out loud, her phone rings. The ugly ring. The secret agent sound from hell.

"Hello," she snaps, turning to walk back into her bedroom so no one will hear.

Nan watches Margo strut back to her room and hears her slam the door. Then she looks up. She sees Cathy leaning over to say something to Holly, and Patti comes plodding up the hall with her wet hair, looking as if she might want to throw the coffee on her face to wake herself up before she drinks it. Nan hears Margo's voice sounding like an amazingly calm but muffled presence in the room, even though she is down the hall.

Nan is seized with the knowledge that without these women, without what they did for her, starting in the airport restroom, her life may have gone in a totally different direction. She might never have turned in the crooked financial people, her husband included. She might have bought another cell phone, called all the wrong people, said all the wrong things, moved in the same old well-worn direction for another twenty years, until the day she woke up and could no longer look at herself in the bathroom mirror.

All of that because of these four women. Even that damn Cathy who needs to duct-tape her little golden kingdom shut and take a break, for Christ's sake. Even Cathy the slut, who was bold enough to risk life and limb looking for her in the wild storm around the hotel.

Maybe, just maybe, she'll have to get another phone so that when she leaves this place she can call these women. And to say thank you, over and over again, for what could very well be the biggest turned corner of her life.

"Hey," Holly heckles her, "you look like you're dreaming. Eat something before I eat it all. I'm a pig. I don't think I've ever said no to a sweet roll or a doughnut my entire life."

"Wait about twenty more years, girl," Patti warns, grabbing the sweet roll Holly is about to put into her mouth. "One day you will be scarfing down anything you can get your hands on and your hips are still locked and lovely in the same place they have been for years. And then the next morning, just like that, it looks as if someone put a spreader in between your thighs and cranked it all night."

"Gross," Holly groans, reaching for another roll.

"People like Margo who have the hips of twelve-year-old boys don't have to worry too much," Patti continues. "But I'm telling you, if I knew then what I know now, or if I had some old broad like me to talk to, I'd be *half* the woman I am right now."

The thought of Patti being anything or anyone but who she is makes Holly drop her sweet roll. Holly sees Patti in a way she believes no one else does. There's a soft golden light around

Patti's face and when she falls asleep, it turns into a very pale shade of white. It's almost as if Patti is recharging herself for the next day's events, or a rehearsal, or a big event she has awaited a very long time.

And even as she sees Patti as a kind of a childless mom, Holly sees her even more as a friend. Someone who doesn't just like to keep things organized and moving but who likes to make sure everyone has a good time, even if they are sidestepping tiny pieces of glass from a broken sliding glass window, running through a storm with dull knives, or worrying about broken windows and bad men. Patti, Holly knows, is fun, light, and lovely. But underneath all of that, Holly is certain, absolutely certain, if Patti had the chance for a life do-over she would change the direction of her heart.

For three days now, Holly has wanted to lean over and ask Patti if she could go with her sometime when she did a traveling gig. She'd promise to be as silent as possible. She'd carry Patti's bags and make sure her slip wasn't showing and have a warm glass of brandy ready for her before she went onstage, so her vocal cords would be loose and ready to go. She'd set up a little stand and sell some CDs and have Patti autograph shirts and cards, and then they would eat dinner together and talk and talk.

Of course, that whole scenario would probably drive Patti nuts because she is so used to being alone. Alone and lonely, Holly thinks. But after a while she'd love having Holly there, and not just because Holly can do her hair. Because she would have someone to laugh with and she'd have someone to talk to after her performance, and someone to walk her to her door, besides a beer-bellied guy who has always wanted to sleep with someone he saw onstage. And when she got up in the morning, very late, Holly would be waiting in the coffee shop to talk about dreams and all the places they could see during the day that Patti had never bothered to see when she sang there the last time. And Patti would always have someone to hear her sing whenever she felt like it.

But just as Holly's about to tell her how much she'd love to do that, Margo storms up the hall, and demands to know if there's any booze to dump in her coffee.

"Now what?" Cathy asks. But she's reaching for the pot and then checking to see if there is any whiskey left.

"Reports and follow-up briefings and questions and answers and all the office kind of crap I have to do that is important that I'm too tired to deal with right now."

"I think out of all of us, you slept the least," Holly says, handing Margo coffee and then holding out her own cup for some of the whiskey. "You must be made for this kind of action."

"Maybe it's because I live in a state of constant terror," Margo explains, sipping her coffee as if she is tasting liquid gold. "Thanks to three kids."

"And you still have years to go with teenagers," Nan says, laughing wildly as if she has a secret. "The stories I could tell you!"

"You haven't really said much about your son," Patti notes, holding out her own cup for some of the whiskey Cathy is pouring.

The color of Nan's skin drops several shades and she closes her mouth.

Cathy looks at her and feels her heart doing that same flutter-flutter thing it did right before she told Nan she had slept with her husband. She knows things were rough with the son, and that he is a wound Nan is not sure will ever heal. Cathy has an uncontrollable urge to reach out and put her hand on top of Nan's—an *almost* uncontrollable urge, because even though she wants to, she doesn't let herself do it.

Instead, she pulls back emotionally and physically and, without asking, silently reaches over and fills Nan's glass with whiskey and then tips what is left of the bottle into her own glass.

Cathy looks from Nan to Holly to Patti and then to Margo, and her heart accelerates. She likes these damn women. She's told them her deepest secret. They've shared intimate moments with one another that supersede any intimate moments she can remember having in a long time. Maybe ever. Cathy is so ignorant about female relationships, she's desperately trying to remember—from watching all those stupid-ass chick flicks when nothing else was on television—what she is supposed to do now.

And this makes her feel even more inadequate and ridiculous. What is wrong with her heart? Could she really be this shallow?

Cathy knows she's been pushing her luck physically and emotionally for years. Her boobs, waistline, legs—pretty much everything from her neck down—could hit the floor at any moment and even though she's the kind of woman who would not hesitate to go under the knife, what does that really say about her?

And men. The parade of men is so long she'd have to call out for a pizza and eat it by herself to watch the entire thing, for crying out loud. She looks around the room again and sees this wealth of light and love that either never existed before or was extinguished because she is an ass or because of some horrid suppressed childhood memory. She feels a connection to them that actually accelerates her heart.

These women are, like, perfect. They swear and drink and tell stories and run into the heart of a storm with knives and they call her on her shit. This is when a bolt of emotional lightning hits her and makes her choke on her coffee. She's missed so much by ignoring women as friends that she could drop to her knees.

Cathy coughs, spits her coffee across the entire top of the

kitchen counter, and is so embarrassed she wants to crawl on her hands and knees right out the door.

"Are you okay?" This comes from everyone at once, which proves her point, and before she can even open her eyes, the counter is wiped up, her cup is refilled, and Patti is dabbing at Cathy's face with a clean napkin.

Cathy remains speechless.

"Clear your throat, honey," Patti orders. "Someone used to always say it went down the wrong pipe or some damn thing. Can you nod your head or something?"

Cathy nods her head and is so glad her coffee went down the wrong pipe because she now has an excuse for the tears in her eyes.

This is usually when Cathy would launch into some ridiculous story about a dog catcher in Ireland that has nothing to do with coughing or whiskey or getting ready to leave for the airport. But she can't speak. Without hesitation, Holly, of all people, takes over.

"Once this lady came into the shop for a cut and color and wouldn't speak but in a tiny whisper. I knew there was something odd right away, but I couldn't figure it out."

"This is prior to your new hocus-pocus days, though," Margo points out, starting to like how the whiskey is making her feel.

"Well, anyway, the client sits down in my chair and then I start to notice things. Like a huge Adam's apple, and a five o'clock shadow that could blind an army, and eyebrows that really needed to be taken care of with a lawn mower."

"Oh my. That woman was a man."

"Yes."

"So what did you do?" Patti asks, wondering what they

would say to her ten dozen cross-dressing and transvestite show-biz stories.

"I gave her a makeover for free," Holly says proudly. "I just said, 'Look, sweetie, this ain't working, let me help you.' And when I was done, she wept. And I got my first hundred-dollar tip."

"How sweet." Nan can see the whole thing happening.

"Did she come back?"

"For years. And then one day I got a postcard from the town in Colorado or wherever it is where they perform so many of those surgeries for transgender people—my little-girl-wannabe had become a woman."

"And you told us this story...why?" Patti likes the heady feel of the whiskey too. She may even start looking for another *la* pretty soon.

"Because Cathy has temporarily lost her voice, which re-minded me of the woman in my salon, and because it's a great story to tell when you are having whiskey and coffee with your new friends on a sunny spring morning a hundred yards from a beach."

Friends.

It's the first time one of them has said this sacred word out loud. Holly is smiling. Everyone else takes a hasty sip of coffee, and Cathy rearranges herself and then starts looking for more whiskey so she doesn't have to say anything or look anyone in the eye.

This time it's Holly's phone that rings. She answers it, listens, nods her head as if the person on the other end can see her, says "Okay" twice, then shuts the phone.

"I almost forgot. I have to go get something. It's kind of im-portant," she says, without putting down her spiked coffee, which she apparently likes so much she intends to take it with her.

And she's gone out the door so quickly, no one has a chance to say anything.

And one by one the women slip off to throw their meager belongings into their carry-on bags and pray that Holly makes it back to the room in twenty minutes, because that's when they have to leave for the airport.

"Please use the bathroom before we depart," Nan hollers from down the hall about ten minutes later. "You know how dangerous airport restrooms can be."

No one laughs.

eighteen

The look on the face of the unfortunate guy behind the car rental counter when he sees Nan,
Cathy, Margo, Holly, and Patti striding toward
him like a herd of potentially dangerous Charlie's
Angels is so priceless that Cathy flips open her hated cell phone
and catches his terrified wide eyes with her camera.

It's the same man who rented them the last available vehicle
back what seems like twelve years ago, when they literally ran
from the airport to try to beat the other three thousand people
who also needed to rent a car.

The startled man smiles wobbly, asks them if they had a nice
stay, and is immediately traumatized by the simultaneous loud
laughter from five women who look as if they could jump over
the counter and throw him over their shoulders without even
breaking stride.

"It was grand," Nan answers when her laugh slows down to a giggle. She slides the keys across the counter. "Just a lovely quiet respite while the storm blew the living hell out of the rest of the world."

"Great," the man practically whimpers as the women pivot to head into the airport terminal.

"We must look frightening," Cathy remarks.

"Well, here, take a look," Patti orders, as she jumps out in front of them, snaps a photo with her cell phone, and then hops back in the little circle they have formed.

Cathy steps up to look at them. Then Nan, Margo, and Holly do the same thing.

"We look kinda tough," Holly decides. "Everyone has on sunglasses. We are carrying bags that could hold guns. And pardon me for saying, but there's a hint of wild energy I pick up when you are all standing together."

"Wild shmild." Patti laughs again, not quite convinced Holly has a grip yet on her new powers. "Let's get on with the plan, ladies."

The plan was conceived during the ride from the hotel to the airport, which was more like a blur of traffic, and trying to remember the route, and Cathy slipping back into her crazy driver, brassy chick persona, and Nan finally telling her to shut the hell up. After that little episode, loaded thoughts could have blown out the windows.

Holly finally spoke up, and said she had a huge favor to ask them. This after flying into the suite with barely enough time to grab her carry-on bag and race to get in the car that Nan had already pulled around to the front of the hotel.

"Can we please, please, please get our tickets and then maybe all have one last drink together in the bar?" Holly asked this with such a sweet little whine, it would have been impossible for even the most hard-hearted traveling companion to say no.

"If we do, will you tell us what's in that secret bag you brought back to the room?" Margo asked.

"Maybe."

"Please tell us it's not some mumbo-jumbo mess of herbs and spices you went down to gather from your new boyfriend," Patti pleaded.

"He's not my boyfriend, and I'm not saying another word until you agree."

"Oh, all right, you big baby," Patti finally said with a half smile.

"I'm only going so I can have something else to drink." Margo sounded like she was pouting. But then she told them she would have no choice but to get off the plane when it arrives in Milwaukee, and immediately begin jogging. Her kids would be waiting. Most likely there would be laundry as high as her neck. She was certain there were also thirty crises she didn't yet know about, and most of them would center around an item that broke, a bill someone forgot to pay, or a huge fight about something stupid, like a discarded towel on the bathroom floor. And they wanted her back in the office for a debriefing before nine in the morning.

"Thinking about that makes me want to do shots," Cathy said in all honesty. "I can barely take care of myself. But you all know that, don't you?"

No one responded at first and then Holly told Cathy that she can handle more than herself. "Look what a good job you did getting dressed today," she joked, trying to get everyone to lighten up.

Patti saw what she was attempting to do and was grateful,

but at a loss to keep the conversation moving along at a normal pace while the car wheeled into the airport entrance.

Cathy had merely shrugged, and by the time they'd shocked the car rental man and took turns checking out their appearance, it seemed as if they were all about to waltz backward instead of forward. Everyone went to check in and discovered that they were scheduled to fly back home on the exact same flights, just days later—same times, same seats as before they were stranded. This meant, of course, that they would all be leaving within twenty minutes of one another, from the same terminal in which they'd met.

Airside A at Tampa International Airport. The place where it all began.

A coincidence? Not even Cathy has bothered to imagine that their initial meeting was more than a coincidence. Five unlikely women bumping into one another in an airport restroom at that particular moment in time? A time when the moon moved into position for its next dive around the earth and sixteen stars grouped together and the pull of gravity dragged them by their ankles so they would all be in the same spot, at the same time, for the same reason.

Except Patti is now remembering that she didn't even have to use the restroom that morning. And Holly is remembering that she was merely walking by and decided to go in to see if she had something stuck in her teeth. Cathy had already checked her makeup twice and is certain she was ducking in there in hopes of losing Nan. Nan had joked with Cathy at the bar but there was something, Cathy remembers now, something that made her want to go into the restroom and close the stall door and be alone for a little while. Margo had watched the door for a few minutes— not enough minutes, apparently—and is now recalling that she was going to cop a smoke before she had to get on the airplane but had decided against it and hadn't really even planned to go into the restroom at all.

And the reason they were all there at the same time is as apparent to each one of them right now as it was all morning and last night. Especially to Patti and Margo, who dissected everyone's heart while they were sitting on the balcony and listening to the waves.

If only they had not all been so damned angry and so damn frightened and so weary and so caught up in whatever it was that was keeping their hearts tied in a place of unmoving familiarness. If only they had each taken one step forward and said what they really wanted to say, embraced one another in a way that offers openness and forgiveness and leaves room for a relationship that embraces the good, the surprising, and even the ugly.

If only.

Now, everyone but Holly thinks there is no time left. And so four days after they last saw it, the five women walk into the bar in a blind daze. It's as if a huge bold light has gone on and their eyes are so dazzled they're afraid to look at one another. Because now they know something. Something very important. Something that is remarkable and lovely and a chance of a lifetime. They just have no idea what to do about it.

Holly walks right up to the bar, does not even ask the other women if they want a table, and orders not five drinks but a bottle. A bottle of Patrón Silver. Really, really good tequila. It's probably about half a day's worth of her wages and yet she flips out her credit card and is adamant about paying.

"I'm buying, and if we don't finish this bottle in the next ninety minutes then we do not deserve to be called women."

"A whole bottle?" Cathy gasps.

"Oh, come on," Nan chides. "I bet you put half of that on your cereal when no one is looking."

"Really, I like to have my cocktails, but I try to be careful," Cathy snaps, thinking Nan is serious.

"Cathy, get with it—I'm kidding. Lighten up before we have to fly back into our real lives, for crying out loud."

"I've had vodka on cereal before," Patti admits. "It was a phase, though. It only lasted one morning."

Holly, who clearly wants to be in charge, asks them all to be quiet for a minute while she ceremoniously fills up the tall shot glasses with tequila. The female bartender has already set up a dish of salt and limes for those who like a little help with swallowing liquor that often makes people take off articles of clothing, say things they may regret if they can remember having said them, leave enormous tips, and swear to every possible deity that they will never ever again for the rest of their lives do tequila shots.

And all these women have done exactly that—more than once. But now they tell themselves a variety of stories to prepare for the stunning sensation of flaming liquid not so much floating as jet-skiing down their throats and attacking their bloodstreams like soldiers on a perilous mission.

It's a celebration. It's a way to maybe say what should be said. It's one more chance to say I'm sorry. It's a way to forget. It's fun. It's a way to see what in the hell Holly has in that bag. It is maybe just as simple as sharing one last drink.

Or not.

"First of all, a toast to us," Holly declares, more or less commanding them to all toss back a shot. "What an adventure!"

The drinks go down as ordered, followed swiftly by a roar of coughs, chest pounding, and two loud cries.

"Blech," Margo squeaks. "I forgot how delicious and horrible this stuff is."

"No time to waste," Holly orders again. "Fill the glasses, please, bartender."

The bartender has not left her post. She's afraid she's going to miss something she will want to call and tell all her friends about the moment she punches out. No women have ever come in and done this before. None have ever purchased an entire bottle of the best tequila before boarding. Shots galore? Yes. But not this. And who are these women? These five look like they were picked randomly from a drawing box or something. One of them looks like a rich hooker. There's the chick buying the drinks who has fabulous hair. The older one, who looks kinda hot for her age, appears as if she's about to cry at any moment. A short, skinny one is an obvious smoker but she has a dual face—one side of it wants to hug you and the other side clearly wants to kick your ass. And the fifth one looks like she's lost in the crowd and needs to take off those damn high heels and put on something that suits her—like hiking boots, maybe.

"More?" Nan gags.

"Consider it a dose of courage," Holly tells her.

"Is there something dangerous in the bag?"

"No. But I'm planning on saying some dangerous things once I have two more shots."

The bartender inches in a little bit closer and wishes she could have a shot too. Just then Holly turns and says, "Hey, grab a glass and have a shot with us."

"Oh my gosh," the bartender says. "I was just thinking I'd love to do that, because you guys look like so much fun." She smiles at Holly. "Are you psychic or something?"

Patti, who was smelling her tequila, starts laughing so hard she sticks her nose in it and starts sputtering. Three napkins instantly head in her direction.

This is when the women remember that all they have eaten so far today are some rolls. The booze is going right to their heads. And they couldn't be happier.

"Holly, do the next toast, for God's sake," Cathy pleads. "And then can we have a little break before the next one?"

The bartender has loaded up the glasses, the six of them clink, and Holly looks into the eyes of these women, these wonderful, wonderful women, and she tries not to cry, but they all see it and so she says, "To four of the finest women I have ever met in my life. You have helped me so much. I want to thank you. And I really want to keep you in my life."

They all drink, with wide eyes. Then Holly reaches down to grab her mysterious bag.

"I hope you aren't disappointed when you see what's in here," she tells them. "But the new me, the one you helped me find, doesn't give a damn, because this is something I wanted to do to show you how much fun I had. And...well, here, let's do this, and then I have more to say."

More to say? Holly?

The bartender wonders what the old Holly might have looked or acted like. She's already hoping she gets invited on their next trip.

Holly opens the bag and says she's probably made too big of a deal about everything, obviously second-guessing herself in spite of her new awareness of *self*. She's young, she admits, but age is just a number, right? And something has been exposed beyond her uncovered abilities to see beyond what most people can see because of these past precious days, because of these remarkable women, because they all were in that restroom right across the hall at the same time, and because they didn't say no.

And because Holly finally remembers a simple, true, lovely

story her great-grandmother told her when she was just a little girl. A story she temporarily lost and has now promised herself she will never again forget. And because, after years of ignoring it, Holly can once again see the string that connects all women.

"None of us said no," she reminds them, pulling her gifts from the lumpy bag.

Holly has designed and then had someone make them tank tops. Bright aqua blue tank tops like the color of the sky and the ocean that they thought they would be looking at every day when they first said "yes." Each top has all of their names on the back, and emblazoned across the front in bright red are the words, *Estrogen Defense League.*

When no one is looking, the bartender quickly pours herself another shot out of the bottle and then stands at attention. She cannot wait to hear what happens next and is secretly hoping there is an extra shirt in the bag for someone like her.

The women hold the shirts in front of them, spin them through their hands, read the back, look at the front, and then lift their eyes to Holly.

Holly has already decided she does not need another shot. She knows she could stop right where she is and make up some story about estrogen and give everyone a hug and then skip out the door, get on the plane, fly back to Ohio, make her early afternoon appointments, and then quietly resurrect all the moments from the past few days she has already gathered in a corral near her heart. She'd pick out one of those moments now and then, whenever she needed it, hold it close, and then put it right back.

But she can't do that. As much as her old self would love to slither away and hide behind a boarding station, it is now actually physically and mentally impossible for her to do that.

So she tells them. Holly Blandeen, twenty-four, the hairstylist from Aberdeen, Ohio, empties her heart right in the middle of the tequila bar, in front of a rather adoring bartender, snuggled next to four women who just a few days ago were strangers.

She tells them that even though they had moments of discord and were trapped in a hotel and were angry and scared half the time, they still had *moments*. They shared meals and space and time. They talked and they laughed a lot and they all drank way too much. They had some fun, and when they were not looking at her she was looking at them and what she saw was a glorious rainbow of life. Of women who have been there and know things and who have survived so damn much and will survive so damn much more.

Holly tells them she has been afraid of actually living for such a long time, that she has longed for a box cutter or a blow torch to set herself free. And it wasn't just her imagined brain tumor that made her so frightened.

"I was around the wrong people," she admits. "People who always wanted me to be like them or live like them and I always hesitated and they took that as a sign of failure. But now I know it was the real me stepping up, because I can't live like them or like anyone but myself."

And even when Nan was pissy and Patti was cranky and Margo was distracted and she'd wanted to drown Cathy when she interrupted her quiet swimming time—she always knew that they would go to the wall for her. Like they went to the wall for Nan.

"Everyone has stuff, you know," Holly says softly. "And you made me think of the power of women, of women friends... and what fuels all of that as Patti wisely told us is estrogen."

Holly stumbles for a moment, catches her breath. "And we have to take care of that, because... well, really, it's what is most important, you know? It's the wild string of womanhood that keeps us connected, that gives us something to hold on to when we are sure we can no longer stand upright."

Estrogen and the strings of womanhood.

For a few seconds, one of those sacred seconds when hearts slow and it's impossible to speak or move because the weight of emotion feels like the hands of the universe pressing down hard on your chest, there is nothing but beautiful silence.

And then that miraculous force that springs from the ovaries, helps create the lovely dips and curves of a woman's body, increases the desire for sexual pleasure, and sways the lush, wild cycles of females everywhere, takes charge. There is an unseen estrogen surge, like the soft spray from the hull of a passing ship that flows around the once-stranded strangers. The almost invisible tie shakes endlessly from woman to woman.

It is a string as fine as the eyelash on a soaring bird and when Margo, then Holly, Nan, Cathy, and Patti open their eyes, they can see the string looping around necks, down shoulders, through arms and ankles, and then passing from one of them to another, until they all know, they really know, that they are tied together in the same way all women are tied together.

They see that the sighs, aches, loves, misgivings, needs, wants, desires, hopes, fears...the everything of all women are looped together from China to Chicago. They see the millions of strings dangling from continent to continent, strings that any woman, anywhere, can pull when she needs to feel the warm hand of another woman on her heart.

For a moment there is a lovely group stagger. Looped together with that string, the women fall together and their shoulders touch and their arms move out and touch.

The bartender, a lovely forty-two-year-old woman with two children, who has three best female friends who she lovingly calls her sisters, thinks she sees the string too and is not surprised when she steps forward and notices that she is also connected to this wonderful group of tequila-swilling women. She knows a thing or two about estrogen and she somehow knows that she will see these women again.

The five women now realize they are not just woozy from their shots of blue agave drink but from the rebirth of something they may have once known and discarded or locked away or simply forgotten to tend.

Patti is the one to speak first. She does so quietly and without the need for more tequila. Although later, when she might occasionally slip back into the place of forgetting, she is now a certified member of the Estrogen Defense League, she will attribute what she is about to say and reveal to the powerful fingers of a drink she will from this moment on absolutely favor.

Patti reveals her *Heart of Loneliness* and immediately hears the lyrics of an entire song parade into her mind. It's Bette Midler telling her, "You got to have friends..."

"I have a life and a glamorous-seeming way to pay my bills, but essentially I'm a lonely, aging lounge singer who cut herself off from her own estrogen flow because I couldn't stop feeling guilty about one horrific incident," she admits. "I'd hate to think the rest of my life will be like that. And if I hurt any of you by being brusque or curt, well, I'm sorry, and I will put extra money into the EDL fund as a penance."

The bartender pours herself another drink. She waves off her male assistant, who is lingering near the women and trying very hard to eavesdrop.

Patti says more. She talks about lost moments and how they probably already know it's okay to disagree and live differently but how all things female really are like an invisible bridge that helps you realize none of that matters.

"Like those fuck-me shoes you girls wear," she says, pointing to Cathy's and Nan's spike heels. "You couldn't get me in a pair of those if you handcuffed me. But it's okay if you wear them."

"And ruin your feet," Holly adds, not wanting to stop herself anymore.

"Exactly," Patti replies, slipping off one shoe and exposing a bunion that looks like a sixth toe.

Nan decides she needs another shot. She's definitely got something to say. The bartender pours a drink for everyone and then stays close, at total attention. If someone else but these five women needed her right now, it is clear they would get hit in the head with a half-empty tequila bottle.

"I need a little extra courage to say what I need to say, and I *really* need to say it." Nan sips on her drink, then finally gulps what is left very quickly.

"You all saved my life," she tells them. "And you already know how grateful I am for that, for the risks you took. Even though you looked absolutely hilarious and demented when you were running around in the rain with your weapons like that."

The bartender is now so mystified and mesmerized she is absolutely immobile.

The four other women are nodding, sipping quietly, but their hearts are pounding like a drum.

"But you saved my life in other ways too. I was so busy sorting it all out, being pissed at Cathy, worried about going to prison or whatever might happen, I didn't think about what it meant or could mean way beyond these days."

And then Nan confides that she dropped her phone in the toilet on purpose when it started ringing and she saw the caller was her husband. She was as afraid and as alone as she'd ever felt in her entire life. And the next moment they had all appeared in that bathroom like the miracle she never believed would happen to her.

"I already had a feeling about you, Cathy, and what had happened with my husband, but like many things it was something I shoved to the side. I ignored it, hoping it would go away, but knowing that it wouldn't. You know, though, you really should stop messing around with other people's husbands. There are plenty of single men around."

The bartender lifts the golden bottle to her lips and does not take her eyes off the group she is guarding.

"I'm—" Cathy starts, but Nan cuts her off.

"Give me two more minutes here. You are ballsy, Cathy, and I like that," Nan continues, gently. "In some ways what you did and who you are helped me too. I imagine you felt as lonely as Patti did, because you probably didn't have two women in the whole world to call friends. But I'm your friend now, and so are the women you see standing here, and without the power of all of you I might never have had the courage to turn in all those bastards so they get what they deserve."

Cathy looks a little stricken. Her gorgeous face is drooping and she knows if she does not say something, she may simply drop over and die.

"I'm a shit. I know I'm a shit and I need to figure out why and I am going to do that and I know I have said I am sorry a mess of times already, Nan, but I am sorry, and I'll try hard to confine my obvious need for happiness via sexual gratification and male adoration in the future."

She sticks out her glass and the bartender steps forward in total awe of the most honest conversation she has ever heard in her life.

"Up until now I sort of thought of women as competition," Cathy confesses. "Every woman. I had no flipping idea it could be so much fun to be with other women and be yourself and not worry. I'm amazed."

Weapons and lounge singers and sexual predators is fun? The bartender is desperately thinking of a way to get inducted into this group, beyond the obvious and already acknowledged estrogen link. What could be next?

Next is Margo. She's twisting her glass round and round in her hand and smiling, and then she leans over and bumps her empty glass against Nan's and tells them she felt at a loss and adrift in her own *Heart of Loss*.

"It's so easy to think about what you are losing and not what you are gaining," she reveals. "All this change and reentry in my life had me second-guessing myself every twelve minutes, until I was very nearly convinced I should step backward and not forward."

She tells them that the night they all decided to go to find Nan, when she realized that she did not have access to her revolver and she felt the electric charge that comes only from a mix of adrenaline and the power of pursuing your own passion, she knew she was finally on the right path.

"I also took great comfort in knowing you were all behind me and if I screwed up you would claw the living hell out of that guy and make him cry like a baby."

The woman holding the tequila bottle would do anything for these five women, absolutely anything. Guns and secret agents and a fight with a bad man in the dark? At this moment, she totally loves her job.

Patti wonders out loud what might have happened if they had realized everything they've just shared sooner.

"Oh, God save the queen, can you even imagine?" Holly squeals. "We could have taken over the hotel or something."

"I think what matters is that you did it." The bartender cannot help herself. When everyone turns to look at her, she apologizes. "I'm so sorry for speaking—"

"No."

"No."

"No."

"No."

"No."

"This is not an exclusive club," Holly says, inviting the bartender into their circle.

"I'm not sure I can keep up, though," the woman all but whimpers.

"You'll catch on soon enough," Cathy assures her. "Click into your own estrogen."

Then Cathy holds up both hands and says that now they are out of time and how sad that is. They should have all stepped it up another notch two days ago, or last night, or anytime before this moment when they had to leave.

"No."

"No."

"No."

"No."

Everyone is shaking their head from side to side very rapidly.

"The thing that matters is that we are doing it now," Holly says forcefully. "Imagine never doing it? Imagine standing on the sidelines and waving to the parade that you have always wanted so badly to join? This is what we have right now. These wonderful few minutes. A chance to say what is in our hearts and to always keep them connected. The only time we don't have is what we gave away, what is behind us."

Holly is speaking so forcefully and with such conviction that the veins on the side of her face are sticking out and have turned blue.

"Look at me, for crying out loud," Patti all but whines. "Holly is just a baby and has already figured this out. I'm an old bag lady who knew all of this a long time ago, threw it away, and am finally being resurrected."

"I wish we had another day, even so," Cathy mutters.

"I love that about you," Nan shares.

"I just wish there was something..."

Nan looks quickly from one woman to the next and checks her watch.

"This all started in that restroom across the hall."

"You have got to be kidding me," the bartender gasps, totally shocked. "You didn't know one another? Haven't been friends for years?"

"Nope."

Shit.

"Can you do us a favor?" Nan asks the bartender.

"Anything. Are you kidding? I'm hoping one of you will slip me in her carry-on so I can go with you."

"If we go into the restroom, will you guard it for a while so no one else can go in?"

The bartender tries with every ounce of her imagination to envision what these women will be doing in the restroom while she guards the door. She draws a blank that could fit into a .38 special.

"Sure," she promises.

Nan looks around and everyone is smiling. Holly is praying to God that Nan is not going to make her throw her phone into the toilet, but she is smiling too.

"Pick up your bags, girls," Nan shouts, laughing. "We're going home."

They follow her into the restroom, juggling their carry-ons and five glasses filled with tequila. Three dazed-looking women shoot out moments later and hurry from the restroom entrance. The bartender does not really want to know what has happened.

She positions herself in front of the restroom door and stands guard with her tequila bottle. Arms crossed, feet spread, her not-so-lovely bartender's uniform looking almost like that of an official restroom attendant, she simply starts waving women away from the restroom with a smile, which works like a charm.

Inside, the women are right back where they started, and Nan tells them she has one last request.

"Please do not make any of us stick our hands in a toilet," Holly pleads. "I'd do it if you really wanted me to, but it's just so icky."

"Don't worry," Nan reassures her. "We never got to model our bathing suits. I really want to do that."

"Are you serious?" Patti gasps.

"Oh, goodie." Cathy will do anything to put on a bikini or take one off and strut.

"Is this some secret estrogen initiation or something?" Margo wonders aloud.

"No. Well, yes. I suppose. I've just got this sudden sense of always trying to do things that are important, and things that I want to do, and it would also give me a lovely moment to remember."

"You're serious?" Holly groans slightly but has no intention of backing out of anything.

"I remember there's even five stalls," Nan says, as if she has been planning this for days.

Margo starts to laugh in a way that is so absolutely loud and borderline hysterical that everyone else also laughs, and cannot stop. The bartender soon is bent over laughing herself, hoping they will tell her what they are laughing about if and when they emerge.

"Isn't this absolutely ridiculous and hysterical?" Margo says one word at a time because she is laughing so hard.

"Of course it's ridiculous. That's why we're doing it. Estrogen makes women do things that appear insane." Patti bends over, flips open her gown-filled suitcase, digs until she finds the bathing suit she will probably never wear again after today, and sweeps into a stall.

There is more laughing, and the tossing of underwear and slacks and blouses, and then the bartender, who yet again cannot help herself, opens the door a tiny crack to peer inside, just as the women begin running in circles in their bathing suits and giggling as if they have sent someone's bra up the flagpole at summer camp. And the oldest woman keeps saying, "This is the best doozy I've ever had!"

So it's a doozy they are having.

After a few minutes Holly halts them. She catches her breath, and holds up her cell phone to get a shot of them all in the restroom that from this point on will be known as EDL Central.

With less than ten minutes until three of them are supposed to be boarding, there's a sudden dash to change again and leave. This is when Holly, who sometimes is seriously just twenty-four, decides to fall apart.

"I don't want it to end," she babbles, pulling at her bra and stepping out of her stall. "I'm like, so depressed now."

"You need one more shot." Cathy giggles, lunging at her so she can give her a long hug. "And this too."

Nan stomps as if she is mad, claps her hands, and wants to make certain that Holly and everyone else knows this is definitely not the end. "This is our beginning," she shouts, and then demands a very fast exchange of telephone numbers. Phoneless, she grabs a pen out of her purse and writes four phone numbers up the side of her arm.

When all five women push through the restroom door, just minutes later, Holly tosses the bartender the one extra shirt and tells her to keep what's left in the tequila bottle. And by the time the bartender has a chance to look up, she sees the women striding down the hall, arms laced, all wearing aqua blue *Estrogen Defense League* tank tops. Then they stop, have a long group embrace, and separate.

And bartender Shelby Kimball, the newest member of the Tampa-based Estrogen Defense League, will swear for the rest of her life that she really did see a thin line of string come out of each woman's heart and then tangle together as if they were dancing in the wind at the very same moment someone with an exquisite soprano voice started singing "I Will Remember You," as if she were Sarah McLachlan.

text-a-logue

Later that same day
Holly to all but Nan: Landed safe. Back to hair-cutting reality
Cathy to all but Nan: Me too! kisses
Margo to all but Nan: Estrogen rules!
Patti to all→one at a time: SGIR SHIT i mean my fst text mgse thsi sucks

Much later that same day
Nan to all: Got a phone. Couldn't stand being away from the EDL. No cops at my door. yet!
Patti to Nan: ! Jst foud how tp make a !
Cathy to all: Cant sleep. Miss you all. Is this normal?
Holly to Cathy: Yes, its called edl love

The next day

Nan to all: Omg! wore t-shirt to get groceries. Everyone wants one and to join

Patti to Nan: What is omg? Do I ned one?

Nan to Patti: Lol! it is oh my god

Patti to Nan: What is lol?

Nan to Patti: Laugh out loud

Patti to Nan: Omg I jst lolled!

Margo to all: Busy as hell. More asap

Holly to all: Me too and ditto about the shirt, was offered fifty bucks

Cathy to all: My husband thinks i am nuts. Won't take my shirt off

Nan to Cathy: Thats a first for you, girl!

Holly to all: Conference call sunday night? Eight est—i arrange?

All to Holly: K

One week after hour-long conference call

Patti to all: Cincinnati gig all week

Holly to Patti: I can really come?

Patti to Holly: Bring tequila

Nan to Holly and Patti: Take photos. We are all j e a l o u s

Cathy to all: Still thinking about my edl idea?

All to Cathy: Yes

Nan to Cathy: Did you get my edl notes?

Cathy to Nan: Holy shit yes!!!

One month later

Nan to all: Husband arrested. Had offer on house. I am feeling light

Margo to Nan: No worries. My peeps tell me you are going to end up very happy

Holly to Nan: Remember, we will all be there for trial. Lets stay at a rivera!

Nan to all: Great restrooms at chi airport!

Patti to all: But how r bars?

Cathy to all: Burgers are on me

Nan to all: U all make me feel safe

Cathy to all: We are dangerous 2!

Margo to all: No shit

Three months later

Cathy to all: Nan moved in2 her new condo-sending photo-she is so happy!

Margo to all: Go figure! nan in denver! money in bank! bad guys in jail! nan living down street from cathy! edl forever!

Patti to all: Anything is possible. Tequila helps

Holly to all: When is housewarming?

Nan to all: Next month-all weekend? 7 9? third wknd? k?

All to Nan: Yes!

Margo to Nan: May have to work, kids, life. Will try

Nan to Margo: Bring the girls! Neighbor has daughters

Margo to Nan: Really?

Nan to Margo: Big y e s

Six months later

Holly to all: Finished gvt class with duffy. Stepping lightly. They offered me fulltime job. Thinking

Patti to all: Hair?

Holly to Patti: Would miss it. But maybe on the side

Margo to Holly: Look at me. you can do it all

Nan to all: Go for it, and oh! Final EDL plans and papers and stuff ready soon!

Cathy to all: Go for it, hol! My volunteer job at domestic shelter has changed my life yet again—good advice naner!

Patti to all: I'm dating, by the way

Nan to Patti: That's btw and holy shit!

One year later

Nan to all: It's edl anniversary month! Booked rivera for next year. 100 rooms already confirmed!

Margo to all: Cannot believe how the edl has grown so fast! Women really needed a place to just have fun!

Holly to all: My estrogen level is soaring! Love this job, and am making bundle doing hair on the side

Cathy to all: Girls…u all rock! guess what? i am happily married! i had no idea it could be like this

Cathy to Margo: Nan adores your daughters and has them helping her with edl stuff when they are not hiking or playing—what a summer vacation!

Patti to all: Have i shown u my very first ever engagement ring?

All to Patti: Yes! Maybe 10 times!

Patti to all: Lol! I luv to lol

Nan to all: That's it, girls! Everyone to the restroom…right now!

Acknowledgments

I had an absolutely wonderful time writing this novel, and so many people who supported and helped make that happen need to be thanked.

Pat and Marc Steuer offered shelter in California when things were a little desperate. You are both absolutely wonderful friends.

Robin Fash-Boyle opened her heart, home, and wine cellar during more than a few bleak moments. You, I treasure.

Shelia Oliver fixed my computer long-distance so many times it's not even funny. I kiss her feet.

Shari and Ray Collins were amazing during the move to Florida—my light is always on for them.

My sister, Maureen Zindars, and my mom, Pat Radish, get a medal for listening to me whine.

Lori Livingston and her sister, Amy Swartz, came to the rescue in the middle of Colorado. I love both of you.

The real Patti Nuttycombe Cochran placed a bid at a charity event and won the right to have her name in this novel. Your family name will now live on. Congratulations, you wonderful woman!

Madonna Metcalf is a true, kind, loving heart and champion of my work, under *all* circumstances. She makes everything better.

My fans, who are all my friends, keep me moving forward with their powerful, loving, open words of encouragement and support. We are all tied together with that lovely white string. Your words mean so very much to me. Thank you from the bottom of my grateful heart.

During the time I wrote this book, a wonderful man, Steven Fredericks, who has been a dear friend for forty years, died. We called him Duffy, and the Duffy in this book is a tribute to our lovely friendship and all the wonderful conversations, laughs, and glasses of beer we shared.

And lastly, the other half of my two greatest accomplishments, my daughter, Rachel Carpenter, has left the nest. I can only hope that you, sweet woman, are as lucky with the women you claim as your friends as I have been. Fly like the wind and never lock the door to your own heart.

about the author

KRIS RADISH is the author of *Hearts on a String, The Shortest Distance Between Two Women, Searching for Paradise in Parker, PA, The Sunday List of Dreams, Annie Freeman's Fabulous Traveling Funeral, Dancing Naked at the Edge of Dawn,* and *The Elegant Gathering of White Snows.* She lives in Florida, where she is at work on her next novel, *Tuesday Night Miracles,* which Bantam will publish in 2011.